'TIL SUMMER COMES

'TIL SUMMER COMES

Seven Spoon River boys wanted fun,
laughter, and adventure any day of the year.
But the best would even get better…

David Chapman

iUniverse, Inc.
New York Lincoln Shanghai

'Til Summer Comes

Seven Spoon River boys wanted fun, laughter, and adventure any day of the year. But the best would even get better...

Copyright © 2005 by David G. Chapman

iUniverse books may be ordered through booksellers or by contacting:

iUniverse
2021 Pine Lake Road, Suite 100
Lincoln, NE 68512
www.iuniverse.com
1-800-Authors (1-800-288-4677)

This is essentially a work of fiction. Some of these characters, incidents, and dialogues are based on historical record; but the work as a whole is a product of the author's imagination stirred by many and varied memories.

ISBN-13: 978-0-595-36346-9 (pbk)
ISBN-13: 978-0-595-80783-3 (ebk)
ISBN-10: 0-595-36346-6 (pbk)
ISBN-10: 0-595-80783-6 (ebk)

Printed in the United States of America

Preface

Doing something like this is a lot of work for anyone who thinks they can write a book. But I don't think anyone can honestly do it alone.

Writing the story is one thing, but solving countless mistakes the writer didn't see is even more important. My family has been wonderful, and I certainly must compliment them. My wife Dorothy visited Bradford many times with me in the 1980s. I began telling her so many of the hilarious, incredible stories I remembered that she thought I should write this book. Byrdena Schuneman, the wonderful lady who was then working on a collection of her historical stories that became the great book, *History of Bradford 1850-2000,* also said I should write about our amazing adventures.

I shrugged this off for those first few years, but then I started my first attempt. After a few chapters it somehow slid down in a drawer. Dorothy gently nibbled and nagged me over the years, but her persistence finally happened when I hit my 50th high school reunion in September 2004. Since she said I was certainly not getting any younger, I had better get going or it will never happen.

It began as simply a collection of memories for the reunion group, but wound up being serialized by Jim Nowlan, the editor and publisher of *The Stark County News,* the excellent weekly newspaper. A number of friends said I should turn this into a real book, so I finally decided to go to work.

My cousin and her husband, Ruthe and Lee Utt, went through editing the entire book twice, and my daughter, Susan McNulty, Dorothy, and Phil Sharkey all gave other versions countless suggestions or corrections. I could not have done this without these five. Somehow, it now seems as if the sunrise has finally lifted.

All I can say is thank you to each of these relatives and friends, from the deepest, most important part of my soul.

The Prologue

"The end of all our explorations will be to come back to where we began and discover the place for the first time."

T. S. Eliot

Are the cycles and seasons of nature merely a mask disguising the much more ironic revelation that, for most of us, life itself is also cyclical in which we have but three seasons: twice a child, and only once an adult? No one who has observed the aging process could doubt the truth in this subtle discovery that each one of us has to do. Yet, if we can accept the special, caring needs created when this happens, is returning to a form of childhood such a bad way to end one's stay on this planet?

While I am currently suspended between these twin bookends of mortality, Eliot's great line has encouraged me to look back to the special place in my memory where I lived during my first opportunity at being a child. There is as much to discover in retrospect as there was initially. At six years of age, I stopped believing the beginning of each year was January first. I soon realized this date is really an overrated impostor. That's not so difficult to explain, because my next sixteen years ingrained a feeling that the calendar's annual tour really started in late August or early September with the first day of school. It ended, not on December 31, but on the last day of school. Nestled snugly between these two points of time were three special and miraculous month's called summer.

They become a second bookend holiday for me. It began on Memorial Day, and ended on Labor Day, at the same time two other opposite experiences also happened...school ended, and then had to happen again once more.

By 1948, when I was teetering on the edge of puberty, summer was the most eagerly awaited season in my life. Actually, everybody loves summer, regardless of which way Mother Nature flips the hemispheres. Its sunny days and starlit nights were filled with things of wonder and adventure from cotton candy and county fairs to fudgesicles and fireflies. Of course, sneaking a few kisses and getting up the courage to snap a bra strap for the first time coincided nicely with the laid back ambiance of the season. Most of all, however, summer offered freedom from the perceived tyrannies of school. June, July and August obviously did not belong in the regimented pace that dictated the remainder of the year, because my summer world was as carefree and unstructured as the rest of the year wasn't.

Summer was a time to play and dream. Kids could just do something as simple as lying on their backs in the grass with their friends and say, "That cloud looks like a mountain or a person or whatever they could imagine." All of my early, special places touched marvelous memories for me, but our town's nearby creek with its surrounding pasture, or magnificent wooded hills bordering Spoon River were the best. Actually, even though our local tributary was only half of the river, we now have signs that say they are an East or West Fork, but back in those days, we called with a respectful mixture of jest and reverence, "The Mighty Spoon." Each year the river had been patiently developing it's decorative foliage since spring's first buds. By the first of June they were all now majestically adorned in well-tailored outfits of green in all its shades.

Those soft breezes that rustled through leaf-filled boughs sent waves rippling over a sea of new grown hay which also filled the sails of excitement in my mind. There were fish to be caught, dams to be built, railroad tracks to be walked, trees to be climbed, balls to be hit, and, of course, grass to be mowed, fruit to be picked and gardens to be weeded. But even the chores of summer were only temporary distractions, minor blips on an otherwise uncluttered agenda. Nothing could long deter the next make-up ball game, fishing trip or skinny dip. Unfortunately, a potential disaster called Polio was hanging over every person for the next few years. No one had any idea how or where it would happen, or what it could do to any of us. Probably, the best way kids could handle the threat was just play, and play, and play. But in small towns, when it hit kids all over America, now we couldn't even go back to creating those cherished memories in county fairs again.

After this, what could we do? Playing in small towns anywhere in our country kids chose a special traveling companion. It never complained, and went anywhere we wanted to go. Yep, mine was a fire engine red, Elgin bicycle, and seemed it was a crimson chariot that carried me anywhere within my allotted bounds, from backyard to park, boredom to escape. My friends were constant mates, and new adventures were always developing because we had been trained to look for, even expect them.

Thanks to the power of suggestion constantly being transmitted through our radios, or flickering across the Saturday afternoon screen at the town's only movie house, excitement and action were daily staples of life. However, radio had a stronger role in stimulating my young imagination than movies simply because it was free and available on an every day basis. At the Brad Theatre, movies cost a whopping sixteen cents, and, on a weekly allowance of twenty-six cents, (a dime extra for popcorn and a coke, or a box of Milk Duds), it made the afternoon's double feature a highly anticipated event.

However, if attending a movie was my weekly pilgrimage to the Brad, our own 'Mecca,' listening to the radio was my daily salvation and inspiration. Because of the numerous action-packed serials we could join Terry on the decks of a pirate ship, sit in the cockpit of a "Flying Tiger," or ride the great white horse Silver with the twist of our dial. Every Saturday morning, thanks to "Let's Pretend," we scaled castle walls, fought multi-headed dragons, and saved beautiful princesses from fates too horrible to contemplate. Even the icy crevasses of the Yukon held no fear for us, because we had patrolled the wilds of the Canadian Northwest with Sergeant Preston for years.

On a lighter side, radio let us chortle at the absurd antics of Froggie the Gremlin on the "Smilin' Ed Mc Connell Show," or try to match wits with "Dr. I. Q." and "Quiz Kids." Of all my childhood diversions, radio had the most significant influence, because of what it did for my imagination. Like all the other listeners, I was creating my own mind's version of the drama. But films, radio and comic books relentlessly urged us to help America meet the challenges of World War II, and we did. Our Victory Gardens, stamp books, war bonds, scrap metal and paper drives were vital. However, they didn't seem as crucial as deciphering special messages from Captain Midnight, or cheering the heroism of allied fighter pilots as they sent countless Zeros and Messerschmitts flaming earthward in the weekly "Eyes and Ears of the World" newsreels.

Whether it was, because of growing up in a long period of wartime, or boyhood's normal disregard for risk I'm unsure, but personal danger was only fleetingly acknowledged, and parental warnings of what could happen were given little heed. Why should we worry? If an emergency arose, we had belts that glowed in the dark, and rings that fit any finger and whistled when you blew through them. Secret decoders allowed us to pass messages or send signals to our fellow commandos. Even Dick Tracy's son, Junior, showed all kinds of neat cop equipment for kids in his dad's comic pages. I finally got my very own genuine fake handcuffs. It stayed in a special small pocket in my coveralls…but when in the world I actually wondered: would I ever really need it?

Other problems seem to occur. The fact that the special belt quickly lost its ability to glow, the ring turned your finger green or the secret messages were usually to buy more Ovaltine didn't deter us. That was when our trusty, multipurpose, Boy Scout pocketknives came to the rescue. They could be counted on to clean fish, cut vines, and play mumblety-peg or the dangerous game of "chicken." As for bandages and casts on broken limbs, they were almost as good as the Congressional Medal of Honor. We subconsciously felt any moment could beckon a new adventure whenever we slipped into a tee shirt, buckled up our bib overalls or tied a double-bow knot in our high top sneakers. Then, a few years after Hiroshima, a bomb with even greater personal import began ticking inevitably within us.

It was also our time to think about sex. But we had to learn about the facts of life on our own, and summer, with it's carefree mood, was as good of time to learn as any. Maybe it was the best. Most of our parents were too inhibited or ill informed to pass along anything close to the straight facts. What we heard from older brothers and sisters or their friends never made any sense. Predictably, our sexual orientation began earlier by playing I'll show you mine if you'll show me yours, trying to see through a sister's blouse that was beginning to fill, or secretly reading comic pornography. These wondrous works of art featured incredibly explicit sex acts between such unlikely pairings as Little Orphan Annie and King Kong, or Pop Eye and Wonder Woman. They were euphemistically called "eight page bibles."

For young boys entering the pubescent years the worst aspect of the contraband booklets was not their raunchiness. It was the depressing effect the overly exaggerated drawings of male genitalia had on us while undergoing our own physical changes. When it came to sexual relations, none of us were sure of what went where and if ours would be big enough to do the job if we ever found out. One only need recall this was the period of time when America's long slumbering age of innocence was about to come to a sudden, screeching halt. Television was very much in its infancy, Korea was an obscure place somewhere in the far east and the Big Band music was still wonderful because rock and roll were just two unrelated words not yet used together as the name for a new era.

Only nine years earlier Clark Gable had broken the ban on movie profanity by telling Scarlet he didn't give a damn. And, as far as sex education was concerned, neither did a lot of others. Freud was way over my head then, and, for that matter, still is. But in 1948 an Indiana professor named Kinsey published a new book that became the biggest shock in America. Looking back, none of us, and most of our parents had not read 'the sex book.' Virtually everyone would have had a heart attack if we realized that a bright, new world about sexual connotations opened our eyes the same way Dorothy crept out of her black and white house, and suddenly saw other different people in Technicolor. We boys were on our own and extremely perplexed. As for our classmates of the opposite sex, though we were unaware of it, girls, too, struggled with equally serious concerns about the many changes that they faced on the road to womanhood.

Therefore, I feel we can read about seven juvenile boys who have a simple, heart to heart conversation. Why? Because we all talked about it, a lot together in those years we just didn't tell any of our parents that we did. The only sad part is that what we talked about was probably 80% wrong. Not immoral, and certainly not stupid, it was that we were just plain confused, because no one told us *anything*. The main part of this is in Chapter 18, and if you still cringe about this, just skip it and go to Chapter 19.

I find myself reflecting on those old memories more often as summer approaches each year than any other season. I suppose I am still held captive by its mystique, though I am resigned to never again fully experience those wonderful feelings of release and freedom. Feelings that used to burst from deep within the moment school issued its annual three-month reprieve from what seemed to be a life sentence. While I hope my retirement years will recapture something of that same exhilaration, long years of adult responsibilities have prepared me for the inevitable fact that nothing will ever be quite like that again. The unbridled audacity and limitless energy have dimmed a bit, but still I hope. In the meantime, I have many memories filled with the profound experience of living my first eighteen years in a small village on the great Midwestern plains of Illinois.

The welcoming signs on each side of town said our population was about 870, but what an amazing collection of intriguing individuals. It included a number of special personalities, some of whom were true Dickens characters in their own right. It was as if a group of remarkable personas from a treasury of outstanding fiction had miraculously sprung to life. How so many of them could live simultaneously in one little town will forever remain in my personal mystery.

Fortunately, years before me, someone did write an outstanding collection about people who lived and died in a remarkable, but composite town called Spoon River about 75 miles south from Bradford. His name was Edgar Lee Masters, and his masterpiece is "Spoon River Anthology." He wrote it in 1914, not as a novel, but as magnificent poetry, and simply told about 250 people's lives on each page, good or bad, happy or sad.

Masters was born in Garnett, Kansas in 1868, and his family soon migrated to Petersburg, Illinois, about forty miles from Pekin. They eventually moved to

Lewistown on the Spoon River in 1880. Later, when Masters began to write his major work, Mr. William Reedy, the editor of his town's newspaper, serialized Masters' book in 1914-15. Reedy realized this book was sheer genius, because he believed Masters had been virtually mesmerized by the amazing memories of his youth.

That is exactly what happened to me as a little boy in Bradford, Illinois.

I have returned there for countless visits over the years. One of the best comments that happened more than twenty years ago is this. The owner of a cafe in a nearby town casually said, "Your hometown produced more characters per square foot than any other place in the universe." How right I believe he was. Maybe it is a yearning to return to that time of innocence, both in my own life, as well as our nation's, that has propelled me into this excursion back to the unspoiled and unhurried village of my youth.

This work is definitely not an autobiography, however, but a gentle blend of fact and fiction, reality and myth, based on many actual people, places and events. While the book is about young people on the brink of discovery, it is not written with younger readers in mind. It is here if they wish to see how life for kids in postwar Middle America may have been, but my hope is to penetrate far deeper than that. 'Til Summer Comes is really for the hidden child who still secretly lives inside every adult. Therefore, with tongue sometimes firmly in cheek, it will explore some of the monumental issues that confounded adolescent girls and boys of my generation.

On a more serious nature, though our village population's size at the time in my story had around 850-900 residents, I decided to name only one person who lives there, is black. Even today, racial imbalances like this are common occurrences in many rural towns throughout America's northern states. How seven boys, who have let ignorance and superstition introduce themselves to racial prejudice, learn the true insignificance of skin pigmentation is a lesson that has relevance in any era.

At the time where I lived more than 50 years ago we actually did only have one black family whose family name is Moody. They lived seven or eight miles south of Bradford, and sadly moved away around 1950. My memory as a young boy is that the entire household was wonderful, and no one had any aspects of prejudice. Several of their kids graduated from Bradford High School., and countless people in town felt their entire family was friendly and pleasant. Being the *only* Bradford area black family living there must have been a challenging experience in their lives.

While the Moody's were alone in those Bradford years, Jim Nowlan, now Editor of *The Stark County News* in Toulon, and a professor at the University of Illinois, wrote a very interesting front-page story at *The Prairie Times*, another weekly paper in the same county on May 4, 2000. However, Nowlan not only wrote about a Toulon black family in those days that he titled "The Harrington Heritage in Toulon: We didn't know the difference," he interviewed the main man in the story, Don Harrington. Mr. Harrington is now retired, and lives in Peoria. He had several other brothers and sisters who also attended Toulon High School then, but Mr. Harrington was crowned King of the 1948 Homecoming Court!

Accordingly, for the story I want to create, a man who really lived in an exceptional 'shack' above the Spoon River only a mile away from town was white, but in this story he is black. His name was Gib Jones, and people still today shake their heads with memories and stories about the man. Amazingly, he probably had no electricity and certainly no running water. I met him many times, and even went into his 'trolley' deep in the woods after I fell into the river. To exist, he had to dig free coal just for cooking and heating on an old stove. As an honest-to-goodness 'coal miner,' his face and hands were often so black he almost did look as if he could have been an African-American.

There are a couple of other reasons I decided to change these facts into fiction. I have always loved Spoon River, but the Moody's and Harrington's didn't live anywhere near there. Additionally, the Masters book has one extraordinary and special fact. One of the 250 or so 'living' dead in the famous book was Shack Dye, and he had a blacksmith shop. If you wish to experience "Spoon River Anthology," you can read about him, too, but the author wrote us very little about what life was like before Mr. Dye died. Interestingly, *Shack Dye is the only black person mentioned in Mr. Masters' book.*

Consequentially, the supposed black man you will read about in this book also had a father whom might have been born a slave in Georgia about 1850. However, since no one in Lewistown has any retrospection or actual facts that proves Shack Dye was a real person, I decided his 'fictitious' son 'Sheck' was born in 1883 and can be in my story, too. I felt this new born boy would be named by his son, so I called him Sheck, and said he eventually moved about 75 miles north along the Spoon River when his parents died.

Because of many hidden circumstances like this, reading "Spoon River Anthology" is a brilliant experience. It is even better to read an annotated edition, and John E. Hallwas, in 1992, has done a tremendous achievement. For example, when Mr. Masters wrote his stories, he did not use his grandmother and grandfather's real names or even mentioned that they were married. Also, as a young man, the teenage girl Masters fell in love got married…but not to him. She wound up spending her life with another man who hurt Mr. Masters so much he hated him. In his book, that man is actually *four* fictional people who cover a number of negative aspects about him. Sadly, his lost teenage girl friend is moreover written about four other different, imaginary dead women. After perusing "Spoon River Anthology" for the third time, I decided to not write a factual book, just an honest story.

Two women novelists have greatly impacted my decision to actually try the difficult task of writing. A. S. Byatt, after years of struggling under the pressures of teaching, raising children and trying to write, at age 47, finally broke free from the bonds that restrained her efforts. Ms. Byatt calls her glorious moment of self-realization, "Silver Power." She describes this as "the moment of freedom when you are sure you are what you were meant to be."

The heroine in Daphne du Maurier's novel, "Frenchman's Creek," at the books climax, deserts her husband and two small children and runs away with a swashbuckling pirate. She responds to an initial doubt as to whether she has done the right thing by saying with power and conviction, "I am alive who was never alive before!"

Though it is obviously an entirely self-centered approach, what more can anyone can ask of life? I will offer but one other thought as to why I have tried to let the characters with which I grew up tell their story. In reality, my book is a love letter of sorts, to my childhood, and the wonderful people who made it so incredibly special. They are the hearts of 'our' story, certainly not me. I have desperately tried to write this by many different 'third persons', not my own first tense. Therefore, this is an attempt to be totally omniscient.

In Irving Stone's "The Agony and the Ecstasy" Pope Julian II tells Michelangelo he feels history might decide his great mistake has been a tragic failure trying to get the Sistine Chapel painted since his papal wars were almost ruinous. My miniscule attempt here might also be called a failure. But at least it is to bring alive that wonderful feeling of personal and creative freedom, which smolders in the soul of would-be writers, reaching back to the first moments of cognizance that such a feeling exists.

The time now is September 1948, and the place, Bradford, Illinois in Stark County. Another wonderful summer has ended, and a wistful sense of mourning lingers in the minds of the village's children as they trudge back for the reopening of school. Though coming months will bring happy moments and seasonal joys, for a group of seventh grade boys and girls, this school year is but another long ordeal to be reckoned with until the next summer comes again.

Therefore, a countdown has begun, plodding methodically through the calendar toward the day most of us looked forward to with greater anticipation than Christmas or birthdays…the final day of school. In 1964, at the time he gave his famous civil rights speech, Dr. Martin Luther King certainly wasn't thinking of seven boys running out of school, but no one could have said it better.

"Free at last, free at last, thank God almighty I'm free at last."

CHAPTER 1

▼

BULLET BOB

"Good evening football fans, this is Chick Moriarty, Sports Editor of the Kewanee Star Courier, and announcer of WKEI's High School Game of the Week. Beside me is Buddy Boyer, my right hand man and spotter. We welcome you to tonight's featured tussle between the Flying Geese of Wethersfield and the host Bradford Panthers."

Two men wearing telephone headsets were cramped in a small, hastily constructed plywood booth atop bleachers on the north side of the field. Their attention riveted on a gathering of opposing team captains and officials at the fifty-yard line. A forest green banner with the station's call letters painted in yellow was hanging across the tiny structure's front plywood panel.

"Folks, the sign at the edge of town says Bradford has 870 residents, and Buddy, I'll be darned if I don't think everyone of them is here tonight. And that doesn't count the huge number of fans who made the twenty or so mile trek from Wethersfield."

"Who could blame them, Chick? Here it's early on the tenth of September, just the second game of the 1948 season for these two teams, but it couldn't be more important. Both are heavy favorites to be in the thick of the always tough Blackhawk Conference championship race and tonight's game may determine the eventual winner. And Bradford fans are raring to go. They still talk about one of the most amazing football players anywhere in Illinois, Chick."

"Right you are, Buddy, I know you're talking about Leslie Welsh a few years ago."

"Yes, Chick, Les Welsh lost his arm the summer before his senior year. He was caught in a farm accident around that Fourth of July, and his left arm was cut just below his shoulder. But folks, this young man was able to play so well on offense and defense two months later in Bradford, the whole conference still talks fondly about what he did back then."

"Glad you brought that up, Buddy. Well, we're just about to get this game underway, and as the captains from each team meet in the center of the field for the coin toss, let's go back to our studio in Kewanee for these important messages."

Seven young boys at the far end of the home team bleachers were leaning against a wire fence, watching with undisguised awe as pre-game momentum surged through the crowd of eager of spectators. All of them had short crewcuts or flat-tops and were wearing blue jeans, tee-shirts, and high-top Converse basketball shoes, or Keds, but none of the boys wore the Orange and Black colors so prominent among the crowd on their side of the field. Two were wearing warm-up jackets of green and white bearing the interwoven initials of St. John's Parochial School. The other five sported similar jackets of blue and gold with a simple block B on the upper left-hand front. Because they attended the town's two grade schools, public and private, they were rivals in any athletic competition. However, when the contests were over, they again became the best of friends because all seven knew they would be united as both classmates and teammates at this same school only two more years from now.

"Do you think we'll like high school better than the prisons we go to now?" asked the skinny one at the end. He was also the tallest boy in the group, and they called him 'Dink', because he had been laughed at so many times for goofing off, he now had an obvious and silly nickname.

"Probably not, at least there won't be any nuns to beat on my knuckles," replied a pug-nosed boy with an impish face worthy of a Leprechaun from the land of his ancestry. His combination of shiny, black hair was sculpted every two weeks into one of the perfect flat-tops in town. His dark, piercing eyes gave him an imposing presence offsetting the obvious fact that he was too heavy for his short frame. Because of his portly build, his breasts were larger than those of every girl in his class. One day, while skinny-dipping, someone named him 'Booby'. At first he accepted this new nickname with the grace and calm of a cornered Wolverine, but gradually warmed to its uniqueness and accuracy.

"There's no way I'll ever go out for football," Booby added. "I'd just get killed. But I'll be out there playin' trumpet in the marching band. You can count on that."

"Maybe we'll like it and maybe we won't, but I can tell you one thing for sure," said another, pausing to spit loudly for emphasis, "I can't wait to play high school football." The boy who made this statement was of average height and weight, but possessed a solid, well-muscled body and an aggressive attitude, which he often used to assert himself. This combination made him appear bigger than he really was. He had adopted a number of different nicknames, but the one he preferred most was something of an anachronism, 'Jumbo'.

The skinny kid smiled. "I bet the three best things of high school are gonna be the same three as grade school: June, July and August. It's already only a week into fall, but I can't wait 'til summer comes."

Several of the boys resignedly nodded their assent. Then the one with delicately formed, patrician features glanced covertly around at the others. He was the most handsome of them all, but, because he was so full of devilment, the other boys felt no jealousy. However, though they were aware that most of the girls their age were obviously enthralled with him, they didn't even care about that. What did bother the others was the amount of effort he spent ingratiating himself to his teachers. This had earned him the crudest nickname in the group, 'Suckass'. Suck for short.

"For sure we can stare at those four cheerleaders jumping around. They've got some neat things bouncing around I'd sure like to see." Several laughed, but a couple of them had no idea what he was talking about. Then a new voice entered the conversation.

It belonged to the biggest boy for his age, solidly built boy with penetrating eyes and a broad, imposing face marked with strong Teutonic features indicating his German heritage. He was a human bulldog, the kind you'd want to have on your side in a fight. There was one drawback, however, and that was when he started doing the one thing at which he truly excelled. He was the undisputed flatulence champion of the group. Because of this they called him 'Beaner', whether he ate any kind of beans or not.

"I don't care about cheerleaders, but I love to smack anybody else playing football. There's somethin' tough in that game when you're going to tackle," Beaner emphatically smiled.

"...And, after Wethersfield's initial drive has come to nothing thanks to Jim Swearingen's recovery of Jerry Lake's bobbled Statue of Liberty attempt, we're about to have the first play from scrimmage for the Bradford Panthers. Swearingen fell on the loose ball at Bradford's 32-yard line. This will be interesting, folks, because the Panthers are one of the high school teams in this area to convert to the new T formation. It's out with the old single-wing and in with this tricky, new idea where the quarterback takes the hike directly from center. Okay, Chick, take it away."

"Thanks, Buddy. Here comes Bradford's strong-armed quarterback they call 'Bullet' Bob Murphy up behind center. 'Conch' Craig, the fullback is five yards behind him and flanked by 'Dooze' Malone and J. E. Terwilliger, the left and right halfbacks a yard or so in front of him. There's the hike from center Kenny Sullivan, uh; I almost didn't see it. Murphy is dropping backwards…he, my gosh, he's throwing a pass over at the right sideline…who's he…wait, there's number 89, big Dan Driscoll coming out of nowhere. Driscoll catches the ball in full stride! Bob Mowbray and Harley Rediger are two big linemen running over to block somebody, but there's nobody from Wethersfield even close! Driscoll is racing down the field. He's at the ten, the five; he takes the ball in for a touchdown on Bradford's very first offensive play! How about that?"

"Had to be the old sleeper play, Chick. Driscoll must have been standing around just inside the sideline disguised by all his teammate's orange jerseys. He probably stayed there while both team's switched from defensive to offensive after the fumble."

"I think you're right, Buddy. Bradford has caught the Flying Geese napping with a 68-yard touchdown pass to take the early lead. Here comes the attempted extra point…yes, Johnny Lawson's drop kick just went right up between the goal posts. Let's listen to the Panther band play their school fight song."

Their fans were ecstatic as the band started it off. "So let us cheer for Bradford High School, the very best school in the land. Cheer for the players, they'll show some spirit no matter if we fall or stand. Cheer for the players, they'll fight for all that we hold so dear. Cheer for the black and for the orange, let's go all out for Bradford High!" At least 600 happy fans just finished their fight song, and yet it was only about five minutes into the game.

Now the boys directed their attention at the celebration developing both on the field and in the nearby bleachers. Several of them smiled at each other as they watched some of the town's leading citizens pounding each on the back and hugging each other on the sidelines. These men were engaged in the local custom which allowed fathers of players and local boosters to follow action from the sidelines as long as they stayed clear of the action.

As the excitement subsided, Jumbo, who had been directing his gaze into the distance beyond the football field to a place totally engulfed in darkness, asked, "Remember when those two farmers got so mad at us a couple of months ago after we dammed up the 'crick'? They said we were starving the cows with not enough water."

Jumbo's comment touched a painful memory for several.

"Yeah, but you know what? I'd do it again, too. So what if somebody's cows don't have enough to drink until the water finally makes it over the top?" The quietest member in the group entered the conversation for the first time. He always seemed to have a friendly grin stretching from one side of his thoroughly freckled face to the other. During their many summer afternoons fishing expeditions in the Spoon River or Broadmore Pond, he always seemed to catch more than anyone else. For this honor he was known as 'Catfish'.

"Yeah, that sure was a fun thing to do, alright," agreed Dink. "The cows could have held out."

"Probably, and then again, maybe not. But all we wanted was a hockey pond to use this winter," replied Beaner.

"Which won't happen unless we go down some day after school and dam it back up before the mud freezes." Catfish's big grin reappeared and his green eyes stared wistfully in the direction of the small stream they called, 'the crick', a typical mid-western misnomer. Barely visible on most state maps of Illinois, the creek carried the official name of 'Cooper's Defeat', but none of the boys had ever heard of Cooper or what defeat he had suffered in some long-forgotten battle. It may have simply been one of Bradford's many tongue-in-cheek experiences with local humor that had now entered into a legendary status in Central Illinois.

"Catfish, that's a good idea," said the seventh boy who often was quieter than the others. "But not down at the crick." He was a well-built good looking, red-haired boy who also wore a well-trimmed flattop haircut, and spoke for the first time. As the star of the grade school heavy weight basketball team, he had been dubbed 'Hotshot' in the town's weekly newspaper last season, and it stuck. He was not only an excellent athlete, but regarded as one of the better brains in the group. "Those old farts would just tear it down and get us in trouble with our folks again. I've got an idea where we can make the perfect place for the world's best home-made hockey rink."

The football game that had served as little more than a place for them to gather was now long forgotten. Its importance dwarfed by this statement from one of the two acknowledged leaders in the group. In their band of seven only Jumbo would challenge anything Hotshot said. However, this was a time that even he was silent, and too intent to spit. They began walking away from the field in the general direction of Main Street, because time was the essence. Without comment they each knew they were going to Dorgan's, the town's only soda parlor that would be almost empty now. But it would be jammed within minutes when a local high school game was over.

"Where's it at, Hotshot?" blurted Dink. An expectant hush fell over them as they moved closer to hear his answer.

"I love to explore the woods along the river. You know how often we go out there in the summer. Sometimes I wander around while you guys are fishing, if I get bored. Well, the day before school started, when we were a few hundred yards down from the hard road bridge, I found a stream that sort of wanders off from the main river. I didn't tell anybody 'cause I wanted to see where it went. Last Sunday, I rode my bike out there and explored it all by myself. It's perfect, like our own branch of the Mighty Spoon. It trickles through a wide, low piece of land that would make an ideal pond if it had water in it. And if we cut the brush growing around the stream bed, get rid of the fallen trees, and then dig some dirt to fill in the dam come winter time it would be the best hockey rink anybody ever saw except the one where the Blackhawks play in Chicago." His words carried such authority the boys stood mute as they contemplated the message.

"Yeah," finally responded Jumbo with an obvious twinge of sarcasm. "But what happens when we dam it up? Won't some other farmer get just as mad."

The two protagonists stared at each other momentarily, and then Hotshot grinned, enjoying his game of one-upmanship. "That's the beauty of it, Jumbo. Nobody will know or care. The stream eventually rejoins the river. It doesn't go anywhere." He let his voice trail off and then added, "who knows, it's just far enough out of the way maybe we'll stumble into the place where the old counterfeiting gang hid the missing printing plates. You never can tell what we might dig up." Hotshot knew mentioning the town's greatest mystery was the surest way to totally enlist their wills.

Incredibly, sixty or seventy years earlier, one of the nation's largest counterfeiting gangs chose this tiny mid-western village as the location to print the money. They must have reasoned that no one would ever suspect that an operation of such a magnitude could happen in such an unlikely place. At the time, federal officials acknowledged the gang was making the most sophisticated bogus money they had ever seen. Though they made several different denominations that were duplicated in money, the main printing plant here promoted 6% coupon bonds. Earlier they had even faked $20 'gold' pieces.

Whether these printing plates were ever recovered, destroyed, or hidden when the operation ended was a mystery. Decades later some townspeople still harbored hope they would be the one who discovered the missing plates in case a reward was still in effect. There was also a nagging suspicion in many minds that several descendants of the few local people involved knew more about the operation than they had ever admitted. Rumors that such and such house had a bricked-up cellar wall hiding a tunnel leading to the railroad tracks, or possibly a long sealed storage vault, or if the roof-top cupola on another home down the street served as the counterfeiter's watch tower occasionally slipped into private conversations. It was the one topic no one in Bradford ever talked about openly.

Except for seven boys eagerly looking for adventure.

"My gosh," Dink blurted. "You think the gang might have buried them out there?"

"Somebody, someday is going to find them. It might as well be us. Maybe the government will pay us a big reward," Hotshot added.

"A reward," Beaner muttered. "Fantastic. I could get that new Schwinn bike with the neat horn in its tank between the bars."

"Want to head out there in the morning?" Hotshot asked, certain his fish were hooked. All he had to do was reel them in. A chorus of affirmative reply's settled the matter.

"Let's meet in the Laughin' Tree tomorrow at nine o'clock. Everybody bring a shovel and saw. We can balance them on our bike handlebars for that far. Now it's off to Dorgan's for ice cream. I've got to be home by ten."

That was all it took to send seven boys running west on Silver Street away from the now forgotten football game. Thoughts of enjoying a double-dip, ten-cent ice cream cone had replaced everything else on their minds. Except the ever-present knowledge that if they were lucky they might even win a free cone from the tiny coupon stuffed away in the bottom of the Safe-T-Cone.

CHAPTER 2

▼

THE LAUGHIN' TREE

A few minutes before the appointed hour six boys were already sitting on their chosen branches in a large Maple tree in the village's only park at the east edge of Peoria Street. This was also State Route 88, which began thirty-five miles south in Peoria, the city that became famous by Vaudeville performers for two generations. It sliced through Bradford, serving as the town's main highway, and continued on to the Wisconsin line. But most folks in Bradford called it 'eighty-eight' or simply 'the hard road.' Since they were surrounded by a network of gravel and dirt roads linking farms across the countryside with the nearest town or village, anything covered in asphalt or cement became known as a hard road. Usually however, locals could tell which hard road was the one included in the discussion without further definition.

The tree got its nickname from "Song of the South", a Disney movie in 1946 which had played in Bradford a couple of summers before. When the boys left the theater that year they agreed that Uncle Remus was right, everybody needs 'a laughin' place.' This site was first choice for three equally important reasons: it was their favorite climbing tree, it was centrally located, and it had the rare, unanimous consent of both Jumbo and Hotshot.

"Where in the world is Suck, he's probably got his nose up somebody's butt tryin' to get somethin' out of 'em," Jumbo muttered through a mouth crammed full of Tootsie Rolls. His Uncle Ned chewed tobacco, but chocolate candy was as close as Jumbo was allowed to occasionally imitate him or the other hero he loved. It gave him a puffed cheek and gobs of nasty looking spittle whenever he chose to let some fly. He was sitting on one of the two higher limbs, separated by the trunk across from Hotshot. He sent a wad downward splattering through the leaves careful to avoid hitting the nervous occupants on lower branches.

"Come on, Jumbo, remember the Laughin' Tree rules. No grippin' or arguin'. This is a place where only laughin' is allowed." Dink was confident he could get away with a mild rebuke to Jumbo because of the mystique this tree had already achieved.

No words of agreement were forthcoming from the other four, but Jumbo didn't offer any defense or protest so the matter was settled. A silence broken only by an occasional rustle of leaves ensued. Seconds later it was shattered by a loud backfire as a still unseen car driving east on Main Street slowed to make the turn, and was followed by an irritating scraping sound. After the car began a right turn at the intersection it was now headed in their direction. Each boy knew instantly who was driving. No other car in Bradford ever made a noise like this.

The loud screech caused by the driver's side running board sliding harshly over cement as hard as granite continued. Sparks spewed backwards nearly three feet. It was a living lesson in two of the laws of physics: a powerful centrifugal force created by outward turning pressure coupled with the several hundred pound weight of the man driving the car.

"Spit, Buck Ed, spit!" Jumbo's screams were unable to compete with the ear-splitting scraping noises. However, as soon as the turn was completed the car, though still listing heavily to the left, leveled slightly, no longer dragging metal along the road. Jumbo resumed his chant and was joined by the others. At the same moment Suck rode up below, lowered his bike to the ground, and chimed in with the chorus as he began climbing the tree.

The car was a gray '38 Plymouth two door coupe. How many more right turns on hard cement it could take was a serious, not hypothetical question. For part of the year it served as both transportation and home to the huge man inside. Buck Ed Minister was an enigma to most of Bradford. Mainly, no one knew how much he weighed. For that matter, where he came from, how he possibly lived for months on end in the front seat of his car, and where he went each winter were three more bits of information lots of folks admitted they would like to know. But the terrible odor originating inside the car kept everyone but young boys unconcerned with questions of hygiene far away. The only adults who got close enough to speak to the giant inside were car traders with whom he brokered many deals. It was often said just a sniff of the foul smells coming from Buck Ed's car could make a healthy person sick, and a sick person die.

However, the car's massive occupant always handsomely rewarded any boy with a dime or sometimes even fifteen cents just for running into one of the stores on Main street and buying him three or four candy bars or several bottles of pop. With children's allowances averaging no more than a quarter per week, helping Buck Ed by running for snacks several times each day was considered easy money. There was but one immutable rule in any dealings that brought errand boys near his car: breathe through your mouth.

A human head the size of a big watermelon looked out the open window. Deep, gurgling laughter erupted from the giant's throat. He glanced into the tree where seven of his most willing servants were sitting, and aimed a huge glob of chewing tobacco directly at the driver's rear view mirror sticking a foot out from the car's door. Now covered with so many layers of brown slime, its original purpose was reduced to that of a mere target. The wet tobacco hit with such powerful force its resulting splatter, aided by wind speed, and sent some of the spittle rebounding back against the side of the car. Here the mess merged with thousands of other such successful attempts, and slid to a sickening grave on the nearly ruined running board.

Each boy simultaneously cheered as the car rolled by. Again the fat man's liquid laughter boomed from the car and trailed behind as he began driving down the long hill to the southern edge of town.

"Wow," exclaimed Jumbo. "There's never been anybody like Buck Ed. He's the bestest, fattest, spitter in the world. I'd love to be like him. I bet he could knock a squirrel off a tree limb fifteen feet away. He's even better than Uncle Ned."

"Yeah," echoed Catfish. "He's the champ, alright. My brother says he could knock a crow right off a corncrib. I wish he'd drive around the block and do the whole thing over."

"Have you ever watched him start that car?" Booby asked.

"Not me," said Dink, and a few others echoed the same sentiment.

"He can't even raise his big old fat leg to reach the starter pedal on the floor. He's got a cane that he keeps beside him. When he gets ready to go he grabs the cane and shoves it onto the starter."

"Boy, you must have gotten pretty close to see that," Beaner said.

"Almost too close," Booby replied. "For a while I thought I was gonna puke the smell was so bad. And I don't even want to talk about the flies. When it's parked, that car is a fly farm."

"My mom says he makes her sick just to see him," Suck added. "She says the sight of all that crap running down his door makes her walk all the way across the street if he's parked there on Main Street. She says smelling it is even worse than seeing it."

"When I buy candy for him I always breath through my mouth, and then walk fast against the wind," Dink said, and then nodded.

"That's probably true enough, but I never get tired of watching the fat man spit," Jumbo declared.

"Let's stop it right now," Hotshot interrupted. "Gotta forget Buck Ed if we're going to get working on the hockey pond we gotta hit the road. Suck's here now. Let's go."

After fifteen minutes, they coasted down the long grade approaching the river. Several boys cast suspicious glances at the overgrown clump of trees and foliage above them on top of the hill to their left immediately before entering the bridge. Somewhere up in that dense thicket lived a large, imposing black man called Sheck Dye. No one knew whom or where he came, and because he was the only black person who lived in this area within fifteen-twenty miles. He was virtually also considered the town's hermit, because he was alone, and rarely came to town on one or two visits each month for shopping during the winter. However, he made periodic trips each week during the growing season because the big man pushed a two-wheeled cart loaded with whatever vegetables were currently ripe. These he sold to housewives from door to door until the cart was empty. Then he pushed it back over the one mile road to his home. Somewhere nearby he obviously had a large garden at the place where he lived. Calling it a house would have been a misnomer, because, in actuality, Sheck Dye's home was an original, turn-of-the-century streetcar.

It happened around ten or fifteen years earlier, when a flatbed truck loaded with the streetcar slowly made the ninety degree turn to head west on Main Street. People literally popped out of stores and houses to see this unique sight. It bore part of the name Peoria Transit Company on its side, and the large steel wheels that enabled it to roll through the city's streets had been removed. As it disappeared over the Railroad Bridge, which marked the end of downtown Bradford, a few people there shook their heads, commented briefly, and momentarily forgot it. Their assumptions that it was destined for Kewanee or Rockford were soon proven wrong when a neighbor, Harry McKeever, came into town later that evening. He said another truck had a crane, and unloaded its cargo on the top of Spoon River Hill, which was adjacent to a large farm, owned by a Chicago lawyer named Gilbert Jones.

Speculation immediately erupted in the village's five cafés, two barbershops, four grocery stores, three taverns, and around many family dinner tables during the next few days. The burning question: what does Mr. Jones plan to do with a streetcar? The answer was not long in coming when a black stranger stepped off a northbound bus one day a few days later, and walked into Dunlap's Grocery Store for a bag of staples. He then picked up the bag and his large, battered suitcase, and started walking westward out of town. No one saw him again for nearly two weeks. By then, smoke rising from a bent tin pipe on the roof of the streetcar was seen by people at the American Legion House, a couple hundred yards to the east.

The speed and intensity of rumors regarding this stranger who had moved into their peaceful little town rivaled that of a prairie wildfire. Normally, even in a small, provincial community such as Bradford, the arrival of an outsider would not cause this kind of controversy. But there was nothing normal about this situation. That a man nobody had ever seen before comes to town and moves into a transplanted streetcar is unusual enough in itself, but the fact that a man named Sheck Dye was the first black man to live in this part of Stark County made it a whole new situation.

For this reason, Hotshot still chose his proposed hockey pond site in the woods at the far side of the river. The boys knew every trail on both banks for several miles in either direction, making it easy to stay completely away from the occupant in the streetcar above them on the hill. They also knew it had been several weeks since the boys had seen Sheck Dye, because he usually pulled his large cart to town when the kids were in school at this time of the year. Most of the neighborhood women were happy to buy some of his vegetables, because his obviously were fresher than even some in the grocery stores. A few ladies were concerned about his background, his cleanliness, or maybe even some early aspects about racism, but most had enjoyed pleasant visits with him on occasion.

The project turned out to be too big for one outing. During the first Saturday, after marking the general area Hotshot thought would be large enough to create a usable hockey pond, they went to work, first diverting the stream's flow back into the river, and then concentrating on clearing underbrush away from the muddy area which remained. He estimated it would take a dam at least three feet high to provide sufficient coverage to flood the indented meadow.

An hour or so into the day's work, Beaner did the inevitable. Sounds of small trees and brush being cut was interrupted by a loud noise which seemed to gather momentum and could have been someone ripping a large piece of rotting canvas.

"Everybody head upwind. Beaner's cut a nasty one," Jumbo said.

"At least we shouldn't be bothered by mosquitoes any more," Catfish laughed.

"He's just practicing for the world championship of farting," said Suck.

"Do you really think there's such a thing?" Dink asked, wide eyed and pushing his glasses higher on his nose.

"If there is, Beaner will win it hands down," Hotshot replied.

"Do you think girls ever fart?" Catfish stopped digging as he asked the question and rubbed some sweat from his forehead.

"Good grief, no," responded Booby quickly.

"What makes you so sure about that," grunted Jumbo, chopping down a small tree in one whack of his hatchet blade.

"Have you ever heard one do it?" Booby challenged.

"No, Boob, but just because I haven't heard a girl cut a blaster doesn't necessarily mean they don't. I've damn sure heard my mom cut loose every now and then." Jumbo looked up and then grinned. "In fact, my dad says when mom gets a touch of diarrhea she can turn an ordinary porcelain commode into a booming thunderbucket." They all laughed.

"Well, how come girls always act like you just did the worst thing in the world whenever you accidentally cut one in their presence?" asked Dink.

"That's the way they are. I can't even get my sister to pull my finger anymore. It must be the same reason they don't like spitting either. Dixie gets real mad when I do it, so I do it a lot just to make her mad," Hotshot said. "The way my sister prisses around you'd think she's trying to act like she never even has to go to the toilet."

"My brother says some famous people never have to take a dump," Beaner said. "But that kinda sounds fishy, like he's pullin' my leg."

"Which famous people?" said Dink. "Did he name any?"

"Yeah, Pope Pius, Winston Churchill, and Lana Turner. He says when they feel like they have to go they just sit around and think of beautiful gardens and fields of flowers. Somehow that does it."

"That's the craziest thing I've ever heard," Suck uttered contemptuously. "Every damn animal on this planet has to poop. It's a natural fact. Even flies and cockroaches poop."

"I guess you're sure right about that, Suck," Dink said. "My dad took me and my brothers to the Shrine Circus in Peoria and an elephant took a dump in the middle of the act. Boy, it looked like a pile of chocolate colored bowling balls."

"So what, we still don't know for sure if girls fart or not," said Catfish.

"Well, like my mom does every now and then, especially when she thinks no one is around," Booby said softly. "The other day she didn't know I was in the kitchen behind her and she let one fly. I started laughin' and she turned around lickity split and said the floor must have creaked. But we were both laughin' in a few seconds. Then she apologized for it, but I told her I didn't care, as many as I've let slip when she's around."

"When my Grampa comes to visit us, our dog Tippy loves to sit in his lap while we're in the living room eating popcorn and listening to Charley McCarthy or Jack Benny on the radio," Dink began. "At least until Grampa lets an orphan. He says silent farts are called orphans 'cause he says nobody ever wants to claim 'em. When he lets one old Tip lifts his head, turns and looks up at my Grampa and lets out this low howl. Then he jumps out of his lap and crawls behind the sofa. My brothers and I all start yelling 'Grampa cut one, Grampa cut one.' He just sits there and laughs. So does my Dad. Mom always shakes her head and usually leaves the room."

"I can't imagine why girls don't see anything funny about it. A good old, loud, rotten, fart is one of the funniest things in life." When he finished speaking, Jumbo added his own special exclamation mark by spitting a huge glob of Tootsie Roll juice as loudly as he could. As predictable as sunrise, the boys all laughed as it splattered on a large leaf, nearly hitting a butterfly.

"They don't like spitting either," Catfish added. "My sisters jump all over me about spitting in the corn plant in our living room. I don't see what's so wrong. They pour water into it once a week."

"And I can't stand the way girls hate the Three Stooges," Beaner said. "Don't it make you mad every time on Saturday afternoon at the cowboy double feature when it starts with the Stooges, and all the girls let out a loud groan?"

"And we always try to cheer louder than them," Suck said.

"What the heck are girls good for if they don't like farting, spitting, and the Stooges," asked Dink, a sincerely perplexed look knotting his face.

"We're probably never going to solve that question. Boys think that stuff is funny, and girls don't. It's as simple as that. Now let's go back to work on this dam or it'll never get built," Hotshot implored.

Beaner couldn't resist holding out his hand and making a fist. Jumbo picked up on his meaning immediately, and hit it with his fist. Beaner said, "Oh, a wise guy, eh," and made a circular swing of his arm hitting Jumbo on the top of his head. He concluded the move by making a boinking sound.

Jumbo faked falling over backwards, and Dink began imitating Curly by rapidly rubbing his hands over his face and saying in a high-pitched voice, "woob, woob, woob." Then he saluted Hotshot and said, "Soitenly, Hotshot, whatever you say, nyuk, nyuk, nyuk." They were still laughing when they went back to work. These boys knew the Three Stooges had made movies before they were born in the later 1930s, and felt the funny clowns would soon retire or just forgotten forever. No matter, they and lots of other boys then still laughed at the Stooges antics as if it was new as when they saw it their first time.

An early second work session the next Saturday tackled a number of small trees that needed to be cut. All seven boys arrived that morning, and followed Hotshot's plan. They piled limbs and branches in perpendicular fashion along the lower section of the stream at the exact point where he said the dam should be built. This long pile of wood and branches would serve as its foundation. After a layer of interwoven brush and logs went down it was covered with countless shovels full of dirt and mud. Slowly the structure began to take form.

"Hotshot, it looks like the Cardinals won't be able to catch the Braves," Dink said wistfully. Then he couldn't resist adding, "Of course, the Cubbies have been out of it since the second day of the season." While the other five always were in the thick of every game of Work-up, 500, or even one of the rare times when enough kids showed up to make two teams, Dink and Hotshot were the only two who actively followed major league teams. When he saw newsreel highlights of Enos 'Country' Slaughter scoring the winning run in the seventh game of the '46 World Series with his famous dash from first base after Harry Walker's double, Dink forever became a Cardinal supporter. Hotshot took the other approach. He loved the Chicago Cubs. Baseball fans in Bradford rooted for one or the other of these two teams and the town was almost equally divided.

"Yeah, it looks like Spahn and Sain and pray for rain is going to get the job done for Boston," Hotshot muttered. "Now I suppose I am going to hear about your beloved Stan the Man for the next hour."

"Why not. It looks like he's got the National League batting crown all tied up. He's hitting around .375. Stan the Man is the best hitter in baseball," Dink said proudly. No matter whenever he was with a group of kids who would be choosing up to play that day, the most embarrassment experience was that he was picked last every time. But rooting for the Cards made him feel a whole lot better.

"No he isn't, he's *one* of the best hitters, but he isn't the best. Look at Ted Williams. His average is almost as high as Musial. And you've got to consider Joe DiMaggio and Duke Snider," Hotshot said defensively.

"Don't mention Duke or Jackie or Pee Wee or any of those Bums to me," Dink replied. "You know I can't stand Brooklyn. They're the only team I love to hate. And I'd be happy if Stan the Man hit for the cycle every time the Cards play the Dodgers."

"And that will never happen again," Hotshot said emphatically, and shook his head. Both guys stopped talking immediately.

Beginning in the sixth grade, Dink and Hotshot bet a nickel a game on the Cub-Cardinal series each season, and, though they played each other twenty-two times, the most either could lose was $1.10. But the rivalry was so heated and games so close, winnings had yet to reach even twenty cents. Today, after such an intense discussion, normal arguments of baseball were soon replaced by the hard work at hand.

About noon the boys got a nod of approval from Hotshot aimed in the direction of their lunch pails. They had only really been working in earnest for little more than two hours, but already the area chosen for the pond was taking shape. As they sat on an old log at the edge of the clearing rapidly devouring their sandwiches Beaner noticed a look of great intensity on Dink's face.

"Whatcha lookin' at, Dink. You sure got your eyes peeled on somethin'," he asked.

"Look over there at the other side. I can't quit starin' at that huge old tree that went down in some big storm sometime back," Dink replied. "If you let your mind run loose you can think up a lot of neat things that tree might be."

"Like what?" Jumbo snorted. "It just looks like a big dead tree to me."

"Me. too," chimed in Catfish.

"Like I said, you gotta let your imagination run loose. See how it split down the middle? Half the trunk went to its right and the other half went left. Fortunately for us both halves fell in opposite directions along the side where we want to build this hockey pond. All we have to do is trim the branches on the lower two logs so they don't stick out in the pond. We can let those other ones going up and out in lots of directions stay where they are 'cause they aren't hurtin' our job, are they, Hotshot?"

"No," he reasoned, "they aren't in our way, Dink. And I think the two main trunks will come in handy as butt benches where we can lace up our skates or just take a break every now and then. We can forget the other higher branches and leave them where they are. We'll just clean up the two trunks."

"Just what kind of thing do you see over there, Dink?" asked Booby.

"At first I imagined it was a big, hungry, Tarantula gettin' ready to eat one of us. Then I looked again and saw a giant octopus with its long tentacles reaching out to grab us. But I finally decided it's really a huge moose buried up to the top of its head in mud. We're lookin' at the biggest rack of antlers in the whole wide world." Dink's words came slowly as if he were in a trance, and then, unexpectedly, he ran to the middle of the fallen tree and jumped up on the split stump. "Look at me you guys. I'm standin' on top of something bigger than Babe the Blue Ox. It's just been hiding here all these years. And someday it's goin' to wake up and then it'll lift its head outta all this mud, and let out a bellow that'll have every dog howlin' for three counties."

Suck broke the eerie silence that followed. "Darned if it don't look like he's jumpin' around on top of a big moose head tryin' to hide from us."

"Yeah, it does look kinda like horns or antlers," Catfish said.

"Well, that does it," Hotshot exclaimed. "Dink, looks like you've given this place a name. From now on this will be 'Hidden Moose Hockey Pond. What do you guys think of that?"

Nods of assent settled the issue. Dink was ecstatic as he walked back to the group. Wow, he thought. So I named the pond just cause I've got a wild imagination. That's really neat. He smiled proudly and then said, "The only thing I ever named before was one of Beaner's farts. Remember when we were all up at Dorgan's for somebody's birthday party, I called that one 'Wallpaper peeler'."

Beaner smiled and shrugged. "Yeah, it was a real disaster. My mom said if I ever did anything like that in public again she'd keep me locked up in our bathroom for so long I might go through high school sittin' there taking courses at home. She said it burned her nostrils and made Mrs. Schindler's eyes water."

"You gotta keep doing' it, Beaner, Jumbo said. Don't let your Mom screw up a good thing. You oughta be mighty proud of yourself. You're the fartin' champ."

"Let's get back to work you guys. We've got a lot left to do," Hotshot commanded. Somewhat reluctantly they resumed their previous tasks.

No one seemed to notice the slight grin still etched on Dink's face as he took another furtive glance in the direction of the fallen tree. He could hardly wait to tell his mother. She was the one who encouraged him to listen to a Saturday morning radio show called 'Let's Pretend' which featured a different fairly tale or story each week. It was this program, more than any of the other after school adventure serials, which had the greatest effect on developing his imagination and ability to create scene after scene. She called the best and biggest stage was in his mind. Dink knew she would be pleased, and nothing he had ever done made him happier than seeing her special smile of pride and satisfaction when he told her of moments such as this.

"It's obvious we're not going finish this thing today," Hotshot said as they saw the sun slip behind the tops of oak and maple trees near the river. "But if we come back next Saturday, you're not going to be here, right, Suck?"

"Yep, my dad's bringing me to Champaign for a home football game," Suck said and smiled. He was obviously happy about this. For him Big Ten Football was big time excitement.

"No problem. Six of us can do it next week. We can take the dam two feet higher by working the other side. I bet it'll bring the water level up at least to the edge of the clearing over there. That should give us a large, shallow pool which will freeze quicker and thicker. And this place is pretty well protected from wind. We need the smoothest ice possible."

"Yeah, and I like the shallow part. Maybe nobody will fall through the ice the way Jim Erickson from Galva did last winter out at Broadmore Pond," Catfish said referring to a well-known accident that was almost a fatal disaster the previous January. Hugh Mallett, Jim's grandfather, lived in Bradford.

"That boy was lucky he didn't drown or freeze his ass," Jumbo added, and was answered with several assenting grunts or nods. "Even if we do fall through, we'll be able to stand up 'cause it'll only be about three feet at the deepest spot."

"You sure have thought this out mighty well, Hotshot, my hat's off to you. If I had a hat." Dink laughed, but it was obvious he meant it as a sincere compliment, not just a wisecrack. His comment brought immediate words of appreciation from all of the others. They were accomplishing something none of them would have ever suspected possible, and now the end was clearly in sight.

A few minutes later Hotshot announced there was nothing else they could do. It was quitting time. Each boy was so intent on gathering tools, lunch pails, and canteens no one noticed the tall figure observing them for the past thirty minutes from the security of a dense thicket only 75 feet away. Only when the boys departed for home did he leave his hiding place and enter the cleared area before the dam. Had they seen him they would have instantly known it was Sheck Dye. Slowly he moved along the muddy wall, touching, probing, and finally stepped back with a look of admiration.

Then he pulled on his old woolen cap a bit tighter, and disappeared into the woods.

CHAPTER 3

▼

BIG MAN COMES TO TOWN

Three days later school had ended, and Jumbo was kicking a discarded three-pound coffee can that someone must have thrown there several days ago. The old sidewalks throughout the town were probably built forty or fifty-years, and aging cracks along here was no different. As he was walking back to his home after finishing his after school chores at the pharmacy where his dad worked, he was shuffling along Peoria Street going south after crossing by the corner at Bradford Dry Cleaners. All of the kids had serious jobs to do almost every day, and Jumbo re-stocked some shelves for his father who worked there for Tinker Scholes' drug store.

His cheerful whistling belied the intensity reflected in his facial expressions as he visually followed the erratic path taken by the now deformed can. While rounding the corner as he walked toward Arbor Street it was momentarily blocked by the large clump of lilac bushes in Terwilliger's front yard. Jumbo gave the can a solid kick only to be surprised by the sound created by someone else kicking the can back to him. He peeked around the corner, and was slowly walking around it, but something suddenly stopped him. A big man was looming before him, silhouetted by the low afternoon setting sun.

"Sheck Dye,' he explained involuntary. "Oh, wow. I didn't mean to hit you or your cart. Honest!" Jumbo was clearly shaken by the near collision that his can might have caused a problem with a tall figure standing by the two-wheeled cart hovering directly above him.

"No problem, son. When your tin can hit my cart, I figured I ought to toss it over so you could jus' keep kickin' it." Sheck smiled, but Jumbo was cowering backwards, and slowly started to edge around the bushes.

He started to mumble saying, "I….I didn't mean to do it. Honest." With this final stammering denial of guilt, he turned and accelerated his retreat by breaking into a full sprint in the direction he had just come back from. But in a few seconds, he darted west into the alley that goes behind all the stores on the south side of Main Street, and hid behind Dave Real's backyard, crawling into the bushes surrounding the house. Miss Sallie Vanzant, Bradford's oldest and sternest high school teacher, lived in the second floor of this home. She had just started climbing down the steps to get to her car, and wondered what was this all about. "Young man, why are you hiding under this shrubbery?" she said firmly.

Suddenly Jumbo thought he had just started something like World War III. He didn't even want to try and explain it to her if he could just get away. Quickly he slid under the house and crawled out of it on the other side. He hastily knew he could run farther around the next house before she could walk over to find him, and now he was instantly zigzagging by several trees under twig-like branches between their homes.

As he peeked through the foliage, Jumbo saw the big man's back disappear behind the Horrie house as he was going east by the homes on Silver Street. Miss Vanzant was in her car also going in the opposite direction so the pressure was over in his mind, but now he immediately decided that he needed to call the guys. He started running again over Arbor Street, and jogged on the side yard that got him to Second Street.

Thankfully, he jumped three steps in one big leap, threw open his kitchen door and grabbed the telephone in the parlor. This excitement had been so fast, and somewhat loud his dog named Brownie began barking furiously, thinking a strange intruder had broken in. Jumbo's fingers clutched the telephone's crank, and he spun it rapidly. "Hello, Central, give me 176….and hurry, please!"

Over the thirty-one years she had worked as a telephone switchboard operator in the main office, or Central, as she and it were both called, Beulah Blackburn had heard it all…literally. Buelah's two natural inclinations were gossip and chocolate, and seemed that both of them happily merged in her chosen vocation: talking. Phone call after phone call began and ended for her with every one in Bradford's area system, and these messages she plugged into were never ending sources for new, juicy material with her best friends. Unfortunately, her job was to sit down all day long, and let her eat fifty kinds of candy any time she wanted, which was apparently often. Friends called her the Bon Bon queen.

Years of working in her job created a sedentary regimen, and over indulging her appetite transformed her once lithe body into something so massive local wags wondered if she and Buck Ed should be required to wear truck license plates on their front and back sides. Folks occasionally had to meet at her second floor office for a special call. Someone in one of the bars broke up his friends when he said that he climbed up the steps to make a long distant call, but she was tied up on the phone while he waited behind her. Apparently, he started overdoing his imagination, because he told the men in the bar one day, while she was sitting in the small chair stool from the back, it appeared that her gigantic buttocks were a pair of tremendous jaws in the process of devouring the helpless seat.

Actually, her large torso was never a problem for anyone there, because Buelah was a good and happy person. She was considered the most vital, if not the most popular, member of the group that she and eleven other ladies called 'the Canister Club.' Once a week they all played the card game really called Canasta, and they all thoroughly enjoyed it. But the best thing she did was running the phone numbers, which instantly notified Bradford's Volunteer Fire Department. When an emergency occurred, Buelah could spring the volunteers into action better than anyone else. Or if either of the two doctors had to save someone's life, she was always on the ball.

When an aspect that had to be involved in with Gilly Shaw, the only local constable, she could call him directly. Everyone seemed to realize it was her ever-present, sixth-sense alertness that Buelah could always come through. This was one of those days when the youngest member of the Robert's residence made his call.

"Eddy Jay, is that you?" she asked in her special demanding tone.

"Yes, ma'am."

"Is anything wrong?"

"No ma'am, I just need to talk with Dink, er, Jonathan Edwards, quick."

"I'll make the call for you, but are you two in some kind of trouble?"

"No, ma'am. I promise. It's just to tell him something. There is no need for you to worry. Now can I get 176, please." Jumbo was still sounding a little breathless, but he was losing his patience. Crap, he thought. I might as well run over to Dink's house and talk with him since as this old fatass is taking so long.

"Okay, young man, I'm ringing it right now." Her tone was now so strong Jumbo wondered if she had read his mind. If he had given it an even deeper thought he would have known that Buelah soon knew that Shuck was just a block and a half from where she was sitting.

Twenty minutes later seven boys were sitting behind the low, sweeping branches of the willow tree, hiding behind the adjacent gazebo on the empty lot between Suck's house, and the Rees home.

Since this was a called meeting of the S.M.C.A. club, Jumbo was kingpin. He first read about being a member by joining the Strong Men's Club of America. This advertisement was on one of the back pages of a comic book the year before. The organization was founded by a body builder named Joe Bonomo, and operated through the same mail order techniques as Charles Atlas, the most famous teacher of body building to young men at that time.

Jumbo was not as tall as some of the other boys, but he possessed a taut, well-muscled body if goaded or forced into a fight. He didn't send for any information, however. One day he simply announced he was forming an SMCA chapter and anyone could join.

His intriguing plan was quite simple: he would be called Joe Vice One rather than being a president because he felt Joe Bonomo held that position, and none of them had to pay any dues. Furthermore, in a remarkable and perceptive adaptation of democracy in action, he was extremely content to be vice president. Keeping members feeling as if they had an official role, Jumbo also made everyone else a vice president, and ranked them by his perception or proven strength from two to seven. When these seven boys agreed to be a member, they immediately closed the membership club. Unfortunately, Dink, to his long-suffering regret, was known as Joe Vice Seven.

"This better be good, you guys. I'm not thrilled about giving up Superman and Captain Midnight both," Beaner said. He was Joe Vice Three.

"Yeah, I hate missing any of my radio shows more than anything," added Catfish, also called Joe Vice Four.

"Just relax, will ya? I thought it was the perfect time to have a great meeting of our S.M.C.A. club. We've got a chance to do some real Junior Tracy detective work now." He glanced at Hotshot for just a second. Hotshot recognized both the statement and the kind of sarcastic look were in reference to his announced plan to find a secret entrance to the old coal mine, but ignored the barbs. "That's why I had Joe Vice Seven help me call you guys, and make a quick meeting right now." Jumbo raised head slowly, and tilted his eyes down. He paused, and then said, "Sheck Dye is in town. I believe it's the first time we've seen him since school started around Labor Day."

"What are we going to do?" asked Catfish apprehensively.

"Follow him. We've got to find out what he is up to. If we hit our bikes right through town on Main Street, we can hide along the only street he will be pushin' his cart. For sure he'll have to go back to the river where he lives at his trolley trailer. Remember last year when we said he must be up to somethin'. It's time to find out now." Jumbo's voice and mannerisms were directly copied from B-movies in numerous scenes he had carefully observed each Saturday on the afternoon double-feature shows. Red Ryder, the Lone Ranger, Lash Larue, the Durango Kid, and other stalwart western heroes informed their side-kicks and subordinates of their plans in this same precise, tight-lipped manner. "He'll be going right in front of us in a few minutes because he has covered all the way down Silver Street.

After a few more moments, they could hear the creaks and squeaks of the large metal cart as it slowly rumbled past the high school making a couple more homes toward the place where they were. Each boy lapsed into silent concentration following the unseen carts moving path in their minds. At the last home there, the cart left a nearby grass covered driveway, and it started clattering loudly over the hard sidewalk cement turning west going toward Main Street. At this minute, Shuck Dye and his cart emerged from the corner clump of bushes and were in full view of seven hidden pairs of eyes.

No one knew if Sheck's age was fifty-five or seventy-five. Years of backbreaking manual drudgery had taken its toll, and his steps were labored and methodical. However, he was tall and still strongly built, with broad, powerful looking shoulders. Each visit by this time of the day, he usually was now slightly sagged from the big load he always began in the morning filling his cart. His close-cropped hair curled into hundreds of tight ringlets each as bright as a newly burst cotton boll, and his short, fuzzy beard was equally white. Its glistening color enhanced the abrupt contrast with his Hershey's colored skin. The man whose presence held seven barely breathing boys in rapt attention was the only black man living within fifteen to twenty miles of Bradford. Jumbo whispered, "He's stopping at the Schuneman's home' over there 'cause she's home."

"What's he got in his cart?" Booby asked softly.

"All I can see is carrots, tomatoes, potatoes, and some flowers, maybe. But I bet he's got something a lot more neat things than that. I've always thought he might be a crook," Jumbo said.

"You always dream up bullshit faster than a duck with diarrhea," Hotshot hushed. "He may be just a hard working old man."

"Yeah," added Suck. "From what I've heard no one ever even causes him any problem anymore. My older sister said about three years ago some of the guys in her high school class threw some green walnuts one night against his trolley trailer. He suddenly came from out of somewhere in the woods, and asked them to please stop doing that because it might break one of his windows. Sally's friends were so surprised they told him they were sorry, and no one does it anymore."

"Well, I still bet he has something else going on in our town, and I think we at least ought to study it. If he's a crook or a thief, we can get him arrested." Jumbo was relieved when he saw all six of the boys were now studying more closely at the person rolling across the street.

"He's coming right over next door, and I bet he will ring the door for Mrs. Rees. Better squeeze even flatter, guys, or he'll see us for sure." Dink quietly finished this and even turned his head to the side.

Now Catfish asked a version of the same question again. "What else has he got in his cart?"

It was silent for a few seconds, and then Suck softly said, "Flowers. At least that is all I can see beside the small bunch of vegetables."

"He's ringing Mrs. Rees' bell. She opened the door. He's tipping his hat to her. Now he's holding up a bunch of flowers. She's nodding, yes, and...", Dink blabbered out.

"For Pete's sake, Dink, just shut up!" Beaner exclaimed. "We can see what he's doing. You act like you think you're Bill Stern or Mel Allen or..."

Jumbo interrupted him, and was angry. "You guys stop talking! Be a lot quieter. He'll be seeing or hearing us," Jumbo uttered.

Mrs. Rees handed Sheck some coins, and then she took the bouquet he held out to her. The flowers were a beautiful mixture of prairie flowers and some interesting weeds, blended into the bundle. Sheck again tipped his hat, smiled and walked back down the steps to push his cart away from the house.

As he slowly rolled away past a couple of more homes farther away, Booby spoke softly. "Do you think he saw us?"

"I doubt it," Jumbo said, "but he might have heard that idiotic play by play broadcast. It's a good thing, Dink, you weren't involved in talking too much to the Japs, or Pearl Harbor would have even been sooner."

Dink frowned at the rebuke, but didn't respond. He knew he couldn't control his mouth. But then he simply said, "I was only five years old when they bombed the boats there. I doubt anybody thinks I caused the problem."

Hotshot shrugged off Dink's ridiculous comment, but his face was now also screwed up in a deeper scowl. Then he looked directly into Jumbo's eyes, and said, "What's so sneaky or worried about an old man selling flowers and toma- toes. That what I'd like to know?"

"I think his flowers and vegetables are just a trick. I bet he's up to somethin' else just like all the crooks who live in Chicago, and maybe he had something involved in the counterfeiters we heard about before." Most of the other guys started staring at each other with a doubt rising into their minds, and Jumbo cashed in with his strongest question. "What if he's part of that old bunch of money makers? He's old enough to have been right into the mess"

"Yeah, maybe he's got dynamite in the wagon and he's going to blow the vault at the bank," Dink said, his face brightening with enthusiasm.

Snickers, heads shakes, and moans greeted Dink's pitiful suggestion.

"You are easily the biggest nutcase anyone has ever known in Bradford," Suck muttered.

"Listen, you guys don't know whether this man is right or wrong either," Dink instantly replied. "Maybe he ain't gonna blow up the bank, but what if he's a burglar and he's just going door to door selling petunias and radishes to just see what's what and who's who."

"That's the best thing you've ever said in Bradford, Joe Bonomo Seven, and this is why we have to find out what he's doing," said Jumbo, and his words had instantly rebuilt Dink's self esteem with that quick reply. Jumbo also let his com- ment gave him a better way to get the game plan back in order.

'Yeah, Joe Vice One. Maybe Sheck's casin' the joint," Dink answered giving a short imitation of Jimmy Cagney in one his recent crook movies.

"That's just what he might be doing, guys. It sure adds up. It's the same thing the Jesse James gang did before they robbed the banks. Remember that movie a couple of Saturday afternoons ago? A crook cowboy checked all around the town before he robbed the place." Jumbo was actually thrilled that Dink had somehow made it sound better than they even knew. If Dink's fertile imagination was going to crank out possibilities faster than the others could shoot them down, what was the harm in speculating? But mainly he didn't want to take control of the SMCA.

"Heck, what if he's a crook from Chicago hiding out down state again til the heats off," Suck said, and almost had a surprised look that the words had come out of his own mouth.

"You guys are nuts," Hotshot said exasperated.

"No," Jumbo explained, "That does sort of fit. Remember hearing about that guy from the old Chicago mob that got blown off a tractor after he tried to start a new life? My dad told this to my older brother when we went duck hunting last

Sunday. He said it happened south of Springfield, I think, and that guy was blasted by a double barrel, twelve-gauged shotgun." Jumbo knew more about guns than any of his friends, because his family loved to hunt even more than fish.

"Yeah, somebody else got blasted in a barber shop while getting a haircut in a small town no bigger than Bradford," Catfish contributed. "When I was fishing with my dad a few months ago he told me about it. You can't deny that, Hotshot."

"Sure, I know about that stuff," Hotshot mumbled, "but those guys were supposedly double crossing Al Capone's old gang, and some of his bunch rubbed them out." Each of the boys had picked up the routine lingo of mob-talk from recent news events in periodic gangster movies, and double-features thanks to something called the 'Eyes and the Ears of Movie-news.' Hotshot then added, "I think this old man is just harmless. Besides, I don't think darkies do crimes like this."

The other six guys were thrown for a loop with this statement. None of them knew anything about black people, because they had never lived nearby or studied in school with anyone black before. About the only book they had even learned to read in first grade was about a boy named Black Sambo who had to run so fast as he tried to get away from a tiger. Unfortunately, the tiger turned him into a tub of butter.

After several long seconds, Jumbo broke the silence. "Let's just try to figure out if he's got any other plan we don't know about. He might be hiding somethin' along where he lives by the river." Jumbo's words were with such conviction the others were caught in his spell. However, Hotshot was not impressed. He remained as skeptical as ever, and sat there shaking his head.

"What if Sheck Dye killed Al Capone?" Dink suddenly blurted.

"Wow," Catfish said.

"Well, big Al died last year and there are lots of rumors how it happened," Jumbo added.

"Oh, my aching ass," Hotshot groaned. "You guys are as full of more crap than a Christmas goose."

"But how Big Al went down is a serious possibility. I mean look at this. If you hear that a Chicago crook needs to go into a hideout, can you do any better than an abandoned street car in the Spoon River woods?" Jumbo stared at the others as if he had made a very logical assertion, but Hotshot rolled his eyes once more, and acted as if he was suddenly barfing.

"Do you think any famous crook in big, old Chicago would want to be living in a crazy dump like the one out by our river? I bet the cops wouldn't even want to see that place."

Jumbo looked over at Hotshot, and then didn't even stop because he knew they were running out of time. "Let's go and find another place to watch him again. We can ride south to Silver Street, then go west to go on a different back way from him. We can shoot right by St. John's church, and go past the old harness factory by the train tracks. We ought to be able hide out near the Kidd house. Sheck has to go right by there."

Five others all nodded, and then ran behind Suck's garage where each of them had hidden their bikes. Each went quietly across their street where Sheck was now a half dozen homes farther west of them, but Hotshot said he was not coming.

"This is simply a waste of time, and I am leaving, "Hotshot called to the others as they were speeding along. With that he turned south and began going slowly as his home was in that direction. It was a bit of a shock, however, so the other six guys stayed together, and soon were creeping through the Kidd's big yard, facing their only road possible. A large section of the beautiful arbor was brimming with concord grapes as they carefully crawled, single-file up on the rows in to a line behind the big garden.

"We'll, we're hiding around between growing some tomatoes on one side and big pumpkins on the other," Jumbo whispered. They nodded, since they had reached the garden's northern end, which faced the street. Jumbo singled, and they each spread out a few feet from one another, and took prone positions, which separated garden from yard. They were now about thirty feet from the sidewalk.

"These bushes don't have many big leaves. I just hope he can't see us," Catfish said.

"If we stay low and quiet he won't," Jumbo countered softly. "We're ahead of him by at least ten minutes. Joe Vice Seven, you go out on the sidewalk like nothing's wrong. Just walk normal. See if you can see him comin'."

Dink was on his feet instantly, happy with the assignment. He hurdled the hedge, and jogged rapidly up to the aging concrete sidewalk. He then turned towards the center of town, and began walking in the direction Jumbo was sure Sheck Dye would appear. Each of the other guys could see him as he slipped into the street, and walked over to the northern side of that pavement. However, if Dink was trying to appear nonchalant by cramming his hands in his pocket, strolling along in a jointed, uneven goose-necked shuffle, and simultaneously making a pitiful attempt to whistle, he was a total failure. He had transformed himself into the epitome of conspicuousness merely by attempting to achieve the opposite effect.

"Holy Moley, Jumbo. You shouldn't have sent Dink. Clowns in a circus won't be that obvious," Suck uttered.

"Yeah, all he needs to do to stand out more is tie a cow bell around his neck and take a dump right in the street," Beaner said.

"Yeah, but it's too late now," Jumbo agreed, and shook his head.

Dink was so intent on looking for Sheck on the north side of the street, he almost didn't see the old man and his cart rolling towards him on the other. Sheck had stopped so suddenly, he was able to clearly stare at Dink. Obviously, something was different, even though Sheck and his cart was a block farther east. As Sheck started moving the cart again, Dink froze momentarily, then spun around, and began running full speed back through the three or four front yards he had just passed over. Sadly, his frantic retreat was not lost on the other alert eyes in his group.

At the last second, after racing across the street, he ran pell-mell toward his supposed hidden comrades behind the garden, and jumped over the hedge. Dink would have almost cleared it, if he was a lot more athletic, but his attempt tripped, and he nearly fell headfirst into several baskets of fresh apples that would have been the last growth this year. Between the noise, the chaos, and a half dozen boys rolling away in every direction, Sheck immediately stopped. As the boys began to reorganize, he softly pushed his cart from the north side to the south, and across the street. His quietness kept them from realizing he changed sides. Then he decided to figure out what was going on.

"Gawd-O-Mighty," Jumbo said exasperatedly. "Dink, you must be the clumsiest a-hole in three states. You might as well stand up and start screaming 'hey Sheck', we're over here spyin' on you."

"He's comin', he's comin', guys! That's why I hurried," Dink gasped through quick panting. "I saw him coming on the other side of the street. He's not on this side. He couldn't have seen me 'cause I ran in front the other yard and ran back here, not out in front of everyone." Dink was now sitting up, and brushing himself off. Somehow, he found dirt into every uncovered crease in his skin. Fortunately, his glasses had fallen off, but were not broken when he fell. However, two sections of fresh, tilled soil smeared over his face, and he looked like a dirty, blonde raccoon.

"Dink, the only way Sheck Dye didn't see or hear you if he's deaf as a post or blind as a bat," Catfish said.

"Or both," Booby said.

"Boy, I risk my life for you guys, and this is all the thanks I get. Look at me. I'm so dirty I bet my mom will make me take a bath tonight, and we all hate that." He grabbed his glasses and began to wipe them on his already filthy T-shirt.

Beaner scoffed. "Oh, sure, like you risked your life. Maybe you ought to start wearing a tank helmet like Mr. Huey says you guys will have when he coaches your grade school football team next year."

"What you boys doin' here layin' down in the dirt? You tryin' to get on talkin' terms with a mole, or a rabbit?" The husky sound of Sheck Dye's voice behind them shocked all six boys instantly, and they were flat on the ground. Their chins dropped in stunned silence as Sheck immediately added, "If you were tryin' to sneak up on old Sheck, you better get a mite sharper at your trackin'. You all make more noise than a roomful of womenfolk at a 'quiltin' bee. Don't leave up yet, 'cause you all have to be okay. I jus hope you were not goin' to do somethin' silly against me. There's a lot of good things in life, and, boys, we all can be a happy bunch right here in America." Sheck's low, soft chuckle was now the only sound they heard.

He had a rich bass resonance, and his words flowed easily in a slow, friendly drawl. Then he winked at them, and was genuinely amused at their surprised transfiguration.

"We're sorry, Mr. Dye. We made a mistake," Suck gently said.

"Yeah, I'm the president of our club, and Dink is the idiot who said you were a crook from Chicago," Jumbo said.

"What," Dink yelled, and stared at Jumbo. "You're the one who dreamed this plan up." Then he sheepishly looked right into Mr. Dye, I had to see where you were comin' by here."

"What you askin' about a crook from Chicago? Boys I ain't never been even close to the city called Chicago, and I never have stolen even one green apple…all my entire life! Forty or fifty years ago my daddy brought our family to live in Lewistown about 75 miles south of here on the same river. He was an honest blacksmith, and none of my family has ever done any wrong things. I think you boys are listenin' to your radio shows too much. You may be dreamin' too much to even be think'n."

Now the boys were embarrassed as each of them stood up, and shuffled from one foot to the other.

"I hope to see all of you soon, boys," Sheck smiled. "Go get your bikes, and run out now, 'fore Mrs. Kidd takes a broom to ya. You broke some nice, big heads of lettuce that she'll be eatin' or given to one of her friends. I'll go to her back porch now, and offer to sell the good ones just to help her if she wants to do it. But, boys, I know you would never do somethin' like this again. And be sure to tell anyone else, nobody ever throws no more green walnuts at ol' Sheck's home again, you hear."

"You bet," Jumbo said.

"Yeah, we'll tell that to anyone else, I promise," said Suck. With that the six boys were running to their bikes, and in seconds were out of sight.

Sheck picked up the spilled vegetables, and carried them to his cart where he had left it when he found where the boys had been laying. Mrs. Kidd laughed when she heard about the boy's mistake, and thanked Sheck for his consideration. She offered to split it, and he could sell them to someone else the next day if he wished. He tipped his hat, smiled, and resumed his homeward journey.

As the old man who was wearing a checkerboard, flannel shirt, and faded bib-overalls walked back to the cart, he pushed it for a few feet on Phoenix Avenue, and turned directly west on the main road. He was suddenly greeted by as majestic a sunset as he could have ever remembered. Countless rays splintered into a semi-circle from behind a huge, billowing cloud back-lit in swirling, pastel hues of pink and blue and red covering the tops that filled the big trees in Harper's Woods. Even though his home was less than a mile further, and it would be dark before he reached it, Sheck Dye was so filled with wonder and gratitude he simply stopped and stared.

"Praise the Lord," he said softly, his radiant face reflecting the skies golden brilliance. "Praise the Lord."

CHAPTER 4

▼

THE BRADFORD
BREAKFAST CLUB

Levi Iodor reached for the screen door with one hand, and, with the other pulled the dangling chain of his railroad watch to remove it from it's special pocket on the front of his bib overalls. As he strode through the front door of the Bradford Café, he flipped open the engraved lid, glanced down to check the time, and nodded. It was just as it should be; six-thirty in the morning, and his regulars would be awaiting his arrival, their morning chores completed.

He'd been telling time from the location of the sun from more than 60 years of working in the fields, and, even though it hadn't yet risen, he didn't need to look at the watch. However, by now it had become such a habit each time he reached for the restaurant door he was caught up in a self-perpetuating action. Levi's farm was the farthest out of town, at least six miles east, and he was usually last to take his place at the table.

Fourteen years, Francis Clark, a long-time agricultural icon and one of the high school's best teachers, decided this town needed a Horse Show. Levi and Ralph Kopp helped him every year from that day to this. Now the big Labor Day weekend virtually had turned into a miniature country fair. Wyoming had its Corn Boil every 4th of July, and Toulon did 'Old Settlers Celebration' a month later, but Bradford felt it was just as proud.

Sadly, seven years previously, the whole town was stunned when Mr. Clark was struck by polio. In just five days he died in a Peoria hospital. World War II began less than two months later and it also seemed the second Decade of Depression might still continue. Now polio was just another sad problem in town.

Judging from the many stars still visible in the pre-dawn sky it was going to be another sunny day that already was alive with the sounds of tractors and corn pickers chugging along off in the distance in every direction. If the first week of November could bring a repeat of the final days of October, an additional week of dry weather meant an early harvest this year as crops would be stored for future sale or use or off to the elevators for immediate sale.

"Morning, Mr. Iodor. You're just about as punctual as those Swallows I've heard about at Capistrano, wherever the heck that place is." She rolled her eyes playfully, smiled and nudged the older man as she flitted by him.

"Good morning yourself, Lynn," Levi said to the waitress now hustling to a table a few feet away. "You look as pert and cute as ever." Then Levi warmly responded to the presence of at least a dozen other friends sitting at tables throughout the long I-shaped dining area. But he headed instinctively for the same two tables with nicked chrome legs which had been carefully pushed together to form one specifically for his little group. Years ago he and his companions were branded "The Breakfast Club" from a radio show out of Chicago hosted by Don MacNeill. These tables were where he'd had breakfast almost everyday for more than thirty years, most of them with the same men he joined again this morning. He offered some gentle hellos around the group, and pulled back the waiting chair. No one else would have sat there even if he'd been sick. Once a person had sat in a chair as many years as Levi had, it was considered his private property.

Lynn looked over her shoulder and smiled again at his group as he sat down. She had a glass coffeepot in one hand and a small tablet in the other. A pencil protruded from above her right ear, almost lost in the strawberry-blonde upswept hairdo. Though frost had gently covered the ground early that morning, for some reason she was almost bursting out of a summery, navy blue short-sleeved blouse with white polka-dots and a tight fitting white skirt which appeared it would split a seam any second.

"Maybe you oughta get those coke-bottle glasses of yours adjusted, Levi. Or are you just showin' your age? Has to be either eyesight or old age since you're callin' something like that cute and pert. Why man, you talk about Lynn like she's one of your granddaughters. That's a full-blown, beautiful woman slingin' food around here." Carl Hensley, another farm owner, couldn't resist taking a jab at his long-time friend and contemporary. He blew over a saucer full of still steaming coffee, and winked at a couple of the other men.

"Your damn sure right about that, Carl," Ed Dunn, a dairy farmer from a few miles north of town muttered. "I have a mighty hard time keeping Christian thoughts in my head as long as I can't seem to get my eyes off watching her move that fabulous body around this place."

"Much as I like ya, it sure isn't you guys who draw me back here every morning. She's a welcome feast for my woman starved eyes," Jess Copplestreet interjected. "You gotta remember, the only other women I ever see in my farm stacked like she is are the gals wearin' their underthings in my outhouse's Sears catalog." Jess was one of the few middle-aged farmer bachelor men in the area who had never married.

As if acknowledging the fact their eyes and minds were firmly trained in her direction, Lynn casually looked back, smiled and sped around the end of the counter into the kitchen.

"Look at that fanny in action, boys, you're looking at two woodchucks tryin' to fight their way out of a small gunnysack," Tiny Hartman said. Like so many before him, Tiny got his nickname because he was anything but tiny. He probably didn't weigh a pound under 280. However, his laugh was infectious, and the others quickly responded even though he had used that line ten or twenty times before in the same situation.

"Boys, boys, let's not let this breakfast take off on such a low road. Remember, this is the day the Lord hath made," Levi said in mild rebuke.

"Levi, I don't spend much time around the Methodist or any other church the way you do each week," Carl said slowly. Mirth had left his face, replaced by a look of mock seriousness. "Naturally I respect you for it," "but I'm just a bit confused over what the Lord was thinkin' when he made a wild piece of excitement like that young woman we call Bradford's answer to Betty Grable?"

"She's well fitted into his plan, I'm sure of that," Levi retorted. "She'll make some lucky man a fine wife one of these days."

"Maybe it'll be me." Dusty Sweat, the youngest person at the table, and one not wearing bib overalls and a long sleeve flannel plaid shirt finally spoke. Dusty was a contract truck driver who worked for Gib Hall, owner of several hog and cattle transport trucks. He also had an ominous reputation for racing stock cars, cavorting with wild women, fistfights, and drinking people under the table. He was not a regular at their table, but was always welcome whenever in town because he was an engaging and personable young man. Many of the men at the table had hired Dusty to take livestock to market many times over the past ten years since he graduated from high school. If any man in town qualified for the term handsome, it was he. His dark eyes could pierce into those of another person with raw, unchallenged power. His black hair glistened from a generous amount of dressing, and was longer on the sides enabling him to keep it combed back in a windswept look.

A sense of excitement clung to him like another shadow. Not particularly imposing in stature, still he exuded a sense of strength rippling beneath his western style shirts and jeans. Almost anyone would have thought twice before having angry words with Dusty Sweat. Or said his nickname that only a few pals ever used…'No.'

Lynn walked up to the table, tablet and pencil prepared to take their orders in case someone didn't say, 'The usual.' It hadn't happened all year, but she was always ready.

"Dusty, you gonna order this morning or you got any idea of what you'd like?" She tried to put a careless lilt to her words, but it was clear to all present she was toying with him.

"I know what I want, but it's not on this menu."

"Woooooeeeee," exhaled Tiny Hartman. "Getting' kinda' warm in here for such a chilly morning. Yes, sir." He slurped from his saucer of coffee. "I can feel the old thermometer about to jump right out of the coke sign over at Dorgans, boys."

A number of them smiled, but no one else said a word. The entire restaurant was suddenly staring at the woman and man staring intently at each other.

"What if it was, would you be man enough to order it?" Lynn said evenly.

"I would, and I believe I'd want the same thing over and over again," Dusty replied. "Maybe the rest of my life."

Lynn smiled and shook her head. "Dusty, I'd better bring you some eggs and bacon. It's obvious you're going loony from bangin' your head driving on those wrecks down at the Mt. Hawley Speedway."

"You give me five minutes alone, and I'll prove I'm not crazy."

"Honey, five minutes alone with me and maybe I'll cook what's left of your brain into something about the size of a potato patty and have it for *my* breakfast." As laughter erupted throughout the room, Lynn turned and sauntered toward the kitchen. Other conversations then quietly took over for a while.

After eating fifteen minutes later, Dusty stood and called over the subsiding noise. "Darlin', I was thinking about that five minutes opportunity. Alone with me about that long, and maybe you'll want breakfast three meals a day." He reached into his jean pocket, removed a half-dollar, and tossed it on the table so it just rolled and rolled. Then he turned for the door. "See you guys." With that he was gone.

All eyes turned back to the beautiful young woman standing in the kitchen doorway. Slowly she smiled back at them. "He'll be back, if not today, tomorrow. If not tomorrow…" She shrugged and then disappeared behind the door.

It was completely silent for a few moments. It was Levi Ioder who broke the hush. "Things like this just don't happen in Bradford."

"They happen, Levi. It's just that we're getting so damn old they don't happen to us anymore," Carl said.

"That's as close to having an honest to goodness boner as I've been in five years," Jess whispered. "Just listening to wild stuff like that gets me excited."

"Good Lord," Levi exclaimed, "What has happened here in the Bradford Café early on the last Thursday of October? Maybe it's a sign of the end of times."

"I doubt that, Levi. More like Lynn's wise to the rise in Dusty's Levi's. Believe it's something more simple and basic like that," Ed Brownlee opined.

"I think I'll just talk about something else right now, boys," Tiny suggested. "How about when the Packers come back to Chicago this weekend. Sid ought to kick their ever-loving butts."

"Sure Sunday we can listen to the radio. The Midway Monsters will do what they usually do, but this is even more important. Who you voting for come next Tuesday, Tiny?" Leo Finnegan was sitting in another table as if he desperately wanted to bring some sense of normalcy back to the routine. As Bradford's postmaster, number one Democrat, and main instigator of political arguments Leo had chosen Tiny as his first target of the morning.

"Finnegan, it's none of your durn business. A man's vote is as personal as his bank account," Tiny said with a chuckle.

"Well, I just wondered if you forlorn Republicans were going to throw away your vote on this little pop in jay from New York," Leo continued, unfazed. "He's the cockiest pip squeak I've ever seen. He's even smaller than Harry. You know, I read the other day where some smart feller said Dewey looks like the groom doll on the top of a wedding cake." He laughed again as he viewed the obvious discomfort on the faces of most of the other men. "Boys, Harry's been giving everybody hell, and America loves it. Loves him. He'll stand up to anybody. He's a pug, and that's why he's gonna win. Harry may not be Irish, but he acts like one. He's got a pair of cannon sized balls. Look how he thumbed his nose at the Rooskies and pulled off the Berlin airlift. Or dropping the A-bomb. I predict he'll have the Republican New York yankee for lunch without even so much as a belch or hiccup. I just got three words for all you sad bunch of Republicans, phooey on Dewey." His gentle cackle was the only sound except for Lynn clearing some dishes from a table in the back.

"Leo, you may be right, but these polls I keep hearing about still have Dewey with a comfortable lead," Carl said. "The Chicago Tribune says it's all but over."

"Oh, to hell with those damn polls, Carl, and Col. McCormick, too," Leo quickly retorted. "My guess is some guy with a clip-board has his head stuck all the way up some Park Avenue phony's ass. These so-called pollsters are not talking to real people. Come out here to God's country and see what you hear. The ordinary, working man in America isn't going to elect a guy who..." He was interrupted in mid-sentence by a familiar figure bursting into the restaurant. Many of the patrons glanced at their watches.

"Well, if it isn't Romeo himself stumblin' home with his magic wand danglin' loose and small between his legs, and right on time, too." Lynn's comment sent the room into gales of laughter. Bob Forbes, one of the town's two most eligible bachelors, had just returned from another all-nighter in Peoria. Then she added, "Boys, with customers like you who never vary as much as three minutes a day in your schedule, I don't know why I even wear a watch."

"Can the wisecracks, I need coffee fast, Lynnie," Bob mumbled as he slid into a chair at the table where Leo Finnegan was sitting with Ed Ehnle.

"I don't know how you get home safely, lad, stayin' out all night and keeping the bizarre ways of womanizing that you do. That damn car of yours must know every pot hole and bump between here and Peoria," Leo said sympathetically.

"Hell, don't criticize the boy, Leo, just because you wouldn't remember all niters anymore. Bob ought to be award some kind of medal for bravery just for going over the Camp Grove bridge two times a day," Tiny said. Everyone chuckled and nodded as they recalled the terrible bridge seven miles south of town that shook and shuddered with every vehicle, large or small. Why it hadn't collapsed years ago was one of the big mysteries in that part of Illinois. Almost as big as why the state road department didn't repair or replace it immediately. The oft-repeated joke was that it'll take a Greyhound Bus to go crashing through before anybody in Springfield even hears about it.

Lynn brought a special mug with a large Valentine on it over to the table. "Here, lover boy, get the transfusion going. I've turned in your usual order in to Minnie. She'll have it up in five minutes. Who you favoring with your attention these days?"

"The same gal, but she's gonna be the death of me yet," Bob replied, inhaling the steam swirling from his coffee mug. "Too bad I'm 15 years older than you, Lynn, we could settle down and save my life."

"My God, gentlemen, if I'm counting correctly, that's two proposals of marriage, or something like it, on the same morning, and it isn't even seven-thirty. I think I'll get into the poker game in the back room down at the DogHouse tonight. This must be my lucky day." Still smiling, she mused about actually sitting in on the low stakes game held almost every night in the back of Rat's tavern and restaurant. Rat, and his son called Mouse, nicknamed it the DogHouse.

"Marrying Forbes-boy would be just about the last thing you'd want to do, Lynn," Tiny said. "You couldn't trust him anymore than you could reform a wild bull. Besides, you'd be wondering what bed his shoes were under every night if he wasn't with you." A lot of the boys started guffawing.

"And he'd be wondering what happened to his family jewels the first time he did it," Lynn laughed. "Guess you're too old to start a new career singing an opera soprano," she said as she looked down at the pathetic creature holding his head before her. "So I think I'll pass on your offer, Forbsie, and let you stew in your own mess. Don't forget you're supposed to open up your gas station at 8 o'clock."

Bob Forbes winced at the thought. "Wish it wasn't a school day, I could get Bill Real to open for me, but that's out of the question," he muttered, "I'll have to do it."

Suddenly the front door flipped over against the wall, and Bradford's mayor, or at least what he and a lot of other folks call him, walked in. Everyone realized that humor was the main thing this man could do faster and funnier than anyone else. His name was Sean 'Belzy' Hooligan, and he was the most hilarious Irishman in a town of many equally funny other Irish folks who lived here nearly a hundred years. He did every kind of job a man could do whether it was right or wrong. He said he had been nicknamed by his father because he was a wild Beelzebub of a Jack of all trades. That statement confused most of his friends, or how he got a huge scar on his right cheek so it was out of the question. He easily could have looked like a pirate, but he told anyone who asked, or didn't even care, that he liked Belzy better than his real first name. Mainly nobody in town even remembered that he was named Sean.

"What's up, Mr. Mayor?" Jughead Johnson asked.

"Coffee, black and strong is as good as I can figure out right now," Belzy said. "I don't have too much to be concerned about for about forty-five minutes. My brain is taking a break."

"Ha," Leo Finnegan said quickly. "Belzy, your brain has taken a holiday coffee break for the last two years." The room laughed loudly. "If Truman gets elected he might get you to find a real job."

"Sure and I'm agreein' with ya, Leo, my friend. A real job is kind of a scary opportunity, as I hope that I don't frighten somebody too much who might be tryin' to make me work everyday. Since my beautiful bride has a real, honest job teachin' third grade kids, I can pick and choose as best as I can."

"Well, Belzy, I'll bet you will be the only other man in town who votes for a Democrat next Tuesday with me since our town's newspaper is the Bradford Republican," Leo offered.

Believe it or not, some of the others in the café nodded, and winked a little here and there. "Heh, heh," Belzy laughed. "I will for sure be votin', Leo. This is a very important election now our old president has gone to his reward. But even Roosevelt won big the last few times, and maybe what we ought to do in Bradford is do just like Chicago folks do: vote early and often. And like the way they do it, too, why don't we write names off the tombstones at the cemetery every two years, and just get voting over with."

Everyone laughed again, and they all were nodding at that. Chicago and the rest of what they called 'downstate' were as opposite as two crazy wild men in a boxing ring. It was obvious that Bradford certainly realized bizarre elections could be as close as others, but this one here was going to be simple. Belzy would be elected the village's Mayor since no one else wanted to run for it.

"Belzy, have you seen the hilarious sixteen millimeter film that Orville and Ralph Chapman did? They had a camera that shot black and white film, and were showing some old film they did. It played last Saturday night, and I laughed until I cried. They said they took some funny movies right here in Bradford," Levi said.

"Sure and I've heard about this, Levi. I bet some of it is so funny they will run it on a weekend show, maybe right in the theatre."

"Good idea," Jughead said. "Bet he took shooting movies of old Goose Neck Turlington." Just mentioning his name put the café into laughs.

"Yep, Jug," Belzy said. "I have seen that meself. The two of them said they took these pictures back in the '30s. Goose Neck is the bald headed guy with almost a foot long neck who could wiggle one ear at a time. Boys, that is a wonderful memory."

"How about Fast Fingers McNeef," Levi asked. "The Chapman's movie shows Fast Fingers was famous for stealing pies off kitchen window sills while they were cooling for some wonderful lady. He just runs out with the pie and keeps on going."

"They also told some of the good old days over in one of the town's pool halls. A wild man we all remember was Bullfrog Duke. He told folks he could hold fifteen billiard balls in one hand and grab a loaded pistol if he wanted to shoot mice under the tables," Leo said.

"Yes, lads, these are memories that all of us love to have from time to time," Belzy sighed. "Time are changing, I guess. It's kind of sad here now. Lots of funny folks in Bradford were silly or crazy then, and lord knows, they were *boisterously* entertaining. But now, friends, they've gone to heaven. Sure and it's melancholy to me, but this fine town is just not as funny as it used to be."

"Well, that's possible, I suppose," Carl said slowly. "On the other hand what if most of those crazy nutcases who died ten or twenty years ago might realize that heaven for them is pretty darn near empty. They might have gone in a different direction."

Things got very quiet with that statement. Then Belzy offered a thought. "Thank you for saying such a pathetic bit of information, Carl. It makes me recall what my dear sainted old mother said almost every day of her life. If she thought something was not going quite right, she always said, 'Son, it looks like things are going straight down in a 'mellovahess'."

The entire room nodded and chuckled. Every one of them remembered that funny comment. "Okay," Levi said, "the town may not be as witty as it used to be, but we've still got a few fine nuts in Bradford, and I'm sure not talking about walnuts or pecans." Several shook their heads, and smiled, but it got kind of quiet again.

Over the next thirty minutes Main Street merchants began filing in as farmers departed. Every morning about now the customer base made an easy transition from farm to village. Tinker Scholes, the druggist, his brother Doc, one of the two doctors serving the area, Lefty Blake, Tinker's right hand man, Ray Batten, the owner of the Five and Dime, Charlie Schindler, one of four grocers on the street, Ed Mowbray, owner of the town's only men's clothing store, Leigh Palmer, the banker, and the two barbers, Jimmy Hennesey and Bill Carroll, were now immersed in the morning's conversation at several tables.

The sun was hardly at tree top level, but it had already been a busy morning at the Bradford Café.

CHAPTER 5

▼

TWO INJUN SUMMER'S RIDE AGAIN

The following Saturday, October 5, six of the boys chugged back on their bikes to create a hockey dream come true. But in Memorial Stadium at the University of Illinois, a much different scene took place that would have far reaching significance for Philip Carlton. He again was going to enter the most hallowed football stadium in the country, at least for his family, during four or five Saturday football games each season.

On one of these great days, Mr. Carlton would never have called his son 'Suck' under any circumstances, because he and his wife were two of the most refined and respected individuals in Bradford. It probably gave them silent feelings of great annoyance whenever they overheard one of Philip's pals call him that. Both of his parents were graduates of the U. of I., and this was Dad's day in Champaign, a tradition in the Carlton household. For the past eight years in a row, Mr. Carlton first took Suck's older sister Sally to this annual event, but she already had a seat in the Block 'I' Section since she was now a sophomore student.

When this happened two years ago, Suck became his companion. And the Illini not only won the Big Ten Conference, they demolished UCLA on January 1, 1947 in the very first time these two conferences played in the Rose Bowl. Buddy

Young, Dike Eddleman, and Perry Moss scored so many points they made it look easy. The score turned out to be 45-14.

All boys growing up in the mid-west were brainwashed from infancy that nobody plays football any better than the Big Ten Conference. But a continual battle of words and wits broke out every time a fan of Notre Dame met a counterpart from the other ten conference schools. This was especially true in Bradford with its strong Irish Catholic contingency. They took the lads in South Bend so seriously several of the ladies in the Altar and Rosary Society would pray over their beads each Saturday while listening to the football game on their radios. God, in their minds, would never turn his back on the Fighting Irish. And since the Irish destroyed the Illini in 1946, the two teams had not played again.

Another team from Indiana was this week's opponent, the Boilermakers from Purdue. Their band was leaving the field playing their alma mater after forming the initials, P.U. Suck and his Dad were getting a chuckle out of this because Suck said it reminded him of what his pals often say after Beaner breaks wind.Then the Marching Illini took the field for the moment Suck had been waiting anxiously since the day he heard they would be going to the game. Two years earlier, Chief Illiniwek captured Suck's attention in a way he couldn't explain. Today, though, he would have to wait while the band did it's new, weekly routine. When that part of the performance ended, he knew the band would begin marching toward the north end zone. This was an electric moment in Memorial Stadium, so intensely popular virtually no one ever left his or her seats. Half time snacks, drinks, and even restroom visits could wait.

It was show time for the Chief.

Suck squinted to see if he could spot the moment when the Chief sneaked into the band as it performed an about face maneuver on the north side. While singing, "We Are Marching For The Dear Old Illini," they started going back south down to the main part of the field.

"There he is, Dad," Suck exclaimed. "I see him. He's hiding under the goal post, and is running right up the middle of the band."

As the Indian-style theme music started slowly and methodically to play, the Chief jumped from his hiding place, and took his place at the band's forefront. He stood, proudly with his arms folded for only a moment or two, wearing a full headdress of feathers and a suit of buckskin clothing. Then he began doing the famous war dance that began twenty-five seasons ago when Red Grange played in the stadium's first game. This remarkable symbol of Illinois football had performed with the band during the same identical part of their show each week. Suck was so mesmerized he held his breath. When the dance reached it's frantic crescendo, the Chief ended it by standing defiant, with arms folded, and a huge roar of approval sprang from thousands of throats.

"I've seen it nearly a hundred times," Mr. Carlton said, "and I still get choked up, Philip."

"Me, too, Dad. It's my favorite part of coming here. It gives me goosebumps," Suck replied.

"I know what you mean, son. Well, what do you say we go get a hot dog and a coke now?"

"Sure Dad," however he slowly stared at the band and watched the Chief proudly walk away. Suck suddenly realized that he wanted to be Chief when he was in college. At that moment it seemed like a million years from him right now, but time was something he knew would be at the right time and the right place.

All he had to do is wait.

Autumn's magnificent early signs of John McCutcheon's 'Injun Summer' were everywhere as all seven climbed on their bikes. This began the third week's excursion along the two-lane concrete road that took them to their Spoon River site. All of them had practically memorized a fascinating story that had still 'hung' around for the past 36 years ago by an artist named McCutcheon. He wrote and painted what now became one of America's most favorite classic stories. Happily, the Chicago Tribune decided to print it on Halloween in 1912. That year it was so popular thousands of families now had it hanging on their kitchen wall, or even somewhere else in the house. From that year to this, the Trib printed their front cover's Magazine section every Halloween. Kids realize their mothers give unconditional love and personal experiences to every one of them, but memories like this are also special times with their father, and his father, and his father's father.

These days and nights had sounds and smells of harvest filling the air. Thick clouds of dust and pulverized husk swirled behind two tractors pulling combines far off in fields to their left. Another tractor with a corn picker mounted beside it chugged through rows of stalks now dry and brown. In the distance Harper's Woods was ablaze with its annual display of Jack Frost's greatest creations.

As they rode past the American Legion House a straw filled scarecrow sporting a preposterously wide grin on his feed sack face waved his greeting. A phalanx of neatly carved pumpkins and several mounds of recently raked leaves surrounded him. Similar piles were popping up on curbs and driveways throughout the community, and soon the air would be filled with smoke carrying their rich, wonderful aroma. Melancholy over the passing of summer was always tempered by roasting marshmallows and wieners over an autumn bonfire, and sipping warm, fresh apple cider. But the six boys pedaling rapidly toward the bridge spanning the Spoon River were oblivious to everything except balancing tools of labor on their handlebars.

This was the day. They would finish the dam.

Sure enough, late that afternoon they stood back and marveled at the imposing structure which already had collected a large pool of water at its base. A few hours earlier Hotshot diverted the stream back to it's original course so it would again flow into the meadow where the dam was waiting.

"I've never seen any dam but the one at the Broadmore pond, but I bet nothing could be any better than this one," Catfish said. His remark was dittoed enthusiastically by the others.

"Yeah, Hotshot, you did a good job of organizing this deal," Jumbo said sincerely. "My old man told me he never dreamed I could work this hard on anything. He even wants to come out and see it."

"Mine, too," added Booby.

"Why don't we let it fill up first?" Hotshot responded. "It'll look a lot more impressive if the dam holds, and we've got a real pond to show for our effort."

"Too bad we never found hide nor hair of the missing printing plates," Dink sighed.

"That only gives us something else to concentrate on next summer. Besides, I've got a great idea where I think they could be hidden. It's not too far from here." Once again, Hotshot's words instantly commanded their attention.

"Where?" Beaner asked quickly.

"I told you guys about the abandoned coal mine just north of Harper's Woods. What better place to hide something? I went to see Miss Code over at the library, and she told me she remembers they closed up the small, old mine. What if it's about the same time the G-men caught the counterfeiters? I also found out they didn't completely seal it up for several years until after the place really closed. Can you think of a better place to hide something?" Hotshot said, his voice in a near whisper. Though he was now thirteen, and one of the new teenagers in this group, he was well on the way to becoming a manipulator of the first degree.

"My gosh, the abandoned coal mine. When you told us about this at one of the football games, I've had to place my hand on a Bible and swear to God I'll never try to get in that place. My dad told me to never go there again. I told him about it after you told us," Dink blurted.

"Me, too. My folks said there's a mighty big danger of cave-ins. I promised I'd never go foolin' around in the coal mine. My Mom said I could kiss my bike and my ass goodbye forever if I get caught in there," Booby said. His remark was silently echoed with agreeing nods from the rest.

"Don't worry. You know I'm not stupid. I'm going to do more research on how a coal mine works," Hotshot countered. "It won't be dangerous. I've already read that most coal mines have a long passageway at the top that also served as an airshaft. There's probably still a ladder in it that would take us down with no possibility of a cave-in. I'll just bet you that those missing printing plates are sitting in some old mine shaft down there, just waiting for somebody brave and smart enough to figure it out."

"Well, I don't know," Jumbo said, privately happy that everyone else seemed skeptical of Hotshot's newest idea. "We don't even know for sure that the crooks hid the printing plates. And no one has ever found them again. Sounds like we've finally hit on something that even we agree we don't have any business doin'."

Most of the other boys nodded their agreement, and began the trek back to the bushes beside the hard road where their bicycles were hidden. But Hotshot smiled as he brought up the rear. He'd accomplished his goal of building a new hockey pond without dissent, and if it took until the following summer to convince them the mine was not dangerous, he could wait. It was then that he paused. Was that a twig snapping in the distance behind him? He scanned the woods carefully. With a shrug he resumed his course for the bikes.

In seconds the entire area was quiet again, save for the continuing sounds of nearby crickets and a few birds chirping. Had any of the boys quietly returned for a forgotten item, however, they would have found the same imposing figure that had inspected their work the previous week. Sheck walked along slowly examining the finished dam, careful to avoid getting his feet wet from the deepening body of water before it. He stood there and simply rubbed his chin for a few seconds and smiled. Then he slipped noiselessly into the forest.

According to the calendar, fall lasts three full months. But the brief two or three week duration mid-westerners call Indian Summer is the real interlude between summer and winter. As more and more brilliantly colored leaves ended their starring roles in nature's autumn pageant, it was obvious this tenuous spectacle had run its course for another year. Soon trees would become skeletons of brown and black reaching bony; finger-like limbs skyward in a final act of desperation. Winter always claimed the territory for a much longer period of time than allotted on paper, usually by stealing a month and a half from its hapless predecessor.

October dissolved into November days that were gray and chilly, Needless to say, the day's big surprise was that Leo Finnegan was right. President Harry Truman not only won his election, he was happily laughing in newspaper pictures all over America. He enjoyed telling one and all that a huge mistake by the same Chicago newspaper that created a wonderful Injun Summer laid an egg. In a late edition on election night, the Tribune claimed Dewey won, but by the next morning the New York Governor had really been defeated. 'Give 'em Hell Harry' was going to do just that for at least four more years.

But post war America now became embroiled in euphoria from a new and totally different source. Climaxing a buildup of Barnum-like excitement and promotion a year earlier, the all-new 1949 line of new Ford's was about to be introduced nationally. Probably no unveiling of a new product in our country's history had the remarkable effect of this one event. After long years of sacrifice on behalf of the war effort, and the subsequent re-tooling delays required to once again mass produce consumer products, the entire country was brimming with eager anticipation because of the announcement that Ford was completely altering its pre-'41 design.

Bradford was certainly no different. No one could recall any previous local event causing more deception or delirium. People were excitedly buzzing over what they would look like, when they were arriving and most importantly, if they were already in town as rumored, where were they were being hidden? When the big day finally arrived, word leaked out that two cars had been hidden behind Beryl Coleman's barn under huge mounds of hay for nearly a week. This revelation merely added to the enjoyment. Folks said it was a sure sign that things were getting back to normal in America.

Promptly at three o'clock one partly cool but sunny Wednesday afternoon, a good-sized crowd of adults gathered outside the small showroom at Browning and Velde Ford. These partners proudly ripped away the huge pieces of wrapping paper covering their large front windows with a dramatic flourish. Reaction was instant and favorable. The sleek, long lines and squared off trunks were met with delighted outbursts and applause. Rationing, so prevalent on most goods during the war, had whetted the nation's appetite for all things new. Yet those at the festivities were undismayed by the fact that, even if you could pay cash for a new car, production delays meant it would be many months before you took possession.

"Boy, oh boy, wouldn't it be great to be able to drive one of those babies?" said an older teenage boy straining to get a better look. Many high school boys not at football practice now permeated the showroom. A number of grade school kids were also there, noisily jabbering about the spectacle.

"Hey, guys, we've got to get to my house by 4:30! I missed all my radio shows yesterday ridin' around tryin' to find these cars, and it's not gonna happen again today!" Jumbo exclaimed as he noticed the time on a big clock hanging above a picture of Henry Ford. He began running from the showroom followed by all six of the others. Quickly, they mounted and began pedaling furiously as cool autumn air rushed past their faces. They sped southward and round the corner over the railroad tracks onto First Street in a loose, v-shaped formation, coasting when their leader did, pedaling rapidly when he re-started, much in the manner of migrating Canadian Geese.

One by one, the boys trailed each other through a narrow break in a thick hedge, easily dodging the protruding edges of a dangerously close wooden sand-box. After evading the four lines of drying sheets and clothes that stretched across the backyard, they slammed on their foot brakes launching their bikes into a con-trolled skid over grass still thick and green. It was a maneuver mastered through many trials, and even many more errors. Each rider wordlessly lined his bike in a row against the porch, and began running up the five wooden steps leading to the back door.

"Mom, I'm home," yelled Jumbo as the last boy burst into the warm kitchen. "Good, just look at the trays of fresh cookies! Let's eat one whole tray, and I'll hide it. Maybe she won't remember how many she baked."

"I'm down in the cellar, Eddie Jay," a muffled reply arose from below. "First the water went off and then the electric wringer on the washing machine broke. I'm running way late on getting the laundry done. Had to crank the clothes dry by hand. Later, you can help me hang this last load of sheets in the basement tonight. Did some of your pals run into the kitchen?"

"Yes," and he then whispered, "Quick guys, grab those cookies before she yells to not touch them. Looks like we missed Jack Armstrong." Jumbo switched on a small Crosley radio sitting on the yellow linoleum counter top before he finished speaking. He feverishly adjusted the dial, as a glow from the radio tubes became visible through a crack in the wooden case.

Gradually, a voice grew louder and louder. "O. K., all you Ralston Straight Shooters out there, this is Tom Mix saying, remember, take a tip from Tom, go and tell your mom, hot Ralston can't be beat." The western style-advertising jingle ended as a loud thumping noise on the floor beneath them interrupted the show's opening.

"It's my mom pounding her laundry stick on the kitchen floorboards," Jumbo said. "I bet she just remembered the cookie trays. She'll probably call me Edward." He smiled and yelled toward the floor. "You want somethin' mom?"

"Edward, you boys stay away from those cookie sheets, it's too close to supper. I'll be right up and give each of you apple slices with peanut butter on them. And Eddy Jay, I will need you to help bring in all those sheets and towels and underwear on the lines when they're dry."

Seven boys, mouths stuffed with fresh cookies, grinned at each other in silence, futilely trying to brush away crumbs falling from their lips and cheeks. But soon the drama to which they were intently listening began creating its daily magic in each of their minds. Fourteen minutes later they were munching on apple slices when the announcer temporarily lifted them out of their spell.

"Boys and girls, be sure to tune in tomorrow same time, same station. See if Tom can escape from the deadly trap that's been set for him in Horseshoe Canyon. If he evades disaster will he have enough time left to save the stage to Tucson from Black Bart's Gang? All you Straight Shooters can find out by tuning in tomorrow. In the meantime, remember, take a tip from Tom, go…"

▼

BILL DORGAN'S BIG NIGHT

Early on the Wednesday morning before Thanksgiving, the Patterson's household was scurrying through the daily challenge of getting three boys off to the same school. Jonathan was upstairs dressing, as usual, the slowest one to get going. His two younger brothers were already at the kitchen table eating breakfast. Thomas, his middle brother, was a 5th grader, and had been assigned milk duty that morning, mainly because he was the first to get his shoes on.

Late the previous night, Mrs. Patterson placed the metal basket filled with four empty quart bottles in it, along with a note stuck in the neck of one of the bottles, ordering extra milk, eggs, butter and eggnog for the holiday. Each boy was assigned duties, or chores, as they were commonly called, around the house. This was one of the simplest tasks requiring only that the delivery be taken to the kitchen and placed in the refrigerator.

Tom walked to the front hall window, and looked out to see if the bottles were normal. What he saw made him run quickly, but quietly into the kitchen where Mathew was just finishing his oatmeal.

"Matt, it's finally happened," he whispered.

"What?" Matt responded in kind.

"It got cold enough last night to freeze the bottles. They've popped their lids." Both boys giggled excitedly, and immediately went to the front door. Matt only had one shoe on, because a major knot in his left shoe had been put off until their father came down for breakfast. Bad knots were assigned to their dad. Besides, events on the front porch were much more important. He and Tom had been planning for this moment since the first frost a month ago.

Soundlessly, they opened the main inner door, and then pushed open the heavy glass storm door that provided additional insulation on the outside. They crept out onto the porch. A light layer of misting snow was buffeting the red bricked surface. Six quart sized bottles of milk delivered several hours ago by Mr. Wattles had frozen solid, and the darker colored cream now protruded at least two inches above the necks of the bottles like icy chimneys. Tom knelt beside the bottles, and gently removed one of the circular discs sitting atop the column of cream. It now appeared to be more like a paper hat than bottle lid. Tom drew his middle finger back with his left thumb, and prepared to propel the first tube of cream as far out in the yard as he could with a finger flick.

Just as he was ready to launch he heard a familiar voice, and it wasn't happy. "NO, you don't, young man, unless you want to be grounded for the entire Thanksgiving holidays." Mrs. Patterson's, motherly instincts as keen as ever, was alerted by the surest warning sign something wrong may be about to happen with boys this age: silence. She had followed them to the door, and managed to sneak up behind both boys without them hearing her. "I need that cream, and so do you. Bring in the basket, and I'll let it thaw and remix the milk later."

"Awe gee, Mom. Dink does it. I saw him do it last year," came Tom's beleaguered excuse.

"And neither he nor you had better ever do it again, young man. As for you, Matthew, don't even think about it again. Now both of you, go finish getting ready for school, and be sure to get your snow suits out. It looks like you may need them."

Upstairs, slowly pulling on his corduroy pants, Dink heard the entire exchange. Wow, he thought, if the milk bottles froze up maybe our hockey pond did, too. For the first time that morning he began moving with speed and purpose. What better time to begin their ice skating fun than a four-day break from school.

Mrs. Patterson's weather assessment proved correct because by late in the morning, the temperatures had only climbed into the low thirties. The snow, which earlier began as a fine powder, was now coming down rapidly in large, wet flakes. Quickly, a fresh, clean, lustrous coating covered everything, transforming familiar objects like trees, shrubs, mail boxes, lamp and sign posts, fences, and everything else into newly fashioned works of art. Grassy yards frosted into dormancy bearing the depressing browns and grays of winter three weeks ago were soon covered by a great, white blanket.

But everything in nature seems to balance itself precariously between excesses. As this scene continued growing in beauty, it also inevitably began creating havoc, first for drivers, and then pedestrians. Thanksgiving travelers would face stiff challenges as they began their journeys to holiday reunions later in the day.

For those who decided to remain in town for the four-day break from school however, it was the most perfect timing imaginable. As the storm began to gradually subside early Wednesday afternoon, administrators at all three of the town's schools agreed that they should take advantage of the lull, and get the student's home as soon as possible. School buses with newly applied snow chains carefully encompassing each tire, soon began arriving. At Bradford Grade School, old Mr. Peterson, the janitor of many years announced he was going to retire next May, had already shoveled the bus loading area clear from snow. Similar scenes were taking place in front of St. John's School and down the street at BHS.

Within seconds of the day's final classes, snowball fights erupted among those waiting to board buses, or as the town kids walked home. Minutes later, sleds suddenly appeared from their summer storage places. Snowmen began rolling to life in many yards, and two snow forts, strategically facing each other, and separated by only 30-40 feet, were in their final stages of construction on the park playground.

Shortly after 5 o'clock, a slight drop in temperature froze a thin layer of surface snow into a crunchy carpet that broke like thin ice under each step. A combination of encroaching darkness, and impending suppertime began clearing the streets and yards as if a soundless alarm had rung. The acrid smell of mittens and gloves drying on radiators permeated many homes that evening.

Each year, folks from one state to another felt Thanksgiving was a wonderful holiday, but mainly it was as real as America itself. No other country anywhere else in the world ever dreamed up a holiday like it to just be thankful. It began back in 1621, when some people who had just moved from England decided to share their meager food with others who had lived on this land for milleniums. Those people were the first thankful Pilgrims.

Now countless blessings were bestowed from one shining sea to the other over those years. More than eighty years earlier, President Lincoln decided to unite the nation with national prayers after a terrible war had been going for two years then. In 1863, he gave a proclamation to announce it would be on the fourth Thursday in November, and that is just where it stayed. At least, until nine years ago, when President Roosevelt wanted to let people get one more week for

Christmas shopping. A lot of people in Bradford had argued about which week the change should happen, but finally Congress decided our country should all say a simple thank you, and made the fourth Thursday it. Of course, those few weeks earlier on November 1941, turned out to be almost simple, because an even more terrible war began in December 7. The man who wanted to change it so stores could let family members buy more presents was now much more deeply involved. In his incredible speech the next day, he said this was America's "Day of Infamy."

Thankfully, now the biggest aspect of this annual sharing experience was that the terrible war was over. Holiday traditions now wound up even better all around the country, because Thanksgiving on Thursday was of course a wonderful holiday, but for kids everywhere in America, Friday was just a magnificent bonus. School was out, too. They could goof off as much as they wanted to, and still have a normal fun weekend.

The huge storm now rolling across the plains was creating some huge problems throughout the state, however. As it got deeper and deeper, many people realized that driving somewhere else for family or friends might be canceled for the next couple of days.

Happily, no matter how bad the storm, Bradford was a small, but self-sufficient village, and it had as much of the early Christmas spirit as anywhere else. Thanksgiving Eve in the Bradford community was a cherished, seasonal event, and it was handled by an honest-to-goodness elf. William Dorgan, the impish and fun-loving proprietor of the ice cream soda and sandwich shop that bore his name, annually chose this as the night he turned on the Christmas lights, which covered the front of his family's large, three story home on Arbor Street. It was his decree that the lights would continue to glow each night until January 1. Actually, each year he kept them on as long as he wished.

Bill Dorgan was everybody's idea of what a leprechaun would look like if one visited Bradford. He was, as he often said, "As Irish as the Blarney Stone, and damn sure proud of it." Mr. Dorgan only stood a little over five feet six inches in height, but the Mastiff Giant would not have been more obvious in a crowd. He was a perpetually smiling, natural clown who also possessed a quick wit. Most folks thought he was in his seventies, but he never admitted his age, though his thinning hair had been pure white for as long as most could remember. As the town's only ice cream soda shop, his success was assured, but he made a decision twenty years earlier that paid even bigger dividends. He bought the local franchise for ground beef sandwiches known throughout the area as 'Maidrites'. In the opinion of many, it was the best sandwich ever made.

What made his role in the Thanksgiving Eve tradition special however, were three very distinct but related occurrences. The first thing stemmed from the fact that Mr. Dorgan didn't remove his Christmas lights or decorations the remaining 11 months of the year. Lighting them was often an adventure, because of frayed wiring and weather damage. Some folks kindly excused his eccentricity as an effort to let Bradford celebrate Christmas all year long. Nevertheless, if asked by an out of town stranger why he didn't remove the decorations, his reason was far less altruistic. "Too damn much trouble to take something down that you know you're just going to have to put back up anyway!"

Folks usually started gathering in front of the Dorgan house around seven o'clock, already enjoying their first surge of Christmas Spirit. The size of the crowd usually depended on the weather, but on most years it ranged between one and two hundred people. As Bill Dorgan and other family members concerned themselves with plugs and wires, impromptu Christmas Caroling filled the air. Dorgan was a man of many words, and, as the big moment came, it was usually preceded by his cry, "Here she goes."

When power surged through the web of wires that for years had snaked its way across the porch railings and around the columns, he was as surprised as anyone else at which bulbs worked and which needed replacement. Fourteen large wooden candles he made himself supported letters spelling 'Merry Christmas'; each topped with a bulb simulating a flame. The two words were divided by the entrance steps at the center of the porch, creating a jammed imbalance on the Christmas side. Strands of multi-colored lights were attached to decorative latticework along the top of the porch roof and down each column. On this night every candle answered it's call to duty except the Y and T. These were quickly replaced by one of the Dorgan's grandchildren.

Because so many bright lights illuminated the entire front of the house, everyone could see a headless Santa sitting in a battered sleigh disintegrating from years of neglect on the top of the roof. Only three of the original reindeer still remained stalwartly holding positions, their companions succumbing to wind and rot. Back in the '30's this roof decoration was the 'piece de resistance' of the entire project. But disaster struck the last time they tried lighting the four floodlights on the roof's front edge. A badly frayed wire shorted, and, before the fuse box exploded extinguishing all the lights in the entire house, it sent a shower of sparks cascading down on bystanders scurrying for cover. Gilly Shaw, the village constable, was heard yelling, "Bill, this is Christmas, not the fourth of July."

Tonight, with all reachable bulbs replaced, the stage was set for the second step of the Dorgan Thanksgiving Eve custom. Standing at the top of the steps, bathed in a rainbow glow, he tilted his head back and turned on one more set of lights: ten tiny bulbs in his special Christmas bow tie. Pausing only a moment for effect while reaching in his pants pocket to grab the battery connection, Dorgan then made the crimson colored tie spin as rapidly as the little motor in the tie would go.

Each kid present knew this was the signal for his third tradition. He laughed and said, "Now, to get us in the holiday spirit, let's go up to the ice cream parlor where we will be selling double dip cones for just a nickel. Not too cold for you is it?"

A loud chorus of nooooo rose from all the children present. Then, like the famous Pied Piper of old, the short, frail, impish man with the marvelous twinkle in his eyes stomped loudly down his steps and assumed his place at the head of his small army of children. He had donned a Santa Claus cap, complete with a white, fuzzy ball at the end. "Are all you kid's ready?" Again cheers of approval echoed through the light. "Well then, let's go! "Signaling another gesture forward, everyone began the short, one block trek to the store on Main Street.

Partly to avoid the coldness of the night, but mostly to get their hands on a double dip cone, sixty to seventy children crammed into the small shop while parents stood and visited outside. Each child waited as patiently as they could to be served. Tonight, the entire Dorgan family, consisting of his wife Daisy, and daughters Marge and Verna, were working as fast as they could to meet the demand. What brought these children and their parents back year after year was not just an opportunity to pay five cents for a double dip cone regularly selling for a dime. Much more, it was the realization that, thanks to this comical and kind old man, the Christmas season of good will toward mankind had formally come upon them again.

As soon as they had been served, seven boys were standing in a circle a few feet down the street in front of Tom Flood's Bowling Alley. In between licks, Hotshot said, "There may be too much snow on the ground by Friday morning, but let's try and get out to Hidden Pond to see if it has frozen over. The bird bath in our backyard is solid ice."

"Yeah, I bet a lot of us had our milk-man's bottle tops shoot right out of the yellow cream this morning," Dink offered.

Several immediately agreed.

"I suppose we'll all be stuck with family stuff tomorrow since it's Thanksgiving, but let's try to get one of our parents to drive us out Friday morning if the roads are too snowy for bikes," Hotshot said. More nods of agreement didn't slow the cone licking even a tiny bit. Though school would now be closed until next Monday morning, these boys couldn't even fathom how they were going to handle a huge holiday tomorrow, let alone worrying about the day after.

Many wonderful things were happening in lots of towns and cities all over America. In spite of the storm's huge snow here, a lot of people had great weather in many other places, but no matter, the whole nation was filled with a very, very thankful group of folks.

CHAPTER 7

▼

WHEN YOU'RE A KID,
CHRISTMAS AND HEAVEN
ARE ONE IN THE SAME

Friday, November 19 was a special time of year for young fans of Paddy O'Cinnamon and his annual Christmas season radio adventure show from one of the Chicago stations. It was a special syndicated serial program, but it did one thing that no other program did on its first broadcast show: they played it every afternoon at the exact same time for 26 fifteen-minute programs, and included the two weekend days. Now it was heard Monday to Friday like all of the other kids' radio shows. Every year when it was played on radio stations, the last of the special programs ended each year on Christmas Eve. Advertising promoted by Wieboldt's Department Store, one of the biggest in Chicago, started promoting the news to tell kids all over the area to not miss this, even if anyone heard it before.

Each day after school for children primarily ten and under, it ushered in the great period of eager anticipation for seemingly endless countdowns every day to finally arrive at Christmas Eve. Paddy, a small, cuddly, brown bear, was in reality, a tree ornament. After miraculously coming to life, together with his newly shrunken children friends, Jimmy and Judy, Paddy takes them to Mayeland to begin a search for the Silver Star Christmas ornament, stolen by a culprit known as the Crazy Quilt Dragon. For little ones, it was radio fantasy at its best, but, for boys and girls on the verge of their teenage years, Paddy O'Cinnamon was a show they could no longer admit interest in. This was to be Booby's dilemma after taking off his boots and coat.

"And here's the Cinnamon Bear." It was the lilting Irish brogue of Paddy's initial statement that caught Booby's attention. Now in stocking feet, he walked to the bedroom he shared with his younger brother. His mother held his six-year old sister in her lap, and his youngest brother who was eight was snuggled close beside her as they listened to the large, wooden radio console before them.

"Hi, Patrick," his sister said softly. "Want to listen to the Cinnamon Bear? Mickey told me that in the next couple of days their plane crashes in Looking Glass valley 'cause they run out of soda pop gas."

"I know what happens 'cause I 'member it from last year," his brother replied. "No, Kathleen, "I'm going to listen to Terry and the Pirates in my bedroom. Besides, I'm too old for this radio show anymore. I've heard every year forever. It's a kids story."

"One never gets too old for a beautiful tale about a brave Irish lad, Patrick," his Mother countered with a loving smile. "Even if a lad named Paddy O'Cinnamon is a bear."

Booby hesitated, nodded slightly and continued walking out of the living room. His siblings and mother heard sounds of the refrigerator door opening, milk splashing into a glass and the door close after he placed the bottle back on a shelf. Mrs. O'Riley instinctively glanced toward the doorway into the hall. Though the two children and her lap were already transfixed by the show, she tilted her head forward just enough to catch a glimpse of his red plaid shirt. He had silently seated himself on the kitchen floor, almost out of sight, but well within hearing distance. A barely perceptible mother's smile illuminated her face, and she kissed her daughter's ebony colored hair simultaneously tightening her loving caress on both children.

None of them remembered all twenty-six programs during this month of months. However, they all knew Judy and Jimmy would happily find the fixed-up Silver Star was ready to be taken down their stairs from the attic just in time to decorate their family's Christmas Tree every December 24.

Things like this were especially true for kids in Central Illinois who thought Christmas and Heaven were one in the same. And the three best places anybody in Bradford could be taken with their moms and dads were their choices in reverse order: Kewanee, Peoria, and Chicago.

Kewanee was only twenty miles away, and good things happened there maybe once a week. Peoria took thirty-six miles to get there, and was so far for most people a trip to Peoria might not occur more than once a month. Chicago was so far away for lots of kids, it had to be the granddaddy thrill of them all. This was so special and exciting kids went crazy whenever any of them got to go. The standard joke for lots of folks in the middle-west was when we die here, if we've been good, good folks, St. Peter will let us go to Chicago 'cause Heaven is the same place.

These three cities had wonderful holiday lights in the downtown areas, but nobody had ever seen anything like what happened in Chicago every Friday evening after Thanksgiving. This incredible city was aglow for Christmas because 100,000 colorful bulbs lit up an 80-foot big fir tree. Mayor Martin H. Kennelly, lit the annual lighting ceremony, because this special moment marked the 'official' opening of the Christmas season. Once a year thousands of people jammed the main corner of State Street and Wacker Drive just to see the lighting ceremony when the power went on.

But how to get here was even more fun than anyone ever dreamed it could be. Two years earlier some mothers and fathers brought their family to Chicago on the Zephyr from Buda, a town less than a fifteen-minute drive. Others drove to Bureau or Chillicothe, and they were thrilled to ride the Rocket, another fantastic adventure. Many families drove to Chicago for several hours of boring arguments and coloring books, but how could anyone not want to ride a train the likes of which no one had ever seen before.

Diesel power was now another new experience in the 20th Century, and old trains that chugged along with coal fires could run on engines that looked as if they came from another planet. These new trains were so incredible a new word was now invented just to identify what people could call it…The Streamliner.

The Burlington Route stunned the entire country in 1934 when their new train called the "Pioneer Zephyr" left Denver and arrived into Chicago just a little over thirteen hours later. The Rock Island Line was just as incredible. They christened their modernistic powerful engine, "The Rocket."

Lots of folks called The Zephyr a "shovelnose" streamliner. Its engine had eight 'windows' in the front where the engineer could see almost 180 degrees of his sight. Amazingly, the Rocket looked so much bigger and more powerful it seemed to dwarf the Zephyr, but that was not true at all. The Rocket created a different panorama from the front because it only had two, bigger windshields, and it had a stunning color scheme with scarlet, gold, and orange. The Zephyr's engineer simply said, "All aboard the Silver Streak." The other proud man said, "All aboard, it's time to ride the Rocket."

While both of the streamliners entered into Chicago from different directions, everyone arrived in downtown within just a couple of blocks. No matter, which train was considered the best, you could hear a song every now that no one could ever forget. Everyone almost all could happily sing or hum this ditty. "The Rock Island Line is a mighty good road, the Rock Island Line is the road to ride, the Rock Island Line is a mighty good road. If you want to ride, you gotta ride it like you find it. Get your ticket at the station for the Rock Island Line."

In Peoria, folks realized that Santa also rode the Rocket, too. Bradford was snowed in this weekend, but thirty-five miles south in the city and its suburbs, folks could see the Rocket arriving every Friday after Thanksgiving. Block & Kuhl's department store was affectionately called 'The Big White Store' for 364 days a year, but one this special day they called it the Peoria Rocket 'Santa Claus Special.'

A few miles away in the railroad yard Santa climbed in from the North Pole, and his own Rocket rolled in on time at the depot in downtown in Peoria. He then rode in a parade through the city in his sleigh, and ended up at Block & Kuhl's toy department. Bands played, kids cheered, and joy was filled with everyone. Kids knew Chicago was bigger and better, but somehow the decoration committee convinced Santa that the wonderful old man 'would play in Peoria' every year.

No matter who or where people wanted to ride on one of these fantastic trains, it was fine to go anywhere. In 1948, passenger service was so easy and affordable everyone thought it could never ever be any better than this. People coming to or from Chicago or everywhere else could say it was a dream come true experience.

However, today the same snowstorm that just caused many problems in Bradford also made some people unable to come downtown, but Chicago was as busy as anyone remembered.

This year the city once again had two huge Christmas Trees only a few blocks away. Of course, Mayor Kennelly had turned the huge outside version on a few days earlier, but another gigantic tree had given millions of Mid-westerners another chance to see what everyone calls 'The Great Tree.' This beautiful setting stood 45-50 feet high in one of America's biggest department store, Marshall Fields.

Wieboldt's invited delightful kids to enter their huge holiday 'Toyteria', and then have lunch at the Travertine Room or Wabash Grill, but Marshall Field's was the king of rapture.

Each year State Street's block of spectacular Christmas windows magically twirled and turned a number of animated dolls and toys into life. Countless people started at one side, and wandered from one corner to the other just to see it all. No matter how cold it was, this was spectacular. When local Chicagoans or visitors wanted to meet someone else, they met under these two corners at the Marshall Field's Clocks. It also was where Christmas began if parents and their kids wanted to see the spectacular Christmas display windows.

All department stores anywhere had toys…lots and lots of toys. As far as the boys believed, all girls seemed to only love dolls and their many different clothes or paraphernalia. Literally millions of tiny little things that dolls needed to wear and do and go could literally go on and on forever. Boys had a totally different game plan. Any kind of a ball was just fine for them, and the other paraphernalia that was needed in the specific game was also important. However, boys realized really big-time Christmas toys for them was serious stuff. Tinker Toys, Erector or Chemistry Sets, Lincoln Logs, Lionel Trains, and the Red Ryder B B gun were as close to nirvana as any boy would ever have or dream about.

Reluctantly, when the many Toyland's finally had to say goodbye, the crème d' la crème in Chicago was when parents brought their kids into any of the four entrance sides of State, Randolph, Wabash or Washington, and lined up to visit with Santa himself. In Chicago everyone was absolutely sure *he* was the main man in the North Pole.

If this was enough to almost feel like they had found the elusive polar city, Chicago must be the world's headquarters, and everyone felt there was one more major aspect that each wanted it to happen on the Seventh Floor. A top of the line, special experience like this happened no matter how long it took to finally be seated, because they were going to enter lunch or dinner in *The Walnut Room*. This restaurant was almost as strong of a feeling for anticipation as if Santa and eight tiny reindeer would soon be landing on their roof at midnight.

There were two ways to enter the dining room. If kids could make the decision everyone knew they would be running straight to the gleaming stainless steel escalators, and ride all the way to the top, the seventh floor. Adults almost always chose to enter the elegant elevators. Either a well-dressed man or woman operated these famous lifts. Almost everyone who walked into one of them now remembered that just a few years ago a beautiful woman named Dorothy Lamour operated one of these elevators, but soon became a star singing and acting in the movies. Getting a job here was easy because countless gorgeous young women always hoped they could begin in the same amazing story. Unfortunately, almost everyone else with pretty faces and magnificent bodies working in elevators or soda shops were just one in a classic million chances to go to Hollywood.

Whichever families chose to go up on the seventh floor the elegant Walnut Room restaurant was so special even the kids stopped talking. Circassian walnut panels and crystal chandelier sconces enhanced the beauty of the natural wood. Square oak tables covered white linen cloths with silver plate service sets of utensils and sliver-plated condiment sets with cold beakers of fresh water overwhelmed many people. Ever table in the entire room had a vase of fresh flowers.

However, no matter what anyone wanted to do, order food or just gaze at the beautiful surroundings, people were all there to see The Great Tree. Many kids in the Midwest believed that this was the best in America. Regardless of the weather outside, everything in this huge building was breathtaking, too. However, the best view from the spectacular tree each year was to see it from the magnificent Walnut Room on the seventh floor. Folks marveled at it while dining there, or went up to view it from many windows on the next two floors.

Everyone there was staring eye to eye with an amazing man who lived right on the tip-top Christmas Tree…Uncle Mistletoe. Everywhere else in the country their holiday trees had stars or angels or virtually anything else, but Uncle Mistletoe was all by himself. Because he looked like that, people thought he might be singing carols with some other folks in a Charles Dickens novel. He might even be an elf who worked everyday for eleven months in the North Pole, and then stands at the top of the Christmas Tree here every December.

Actually, a copywriter for Field's advertising department dreamed this up two years earlier. Uncle Mistletoe turned out to be a chum to Santa who told him the good and kind boys and girls everywhere. Down at the bottom of the tree surrounding the base his good wife Aunt Holly helped put hand-made ornaments all over the magnificent tree.

As pretty and homey as she, his red coachman's coat also had a tall black top hat touched with mistletoe greens, and his face's bushy black eyebrows with an ear to ear smile mesmerized everyone. Christmas here was fantasyland. But most of all, for all the kids and most of their parents, it was as true as truth could be.

No matter how many millions of people always wanted to come to Chicago or Peoria or anywhere else for Christmas, there was one more final, but equally incredible experience that was the last stop before going home.

Fannie May candy. Most families thought a special law might have been voted in the Illinois General Assembly. Powerful leaders in this great commonwealth secretly could have decided that everyone has to buy at least one box before folks go home. Any kind of box is their decision, but if they leave the city without it, they could probably go directly to jail in Joliet and spend about three eternities all by themselves.

In Bradford it's possible that someone has gone into the state clinker there, but it is sure that no one went there for not buying Fannie May candy.

CHAPTER 8

▼

HIDDEN POND WITH
SMOOTH ICE

Friday morning was clear and cold, a continuation of the area's weather patterns, which developed after the big snowstorm two days earlier. Because Bradford enjoyed the peculiarity of having a small U. S. Weather Station four miles outside town, radio stations as far away as Peoria and even Chicago, often used their reading because it was an official source. This led to the village's dubious distinction of often being reported as the coldest place in Illinois. Mostly in jest, the town's weekly newspaper, The Bradford Republican used the line, "Hot News from the Coldest Spot in Illinois," as the paper's masthead slogan.

Of course, Bradford was no colder in reality than hundreds of other small towns and cities, but the weather station was located on as barren a plot of land as one could imagine. No stand of trees, cluster of buildings, or any other barrier offered relief from winds that often reached fifty miles an hour in a howling winter storm. The term 'wind chill' had not yet become part of the meteorologist's lexicon, but had it been, Bradford might have rivaled International Falls, Minnesota for first place honors in the mid-western deep freeze category.

The boy's spirits were soaring because the temperature hadn't been above thirty-two degrees since Tuesday. Only two of the group had actual hockey sticks, Suck and Hotshot. The rest either brought the best facsimile from the previous game or spent the first twenty minutes after arriving at whatever river, lake or pond they had arrived at hunting for a new, strong tree branch. Limbs that had an oblique crook were always in high demand. The sharpest eye always got the better branch, which meant that Dink, with his thick lenses, was lucky to find anything usable. When it came to finding a puck, any old tin can would work. Ice was the most elusive ingredient. In the months since Dink christened the pond, the name had successfully survived several attempts to change it. Minor jealousies inspired other suggestions such as Mystery Slough and Lost Pond. These were rejected because there was no mystery regarding either location or creation due to the boys ingenuity, and, to as to naming it Lost Pond, Booby accurately reasoned, "It ain't lost. It's been sitting right there since we made it."

They did make one minor change, however. The 'Moose' part of the name gradually became less important as time went by and it was simply referred to as Hidden Pond, a name that seems to fit perfectly. It was completely secluded from view in any direction, thanks to the thick stands of underbrush and trees that surrounded it. They also hoped this natural barrier would protect it from gusty winds as it froze. Ripples frozen into the surface would make the ice rough and slower.

Three Saturdays ago they each took a handsaw or hatchet, and created a new, secret path through the woods to the pond. They wanted to put as much room between entering the pond and Shuck Dye's place as possible. So far, they had never seen him, even when riding on the road to the river below his streetcar home.

Two fathers, Lefty Roberts, and Jack Randall, agreed to drive the boys out for their inauguration of the new hockey rink. Both men secretly also wanted to see what had so captivated their son's time and conversation. "If only I could get Eddie to work this hard around the house," Lefty whispered to Jack as they brought up the rear of the procession into the site.

"Yeah, they cut a heck of a lot of small trees and branches just to make this path." Jack responded. "Pretty impressive so far."

After about two hundred yards the procession came to the edge of the pond. As to be expected, it was covered in a two-inch layer of snow. Hotshot was first out on the ice, stepping gingerly at first, and then, hearing no telltale breaking sounds, moved farther toward the middle.

"Be careful, I know you guys all said it's fairly shallow, but just take it easy. You're not a bunch of little kids anymore, but we still promised your folks we'd watch out for you," Jack called.

Soundlessly, Hotshot continued to the deepest point as the others began taking hesitant steps in different directions. Still no sounds of ice cracking. Hotshot dropped to his knees and pushed the layer of snow away. "Wow, would you look at that! It's perfect. It's absolutely perfect!"

No one spoke as the group stared at the patch of ice before them. Miraculously, the brown, muddy water from the Mighty Spoon was now transformed into thick, solid ice that now appeared to be a pool of frozen milk trapping misty, ghost-like apparitions near its surface. "We did it. Guys, we did it! Our very own hockey rink." Hotshot's unbridled exuberance was contagious, and instantly everyone was yelling and pounding someone else's back or hugging the nearest person. Even the two fathers who had only contributed their services as chauffeurs caught the excited mood.

"Let's get the snow shovels and brooms and clear the snow, and little limbs with leaves as soon as we can," Jumbo cried. "It shouldn't take us more than ten minutes."

Everyone went to work as soon as he grabbed a work tool. The pond was quickly cleared and it was obvious their dreams of smooth ice had come true.

"Boy, I bet the Blackhawks would even be jealous of this place," Catfish laughed, as he looked out over the expanse before him.

"Yeah, we really do have the perfect pond for hockey." Hotshot shoved his arms and smiled as a very proud teammate. Actually, since he fantasized the challenge to really build a hidden hockey pond, he wondered if this small 'rink' might even impress the professional team in Chicago.

The next day had a much different plan for at least several of the special seven. Sunday, January 9, was going to be a special treat for lots of the kids in town, and even many of the parents. One of the best movies ever made was coming back to Bradford almost ten years after its premier: *The Wizard of Oz*.

For nearly fifty years, the book that mesmerized children since 1900 had done an even more incredible transformation into one of the most amazing movies in 1939 this country had ever had. Many people didn't even know that the original book was named, "*The Wonderful Wizard of Oz*," but wonderful might even be the best adjective anyone could ever compare.

Hockey for three hours yesterday had a blast, but going to this movie for two hours in the afternoon was just as astounding. When the early show ended Jonathan Crawford Patterson was unaware of the muted sounds made by his own buddies and other kids and people who were shuffling over crumbled popcorn boxes and bags and coke cups as they left the theatre. Various conversations were shared with the other people who were raving about the movie they had all just seen.

The four large round bulbs hanging high in the old metal ceiling transformed a magical movie theatre into a sadly dilapidated, ancient building. Nearly two hundred people were now leaving the two aisles, but one boy still sitting all by himself had a glazed look of rapturous wonder. Dink automatically decided he had to stay for the second show.

As the last couple slipped out into the sunny afternoon, he walked into the men's restroom and stepped up on the toilet seat to hide his feet. Even if Mr. Winter's glanced into the facilities, he probably wouldn't have checked for someone hiding there.

When about half of the people who had been standing in Mrs. Fannie Winter's office window to buy tickets were already either into their seats, or buying things at the small concession stand, Dink slipped in and took a different seat.

Even before the preview movies started again for him, he stared ahead in the general direction of the blank screen, unblinking and oblivious to everything except the memories of the amazing movie that had just come to life for him. His mind was whirling much like the Kansas cyclone he had just witnessed. Nothing he had ever seen or heard had so profoundly touched or moved him. The characters and scenes cascaded through his mind out of sequence,

Believe it or not, this same astounding experience had happened again for Dink when his second showing was now over. "Young man, you better not be trying to come back for a third show today. We close the theatre in ten minutes so my wife and I can go home for supper. We'll be back for the seven o'clock show about six-thirty."

Mr. Winters smiled down at Dink, and the boy gulped. He knew he somehow had been caught even though he tried to hide himself as best as he could. "You're the Patterson boy. I think your mom and dad are probably already wondering where you are."

"Yes, Mr. Winters, Dink replied as solicitous as he could be. "It's just that I…I…" he stammered. "It's that I was sitting there thinking about….what a great place Oz must be." He changed his answer at the last second for fear of sounding foolish, because Dink could easily tell him that more than anything else in the whole world he wanted to fly over the rainbow and live in the Land of Oz.

Mr. Winters smiled again, and nodded. "Well, son, you'd better leave now so your folks are happy to see you. But I have to tell you that I loved this movie the first time I saw back in '39 when it came out."

As both started walking out into the lobby, the old man placed his hand on Dink's shoulders. "I'll tell you something else. In fact, I have never even told what I am saying to you or to my dear, loving wife after nearly 51 years together.

When I first saw the Wizard of Oz it made me hope that I'd just had a glimpse of what Heaven is going to be like." He smiled and then added, "That is, of course, without any Wicked Witches," with a soft chuckle.

"Gosh, Mr. Winters," Dink said excitedly. "Do you really think it could be. Oh, wow! I go to church lots of times, but I get a little scared about how I would get to God's Heaven. But if it turns out to be the Emerald City there's no point in being afraid to die, if that's true."

Frank Winters smiled and nodded his head, realizing that in Dink's youthful exuberance had also occurred to him ten years ago. It might surprise him that his young boy's remark like that could also sound as if it had been spoken by a 71 years old grandfather.

"You're right, young man. Go have a happy evening with your family. If you come back with your folks to see it again, remember watch closely at the beginning, right after all the credits tell who did what. I think you are a loyal believer."

Mr. Winters unexpected comment had stopped Dink as they were standing in the middle of the lobby. A very cold upper atmosphere in the late afternoon now illuminated part of the sun as it was slipping into the Western view through the two big glass doors. He screwed up his face tightly in his typical questioning frown. "What do you mean? What should I watch for?"

"You saw the first words at the beginning, but the next time read them more carefully. This movie is dedicated to people like you and me, no matter how old or young we are. All we have to do is be true and loyal believers."

Dink stared down at the floor momentarily and then looked back up into Mr. Winters' friendly gaze. "Thank you, Mr. Winters," he said, beaming with a feeling of joy that he couldn't have possibly been able to explain. "And thank you for telling me that. I'll always believe in this story. I promise you that as if you were the Wizard of Oz himself."

With that both of them did the most natural joy grampas and grandsons love to do…a big hug. Though these two were not related to each other, they certainly had begun become a life-long friendship together.

"One more thing," Mr. Winters said, in an afterthought. "Have you been over to see the entire collection of Oz books that L. Frank Baum wrote, too? It's at the Bradford library." He laughed and also added, "The man who dreamed up these incredible stories had the same name as me, Frank."

Dink smiled, but he immediately replied "Gosh, no. I've got just the main book at home. Are there more?"

Mr. Winters glanced over and saw Mrs. Winters was patiently standing a few feet away. Supper was important, but even she realized that her long time companion was just as amazed about the Wizard of Oz as the young boy standing beside him.

"Go over to the Library when Miss Code opens the front door. Tell her I sent you. You're in for a terrific surprise. She will show you where a dozen other books are written about Oz." He grinned, "Jonathan, I have read everyone of the books, and you will, too."

They waved to each other, and Dink was now swept along by such utter euphoria he began to skip and jump and run. As he suddenly stopped skipping he yelled back at the elderly couple walking across Main Street to go home, "What a wonderful, wonderful day this is for me."

Both waved back at his statement, and grinned at each other. Then Mr. Winters reached over and held her beside himself just a little closer as they again walked toward home.

CHAPTER 9

▼

THE HELPING HAND

January brought with it some bad news for the boys: unseasonably warm weather. Hidden Pond's surface not only had turned slushy; it was now becoming a favorite passage way for various woodland animals from raccoons to deer. Each night, when temperatures usually dipped below freezing, their tracks remained until the daily thaw repeated the cycle. It totally fouled up any skating plans, and only a serious meltdown allowing the surface to again go smooth, would solve the problem.

The white in Bing Crosby's song about his dreams for a snowy holiday had turned into a dirty, soppy mess. For the first hours following its arrival, snow is one of nature's most beautiful gifts, but it almost always ends up like an irksome houseguest who overstays his visit.

However, going back to school for the first time since Christmas vacation was even more devastating for Suck. It was this day that he learned the news that Barbara Denson was gone, apparently leaving quietly over the holidays with her mother. Miss Wallace said it was her understanding Barbara moved to Princeton, a larger town twenty-five miles away. This news sent Philip Carlton into the biggest emotional tailspin of his life. A simple trip like this wasn't a formidable distance to a teenage boy with a car, but to a thirteen-year-old she might just as well be in Saudi Arabia. It wasn't until the shock of her departure sunk in that he realized just how much this beautiful girl intrigued him. Because his birthday fell in mid-December, he was the eldest in his group of seven, the first to turn thirteen.

Using nature's time clock, however, he was several years older than most of the others.

Suck decided to find out what happened to the Denson family over the holidays. After casually asking questions at the Drug Store, Peterson's Dairy Bar and Café, and Dorgans, of course, the only thing he could determine was a rumor that her mother was unable to find work in Bradford. Barbara's father disappeared years ago, and, though it was common knowledge among the adult community that her mother was having a difficult time, none of the kids in her class were aware of any problems.

That night at the dinner table, Suck was unusually quiet. It didn't take Mrs. Carlton long to pick up on it, but she waited to see if he wanted to begin a discussion. As they were finishing desert, she sensed whatever it was he needed some outside stimulation. "What's on your mind tonight, Philip, you seem to be unusually quiet."

"There's a problem that has been really bothering me, and I was hoping our family could help. It's a case of someone in need," he replied.

"Why, that's one of the most thoughtful things I've ever heard you say, Philip, whatever it is I'm sure we can be of assistance," his mother said in a mixture of wonder and satisfaction.

"What is it that's concerning you, son?" Mr. Carlton said, attempting not to show any signs of the slight feeling of skepticism he suddenly was feeling. Years of observing friends and employees endowed him with a sixth sense that set off a silent alarm in his mind whenever he heard a statement that was uncharacteristic of the speaker.

"Is there any way we can adopt Barbara Denson?"

Experienced parents are sometimes upset or disappointed by things their children say or do, but rarely are they stunned. This was one of those times when his question knocked them for the proverbial loop.

"What on earth do you mean, adopt Barbara?" his father asked immediately. "Has she suddenly become an orphan?"

"No, but she had to move because her mother is having a hard time. I was just wondering if she could come live with us for a while. Kind of like an act of Christian charity they talk about in Sunday school." Suck decided to roll out all his artillery in a deliberate attempt to mask the real purpose of the idea. But his ploy to mislead his parents was an instant failure.

At the words 'Christian charity' Mrs. Carlton choked while taking a sip from the cup of coffee in her hand. Part of the fluid went into her sinus cavities and she grabbed a napkin to cover her mouth and nostrils. Bob Carlton also reacted immediately, rolling his eyes, first in disbelief at Suck's comment, and then at his wife's dilemma. He was trying to maintain total composure, and yet was struck by a strong desire to throw his head back and begin laughing. Fortunately, he didn't. He rose from the table and went around to offer any assistance to his wife.

She raised her hand to reject any help, and gestured for him to sit down again. "I'm sorry," she said, "I suppose I was a bit surprised to hear about this new charitable idea of yours, Philip. Coming from someone who fights us tooth and nail every Sunday morning to keep from going to your class and then on to church, well, it was too big of a shock for me, I guess." She dabbed the napkin to her lips and nose.

"Yes, Phil, that caught me off guard as well," his father added. "I don't suppose the fact that Barbara is one of the, uh, prettiest girls in your class has anything to do with it?" As one of four cheerleaders for the grade school's basketball team, Barbara's blossoming figure was a well-known fact to everyone attending the games. "Oh, no, Dad. It's just that I know how many friends she has here in Bradford, and it hurts me to think of her possibly being lonely somewhere else."

At this, Bob Carlton was still able to restrain outright laughter, but he couldn't keep from smiling. "When do you think this sudden attack of altruism came upon you, son? I suppose you realize it represents quite a personality shift." From the look on Suck's face it was obvious that Mr. Carlton knew the meaning of altruism had escaped his son.

Helen Carlton, now fully recovered, also developed a twinkle in her eyes, and looked at her husband. "Now Bob, I'm sure he meant it with the best of intentions."

Suck either did not realize the game was over or he felt he was in so deep he had nothing else to lose. "I really wanted it to be a nice gesture to help them out. Besides, now that Sally has gone off to college her bedroom just sits there empty…" His words chugged to a stop like a car running out of gas. "Well," he said, resuming his speech at normal speed, "it was just an idea to offer a helping hand." Suck instantly realized his addendum was the wrong choice of words.

"A helping hand, hmm. Yes, I'm sure you'd like to do that. It's very nice of you, son. I doubt it crossed your mind that next summer up on the lake at Camp Lincoln you could probably use one of her brassieres as a sailboat spinnaker," Mr. Carlton said softly with a wink.

"Bob!" Mrs. Carlton exclaimed in rebuke, but she immediately began to laugh and covered her face with her napkin.

All three of them were now laughing. Mr. Carlton arose and went over to his son and gave him a one-armed hug, and then patted him a couple of times on his shoulder. "Nice try, son. Adopting Barbara Denson. Hmmm. I'll give you credit. That was a heck of an idea. Helen, looks like we're going to have to keep a little closer eye on you know who."

As January grudging gave way to February, the feelings of excitement which greeted the winter's first snowfall or sleigh ride or skating party were replaced by a growing resignation that only time and a new season could bring this dreary period to an end. One sunless day could easily be tolerated. Even one sunless week was to be expected. However, when five or six weeks in a row filled with the shortest days of the year, and skies the consistency and color of molten lead pile up one upon another, it is then that human patience is pushed to the breaking point. It made people wonder how their counterparts living through colder and longer winters further north of Bradford manage to do so without losing mind or temper. Actually, it was a thought no one really cared to contemplate very long.

Valentines Day came and went, and for the younger kids in grade school it was a simple, happy experience. Twenty-five little cards were usually bought in an inexpensive bag at Batten's Five and Ten, and they signed their names with 'Mary R', or 'Jackie W'. They were put into a colorful box that each teacher had made. These seven boys were now being very coy as to which girls they sent a Valentine.

Thankfully, both for Bradford's kids and their parents, basketball was king in the mid-west because Illinois' weather was bad most of the time. The high school gym remained open all day Saturday, and pick up games for all age groups were the norm for dreary winter days. Uniforms were easily created to differentiate one team from another. One team took off their shirts, and the other left theirs on, allowing a game they called 'shirts and skins'. More informal games of H.O.R.S.E., involving four or five kids taking shots at one of the six goals suspended around the floor's perimeter, were always underway.

Fortunately for most people, challenges at work, school, church, and the winding down of the various basketball seasons offered much needed diversions to the dullness outside. If any manmade diversion deserved credit for bringing folks through the moments when cabin fever seemed to be going into the terminal stages, it was radio. After parental patience was long exhausted, and rebellious tempers were causing sibling civil war after school, radio was the savior. By early 1949, programming sophistication had reached the point where there was something for everyone in that miraculous little box containing the glowing tubes. Comedy, mystery, drama, game shows, sporting events, musical variety, children's programming, and regularly scheduled newscasts gave a welcome break from the annoyance of weather related frustration.

Immediately after school, kids had the option to spend up to two hours spinning the dial from one fifteen-minute serial to another. *The Adventures of Superman, Jack Armstrong: The All American Boy, Terry and the Pirates, Tom Mix, Sergeant Preston of the Yukon, The Lone Ranger, The Green Hornet,* and *Captain Midnight* were but a few of the adventure stories available each afternoon.

Housewives all across America also had their own special moral booster: a daytime phenomenon called soap operas, thus named because so many were sponsored by big soap companies. Women could lose themselves in other peoples problems without the guilt of gossip or eavesdropping. Millions were enthralled by the exploits of daily shows such as *Young Doctor Malone, Ma Perkins, One Man's Family, Our Gal Sunday,* and *The Romance of Helen Trent.* Weekly dramatic shows also enjoyed a tremendous following. *Suspense, Light's Out, Inner Sanctum, The Fat Man, Grand Central Station, The FBI In Peace and War, The Shadow, Lux Mystery Theatre;* the list went on and on. All of the famous comedians of that time had shows of their own creating a Sunday evening family ritual. Gabriel Heater, Edward R. Murrow, H. V. Kaltenborn, Drew Pearson, and Walter Winchell were names everyone recognized from their distinctly unique styles of broadcasting news each day. It was a welcome relief to let sounds from a box on the table take you any place in the world, and even beyond. This was truly the golden age of radio.

Most seventh graders had but three normal sources for news stories. The "Weekly Readers" briefing in their history classes using photos and maps the schools received by mail each week, what they overheard their parents discussing, and the best way of all: in the Brad Theatre every Saturday afternoon at the double feature matinee. An announcer/reporter named Ed Herlihy became almost as familiar to them as one of their teachers thanks to "The Eyes and Ears of The World," a six to eight minute newsreel produced each week which preceded the movies. It was usually sandwiched after the pre-views of coming attractions and a Bugs Bunny or Road Runner Cartoon, or another short subject, often the Three Stooges. Weekly serials, which specialized in cliff hanging endings that always left the hero or heroine in a disastrous position, were shown periodically. But it didn't matter what was on the screen, kids were just happy to be there. Admission was sixteen cents and bags of popcorn, small cokes, and most of the candy bars each cost a nickel. All in all, it was such a cheap, safe way for parents to take a break from their brood, and they enjoyed the afternoon as much as the kids.

One cool March Saturday afternoon children from surrounding farms and the village alike were gathering in front of the theater's single box office. The Brad Theatre was on the north side of Main Street filling the space between Dad Tumbleson's Standard Oil gas station, and Kelly's Shamrock Tavern. It was an old, worn out looking building with a red brick front, small glass enclosed ticket booth, and a back lighted marquee. It definitely had seen better days, most likely in the prior century. Before it became a movie theatre in the 1920's, it was called the Bradford Opera House where almost any kind of performance imaginable had been performed.

Matching the building in age were the elderly couple who managed and operated it, Fannie and Frank Winters. Dink had had a fantastic experience with them two months earlier when *The Wizard of Oz* came back again. He now knew them a lot better than any of the other guys. This couple had been there so long most folks couldn't remember buying a ticket from anyone but Fannie Winters, and handing it right back to Frank. Frail and withered, she didn't look as if she would last until the second feature, but always managed to smile at each child in the line. Since most kids eagerly paid the sixteen-cent admission by shoving a quarter and penny through the semi-circular window, she always had a stack of dimes ready to make change. Thus, the line moved quite rapidly.

Mr. Winters wore many hats, serving as manager, ticket taker, usher, and even helped projectionist Arnold Bundee mount the huge reels of film on the two projectors mounted side by side. Arnold stuttered so long and so much he was thrilled to just sit up stairs alone in the flickering machines that made everyone happy. Unfortunately, if an old film broke or the machine itself occasionally stop working, 150 kids always started booing instantly. Poor Arnold started muttering himself so loud that everyone soon stopped yelling, and began to laugh. But breakdowns that everyone always experienced somehow got fixed, and the projection machines eventually went back into action.

'Lights, action, camera' was when every Director called these three critical words on Hollywood sets then. Arnold had no idea what that meant or who it was. However, when he had to suddenly turn on the one light bulb hanging above him in the small room upstairs, he immediately went into serious action, and eventually one of the cameras was finally going again.

Assisting and overseeing the small concession stand was also Mr. Winters' domain, especially between features. He helped whichever part time teenage employee was working that weekend afternoon or evening to get ready for the onslaught of hungry, rambunctious kids.

Seven boys who wanted popcorn and Milk-Duds were seated in the second row from the front. Dink smiled at both of the Winters, but he and the other six were now primed to play a joke on one of their classmates, the biggest girl in grade school. Nature, through the mysteries of genetics, created in Viola Curry a girl with the body of a middle linebacker. Principal Huey, who also doubled as the coach of the fledgling football team, almost weakened and invited her to try out for the team. When he watched her kick a football right over the roof of a two-story grade school building, he got very excited.

Sadly, the Bradford School Board agreed with the plan, but W. S. Perrin, Stark County Superintendent of Schools ended it immediately. He said females will not play in sports....at all! He felt girls should learn how to cook and sew, and play with dolls. In just eight to ten years they would be dropping those sawdust mannequins into recreating the next generation of real kids. Mr. Huey had to quickly forgot Viola's natural ability, and when he took the coaches cap off, he returned to wear his coat and tie in the principal's office.

Actually, it was Suck who dreamed up another challenge for Viola, and shared his idea with everyone else but Jumbo. Today, just as they went into the theater and took their seats, Suck waited until he could find where Viola was sitting. When he saw her near the middle of the front row, he chose seven seats in the second row for he and the others. Walking down the aisle, he dared Jumbo to sit beside her and put his arm around her. Immediately, the others picked up on it before Jumbo had time to react.

Edward Jay Roberts didn't get to be an acknowledged leader without three necessary assets: brains, guts, and an almost unnatural absence of fear. No one ever double-dog-dared him anything, because one dare was always sufficient. This time was no exception. What the others didn't know is that he already was planning a surprise of his own. Today Jumbo decided he was going to win Bradford's unofficial bubble gum blowing championship. His pocket was bulging with two large Bazooka brand packs, each containing six normal chews. What better place to blow this bubble than to sit with his arm around Viola on the front row of the Brad Theater before at least half the kids in town.

Suck, ever the manipulator, already asked another classmate, Dana Evans, a pretty classmate with long, black hair, to sit with Viola, and then, at his tap on her shoulder, to leave her seat ostensibly to go to the restroom. At first Dana didn't want anything to do with it because she was afraid it would hurt her companion's feelings. She had befriended Viola at the beginning of the school year because she felt sorry for the way most of the rest of the class ignored the newcomer to their class. It took fifteen minutes to convince her that it was, in his words, good, clean, fun. What Dana didn't realize is that already, at the tender age of thirteen, Suck's definition of what constituted wholesome entertainment was broadening on a daily basis.

Jumbo's acceptance did not come without a price. He whispered that if he did it, they had to buy him a large box of popcorn as his reward. Even though it cost a whole dime, they accepted because they were dividing it six ways. Hotshot was pondering how they would divide six into ten evenly when Suck tapped Dana. As soon as she excused herself, Jumbo made his move. He strutted in front of the stage, and he was silhouetted by the action on the screen as far back as the first three or four rows. Every kid in these seats watched him sit down by Viola and lift his left arm around her, giving her a quick hug for emphasis.

Laughter that had been building like spring floodwaters behind a damn now exploded. Viola glanced at Jumbo, startled. The fact that she outweighed him by 40-50 pounds, and was at least four inches taller, easily explained why she looked down on him. When the laughter started, she realized she was the brunt of a rather cruel joke. A flush of blood momentarily darkened her face, but it was lost in the glare or the screen and surrounding darkness. Then she got an idea of her own.

Viola, speaking through lips clenched so tightly she could have been a ventriloquist, leaned over and whispered in Jumbo's ear. "Listen, Mr. Smarty-pants, you better sit here through the entire first feature and leave your arm right where it is, or I'll break it, plain and simple. And if you so much as make any kind of dumb move with your hand, I'll sit on you. Got it?"

Jumbo gulped and nodded. This was a first for him. Since the years since they met in Mrs. Peterson's Story Time when they were all three or four, none of the other boys had ever said anything like that to him. Even his older brother was never so blunt. Looks like I'm really going to earn that box of popcorn, he thought. Adding to his discomfort was the worry that one of his friends behind them might have heard her terse command. This hadn't turned out to be such a fun prank.

A few minutes later, he remembered his original project for the day, and started slipping chunks of Bazooka into his mouth with his free right hand. Slowly and methodically he chewed each new piece, gradually incorporating it into the gooey mess growing in his mouth. Eight pieces were now thoroughly mixed offering exactly the right feeling of density and strength. Without fanfare he began blowing the bubble.

Everyone was so caught up in the Lash Larue cowboy drama now fifteen minutes old, no one noticed it until it reached about the same size as his head. Even in the theatre, with no breezes to cause problems, it began to bob and shake slightly each time he paused to slowly inhale through his nose, and exhale into the growing pink mass. As it reached the size of a basketball every eye in the first four rows was now watching the new drama unfold. When it surpassed a large Halloween Jack-O-Lantern, kids were calling words of encouragement. Viola sensed the time was right to literally put the final touch on Jumbo's practical joke. She timed her move to the precise second he again began the slow inhaling motion with his head now tilted slightly backwards, and popped the bubble with her left index finger.

The bubble collapsed in a filmy, sticky mess all over Jumbo's face. His hair, both eyebrows and his left eye were completely covered. Boisterous laughter rocked the theatre, and Jumbo immediately jumped to his feet and began running in a zigzag manner up the aisle, trying to see where he was going. He knew the problem with Bazooka was the longer he waited, the bigger the problem was to get it off.

It wasn't until later in the afternoon at Dorgan's, as he watched Viola and Dana in the end booth drinking Black Cows that Beaner told him his bubble didn't pop of its own volition. This was something he didn't know because the bubbles huge size prevented him from seeing anyone's finger strike it.

Sensing from the look on his face that he now knew the truth, Viola smiled coyly and said, "Hi, there, sweetie. How about another date next Saturday?" Both girls instantly laughed, and tried to cover their mouths with napkins.

In a show of solidarity with Jumbo, the other six boys tried to repress their laughter but failed. They found it impossible to keep from smiling, and several were heard to emit quick giggles or muffled laughs. The worst of it was Jumbo realized there wasn't a thing he could do about it. But, as so often happens, just when you're sure things can't get any worse, they do.

And up to now one silent observer of this scene interrupted the laughter. "What's this I hear about you, Edwards, picking on a helpless, little girl?" The speaker was Marge Dorgan, at thirty-eight the youngest daughter in the family, and every bit as offbeat and unique as her father. "Why don't ya invite me to go to the movies with ya? I might even make a point of putting on two socks that match." This last reference was to her total indifference to what she chose to wear each morning. Clothing selections that showed coordination and fashion sense were not her style. This was particularly true in her inability to wear two socks that belonged together. Her clothes were first and foremost functional in nature, and attractive color combinations or matching items were as unimportant to her as who made them.

With this outburst, everyone in the soda shop began laughing. Marge walked around the counter and over to the stool where Jumbo was sitting. She gave him a hug and tousled his hair. "Just because I'm a little older than you don't mean I won't wait for ya. Besides," she said with an obviously false demureness, "Viola said I could have ya." No one ever remembered a time when Jumbo blushed more than right now.

He tried to get away from Marge, but she held on. He finally used the stool as his ally, spinning away from her grasp and started for the door. The other boys, holding partially eaten ice cream cones, immediately jumped up and followed his lead. Retreat seemed to be the best option they had.

CHAPTER 10

▼

WINTER'S SPRUNG...IS
FINALLY SPRING

"Look! Over here. Oh, isn't it pretty."

One girl said it, and several others ran over to the spot where they were now standing. A beautiful red tulip, with it's bud still tightly closed, had penetrated up to the remains of a sooty covered chunk of left-over snow in a small bank on the north side, right beside the front porch steps. This remaining chunk of slush was covered with splattered mud. Since the location was directly on one of the two main sidewalks that led to school, in seconds a number of kids were standing in the yard, looking at this welcome harbinger of Earth's rebirth.

"My mother says that tulips are the bravest flowers in the world. They pop right up with their little buds through almost anything, even snow, to tell us God hasn't forgotten about us," one girl pondered.

"They tell me to get home and start looking in the closet for my baseball glove," as Beaner said, then turned and began running up the street. He was quickly followed by several of the others.

"Let's grab our gloves and meet in the park. If it isn't too muddy, let's play catch," Dink yelled. Their happy voices trailed off into the distance.

Beautiful songbirds were now returning in greater numbers every day. The first sighting of a robin or cardinal was always a welcome relief after enduring a cold winter with nothing much to eat. Hungry sparrows or starlings pecking around the yards were the saddest of them all. Now, farmers were busy sharpening plows or adjusting planters. Chicks were hatching and newborn calves were taking their first unsteady steps. Farm cats received an occasional reward for maintaining their vigilance against barn mice by receiving a few quick squirts of fresh milk at milking time.

Easter was a perfect Sunday. A year earlier it had snowed so most folks had to wait on the Saturday night weather report to know if they could wear their Easter bonnets. All over town, colored eggs were in baskets or hunted in the backyards. Dink's mother even baked a bunny rabbit cake each year. Everything was white from the cake to the frosting to even its coconut 'fur'. Two little pink jelly beans eyes were the last swallows Matt got to eat because he was the smallest.

On some warmer afternoons you could see kites of many colors and shapes bobbing in the sky above the pasture that was divided by the meandering stream, Cooper's Defeat. The pungent smell of newly spread manure was another reminder of the coming planting season. Sometimes, if the wind was strong enough, it was an odor that could reach any place in town because the fields it fertilized were only a block or two away from many homes, even in the center of the village. But for good people in rural America, manure was a staple, a fact of life. It wasn't the least bit offensive because it was so necessary.

Mud was a far more common source of displeasure and frustration. Boys and girls repeatedly had shoes and boots literally sucked off of their feet if they inadvertently ventured off a sidewalk into one of the many patches of ooze and muck created by the spring thaw. No ground anywhere seemed to be immune to the problem. Cars easily got stuck if their rear wheels left a solid surface from concrete, asphalt, or gravel. On any field, even something as powerful as a John Deere or Farmall or Massey Ferguson could find itself in such a quagmire. It would take a brother tractor to secure release.

For the boys, a local mud problem had temporarily stymied the first baseball game of the spring. Eight or nine forlorn looking boys were sitting on the library steps staring at a playground that gave a decent days appearance of being playable, but they had tested it and found otherwise.

"Boy, I sure will be glad for summer. I'm so sick of slush, and now mud. I'm just fed up," Hotshot said, after the entire group endured a brief period of frustrated silence.

"Me too. This is enough to make a goat puke." Catfish shook his head.

Suck looked over at Catfish, and laughed. "Let's hope nobody pukes any more around here. We've got more than enough mud right now."

Jumbo then immediately sent a blob of brown spittle shooting over the side of the staircase. He looked at Suck, and laughed. "Oh, well, a little more mud won't hurt nobody."

"Guess so. Players are always spittin' all over the baseball fields where the players stand and play in the game. I've been there a few times with my dad, and he says Andy Pafko and Phil Caverretta in Wrigley Field spit tobacco in the outfield or infield even if they are just standin' around or even when they're playing," Hotshot added. "In fact, most all of them do it."

"I bet Stan the Man doesn't spit anywhere, even if the Cubbies might be spittin' when they're playin' against him and the Cards," Dink offered.

"Stop mumbling about that 'Stan the Man' again, Dink. Speakin' about puking, Cub fans will be sick if you start more crap going again this season." Hotshot was the best natural pitcher of any of them, and he wanted Jumbo to be his regular catcher, but if Dink started too many arguments, when they felt it, they would be saying 'adios' to him.

The boys stared at the park, and wistfully hoped that things are going to get better soon. Finally Dink said, "At least we only have two more months in prison. I can't wait for the last day of school. That's my favorite, all-time holiday."

"Even better than Christmas or your birthday?" asked Catfish.

"Yep, because that's the first day of the holiday, and it lasts three months. All the other holidays take forever to get there, and then they go so fast you can't believe they're gone," Dink said.

"Huh, that makes a lot of sense," Catfish nodded.

"Me, I like the Fourth of July at the fair in Henry. All that cotton candy and rides and the fireworks over the river are great. But, I guess I like the last day of school, too, because it means we're free again." Jumbo said.

"Yeah, but next Thursday night I can't tell you how much I'm looking forward to St. Patrick's Day again," Dink said, immediately changing the subject.

"St. Paddy's Day! From you?" The words instantly exploded out of Beaner. He now was a wild, pug-nosed boy, full of freckles, topped by an auburn colored crew cut…and he was mad. "Dink, you aren't even Irish. That's our holiday," he added indignantly. Booby and he felt St. Patty's Day was their own Irish personal property.

"I know it, Beaner, but I still like to go to Irish stuff even if my dad says my brothers and I are mongrels."

"What the heck are you saying, Dink?" Hotshot said as he curled his nose.

"My dad says we have so many family members from different countries over the past hundred years we might just be like a normal mutt. As far as the Irish stuff, my folks always bring me and my two brothers to the Altar and Rosary Society dinner in the basement of St. John's hall every year on St. Patrick's Day. Then, after we finish having dinner, we go upstairs to the show, and listen to one of your Irish buddies who always has a squeaky voice trying to sing 'Danny Boy'."

At this remark they all chuckled and nodded. Booby and Beaner, and a couple of the rest of them remember last year when Jackie Finnegan forgot the words and Mrs. Barnes had to start all over on the piano for him. Then, when he was through, he slugged Mike Mulligan because he was laughing at him. When the boys talked about it for a while, they were laughing even more.

"You know what my favorite part is?" Booby said.

Several instantly replied 'what?'

Booby lowered his voice to almost a whisper. "I love to stay out late as much as I can, and hang around in a corner to see how drunk a few of the town's men get. "Again the boys were laughing together. "Last year, next door to us, Terry Gill got so mad at Sean Shanahan he grabbed a small pile of bricks sitting near the driveway. He was cussin', and threw one at Sean. The problem was he missed, and the brick went right through the right side window of Mrs. Derrigan's car. She lives next door to them, and grabbed a broom in her kitchen and then started chasing both of them from the yard."

Now everyone was engulfed in more laughter.

"Yep, St. Paddy's Day is sure one fun day," Beaner agreed. "I heard about the hilarious time that happened when Mr. Harrigan got so plastered one night driving home to their farm near Milo. According to Mrs. Harrigan, they were only going about ten miles an hour from Buda that night because of a very thick fog. She said she was thrilled he was driving that slow because he was crocked. Thankfully for them, it wasn't running on the Streamliner that night."

Each boy nodded because everyone loved to watch the incredible train from the Burlington Line. It was as if new aliens from another planet had arrived into the Midwest, and they now let folks ride on it everyday.

"Just as they started driving over the two train tracks, he didn't see any flashing lights in the fog, because there aren't any. When she saw a Chicago and Northwestern freight train had stopped on the track, she said she yelled at him, and he hit his breaks. Unfortunately, he drove right into the side of a boxcar. A hobo was sleeping in the open door, and it scared him so much he jumped out, and ran away in the darkness. Mrs. Harrigan says back up you crazy bastard, I am driving from now on."

They all were laughing again, and then Catfish said, "Were they hurt much?"

"She told my mom her knee got bumped, but not too bad, and he didn't seem to know he'd done anything. Actually, she hit him in his head with her purse after she saw the front car's bumper was bent a little. They had to wait for the train to finally leave, and she drove them home. She says he now feels the train hit his car instead of the way it happened."

As the boys were laughing yet again, Beaner closed the book. "Like I said, boys, there ain't nothing quite like St. Patty's Day in St. Johns Hall."

CHAPTER 11

▼

BOOBS, VIOLETS, AND MARBLES...THEY'RE JUST A DREAM AWAY

Gloria Benton tiptoed into her bedroom and gently closed the door behind her. She quietly crept across the room and stood in front of her dresser mirror. Rising to her toes, she was standing sideways as she stared at her own body. As she looked at herself, wearing a very tight, pink sweater, she positioned herself in an even better side profile, and arched back while pushing her shoulders and ran her palms down as she shoved in her stomach.

Her firm, already well formed young breasts strained inside her bra so strongly it brought a slight hurting sensation. The straps cut barely into her skin, but it wasn't a look of pain that formed on her face, it was proud satisfaction.

"Gloria, where are you?" said an older woman who had unexpectedly burst into her bedroom. "Oh, my dear, you surprised me, and I'm sorry." It was her grandmother who had driven over from her home in Toulon. Gloria's mother also walked in as they had just climbed up the stairs to see something in her bedroom.

Now her mother was somewhat agitated by the unexpected happening. "Have you been wearing a two-year old sweater? I believe it's not only old, it's too small now. But I guess you feel it makes you feel bigger. Let me tell you something,

Miss Pin-up girl, those new breasts can get you in trouble quicker than you can say Jack Robinson."

Gloria started to cry, and lowered her gaze. In her mind she couldn't believe that they had found her so quickly.

Mrs. Huffman walked over and put her arms around the lovely 13 year-old girl. "You were my first granddaughter, Gloria. Now so quickly, you're turning into a beautiful, young woman. It's always a surprise for even those of us who became mothers a lot of years ago. Energy and changes are a very strong aspect of your coming life. But don't try to grow up too soon, dear. You're just in the 7th grade."

All three of them hugged, and smiled. "Sweet Gloria, just remember that teen-age boys seem to always talk about sports or fishing or hunting, but when they now look at you it's cooking their brains twenty-four hours a day. All you have to do is stay ten minutes ahead, and they'll never figure out what you are feeling or thinking." They each laughed, and then the two mothers started to walk out.

"Come on down, Gloria," said Mrs. Huffman, "I have to go down in the kitchen, because I think Washington has a serious law that says grandmothers have to bake cookies. Heaven help me, if I get arrested so come down and give me some help."

"And especially change your sweater," said her mother, as both started down the steps. Then she stopped, and looked back into the bedroom. "Actually, I don't think you should wear many sweaters to school. Some of those boys are going to think you are another Lana Turner or Betty Grable." All three smiled again.

In a couple of minutes they were immediately busy. "How about kneading a bag of margarine for me," Mrs. Huffman said, and handed it to Gloria. She lifted the clear plastic bag, and placed her thumbs and fingers on the small, reddish colored capsule near the middle. With a rapid squeeze the tiny, inner container broke, sending streaks from a mixture of red, yellow, and gold coloring food into the putty-like substance. In a few minutes she knew it would be as yellow as a fresh bar of butter.

Gloria said nothing as she grinned and smiled with each of the other women as they worked, but her mind was very involved, and it wasn't about cookies. She said to herself that she could wear whatever she wanted, and it would be the tighter, the better. After all, she thought, mom and gramma don't need to know everything I do.

Two years ago Philip Carlton started carefully reserving one night each year, and as far as he felt it, he was strictly on his own. In fact, he wanted to be as far away from all of the other six pals as possible. It began when his mother told him of a custom she remembered enjoying as a young girl in Peoria, and it instantly appealed to him.

Her story said that something happened just about dusk each night on the first of May. A boy who suddenly wanted to see a beautiful girl would make a small basket of colored construction paper with a pretty handle, and fill it with fresh, spring flowers. He could add a few pieces of candy in the basket, if he wanted to make it even nicer. Then the boy would carry it up to the front door of the special girl of his choice, set it by the porch's front door, ring the doorbell or knock there, and wait. At first sight of her, the boy was supposed to run away, letting her give an immediate chase, and hoped she would catch up with him.

However, boys who were interested in this game, always figured out how to make sure they got caught, and a boy practically prayed that she would then kiss him as a very distinctive thank you. If kissing wasn't on his agenda, a boy could probably outrun her, but it may be that the entire village of Bradford had never had a boy who wanted to run that fast before. This custom was so wonderful lots of boys and girls were thrilled, but for some this was also their very first 'premature mating season'.

The main aspect usually expected a boy to make just one May Day basket, but possibly some might make even a few more. However, Philip Carlton was not just any kind of a boy. He was the first that anyone had ever heard or done before because he now prepared eleven identical baskets.

He created them with interwoven color paper strips of purple and yellow, and the baskets were brimmed with violets, daffodils, and fake grass. Each had a Hershey bar, and some big, bright jellybeans. He placed them into the large wagon, which he could pull behind his bike. The fact that he was going to be stopping at eleven homes that evening didn't phase him at all. He knew that some of the girls would not know if any of the others would visit with him, and that was fun. Even if some of the others girls would know, and might be whispering tomorrow, he hoped it would still be more important that they felt he was the most significant one who came to their home.

As he began out of their side door, he smiled and said goodbye to his mother. He looked back at her and said, "Mom, I don't think I will be running too fast tonight." Both of them laughed, and he walked up to his bike. He even built an extra temporary metal basket on the back bike wheel so it wouldn't spill.

Thankfully, the first home he stopped at was quiet because no one else was anywhere to be seen. As he placed his basket, and pushed the doorbell, he started to back up. Gloria Benton immediately opened the door, and started pushing for the screen door. He suddenly realized that he didn't want to run very far either. But, at that next special second, he said to himself, heck, the darkest part of their yard is certainly the best of all where I ought to be running. And that's just where he......and she......ran together.

All seven boys arrived within minutes of each other at Dorgan's Soda Fountain for some five-cent ice cream cones following school on a warm, sunny May afternoon. They soon would be going to someone's home, and listen to their favorite adventure radio shows. Where they were going hadn't been decided yet.

Amidst a lot of laughing and licking, two pretty girls appeared at the door. They peered through the window, and entered, demurely seating themselves on one of the empty booths along the wall. They were pretending to be unaware of the boy's presence.

Beaner and Jumbo were again having a race to see who could spin their counter stools the fastest. A combination of centrifugal force and body weight placed a great strain on Beaner's seat, and it began to loudly vibrate. Marge Dorgan, the most out-spoken of Bill Dorgan's five daughters, reacted immediately.

"Beaner, you damn fool, stop it now! If you and Eddy Jay want to spin on something, go to a carnival or the Princeton fair this year." She continued frowning, and then started rubbing a rag on the counter top.

"I would, Marge, but it doesn't open for three months," Beaner snickered, knowing his image would be enhanced among his peers by giving a wisecrack to an adult. Marge was somewhere in between for a lot of people. She could joke and kid with some people, and insult others. This day she was furious.

"Then get your fat butt outta here, and go volunteer to be a hood ornament on a semi-truck right out here in Main Street. We're stopping that racket, boys."

"Okay, we'll be good," as Beaner entered a fake submission.

Marge had a nasty streak four miles wide, and it lurked just beneath her surface most of the time. It was particularly exacerbated by the presence of all seven boys at once. She never showed much reaction when only one or two came in, but preferred to have Verna or her dad and mom if it was jammed. Anytime boys showed up together, it usually signaled that trouble wasn't very far away. However, everything had turned out just fine...right now.

The two girls were sucking a coke, and been forgotten in the commotion. As Beaner and Jumbo slipped off the stools, they noticed two big bags with numerous rounded bulges. It was lying on the table between the two girls.

"Whatcha got there, Marlene?" Jumbo asked.

"Wouldn't you like to know?" came her frosty reply.

"Looks like marbles to me, Jumbo," Beaner replied.

"Maybe you boys would like to play a game or two," queried Donna.

"Against who, Donna?" Beaner and Jumbo now stared at each other.

"Against us, that's who. If you're not afraid of getting beat by girls, that is," Marlene said, and she and Donna then looked at each other, and smiled.

"Shoot, I ain't afraid of playing any silly girls when it comes to anything, especially marbles," Jumbo scoffed.

"Me neither," added Beaner.

"Why don't you go get your bags boys, and meet us in the marble pit? Unless you don't know it's called the marble pit under the bandstand," Donna challenged the two boys. But now all of the other five had listened, and this last comment was greeted with several ooh's and ah's.

"And Beaner, be sure to bring your favorite cat's eye big shooter…I think I'd like to win it from you."

Beaner's face reddened, and a serious blush had also appeared on Jumbo's face. Now the additional needling from their contemporaries didn't help matters in the least. Both boys were suddenly ill at ease, and for the first time in this kind of situation, disaster was now a serious possibility.

They were trapped, pure and simple. After a couple of seconds, Jumbo announced, "Sure, we'll do it."

"Me, too," Beaner slowly replied, but his response was not too certain.

The two boys walked across the floor and disappeared through Dorgan's screen door. When they grabbed their bikes, the special push-button tank horn in Beaner's Schwinn had not giving much action today. In fact, not pushing the button was the first day since he'd ridden on his prized Christmas present five months ago.

Thirty seconds later both girls smiled and calmly slide out of the booth, grabbing their marble bags as they stood. Ignoring the other five boys, they marched to the same door with looks of total disdain accented by subtle smiles.

"I hope you gals kick their butts," Marge muttered as they passed by their side of the long counter. "You girls are already the champs at playing jacks. Maybe marbles are next." They glanced at her and she winked.

"We sure can't lose with marbles, Marge," Marlene flippantly said. "If they beat us they'll laugh for about five minutes and it'll be over and forgotten. But," and she paused and then said emphatically, "If we beat them, they'll think the world is going to sink in Lake Michigan." All three roared with laughter.

Minutes later, the confrontation was about to begin. The two girls were patiently waiting when the boys arrived.

Most of the kids knew the so-called marble pit was accessible only by removing one section of the wooden latticework panels, which skirted the bandstand's base. The ground beneath the old structure was never touched by moisture from rain or snow. This dirt had become perfect because it was soft, fine, and dry. The room was a large space with around five feet of headroom. Donna was the tallest, and she had to tilt her head to one side when standing. The other three could barely make it in with any head bumps. But, since marbles are a game played from a kneeling position most of the time, any height limitations made no difference.

As they slid under the building the boys blinked several times adjusting their eyes to the slightly darker surroundings. "Wow," Beaner quickly said. "This place has been raked or somethin'. I never saw the ground look this good. 'Course this is the first time I've been here since last year."

"Yeah, I wonder who did this," Jumbo agreed.

Neither of the girls said anything, nor did they even look up at the questions. They were intently counting their marbles.

"Why don't I play you, Jumbo, and Donna can take on Beaner. Then, if you guys have any marbles left when we're though with the first game, we'll switch." Marlene's tone exuded absolute confidence.

"It's the first time you ever called either of us nicknames," Beaner said as he frowned.

"Maybe we will call you with those dippy nicknames if we wish," Donna replied, and then said, "Now let's get on with the game. Throw your marble out in the center of the circle. First one to seven wins all that are left in the ring after each game. We're playing for keeps, and remember, not for just for fair. And no quitting early."

"And let's have all shooters at the end for the shoot out, if there still will need to have one," Marlene immediately stated.

"Finally, no kings X's either," Donna flatly ended the conversation.

Beaner and Jumbo looked at each other with growing apprehension. Beaner seemed to have gulped in his voice as he simply mumbled, "Well, o.k., we'll agree to all of the rules."

Jumbo was surveying the situation, and then he suddenly remembered a Tom Mix radio show last fall that they all had heard. He quietly said, "Beaner, I just hope we haven't crawled right into Horseshoe Canyon."

The circle was now already marked by Marlene's first right finger in the dirt. She said, "Jumbo, you've got a pitch and lag line. You lag first, and show me what I've got to beat."

He stepped up to the line and tossed his Shooter across the circle. It rolled to a stop some nine feet away, about ten inches from his target. He grinned with relief. Marlene took aim with great intensity, and lofted her Shooter toward the lag line. The large marble bounced twice before rolling to a stop, only inches shy, beating Jumbo's by more that half a foot. It was her turn to grin.

Silently they crisscrossed over thirteen marbles in the center of the ring. Each marble was approximately three inches apart. Six belonged to each, with Marlene volunteering to add one that served as a tie-breaker.

"All right," Donna said, "We're ready. We'll both begin at the pitch line, and then take rounders after that. X marks the spot." She knelt and quickly knuckled down. Her Shooter ker-snipped off her thumb, and smashed into the grouping of marbles, knocking two out of the ring on her first effort.

"Wow, two in one shot," Beaner said in a husky whisper. His attempt was a clean miss.

Marlene was now free to aim from where her Shooter had stopped. As Jumbo leaned forward to watch, her blonde pigtails dangled over her temples, but her concentration was undeterred. She fired a bulls-eye sending the small marble several feet out of the ring. One more ricocheted out before she missed her fourth shot. Her pretty blue dress with the small white polka dots could not hide the tomboyish look of pride and competition that covered her face.

"Your turn, Eddy Jay," Barbara cooed. A few moments of tense thoughts filled his mind, and he slowly assumed a kneeling position.

He then looked back up at her and said, "Gee willackers, four in one turn. We never hit that many before with any guy in Bradford." His audible comment was almost lost in a sigh of amazement.

"Also, we want you to two to know that you've always got to knuckle down on every shot. And there will be no histing or hunching or smoothing allowed," as Marlene rattled to both of them in a dictatorially expression.

"Holy Moley, I don't even know what 'histing' means." Jumbo uttered again, as he looked up in wide-eyed shock. "Where in the world did you two girls learn marble talk?"

"Heck, I'm more important to learn where in the world you two learned to *shoot* marbles, too," Beaner stumbled slightly as he spoke, and the two of them were now stunned into silence, equally lost in disbelief.

For a few seconds neither of the girls said anything, but as Jumbo finally was ready to take his turn, the answer came from Marlene.

"Donna's father taught us this spring, first on the floor in his farm's machine shed, and then right here where we are."

"My dad was the VFW state champion in Iowa when he was 14," Donna said, somewhat smugly.

Jumbo's shot suddenly veered erratically, and rolled across the right side of the ring, missing all of the remaining marbles by several feet.

"I call slips," he said weakly.

"Nope, slips only apply to shots of a foot or less, and only if it's really slipped. Sorry. Your shot went half-way to Spoon River," and both girls laughed, covering their mouths at Marlene's statement of ridicule.

When a boy hears about disasters on a radio show he is quickly interested, but realizes that it either happened to someone else or was just a story. On this day, however, two boys now knew it was real, because it was happening to them.

In a few more minutes, after the final contest ended, the girls looked over and Donna smiled. "Think it's time to go home, Marlene. Since all the marbles are now in our two extra bags, unless someone else is walking into the pit right now, there are two boys over there who don't even have a baseball, let alone even one more marble."

As the boys left dejectedly, they realized they could still hear more laughter than anyone had ever come from two such pretty girls.

"Let's go back to Dorgan's," Marlene said. "Bet Marge will be so happy she'll probably give us both a free chocolate soda."

CHAPTER 12

▼

THE BOYS GOT BEAT

"So you two guys got beat by a couple of little girls, huh…" Suck snickered, and several other boys muffled laughter after he had enjoyed the sarcasm.

It only took about half of a second, and Beaner was exploding. Humiliation was certainly not one of his normal personal experiences. "Carlton, if you know what's what you'll eat those smart-ass, crappy, wisecracks or I'll ram 'em right up *your* butt! They were girls, all right, but they weren't *ordinary* dipstick girls. We never had any idea that they got that good." Beaner was now even angrier that he was steaming, he would have immediately fought anyone including Joe Louis or Billy Conn.

"Now if any of you barf-heads want to say any more crap about this, let's climb down right the Climbin' Tree now, and let's go to fightin' 'cause I'm not scared of any of you. It's your choice, 'cause I'm ready. Boy, I'm really ready."

A reflective silence held for a few seconds before Jumbo added his challenge to the other five. "The same goes for me 'cept I may start fightin' any of you right up here in the tree."

Dink looked around at all of them, and realized, thank goodness, that he hadn't been in any guise of the situation they were now in. He kind of smiled, and said, "You'll never hear nothing from me for two reasons. One is that I'd probably lost all of my marbles faster than you two did, and I can't beat up any boy here in a fight. I'm sure not volunteering to get the crap kicked out of me."

His remark instantly defused the tension, and the other six guys broke into spontaneous laughter.

Immediately, their mood returned to the boisterous, rowdy attitude that seemed to be a normal countenance of their daily experiences. This was the Saturday morning that had followed yesterday's marble disaster. Now they had climbed up the huge, old elm because it served them well in a number of capacities. Today it was solace.

Catfish stared at several for a moment, and then spoke indirectly to all of them, "You guys know what happens two weeks from yesterday," and grinned.

Big smiles spread over several faces, and after a brief pause, the rest did too.

"We get paroled for the summer," Dink exclaimed. "Prison will be closed for three months." Everyone then started cheering, and Suck, who was at the tallest branch, threw his baseball glove, and let it bounce from one limb to another, landing in the grass below. Each of the other did the exact same thing, and all laughed even more.

"That's why I asked the question," blurted Catfish, "school's almost out, and by Jiminy Christmas, will I ever be glad."

"Yeah, we've waited a long time 'til summer comes, and now it's almost here," Hotshot said. "Let's do neat things this time none of us will ever forget. Not just baseball or fishing or camping or even just old, ordinary exploring. Remember when we were kids and Mrs. Peterson was our Story Lady?

All six gave a quick chorus of nods of confirmation.

"Last July, when Beaner had a birthday party, she told us that everyone of us should have a special time where we have a personal experience. She said it would be our very own quest."

"Oh, yeah, Hotshot," Booby agreed. "I remember. It was a man who wandered all over his country and got into a fight with a windmill."

"Yeah," Suck said, "we're supposed to believe about ourselves, and try to be stronger and better."

"Well, I know you guys laugh about how skinny I am, and I'm so weak. That's why someday I am going to mail a letter to join up and be in Charles Atlas's real strong club, not just the silly thing you started, Jumbo."

They smiled at Dink's comment, and Jumbo pressed his palms into a powerful attempt to create pressure like the comic book ad at the back of the cover. "You might even grow up to be a 98 pound old weakling if you eat enough," and all of them but two roared with laughter.

"Stop cackling about him," Hotshot said to the other five. Then he looked over and said, "It might work, if you try, Dink. What I'm talking about is that all of us should try discovering something neat." The infection in his voice changed to one of secretiveness.

They each narrowed their eyes automatically because Michael Randall was so impressive in his manner, and his consistent achievement with the highest grades. He was one of the other two main leaders. He was blessed with good looks, a strong physique, and natural athletic ability. He could almost always sway the group's thinking with the force and dominance of his personality. No wonder he had been called Hotshot an almost arrogant nickname.

"But what are you planning on doing?" Suck immediately asked. And Jumbo leaned forward, and nodded, too.

"I know some of you are scared about this, but I am now getting closer to finding how we can climb down into the coal mine. I have talked to Mr. Wilson who lives over near where the Bowyer farm is. He said he has seen the coal mine personally."

Hotshot's statement almost caused a concussion. "Holy Moley," Jumbo clamored, "I thought this crap was over. You haven't brought it up since back in the fall." Gasps also rolled over some of the others.

"What am I going to do if I have to tell what you want us to do and admit it to my dad?" Catfish quietly said.

"It can be a secret because it won't be scary or dangerous. I have now read about three kinds of mines: drift, slope, and vertical. I'm pretty sure that what they built around here back in the 1920s and 30s are slope mines." He leaned back up and looked at their faces.

"How in the world did you learn this much stuff," Suck softly asked. "My dad is an engineer. He is so smart I get worried I might not ever get as smart as he is. But he makes me study a heck of a lot, especially arithmetic. When I asked him a few months ago about coal mines, he said the one in Harper's Woods was probably either blown up in the main shafts, or just filled up, and covered over. But, it's closed. Period."

It was very eerie. In fact, it was almost too quiet. Somehow Dink could talk much faster than he thought, and crazy things like this happened many times each day. "Wow. Your dad is an engineer, Suck. Guess what? My Uncle Glen is an engineer with the Chicago and Northwestern train. Every couple of days he runs a long freight train just a mile east from Bradford."

The others stared at Dink, but not one of them laughed, because Suck was the only one who knew the difference and, though he rolled his eyes slightly, he decided to not do it either. "My dad is a mechanical engineer and designer. He used to work at the Hall of Science at the World's Fair back in 1933 before any of us were born. The Fair was in Chicago right after he graduated from the University of Illinois."

Again the boys were stunned. Nobody had ever had such a conversation like this before because the two smartest guys here were head and shoulders over the rest of them.

"I don't know about stuff like this. All I know is how to shoot a duck, catch a bass, and sink a basketball shot. But I know this: if climbing down in some kind of coal mine is dangerous, I'll kiss a frog. And guess what? I ain't never going to kiss a frog, just to try and find a princess." He spat a blast of Tootsie Roll juice that hit a big leaf and almost knocked off the limb it was on.

Everyone, even Suck and Hotshot, laughed. Jumbo had a totally different level of danger than anyone else. Normal or scary occurrences that had great potential for injury or calamity, he dismissed with utter disdain. But when Jumbo said something might be considered as a terrible hazard, or even a potentially terrible situation that he might see, he would stop right now. After all, hadn't he been the only one brave enough to urinate on an electric fence? His gamble was sheer luck because the electricity was not turned on the day he tried it for the others. If it had been on, he would have discovered that the power flowed on and off for a few seconds, and he might have been thrown about ten feet.

Or how about when all of the guys saw him wrap his fist with a handkerchief, and smash a pane of glass. He enabled all of them to enter through the window of the empty old farm home everyone called the "Haunted House." And, who could forget the day at one of the swimming holes in the river when he stood on the back of a large snapping turtle, completely naked, and teasing it's darting jaws below him with probing a long stick. If Jumbo said something was too dangerous, that was all the other five needed to hear.

"I guess I kinda agree," Beaner said slowly as to not offend Hotshot. "You can count me out of that idea. I get into enough jams without doing something like climbing around in a coal mine that's been closed for 20 years."

"Me too, besides report cards will be coming out for the end of the last semester, and my folks will probably tell me I'm grounded. And that's as sure as God made little green apples," Catfish said.

One by one each boy continued expressing reservations on being involved in the search for the possible secret shaft. Finally, Hotshot smiled, and said, "Hey, guys, I'm just having some fun. When I do get the rest of the facts, I'll tell you later in a month or so. Then, if you think I'm too crazy or this it is too scary, don't go. But, I am if I can, and I may be the one who finds the counterfeiter's hidden printing plates."

Again it got very quiet. Jealousy, if Hotshot found this concealed or secret part of the town's history, was instantly raring through several of their minds. Simple excitement also lit a flame that was equally intriguing.

Hotshot realized that he was not going to miss the possible day when at least some, if not all of them, would also want to climb down into that covert web of mystery. "I'm tired of sitting on this limb," Hotshot suddenly offered. "Let's go down, grab our bikes, and go for a cruise."

Just as soon as they finished that, everyone began riding home. Hotshot walked into his home, and suddenly remembered an even more imposing order that his mother had given him several days ago. Hotshot found out he was going to a dinner engagement with her to hear a man who sang so resounding and so powerfully that he immediately begged his father to go in his place.

Mr. Randall thought for a moment or two, and simply said, "I've got a headache this year, and I may have to get one next year, too. Actually, that's a woman's idea, but it'll work for me. Sorry about that, son."

CHAPTER 13

▼

A STOUT HEARTED BOY

"Mom, this is not fair. Why do I have to go there?" Hotshot felt so angry he was almost ready to run away. However, he reasoned, that is not a very logical plan right now, since he was going to be the best guard in his grade schools heavyweight basketball team next season. And at least this meeting will have some good food, he thought.

"Our Bradford's Eastern Star's annual dinner is tomorrow night, and several of my friends are bringing our sons and daughters for a special evening," Mrs. Randall said. "And that is final. You will be there, and you will wear that long sleeved yellow shirt with the tie we got for you."

"Ohhhhhh, rats," he muttered. "I think wearing a tie is as close to being hanged like Jesse James."

"You *will* wear that tie, and don't consider that you might look like Jesse James because he wasn't hanged, I think he was shot with a gun. Which way do you want it to happen, son?" She smiled a little, but her forehead was now frowning a little, and her voice was still stern.

Hotshot laughed. "I think I'll wear the tie, mom, but for only an hour or so, okay? What I don't understand is why this dinner is going to happen?"

"A number of women who live here are members of a club...actually, it is called a lodge. Any lady can be a member because it is open to all kinds of religious faiths. We mainly do a lot of work to help raise money or do good deeds for other folks, mainly kids. The foremost reason tomorrow night is that we each had to buy two seats for the dinner, and a lot of us thought it would be a good experience for you grade school kids." Mrs. Randall smiled, and then said, "Got it?" She immediately walked out of his bedroom.

The Order of the Eastern Star Lodge met in the second floor of the big corner building where Main Street extends east and the route turns south. The small star sign that had their name hung on one of the top windows, and it was lit every night for a few hours. Below, Jerry's Dry Cleaner's, was on the first floor. Several weeks ago, the ladies decided to have their annual fundraiser, not at the lodge, but in the lower floor of the Library across the street in the park. However, enough members had sold so many tickets, they decided to have the program at a bigger place. After a few days, they decided that the basement's main room at Leet Methodist Church would be perfect, because it was bigger, and the lodge was open to any woman with their own religious persuasion. Eastern Star, as their small brochure said, was 'neither a religion nor a substitute for one.'

When the big night arrived, it was more than any of them had hoped. Their food was outstanding, and the room was full. Fern Williams, the toastmistress, after dinner thanked everyone for their long and diligent work. Then she introduced Dr. Robert Johnson, a professor at Bradley, who was also a highly successful performer for the Peoria Opera. The accompanist sitting at the piano was his very beautiful wife, Sarah. Several lodge members had met or knew about the Johnson's, and were thrilled that each pleasingly agreed that they could give the program gratuitously. However, the ladies made sure that both of the musicians got a delicious dinner, and gave them a large attractive plant they bought at Thomas' Florist Shop at the other side of the rail road bridge.

As all of the women smiled, nodded, and clapped as the speaker stood up. The main evening was now going to begin.

"Ladies and gentlemen, girls and boys, tonight is a special evening for my wife and I, and we hope this will also be a marvelous program for all of you, too. As Mrs. Williams said, I now teach at Bradley University in the music program, but as a young student in Rollins College in Winter Park, Florida, I had a professor named Thaddeus Seymour who pushed me to the very limit when I began studying music. He loved a number of old standards and famous songs. I hope you may enjoy what my wife and I will offer for everyone. Thank you."

The first three songs were military musical numbers, and then Dr. Johnson introduced a new one that had just been out in theatres around the country. The song was already a hit called, "She Wore A Yellow Ribbon", from a movie starring John Wayne. Many of the boys had seen it here, too, and the movie was simply fun for everyone. Unfortunately, now as the song was becoming a hit for the ladies, within seconds Hotshot was slowly dozing off. In seconds latter, his head lapsed so low he was now almost comatose. Somehow into his mind, however, he was galloping across a road where a beautiful girl was trapped in her horse-drawn carriage. As her panicked horses were running away, he jumped up on the pair, climbed over on one of them, and pulled them down.

"Well, howdy, pilgrim. What's a sweet young thing like you doin sashaying alone out here in the Wild West." Hotshot was wearing a uniform as if he was a cavalry captain.

Amazingly, in his dream the lovely girl was Jeannie Houghton, a girl he was crazy about in his seventh grade class. "Thank you, Captain. My horse won't behave. But I heard this is your last day in the army. Captain...maybe you will come to my house, and stay with me for the rest of your life."

"Ma'am, thanks, but I may be re-up in', again."

"Wait, Hotshot," she softly said, "There's something else you should know...my mom and dad are gone now, and when I walk around my home, all I ever wear is a yellow ribbon."

Hotshot woke up instantly, and it snapped his head. His mother simultaneously leaned over and said, "Stop falling asleep, son," as she whispered firmly into his left ear. At the same time, the entire audience was applauding as the current song ended. However, he was much more astonished at what had just happened. He glanced over where Jeannie and her mother were sitting, and was amazed because she turned her gaze directly at him...and smiled.

The fifth selection Dr. Johnson's wife began playing the most beautiful musical selections that Dr. Seymour, the Rollins College professor, had loved all his life: "Beautiful Dreamer." Unfortunately for Hotshot, the second half of the great song's title was creating a big problem: he was an uncontrollable dreamer, night after night. But now, he was trying desperately to not nod any more, so he kept his neck so stiff it hurt. Alas, in seconds, he was again totally asleep.

Over the past year his parents took him and his sister to see several outstanding movies. Some were so good in the late 1930s or early '40s many of them were being shown again a second time. It was obviously that these great movies seem to control his mind during his sleep many nights in his life.

Within seconds, Hotshot was gliding into another strange combination of a dream and a memory movie. A huge, southern plantation was there, and the front door suddenly opened as Hotshot walked out on the front step.

He was wearing a formal suit, a dressy man's hat, and had a cigar clinched in his teeth. Ginny almost stumbled as she followed him out of the home. She was wearing a crimson dress, and she was leaning against the door, almost crying.

As he turned to stare at Ginny, she looked directly into his face and said, "Hotshot, where will I go? What will I do?

He reached up and held the cigar in his right hand. He looked at it, and then said, "Frankly, my dear, I…" but she interrupted instantly, and she ran over and threw her arms around him.

"Wait. Before you leave, think about this. All of a sudden you might want to really give a kiss, not a damn, Hotshot," and Ginny pulled his head down, so their lips fell together in a deep kiss. Just as he dreamed he threw away the cigar, his mother punched him again and his head flipped up.

"Stop this dozing, son," Mrs. Randall said. "People think you've gone into a coma."

"I'm sorry, mom, but this music is so dull," he whispered back to her.

Almost as if the entire audience wanted a little more action, the next song was much more dynamic. "Road to Mandalay" made folks nod and smile, and Dr. Johnson's version of Kate Smith's hit, "God Bless America," was equally delightful.

Somehow Hotshot had not fallen asleep for the next four or five tunes, and he was thoroughly enjoying his furtively glances many times back to Ginny. She equally stared back at him more than he might even realize. It had been nearly an hour, and the audience realized it would be about the end of Mr. Johnson's program.

A rousing song named "Stout Hearted Men" didn't keep Hotshot any more wide-awake than several other kids who had also come to this concert. In the final act, Dr. Johnson asked if they would like to have one closing song. Several of the women immediately said they would love to hear 'Beautiful Dreamer' again as the climactic conclusion. He happily agreed and began singing it for the last time tonight.

Within seconds, Hotshot was gently falling asleep again. Suddenly, another next dream was now consumed in a black and white, January 1942 hit movie called 'Casablanca.' Dr. Johnson had already performed several songs previously that could be the most perfect movie song women loved more than almost any other: 'Time Goes Bye'.

It had been the theme for Bogie and Ingrid Bergman. The movie was also so popular it had been shown again just seven years ago in many theatres throughout America. Michael's mother told him that this was the best movie she had ever seen. If fact he remembered that she could speak many sentences she had memorized seeing the movie about two dozen times. Even he tried to imitate how Bogie would have spoken its dialect. Mrs. Randall's memories of World War II were still very important for millions of GIs and their sweethearts.

Somehow, after earlier hearing that song, Hotshot was now staring at Ginny who was wearing a wide brimmed hat in his dream. She had a linen suit; he wore a full raincoat and a man's fedora. Suddenly, a twin-engine plane was rolling up to them, and two other men were watching them.

Hotshot grabbed her, and said, "Ginny, I'm no good at being noble, but it doesn't take much to see...", and she interrupted him.

"Hotshot, can all that unselfish crapola. You and I are going on the plane to Lisbon tonight because I've got two good reasons," and she grabbed both of his hands, and placed them open palmed on her breasts.

For the third time waking up in a shock flipped his head, and this time almost cracked his spine. Fortunately, his mother had not noticed it, as the final verse, 'Beautiful dreamer, awake unto me' ended the song. He glanced again at Ginny as he was rubbing his neck, and for the third time she was staring at him with a friendly smile.

When most of the people were leaving. Mrs. Houghton was laughing and chatting with two other mothers whose kids had already walked down the stairs and were standing on the main steps at the church. These four women couldn't be any happier, for not only a large attendance, but the couple from Bradley had literally thrilled the entire crowd.

Dink and Suck had been sitting with their mothers, and now were shuffling down the steps. Dink said, looking up at Hotshot, "Boy, tonight was the longest three weeks of my life."

Suck grimaced. "I hated it, too. What'd you think, Hotshot?"

Hotshot blended a jaunty, confident demeanor, and a pleasant secret. "Actually, I had a lot of fun tonight." He winked at both of them, and walked over toward Ginny.

The two boys were somewhat bewildered, and they shrugged, then walked away. But, as Hotshot reached a few feet away, he held back several feet. "That was a fun evening for me. How about you?" she asked.

"You're a pretty girl, Ginny," he said, and then added, "I've been wanting to do this for a long time." As soon as he stopped talking, he quickly walked right beside her, grabbed just below her shoulders, and kissed her, matter of fact.

When he stepped back, Ginny was stunned. She was actually so startled she moved back for a half-step, and touched her lips with a couple of her left fingers. Both of their mothers saw it too, and were equally staring at both of them. Then they quickly looked at each other and wryly grinned, but did not speak.

He nodded at Ginny, and simply said, "I'll be seeing you...again."
It had been just one more song he had heard tonight.

CHAPTER 14

▼

FREE AT LAST

"Girls and boys, for me you have been a dear, dear joy to teach this class year for the past nine months. I hope each of us shall be equally grateful for enjoying these many challenges and experiences, and…" but then she paused. Everyone in the class eagerly seemed that their teacher was about to offer an additional comment since twenty-three kids were sitting there waiting. However, if several of these boys realized they were hearing what their teacher was thinking, it would have been a much different encounter.

A few more moments went by, as she stared at one and then another, contemplating their faces. Obviously, her main problem was that five boys in this class had given her the most memorable and exasperating school terms she had ever endured in her thirty-six years of service to the Illinois public school system.

She mused, 'Could a frustrated, saddened, single, and shattered teacher who still loves and believes in Jesus everyday of my life, actually strangle several of these wild, pubescent boys?' Her smile was suddenly devious. 'What if I did this hideous act on a lonely, hideous, dark and windy night? Oh, no,' she reasoned, and quickly rejected her appalling contemplation. 'I now have only four more years to teach, and if I do something so dreadful as this, I'm sure I would be immediately convicted by a cruel and vindictive jury. Then, as quickly as this, a judge would throw me far, far down into a black, hideous pit. Hell itself would be better than that. Hmmm. That is not a very good decision, Edna,' she thought, then smiled, and spoke.

"Since we have all finished our work this final semester, we have about twenty-nine and a half minutes until that magic sound will ring, and you will be running out of this door into your own part of heaven on earth on this beautiful summer day. I would love to hear and ask some questions about what any of you hope could happen for the next three months. Just remember, next September, Miss Mayme Fate will be teaching 8th grade for you, and think about her real name, Fate. This word also means destiny, chance, or even nemesis. Therefore, what would you hope will happen this summer? Please, any of you, start telling me right now." Twenty-three chins dropped.

Miss Edna Wallace, in Bradford Grade School, and Sister Regina, the nun who taught St. John's School for 7th and 8th year kids, were almost unknown to each other. Of course, in such a small village, they saw each other once or twice a month but had never visited for any other reason. Miss Wallace was 58 years old, and Sister Regina, a Benedictine Sister, was 34. No one in either of their classes had any idea where the two teachers came from, or how they arrived here. But such information wasn't really of any importance to each of the students. They had to learn, understand, study, and even memorize a lot of things, but a number of them hardly ever thought. For 7th grade kids, however, thinking and doing can be two vastly different experiences.

Miss Wallace annually selected this day as the one in which she would remove smoldering resentments that that had been building gradually throughout the previous nine months. She had done this for many years, but since each class was new every fall, none of the listeners realized they would be targets of her cyclical litany. According to her fellow teachers, and virtually every one of their parents over those many years, Miss Wallace was well-groomed, well-mannered, and well-respected. Unfortunately, if you were a boy whose disposition tended towards disciplinary problems, she was never well-liked. Each school term seemed to bring with it a fresh supply of protagonists for her acerbic wit and rapier tongue.

Normally she enjoyed the challenge, because she had an excellent grasp of the many psychological and physiological changes occurring in her still immature young men and women. But this year had been different. Three boys managed to create more confusion and chaos than any previous group of boys that she had yet encountered. Through the sheer power of their personalities they seemed to choreograph and direct unparalleled moments of disaster within the class. Donald Randall and Phillip Carlton were simultaneously the best and the bright-est boys as far as their education, but they could also secretly dream up the worst and most vexatious situations that their three other pals did. Actually Eddy Jay

Roberts was almost as good as these two leaders in every aspect, and he enjoyed turmoil much more than creativity.

The errant sides of their nature conceived numerous daily trials for Miss Wallace, but acquiring gullible recruits to enact the schemes was left to their brilliant sides. They subtly made proposals and suggestions to the other boys, which resulted in one traumatic event after another. Such as the day when, at their prodding, Jonathan Edwards rang the fire alarm, spewing eight, unsuspecting classrooms of children out onto the surrounding playground. The principal, Russell Huey, quickly spanked him, and sent him immediately home. Another spanking handled that two hours later when his father came home. Thankfully, this was the last stupid decision Dink made, at least the rest of this year.

Miss Wallace was always angry because of the almost daily battles with pea shooters, water guns, spit balls, chunks of art gum erasers, and worst of all, the paperclip slingshot. A simple rubber band stretched taut between one's forefinger and thumb, when engaged with a paper clip bent straight with only one "hook" remaining could almost be as deadly as a very dangerous dart. Two of the boys had been suspended for three days several months ago for that. Some of their plans didn't even involve Miss Wallace. They loved to cause problems for girls.

Freshly chewed bubble gum was occasionally slipped in the center of an unexpected girl's desk seat. Or slipping mice or garter snakes in dress pockets. Or putting a dead cockroach in the old-fashioned inkwells beneath the desktops. Or sticking some unforeseen thing from the classes glue pots. Girls thought boys were easily the stupidest humans of this or any other planet. If one of the girls in this class hinted at it to Miss Wallace, she would have laughed robustly, and immediately nodded and hugged her.

Her main problem was that after she discovered who the three ringleaders were, she could never catch them in the act. Sadly for her, it was always one or two of the other dupes. Being a dupe was Jonathan's strong suit. Miss Wallace certainly suspected he might someday be tapped by 'I Felta Thigh' instead of Phi Beta Kappa, if he ever did finished college. But she also certainly realized that he and any of these current boys were not stupid. That first realization more than twenty years ago changed her understanding that some kids are just plain naïve in their early years. Stupidity however, might be almost a terminal disease for others.

Once before, speaking in a county faculty meeting, Miss Wallace said that her observation of more than thirty years, here is an undeniable fact. A new father, who has an IQ of 80, and a new mother, who might have married him, and also has an IQ of 80, will not have a baby who turns out 160. The other room of educators not only laughed, they applauded. Later Mr. Perrin, the superintendent, congratulated her, and agreed, while it was certainly a million in one shot, neither of them had ever seen it yet.

Unquestionably, it wasn't that any of these boys didn't have even an ounce of brains that kept themselves in trouble. No, it was their own highly active and mischievous nature. Eddy was just as sharp as the other two, and Jonathan and Billy were equally alert, it's just that they were easily beckoned into virtually any scheme concocted by the other three. Each day it seemed as if one of the three leaders was a new, young P. T. Barnum.

"It's been a little quiet since I suggested that we could hear about your future plans. I think even some of you girls are unusually silent. Maybe I think I will pick and choose with some of you to help me better understand what you hope you will someday do. While I certainly understand and concur with the old adage 'boys will be boys'…" she paused again, and then silently added, 'in your case some of you will be incarcerated after an even worse wrong decision.' "Truant behavior inevitably leads to problems with the law, something several of you should ponder with great concern. Another of my own truism could be stated thusly, classmates today, cellmates tomorrow. In a phrase from one of my nephew's who served honorably in the Navy until 1945 might say…to a few of you. 'You guys better shape up or ship out."

Miss Wallace's change to a guttural growl on her last sentence brought bursts of humor to a few of the boys, some personal relief. Even she laughed, but then began speaking again.

"Seriously, I am sure you know who you are because we have had some amazing experiences together this year. That isn't important now." Once more she paused, and glanced across the room. Her musings slid into a touch of anger, and thought, 'How distressed I feel for Mayme Fate as she will be the next to inherit this gang of miscreants. Oh, well….' "I can only say how thrilled I pray for almost a miracle to happen that might open your heads and minds to a deeper awareness of the feeling of others."

Again it was quiet. Every window was open, and a warm breeze fluttered the leaves along the well entrenched ivy vine which grew across many mortar recessed through the old, red bricks that covered the school's exterior. Once more lost into her thoughts, she contemplated decidedly unchristian thoughts that might encourage several of the boys to play in heavy traffic.

"I suppose it would be overly optimistic of me to hope, but to my very last thought I will hope and pray for each of you. Girls, how let's hear from Ginny, Jeannie, and Susan, and then the rest of you. Then some boys will have time to tell us their plans. Unfortunately, some of you will have to speak," and her smile was very ominous.

As each girl stood beside her seat with plans that were almost so well arranged and sparkly clean the boys were embarrassed. They were going to be running around in almost anything they would do that somehow always ended in mud. Even if it hadn't rained in two weeks, boys could somehow find mud.

After ten minutes, Miss Wallace turned her attention directly to Michael Randall. "What are you going to do, Hotshot?"

Surprised giggles and partially suppressed snickers immediate erupted in the entire class. Hotshot sat in stunned silence. In the entire nine months of seventh grade classes, Miss Wallace had never mentioned his nickname or any of the others, either. His look of bafflement prompted her to continue. "That is your nickname, isn't it?"

"Yes, ma'am," he responded, while squirming self-consciously.

"What will Hotshot be doing this summer?

Again the sound of this bastion of education protocol quizzing one of her students through use of his alter ego, evoked laughter and good nature jibes at the embarrassed recipient. She stared relentlessly at him.

"Uh, I guess, uh, we'll play a lot of ball, and uh, do a whole bunch of fishing, too at the river." A couple of drops of perspiration were mounting on his forehead. One of them skidded down his left cheek, and ran into his tee shirt as it touched his collar. He now unconsciously wrung his hands slowly, and then started nibbling on one of his fingernails. In spite of the fact that he had next to Ginny the highest tests in this class, Miss Wallace had quickly learned that he had only two flaws in the otherwise endless list of positive characteristics at which he excelled. Speaking in public for Mike, even simple class recitations, was an agony in the category of cruel and unusual punishment. The other was biting his fingernails so close he sometimes caused it to bleed.

"Go on," she commanded, knowing full well what she was doing.

"Uh, well, uh, we liked to go to the Spoon and at Broadmore for catfish and bullheads."

"How about skinny dipping there?" At her question he went as red as a Washington Apple or the town's fire engine. None of the boys said anything, but the girls were giggling and laughing.

"Probably not this year," he said nervously. "Snapping turtles are kind of scary at either the river or the pond." At that she smiled, and then everyone laughed.

"With boys it would be lot more scarier for them, 'cause girls never do it to anybody," Ginny said, and the girls laughed even louder.

"Sit down Michael, thank you. I have heard that you are a very good baseball and basketball player. You've got a good arm, young man," Miss Wallace smiled and then looked to Philip.

"What does your nickname stand for, Philip?"

"Ma'am, I don't want to offend you."

"It's far too late for that, Philip. Some of the other teachers seem to have over-heard your friends call you something that starts with…suck?" Some giggling was back in action, and the entire class stared at him, not her.

"Yes, ma'am. But, I don't like it, and I don't want to offend you, ma'am." Now it was Suck who was sweating.

"Well, pray tell, if this is too embarrassing let's change the subject," and Miss Wallace. "What will you be doing this summer?"

He was so relieved he would have said anything to make her happy. Of course, that is exactly how he had been nicknamed because his 'brownie' experiences were now in a category with most teachers that some students were so famous they had turned it into personal legends. "I will be going to Camp Lincoln in Northern Minnesota for two weeks in late July. I have hidden a secret to every-one here, even you Miss Wallace. I have been studying piano lessons for more than a year with Mrs. Peterson in her home. Two weeks from Saturday morning I will give a recital for her, and my mom and dad, and some other kids who are also studying. And their folks will be there, too."

"My, my, that is incredible, Philip. I certainly did not know about this until right now. I want to come to the recital, and see you."

As Miss Wallace finished this the other four boys were not only stunned, they were almost ready to vomit. All of the girls were equally quiet, but they were once more amazed at what Philip could churn in their minds.

"No wonder how he got the nickname, Miss Wallace. He does this kind of brown-nose stuff. The girls love it, and the boys hate it." Jumbo was so fed up he couldn't control himself. Immediately, the other guys nodded. No one felt they were getting into any trouble today, it was truly the last day of school.

"Well, isn't it Mr. Jumbo, I presume?" Miss Wallace frowned slightly.

Now Eddy Jay was in the center of action. He looked down and realized he if he had kept his mouth shut he might have not even had to say anything. "Yes ma'am." Suck quietly sat down, and didn't even glance at any of the other guys.

"Please stand up, Eddy Jay. I've always wanted to know not only where Jumbo came from, but also I believe there are a few other gems in your repertoire. Sev-eral of us have heard about, Brown Gut…and something about a Bonomo strong man, even a vice-president. Bradford is a famous place with more crazy nicknames than I've ever heard or even read in Charles Dickens or Edgar Masters' books, but how did you get more strange versions than even here?"

The entire class was now laughing. "It's not me, ma'am, it happens from my buddies," Jumbo mumbled.

At that everyone was happily ridiculing and yelling back at him. Dink stood up without realizing what he was even doing. "Yeah, Miss Wallace, even if Bradford has some funny folks, Jumbo is the craziest guy in the whole town. Maybe the whole state." Many of the kids started clapping.

"My goodness," Miss Wallace replied, "for a class who was so quiet ten minutes ago that I asked for an answer and then had to verbally reply, things have gotten pretty exciting around here. Jumbo you may take your seat, since another boy who I think I know is called Dink can tell us what he is going to do."

As everyone knew countless times, Dink never was tongue-tied. He simply had never spent any time to really think about what or why he was going to speak. These two aspects always got anyone into trouble. But now, suddenly shocked that *he* was on the spot, Dink was also standing alone since Miss Wallace quietly had sat down behind her desk.

"How did you get a nickname called Dink, Jonathan?"

"Well, he, my dad, that is says that I'm a natural born goof off." Again laughter filled the room.

"That's for sure," Hotshot said, and more chortling had kids shaking their heads.

"Go on," Miss Wallace said quickly.

"Dad says I never get anything worthwhile done. I have to do all my chores, but somehow I just stumble around and forget to do what they tell me I have to do. My dad said one day that I was just a 'dinky' person around here and a 'dinky' person around there, and never got anything done. Once my dad started calling me 'Dink', and that's how it happened. Even my mom calls me that every now and then."

"You certainly know you have been sort of a class clown, Jonathan. Somehow, one in almost every class takes on that job. I hope you can offer the position to someone else next September."

As she finished this, a smile also gently creased Miss Wallace' normal stoic features. This time it held no hint of sarcasm. Dink's explanation unexpectedly opened a long dormant drawer full of student memories. She contemplated it as she suddenly remembered these years of kids offering tardy attendance records, preposterous explanations, and other answers that were simply stupid or outright lies. She knew virtually everyone in town, and Dink's father must have been a challenge for this skinny boy who couldn't get himself together.

Like thousands of other small towns in America, Bradford had many successful, influential fathers and mothers who formed lengthy shadows over their growing children. Edna Wallace, an only child, remembered very well how her father expected that she would equally also offer high standards and successful expectations for herself. His strength of character and powerful adherence to the ethic that a reward of hard work and honest dealings, now formed a giant, monolithic beacon of judgement for most of her actions.

After all these years, she realized her goal of pleasing him had never ended, even though he died twenty-one years earlier. He was now gone, but his spirit still influenced her everyday deep into her mind. She silently chided herself for not earlier conversing together years ago about the influence he had for her. Unfortunately, she didn't recognize this mutual happenstance, and it could have created a better and bigger human bridge together, not a closed wall. Developing a deeper understanding between them would have been the ultimate connection, but frustration caused too many problems. And now, at this moment, she was also sorry for her earlier nasty thoughts about several young boys who could simply be the next generation of what happened to her and her father.

"How about the last of this quintet, who was named Billy Curtis all these days for nine months. May I ask if I am speaking now to Catfish?"

Catfish slowly stood up, but before he could even acknowledge her question, an amazing sound happened that almost rocked their lives. The school bell started ringing, and cheering erupted. Some of the kids were all ready out of the door before it had actually stopped.

Believe it or not, the happiest person in this room was a 57-year-old woman who was also free at last.

CHAPTER 15

▼

PRAYING FOR NOTRE DAME

The same day five happy boys burst out of the front door at Bradford Grade School, they were screaming and running like wild cats or dogs. Father Cleary, and the five nuns, who taught kids in St. John's School, would agree. When school ends every spring, kids are equal opportunity people; they are simply crazy. As for religion at any church in Bradford, or the rest of our country, it certainly was the same basic grade school experience. Anywhere, you could watch kids jam themselves through every front door, as they ran out of the last school term.

Today Sister Regina Theresa smiled as she looked over the beaming faces before her. The room was supercharged with excitement, as the 1948-49 school year was coming to its logical conclusion. At 3:00 the final bell was only minutes away.

For fifteen eight graders, a formal graduation ceremony was scheduled that evening in their parish hall next door. Twenty-four others at Bradford Grade School would be sitting in the high school basketball gym, and they would also be wearing pretty dresses or their first suit and tie.

However, fourteen seventh graders who shared the room would be scattered to the wind seconds after the bell rang. Their eighth grader friends had already gone to get ready for tonight's big show. Sister Regina was wearing the full habit of her

Benedictine Order, and her crisp, white coif and flowing black veil obscured everything except her face. Her charming smile radiated such a Christ-like warmth, and her genuinely compassionate nature sprang from convictions of sincerity and empathy so deep within her soul. In spite of the fact that everyone knew she was a lovely and beautiful woman, Sister Regina's glorious face was merely accepted as a reflection of God's great glory.

She did nothing to enhance it, but the blush and color of nature's life had found a perfect home in her face. Her unaffected and friendly countenance had almost immediately quelled initial doubts among her four older fellow sisters, ranging from concern about her calling to the darker, more human emotions about how beautiful she was. But her first year she quickly won them over by merely being the loving, obedient servant she had promised to be only eight years earlier. Now everyone, who was touched by Sister Regina's life, expressed feelings of admiration, gratitude, and joy for her presence.

Today, while it was an eagerly anticipated event in the life of every girl and boy in the room, this was also filled with a potpourri of ambivalent emotions in Sister Regina's heart. She would soon be leaving Bradford because a doctor had recently given her a shock. After doing some tests, two other doctors in Peoria at St. Francis Hospital had to tell her mother superior that Sister Regina has cancer.

Several days ago she was told that she would be returning to the convent in Nauvoo, where she had taken her vows. Her transfer would take place several days after school let out, and she purposely did not inform the children until this moment. She looked up at the poster board facing her on the back wall. Her carefully arranged series of colored prints depicting the seven sacraments gave her strength. She cleared her throat and began to speak.

"I have a difficult announcement I must make today. I know you are all excited about your plans for the coming summer months. The eighth graders have left and will graduate tonight. They will begin four years of study a few blocks away in Bradford High School. Next September, you will now find yourselves moving over two rows since you will be the big, smart eighth graders then." She emphasized big and smart with a good-natured twinkle in her eyes. But the fourteen kids were only chuckling nervously because a strange feeling of apprehension now clouded their previous mood of happy anticipation.

"Sadly for me, I must admit, today will be my last day as a teacher here at St. John's." The room was so quiet it could have been an empty room. Then several girls were already crying, and even drops of tears were filling the eyes on a few of the boys. "The Mother Superior at the convent where I was trained has new challenges and plans for me very soon. I accept it as God's will for me." Now a chorus of oh, no, and don't go instantly echoed through the room.

Sister Regina lifted her arms, palms out, to end their heartfelt protest. "Thank you for your love and concern. I want you to know, I, too, have a special closeness with each of you. I'm going to keep an eye open on what you're doing with your lives from now on. And, if any of you miss confession or forget what you've learned in catechism classes, you need to know that I have asked Father Cleary to call me, and I'll come back and pull you to mass by one of your ears!"

Scattered laughs followed her forced attempt at levity, but every girl was dabbing tissues, and some of the roughest and toughest boys were blinking rapidly as they assimilated the news.

"Now, now, we can't have tears on such a lovely spring day as this. Since the final bell will ring in about twenty minutes, and we've finished our work, let's let the seventh graders tell us what your plans are for the summer." Some folks laughed that this almost could have been a law for all grade school universal teachers to share interesting plans for everyone's final hour of class this year. Certainly Sister Regina and Edna Wallace did it whether there was any national act or not.

"Is anyone going on a trip somewhere exciting especially far enough to leave Illinois." Her question was needed because the quietness for a few seconds created an awkward pause. Several girls began raising their hands, and telling that one was going to Chicago for a week, another to Lake of the Ozarks in Missouri, and finally a boy said his family was going to visit relatives in Denver and go see Yellowstone Park.

Others hesitatingly offered summaries of their plans. The pall, which had covered the classroom like a thick, oppressive, invisible blanket was lifting. However, Beaner and Booby were about to be involved with their own interesting minor inquisition.

"What about you Richard, what do you think you'll be doing?"

Beaner stood quickly, and looked directly into Sister Regina's eyes. "Well, Sister, we're going to visit my cousins in Evanston sometime. Mainly I guess I will be fishing in the Mighty Spoon with my buddies." He then gave her a big, toothy grin that spread all across his face full of freckles. His blue eyes sparkled because a bit of the moisture that had accumulated was still there after Sister Regina's announcement.

"Would your close friend, Mr. O'Riley, be involved in this plan, too, by chance?"

"Yes, sister, he will want to do it, too," Beaner smiled, and so did she.

Then she turned to Booby, and twinkled. "This is probably against some unknown rule here, but I have to ask a question. Patrick, I suspect I already know how you got your nickname." Many of them snickered, and looked at each other, hiding their laughs. "I'll pass over yours, but why does Richard have such an interesting moniker, if I may be so inquisitive?"

Once more she was actually being a bit coy, something most of the other nuns rarely did because they were more serious. It may have been her enduring youth, since the others were twenty or so years older.

"Uh…uh, we call him Beaner, sister." At this titter rippled through the room.

"Stand up again, Richard. You can help us understand."

Beaner was again standing up, but this time he was very embarrassed. "My nickname is strictly for only boys. I don't have a sister or any girl cousins who ever calls me it. I even have smacked a couple of guys who….." Oops, he thought. He realized his usual uncontrollable anger had gotten him caught again.

Now they were all giggling, and Booby said, "He probably deserved it, no matter who he slugged." Outright, uncontrolled laughter erupted even louder.

"Class, class, let's hold it down. Control your noise. Father will be coming in here to see what in the world is happening." Returning her gaze to the two boys, she added, "I won't pursue your nicknames any further. Who else goes fishing with you two?"

"Sister, the two of us have five other pals who go to grade school. One of them, Catfish Curtis, is some kind of genius with fish. He can almost talk 'em into jumpin' right into his dad's boat. He tells us what kind of bait or which hook or anything else. That's how he got to be called Catfish."

"I see," said Sister Regina. "It's nice that you are playing so well with all of the others. In little more than fifteen months you all will be freshmen together, as long as you all stay in Bradford. Maybe some boys here might be going to St. Bede."

"Well, sister," Booby interrupted, "I bet we stay here, because Bradford probably wouldn't have a high school football team if all of us Catholics didn't save the team every year." Some of the others clapped, and quietly cheered at that. Then he briskly continued. "But we all have lots of good friends, even if they are Protestants. Sister, I know you have heard me playing the trumpet for two years already in the high school band because the music teacher needed somebody else 'cause the band is so small."

"That's wonderful, but my goodness, let's never start arguing with any Protestants in Bradford. They are fine people, wonderful people. They believe in the same God we do, they just understand a different countenance from our church.

The problems erupted more than four hundred years so it is almost old history. We love our church, and I am sure they do, too."

"Sister, I know all that, and we have a lot of fun, but we have had a bunch of arguments because all of us in St. John's think they're goin' to hell when they die because of this guy named Luther, and they think we're going to be wandering around in purgatory for a zillion years."

"What?" The shocked look on Sister's Regina's face was accentuated by her right hand now covering her mouth. "Patrick, that is not for you to judge. God alone, and our savior, Jesus Christ will be preside on the final judgement day for us all." She stopped and automatically blessed herself.

Whether buoyed by the knowledge that this was the last day, at least for this school year, Beaner wouldn't quit. For him the past two or three years had become long suppressed convictions that silently nurtured, and were now released. "I'm sure you're right, sister, about God judging everybody. But these pals of mine don't ever go to confession, ever, because their church doesn't even have one. On top of that they never ever speak Latin in their church. They eat meat; real meat on Friday's while we have to eat fish we didn't even catch. And they don't wear any medals around their necks even playing basketball games."

Booby immediately interrupted. "Yeah, and they don't have any statues, big or little even like St. Christopher on their folk's dashboards. And they never pray the way we do with the rosary, and they don't even go over to kneel and pray at the Blessed Virgin. Heck, sister, they don't even have near-enough candles."

"Stop all of this, boys. You have to trust *your* faith, and not try to re-invent anyone else's beliefs, especially your own. Class, just because we feel Roman Catholicism is the true faith, it doesn't give us the right to judge others. As I said before, only God can do that. All that you or any other of the rest of us should do is live our lives being the best Catholics we can." Sister Regina slowly sat down in the front chair beside her desk. This had totally drained her.

"Well, Sister, I know you are moving, and you want us to stop, but there's one more thing you should know about Protestants," Beaner almost whispered.

"Oh, Patrick, it distresses me tremendously to hear you say more about that. You *must* stop."

"Sister," Beaner said softly, ignoring her stern reproach. "Each Saturday after-noon during football season, Suck...er, Philip Carlton, roots for the Illini team. He says no matter who they play, he hopes that Notre Dame will get killed every week."

"Oh," replied Sister Regina as the bell sounded, and a quizzical frown gently creased her forehead. Everyone was now screaming and running out of the class, but she covered her mouth slightly with a couple of fingers, and glanced up at Beaner who was silently standing there. "I guess that *is* a little different."

CHAPTER 16

▼

REMEMBERING MR. LINCOLN

For a number of years before 1948, no matter who the principal was at Bradford High School, Miss Sallie Vanzant operated her room the same way strong wardens would run their prisons: tough.

Any person, any time, any place who goofed around in any spot at this town's high school suddenly realized they had made a huge mistake. Miss Vanzant was already well over 60 years old, and was thin enough that she probably didn't weigh more than a hundred pounds, but age and size had nothing to do with her strength or determination. Happily for her, she now had a new principal this year that had proven that he was the perfect man for the job. They worked well together. His name: J. A. Jones, and with Sallie Vanzant, they were a great pair. About a dozen other good teachers also ruled their own part of the roost, and brought this group into such a perfect high school operation that everyone in town felt 181 students could never be one bit better anywhere in America.

Fortunately, the two schools where the seven crazy seventh grade boys attended were also just as firm in control over the kids in all eight classes. Unfortunately for them, these boys always hoped the next school year would be easier, but they now realized that life for them was never going down hill work-wise ever again. If they did fall behind, it was their sad demise and they would be in trouble.

The day before these grade school boys ended their normal school year, thousands of other high school seniors throughout our country held the wonderful realization that they had finished twelve years of study, and now had graduated in the first big moment of their adult lives. Graduating from eighth grade was nice, but it was more like a continuing job in a different place, not a great happening. High school was the end of the line for a lot of these young men and women.

Since the graduates had departed, and the other three classes also had finished the previous afternoon, most of the teachers were closing up their offices today. The previous nights celebrations for the proud graduates, offered new jobs, new dreams, and several of them knew the classes first marriage also would be on high on their wish lists. However, some would be studying more because college was already a new, tougher formidable task. And some of the boys were now already accepting the military draft, because two years in the service had to happen before they could determine what the real world could transpire. However, figuring how one of the new college boys would keep himself in school before he, too, had to go into the military, was the gamble. Would his grades be high enough to be able to come back for one more semester, or had he been screwing around with too much beer, and too little study? Time would tell.

The same Friday afternoon that watched those seven boys run into joyful oblivion, Miss Vanzant had a much different challenge. She would be meeting with Bob Lee, one of the young men in the senior class which last night that had its commencement ceremony in the basketball gymnasium. His parents had a great restaurant on Main Street right beneath the only bank in town. Bob didn't know it yet, but he would be asked by Miss Vanzant to memorize Lincoln's Gettysburg Address, and deliver it by next Tuesday morning in Bradford Park.

This was always a consecrated experience for most of the town. May 30th, whenever the day arrived on the week's calendar, was Memorial Day, and it was the big day for the American Legion members. World War II ended less than three years ago, and about two dozen soldiers and sailors who left high school as a boy now had come home as a man. Sadly, four local boys in that war came back to be buried. From 1941, a number of homes had small flags hanging in one of the home's front window with a red star. It signified someone from their home was serving our country. Tragically, these four flags still showed the saddest part because their stars' were gold.

Though Miss Vanzant never served in the military, she finally got the women's opportunity to vote in 1920, and was proud to do whatever she could to make America stronger and better. For nearly her 35 years as a teacher, one strong schoolmaster had convinced one nervous student to join these hallowed steps, and stood before the ancient octagon bandstand. A knocking sound came which gave her a bit of apprehension. Bob walked in as straight as an arrow.

"Hello, Bob, I am so glad you could come. Congratulations for winning the Salutatorian of your class. Your ability and intelligence is exactly what I am thrilled to see." Miss Vanzant smiled briefly, and then got right down to the point, because he already knew what was about to happen.

"I didn't think I would see you so soon, Miss Vanzant. But I think I heard today that Grace Hopkins has come down with the flu," Bob replied.

"Yes, her mother called about eleven o'clock today, and said Grace had a very high temperature. As you know, she was going to give the famous speech President Lincoln gave our country eighty-six years ago. Bob, she had memorized this since last month, and now she's so sick we can't gamble if she'll be good enough to be able to speak."

"That is very disappointing for her. She and I have been good friends since we were both in grade school together. I was so relieved that she got the assignment. I was planning on just standing over in the park to hear her next Tuesday. Now I am really nervous." Bob was very uptight as he looked into her face, and he glanced up to stare at the pictures of two great presidents who were joined together on the classroom's front blackboard. Though both were fading portraits serenely hanging there for a number of years, these were American's patron saints, George Washington, and Abraham Lincoln.

Miss Vanzant suddenly realized it was a golden opportunity to confirm him immediately. "Look up at them, Bob. Look deep into their eyes. You will absorb their souls as you let them enter into you. I know that four years ago you and your 8th grade class rode the Illinois annual school bus trip to Springfield, and saw his home, tomb, and the early days at New Salem. I'm sure that trip changed your life."

They both studied the two portraits. Washington exuded strength, leadership, and heroism as the country's first commander, but Lincoln's craggy face gave a taciturn appearance with compassion, humility, and an almost overwhelmingly feeling of sadness. Virtually all classrooms throughout the northern states used these two pictures, but, in addition to Washington, every main picture in the southern states proudly showed Robert E. Lee. A terrible war was over, but many aspects of its morose heritage still held on.

"Historians say that Washington's impressive physical stature and the power of his intense gaze could instill such a feeling of confidence that he became the dominant leader of his age, not only to his friends and contemporaries, but a powerful adversary for his enemies, as well. Mr. Lincoln was also tall and strong, but in a different, gangly and raw-boned way. To some he looked more like an ordinary prairie farmer than President of the United States. You are a native son of his adopted state. Illinois is where he matured into the man, and I feel is the greatest human being who was born since Jesus Christ. Mr. Washington's strong hands guided this nation into existence, but Mr. Lincoln held it together with both of his." Miss Vanzant then lowered her eyes, and slowly turned to Bob. She had done this version of her own memorized talk so long she could tell it any time or day. The message that she gave was so powerful a smile of wonder and admiration now radiated from her.

Bob was now so mesmerized he couldn't even speak. Two powerful presidents from our early country's history were now hovering over the shoulders of the one woman who could talk this young man to stand and speak with *the ages*. Miss Vanzant had long ago understood what those two words meant to her. The morning after the previous disaster in Ford's Theatre, Lincoln had just died, and Vice President, now to be President Johnson said, "We have been struck a mighty blow."

Stunned by this shock, Edwin M. Stanton, the Secretary of War, agreed, "…He will belong to the ages."

"One man was the guiding force in forming our country's union, and the other in preserving it. My heart goes out to each, but there is something in the poignancy of Mr. Lincoln's eyes that has always touched me. No man since Christ ever loved humanity more or made a larger sacrifice for them, than Mr. Lincoln. Look into those warm, wonderful, piercing eyes. You are looking into that man's very soul. I firmly believe that it was providence's great plan that Mr. Lincoln would have to sacrifice his life in order that the entire state' union which he so desperately sought, could be saved. Like Christ, he gave himself for the many."

Bob gulped. It was an involuntary reaction to the breathtaking sense of pressure and confusion he now was feeling. Was it possible that Honest Abe and Jesus Christ were now reaching out and personally selecting him to deliver this famous speech? The thought almost petrified him.

She quickly sensed his apprehensions, and went right for his proverbial throat. "Now all President Lincoln asks of you is to stand up for him next Tuesday morning and repeat his potent words on this coming Memorial Day. Bob, it's only ten sentences long. One hundred seventy-four words. I will help you work on it tomorrow and Sunday. Then you can practice on Monday with your mom, dad, and me. I know you can do it, Bob…"

Her words trailed into silence so quietly the only sound came from the rhythmic ticking of the old pendulum wall clock with the Roman numerals on its face.

"I have to admit I am almost frightened beyond belief, but I wonder do you really feel I can do it?" His reply was barely audible.

"Bob, as I said a few seconds ago, I know you can do it. The way you walked into this room told me that you were the one who could do it. Now think about this: someday you may be in an important position of leadership. Good leaders begin their lives with challenges just like what you are doing now, and will again and again. No one knows what will happen in these serious challenges, but they know it takes the first powerful step to make something happen right. In these four days you can be so strong you will realize that your initial step will be the first of many that you will take, young man. And, I'll help you any way I can." Miss Vanzant then reached over and squeezed his closest hand gently.

He looked back up into the touching eyes of Abraham Lincoln, and then he looked back to her. "Miss Vanzant, uh, uh, I'll do it. I'll do it for you, and I'll do it for him, and for what he did for all of us."

"What a wonderful decision you've made. Everyone will be so proud." Miss Vanzant smiled and stood for a hug.

"I'll go home now and tell my folks. Then I'll start memorizing so I will say it on Tuesday," Bob said and nodded. "Goodbye, Miss Vanzant. I promise," as he called over his shoulder.

"Thank you, Bob. We'll talk again tomorrow. Just call Central or walk over if you have any questions. I used my mimeograph copier, and made you this copy of the president's hand-written Gettysburg Address."

When he reached over and picked it up, Bob looked down at the two page of paper, and almost felt trembled. But he smiled to her, and walked quietly out of the room.

As the large door with the frosted glass window slowly closed, Miss Vanzant reached over and pulled the middle right hand drawer in her desk. She removed her pocket book, and took a small hanky from it and dabbed her eyes. Again she looked up into Mr. Lincoln's serene, sad, countenance, and blinked as another tear streamed down her cheek. The hanky caught it instantly, and she softly said, "Please, sir, give him a hand." Then she somehow smiled, and gave his picture a slight nod as if he had given his consent. "And like I told him, I'll do everything I can, too, Mr. President."

"…That we here highly resolve that these dead shall not have died in vain, that this nation shall have a new birth of freedom, and that government of the people, by the people, for the people shall not perish from the earth."

As Bob finished what many have always felt was Lincoln's greatest speech, the powerful conclusion was so strong that even he was suddenly stunned. He closed his eyes, and simply tilted his face down in awe. After what seemed to be its own private eternity for a second or two of total silence, instant cheers and applause now filled the park.

Though Sally Vanzant was one of four other people sitting on the podium, she was the first to stand and clap proudly. Interesting, the same hanky that had been needed just a few days ago was still in her purse. Everyone around was now up on their feet to applaud Bob. When Mayor Hooligan spotted Miss Vanzant's blinking eyes, he smiled and leaned over to her.

"Sure an you did it again, dear lady. Thanks for turning this Memorial Day into another memorable experience."

Belzy was a very simple, basic politician, but more importantly, he was one who was also true and honest. That combination was so rare he could equally say a flattering compliment or a serious statement, and never be considered false either way to anyone else, or himself. As the applause subsided, he now had to give another speaker's due. For the first time in the history of Bradford, U. S. Representative Everett McKinley Dirksen from Pekin, was going to speak today. Many people from all over Stark County were already here because, amazingly, he was such a very important person and this county was the smallest in his district.

Rep. Dirksen gave such an incredible speech, people would always remember this day for two distinctive reasons. Certainly his linguistic ability was now very apparent all over Central Illinois. His extraordinary speaking capacity could roll certain words of even one or two syllables so long that they almost became a personal paragraph. But the main reason was unexpected…it was only eight and a half minutes longer than the one Bob just gave for the sixteenth president in 1863. Lincoln spoke on that Pennsylvania gray, chilly November day, but today was simply magnificent, and Dirksen's reception was ecstatic. People probably didn't realize that the good congressman was giving this same speech today six or seven more times in other nearby towns, but that didn't matter.

High school band football games at home were routine performances, but two special times a year were the only times they marched through Bradford. One went from east to west through Main Street at Labor Day's celebration, and the other marched at a different date in late May from the Park straight north to the town's cemetery. This annual event was much more reserved than the second parade in early September. It took less than fifteen minutes for the forty-one band members to perform immediately behind the several different flag corps, and many in the park followed along. John Phillip Sousa would have even been thrilled that such a small, but gallant band was as good as any else in a challenge like this.

As was the custom, after they arrived and crowded together, everyone stood anywhere in the cemetery, except on a grave. The American Flag was already at half-mast on the main burial grounds. Military ritual is very important for a lot of people, and though the 'retired' soldiers and sailors here were now normal, working men, today was singularly special. Warlike leaders in Egypt or China or Mesopotamia probably created exercises like this more than 5000 years ago, and even the simple, but prestigious Roman Salute was created several centuries before Julius Caesar had been born.

Maybe those other customs and decorum were of another time and another place. Bradford had it's own private version, though somewhere else it might have been with a bit more 'spit and polish.' Today, however, the saddened and bereaved people who were standing in their own cemetery knew this was a very special place for them.

A brief, but touching prayer was given by Bernard 'Bummy' Fuertges, the Chaplain at Bradford's American Legion Post 445. Lee Ely, the band's best trumpeter, stepped up to the main spot. He began softly, but proudly, playing 'Taps'.

As he stepped quietly back into the band, the main American Legion Rifle Squad and Color Guard who wearing their own various military uniforms, were now standing in line at parade rest. Francis Webber, the current Commander did a sharp about face, and turned directly toward the most people standing in the crowd. He held up a small, imitated, red flower, but anyone there knew this was a famous "Buddy Poppy" that was sold all over America as far back as 1920 by the VFW. This great organization collected needed funds for veterans who sadly didn't come home, or those who were crippled or scarred for life.

"My special poppy has stayed with me for nearly twenty years. I bought it for a dime as a kid in this same cemetery, and now I buy a few new ones every year, and give them to other folks such as you. When I went into the army in 1942 I promised myself that I would secretly place it in my shirt pocket whenever I had to go into a battle somewhere in France or Germany, just for some additional courage and hope. I am here because of the Grace of God...and this Buddy Poppy. Some of my best *real* buddies in that war are buried across the ocean, and two of them are a few feet away from us. I wanted to ask that each of you keep it in your heart and your prayers, and buy some for your own family and friends."

He paused, and then slipped the old, almost crumbled little poppy into his same top pocket, and took another piece of paper out of a back hip-pocket. "Before we give the solemn 21 Gun Salute, I would simply also like to read the third stanza of a famous poem that was written back in 1915 by a Canadian Colonel named John McCrae." Commander Webber cleared his throat, and then turned his face slightly to the left. "AhhhhtenHUT," he exclaimed, and the other men were all instantly at attention. Immediately, he called "Present arms," and the entire squad brought their M-1's up in front of them. Then he began to read.

"Take up our quarrel with the foe:
To you from failing hands we throw
The torch, be yours to hold it high.
If ye break faith with us who die,
We shall not sleep, though poppies grow
In Flanders fields."

Commander Francis Webber was unapologetic as he brushed a tear that was running slowly down his left cheek. He did a sharp about face, and gave the correct orders to raise their weapons.

"Ready….aim….fire. Ready…aim….fire. Ready…aim…fire."

CHAPTER 17

▼

SUMMER SATURDAY NIGHTS

Four days later, the first 'early summer' weekend was now about to happen again. Annual events in lots of midwestern small towns were so well planned nobody needed a calendar for anything, except for a few folks who might want to know what day it actually was. People, from kids to the oldest people in their village, would say instantly that there wasn't anything better in the entire world than hanging around downtown Main Street on Saturday night.

That was sure true for good, old Bradford, Illinois on a Saturday night summer evening in June, July, and August. It almost seemed like it was a fantasy, but the best part of this so-called dream was this: it was true. If heaven really happens when these seven boys find their lives are over, they will easily beg God to let any of them back to these incredible days and nights again.

Catfish lived right on Main Street, and the rest of the others easily walked there. On Saturday night lots of others people arrived with their family in a car, pickup truck, and some folks even rode to town on a tractor. It was so crowded by 7 PM two or three vehicles would be jammed in any parking lane. People happily sat around their cars or in them, and everyone visited with countless other friends who were strolling along from one side of the street to the other.

Virtually all of the businesses, from the old, rough and noisy train bridge at the top of the western end to the only one block 'hard' road corner from Peoria on Rt. 88, were busy. People could do most anything, eat ice cream at Dorgan's, buy a suit from Mowbray's, take in a movie at the Brad Theater, or just enjoy a delicious cold, beer from one of the three bars.

Dink told his pals that some day they all will walk right in and get a real drink, but it'd take almost nine more years before they could. He quietly didn't admit the mess he had when he was six, and drank his first, and last beer. His dad said he was going to work for a couple of hours at Heaton's farm with five other men, and he could go fishing by himself because a nearby creek was only about a hundred yards away. However, Dink stole a beer from a fifty-five-gallon tank filled with ice that the workers used, and after catching a ten-inch catfish, he decided to celebrate and drank the entire bottle.

Unfortunately, he later told his dad he had fallen asleep, but his dad laughed and told his mother that passing out is more likely. Dink also had to admit that his planned future supper was already covered with thousands of maggots right beside him. Between the beer headache, and the terrible, newborn flies he promised that this would be his last beer ever. What he didn't know is that his mother and father glanced up at each other, rolled their eyes, and said a simple silent prayer to save another crazy kid doing one more wacky day.

Most people in towns all over the Middle West felt the same way. Like the kids in Central Illinois, they had special prayers. Some were doing their rosary, some others memorized prayers and some only said it when they wanted some serious help from God. Lots of girls and boys thought a trip to Peoria was Treasure Island, and if they ever got to Chicago, it was heaven. Prayers were probably the best things they could do to keep lunatic kids from driving their towns to distraction and possibly destruction. However, a thick belt or wooden paddle might actually get a lot more immediate action. But every set of parents kept thousands of wonderful memories, despite two terrible wars, and the Great Depression. In spite of it, many often felt they were the luckiest people anywhere in the country.

Some had so many memories that lots of people got worn out hearing about them, and some didn't even believe it. Nevertheless, every now and then somebody who lived in Bradford would simply say that something or some person they saw or met as a kid was *honestly sure that these crazy stories really did happen.*

No matter how many wonderful recollections, just plain fun, or visiting good neighbors in any town in America, Bradford would happily say that life is sweet.

Well, actually, there was one man who couldn't ever be called sweet. Any time, day or night, people on Saturday nights could stare at the fattest man in the town's history. These seven boys loved Buck Ed Minister, whether he was 450 pounds or even 550 pounds. But those Saturday nights caused strong problems for girls and women. His powerful odor, and tobacco chaws with it's ancient juice probably had turned into such a stain in his chin it was now a permanent part of his skin.

At least the fat man seemed to get the most flies on Main Street so the rest of the folks, who were walking around for a stroll, enjoyed a break.

Bill Dorgan, The King of Maid-Rites and Nickel Ice Cream Cones, was a show all by himself. The weekend after Memorial Day still had people laughing when he announced he had seen a real "Flying Saucer". He told anyone who would listen to him that it had come in from a space ship, and he saw it! He even hoped it would give him a ride. Unfortunately for him, he was the only person in town to see the thing, and even a few friends who enjoyed a beer everyday said they and no one else believed him either.

It may have helped his aging eyesight quite a bit better sipping a glass of his own special 'green beer' each evening on March 17th, and the Irish bow tie he only wore on that special day.

Saturday afternoon and evening was actually the busiest time of the week. Two barbershops were full of customers all day, and late into the night. Jimmy Hennessy owned and ran his renowned "Auditorium" at the smallest store in town, and Bill Carroll's shop was on the opposite side of the street. Tom Flood owned and operated his great bowling alley, and teenage boys thought they might get killed several times a night working there as a pin boy. The only constable within fifteen miles was Big 'Gilly' Shaw, and he could throw a bowling ball so hard it seemed as if pin boys gambled their life every time he rolled it down the lane.

Ed Mowbray's clothing store gave away a free suit if people bought the first nine. How many men in Bradford, or anywhere else for that matter, ever owned that many suits in those days? Mr. Mowbray had another incredible drawing every Saturday night. He froze a huge pair of big boots in a large block of ice, and it sat in front of his store on Main Street. People bought tickets to see who could guess when the boots could be melted enough to get out of the ice. If they were still having fun in downtown late enough, kids loved to see when the last bit of ice was considered melted.

The important Main Street volunteer fire station was on the south side of Main Street. Every kind of worker in the town could fight a fire or help at an accident within minutes. The two trucks were gems, and always were kept as shiny as the first day that either arrived. They stood out about ten or fifteen feet from the big front open door.

People wandered in and out of almost every business on the street. Some wanted to see Art Marsh's funeral home and furniture store, who ran his business with his son-in law, Bob Dunlap. The whole town knew Mr. Marsh was the most distinguished looking person anywhere here. The previous year Gale and Alberta Ray bought Batten's 5 and 10, and everything folks needed was there even if it cost a little more than a nickel or dime.

Greg Owens' Insurance and Real Estate office also opened last year, after he got out of the army. When Bradford folks needed to get some meat they had previously butchered or prepared vegetables they canned and froze months ago at the Locker. Now, if they wanted to cook something tonight, it was a snap. Jesse Rouse ran his Maytag Store, Sullivan and Bucher owned and ran Bradford Community Hardware store, Manning's and Lehmans' both ran feed stores across the street, and the automobile business that what would become the most successful dealership that ever happened in Bradford was Browning and Velde Ford.

Four and maybe five grocery stores operated at the same time, and five or six restaurants ran everyday of the week, except Sunday, and all but one of them were no more than about 200 feet away from each other! The lone location was just a half-mile away at Johnston's Café, beside the intersection of Rt. 88 and Rt. 93. Folks knew since three churches controlled those Sabbath days, every restaurant was closed, but suspected they could still get a big bag of Maid-Rites even that night at Dorgan's.

Anyone sick had lots of good health advice because Bradford had two doctors, one dentist and a pharmacist then, and they were all on the North side of Main Street. Dr. Ross Herrman, a dentist named Dr. C. N. Heinzmen and two brothers: Dr. J. E. Scholes, and Clarence 'Tinker' Scholes, who had a pharmacy. Wayne 'Lefty' Blake was then his right hand guy, and Lefty bought the store a year earlier.

In 1949, Bradford Banking Company was run by Charlie Rees, and Leigh Palmer was the Cashier. But Lucille 'Casey' Scott, and Bill Tumbleson ran the day to day services. Since 1907, R. L. 'Bob' Breen ran the Bradford Republican weekly newspaper, but three years ago he sold it to a young veteran named Jim Fulks. Jim was a pilot, and completed 28 bombing missions over Germany with his B-17. His plane was shot down, and he spent nine months in a prison camp. When he got back, he bought the paper from Mr. Breen. The town loved Bob for more than 40 years, but was just as happy when Jim came back to town and took over the paper.

Amazingly, the two biggest businesses that had the more employees, and best job were both only about a block or two away from Main Street. Hotchkiss Steel

Products Co. made several kinds of serious machinery, and a number of folks were thrilled that they could get a good job right here in town, though a lot of others were driving all the way to Caterpillar in East Peoria. Most kids at this age could not even grasp at what this company did, but these seven boys knew instantly what the Jim Dandy Collar Factory made.

It was built in the southwestern section of town along the railroad tracks, and though it was still working everyday, folks knew that horse collars, halters, and bridles were nowhere as important as they were even ten years earlier. A decade ago between thirty and forty people worked there, but by 1949 the company was down to just three people. Millions of cars, trucks, and tractors had practically left horses for no other serious business than riding or racing them. Even so, lots of people loved to walk in and just smell the powerful and incredible aroma of so many different uses of leather goods.

On this night at the first Saturday evening in June 1949, Main Street was just as full and fun as it's ever been. These Bradford neighbors were enjoying laughter and friendship everywhere on Main Street. Even with so much merriment and vocalizing most people could hear a sound about half a mile away that it was so much of a routine for one unique young man, anyone who heard it would have automatically said, "Poop Deck's car is ready to roar."

It's because these several hundred people in town knew exactly how he was making the hullabaloo, and where he was going to do it. Two years ago, everyone was just amazed at what he enjoyed doing, and kids and adults would stop and listen wherever they were when they heard the sound. Interestingly, a lot of people laughed about it, and didn't seem to care that much now. Even Big Gilly, the single cop in the town, wouldn't give him a ticket for breaking those two certain laws: speeding at 50-60 miles an hour on South Peoria Street, and making a sound that would blow some folks right out of their seats or beds. This probably would have been against the law anywhere else except in Bradford.

Donald 'Poop Deck' Runyan was a twenty-year-old madman who thought his '40 Ford V-8 made the most beautiful music he had ever heard. Of course, a lot of other people in Bradford didn't agree, but Big Gilly finally agreed he would only let him do it three times in a row, and then only when there was no car running south then on the Rt. 88-Peoria road. Traffic was usually so light this was not a problem.

What was it that made this amazing experience almost as habitual as the town's noon whistle every day? His friends don't even seem to remember how he got such a crazy nickname, but in this town no one was overwhelmed with crazy nicknames because everyone seemed to have one! But his car's changes rocked the rest of the town. Poop Deck somehow discovered something called Dual Smitty Glass Pack Mufflers. They may have been invented for crazy young men who went out of control with that horrendous but intoxicating sound.

Every Saturday afternoon for three summers, Poop Deck brought the town to it's edge roaring down the empty road to about 60 miles an hour, and then slammed his second gear into action as he came back up the hill into town. He even made it sound even better for himself when he rolled his left window and leaned his head out just as the wind hit his ears. The roar that happened with this was a truly powerful sound that was singular unto itself. As it began to go slowly and even more slowly, Poop Deck would do a u-e and go back south to Ehnle's corner, and do it again.

Last year he topped himself with an action of sheer genius, and pulled the hoses that operated his engine's windshield wiper. For some reason, this aspect was completely unknown by any driver in town, and he knew had hit the ultimate achievement. After the third run, Poop Deck was as normal as any other young man in town, because this week his performance time had run out.

Naturally, other folks in Toulon and Wyoming and LaFayette felt their town in Stark County was pretty special, too. But Saturday nights made a lot of people in Bradford convinced it had to be better here than anyone else in the entire world.

CHAPTER 18

▼

THAT HIDDEN CLOCK WAS RINGING OFF THEIR BELLS

The first week of June had been so good everyone around seemed to be even a little bit happier than they were just a few weeks ago. Summer was thoroughly here, and no one cared that it actually didn't officially arrive for nearly three more weeks on everyone's calendar

Maybe, and maybe not, but something new happened about that time, and it was now a different experience with several of the seven pals. In fact things were getting into a new level of conversation privately with four of them for the past few months. Hotshot, Suck, Jumbo, and Beaner were now closer to their age of 14 than 13, but the other three were either falling a little behind, or they were just perplexed to talk about it to anyone. Thanks to several older brothers, these four shared some quiet news that fishing was fun, but sharing these new eight-page 'comic' publications was a heck of a lot better. Adults would have announced that they should immediately confiscate this stuff, and call it plain, simple pornography. Of course, that is just what it was, though most of the fathers would probably have at least glanced at it before they, too, destroyed the junk. Unfortunately, some of the fathers might hide it themselves. This is why mothers everywhere knew that they should demolish the smut quickly, and lots of fathers didn't even know it had happened.

Several of the boy's physical body's were certainly changing, and while their voice octaves were going lower, their carnal brains were running about two levels higher. With this in mind, the boys were riding their bikes as they held fishing poles, bags of lunch, and canteens for water. But this trip was to Lake Broadmore, a four-mile ride most of which was gravel roads. This usually took about thirty minutes, but today they were so full of equipment they were chugging fairly slow.

They were now fishing around the East Side of the lake. They could bait their hooks for whatever they could catch. Big night crawlers, peewee dough balls, or even a small bucket of little shiners was fine if Catfish felt that one was better than another. Three of the boys were a few feet away on the causeway, and the rest were nearby.

Even though no other person was within three hundred yards, Suck's voice was barely above a whisper. He said, "I'll tell you what the two best things are going to be this year in eighth grade." Each boy turned toward him, and moved closer, sensing something important. Suck paused for additional impact. "Boobs."

"Boobs?" The response had been given simultaneously by at least three of the group. It was loud enough that a couple of them raised an index finger to their mouths for quiet.

Suck looked around the group before continuing, checking again to see if anyone in the lake was trying to eavesdrop. "Boobs this year. And by the time we get to high school a year from September, every girl there will have grown a pair." As they grinned and snickered, the boys exchanged sheepish glances containing the strange mixture of self-conscious embarrassment and expectation that sexually inexperienced males have shared since the beginning of time.

"Suck, I bet you hope they'll all be built like Barbara Denson was. It's just a tragedy that she moved away back in late December. I bet I've seen you snap her brassiere strap in the cloakroom a dozen times. My brother says she's already grown a pair of cantaloupes. He's just sorry he'll probably never see her again. He bets she will turn into watermelons." As usual, Jumbo spat convincingly when he finished. They were laughing again.

"Maybe not that good, but they're all gonna have 'em. It's a natural fact, "Suck said, with a disposition of authority. "So what if she moved. The rest of them are going to happen."

"Wow, imagine," Dink exclaimed. "Room after room full of boobs. That's all I ever dream about. What do you think they feel like? Are they soft or hard? If I only had a teenage sister. All I've got is two stupid younger brothers. When I bend my arm and feel my elbow, it sorts looks like a boob, but I don't know if they're that hard. I never dream about sports or fishing, just boobs." His unbridled honesty was a continual problem for him as he often blurted his thoughts without benefit of discretion.

"That's all you dream about?" Hotshot asked skeptically. "Whatever happened about baseball or fishing?"

"It's probably because of the calendars my dad gets for his office with pictures of beautiful women naked as a Jay bird. He calls it a calendar, but it's really a bunch of smiling naked women." He pushed his glasses higher on his nose and added, "I sneak a lot of looks at those pictures. I got caught when I was in first grade. I drew my first good picture. It was a naked woman, and drew everything right except her feet. I thought women who wore high heel shoes had real feet that filled their heels down about three inches. Miss Ternus saw my picture, and made me sit in the cloakroom for a whole hour. Then she sent my picture and a bad letter to my mom and dad."

"Wow, did you get whipped pretty bad?" Catfish asked.

"No, because my mom was so embarrassed she asked my dad to handle the problem, but my dad thought it was funny. He just told me to never draw any thing like that again in school. I haven't done it again, but maybe it's okay with him to let me draw some more at home."

"Dink, I'll bet you go upstairs and lock yourself in the bathroom every time you walk through your Dad's office. As often as you flub your dub, you might even have to put it in a sling one of these days," Beaner guffawed.

"A small sling," Suck said.

"Yeah, about the size an ant would need," added Jumbo.

When the laughter subsided, Dink was now glaring defensively at Beaner and Suck. "I don't do that any more often than you two or anybody else here does."

"Bullshit, Dink," Suck said. "The only guy in the world who beats more meat than you is in the A & P butcher shop."

This time everyone, including Dink who was usually the brunt of a joke, broke into hearty laughter. This was familiar territory for him. No one in their group was the butt of more jokes and pranks than he, but it was Jonathan's parents, not his friends, who gave him his nickname. Their patience with his habit of stalling on every chore or duty he was expected to perform in their home finally gave way to accusing him of always 'dinking' around instead of immediately getting the job done. It didn't take long before he was Dink to almost everyone in Bradford.

However, for at least one practical purpose, they all had turned 'dinking' into a sexual adjective. But Dink was definitely not alone. Masturbation was now as normal for all of them as if they were going to the bathroom or just playing with one of their toys. Nevertheless, part of their own body was now the most interesting 'toy' they had. Baby boys figured out how their penis actually felt within weeks or months. Their first orgasm encounter could be anytime, even a few years later or some as far as ten or twelve years later. None of the seven had ever done anything like this all together, but several had masturbated together, just for fun. Relief hadn't yet begun to give them a new level of action. And, for these 13-year-old boys, homosexual experiences were as far away from their minds as if it was happening in another planet.

The big problem was very simple: none of their parents had told them anything honest about sex, and older brothers or cousins only told bizarre lies.

Hotshot began speaking with his habitual trademark, a soft mixture of snicker and giggle, "if boobs are the two best things, I wonder what the one best thing a girl has is going to be?" His glance and quick wink in Suck's direction indicated the question was rhetorical. Suck caught its meaning and nodded, his face beaming in a knowing grin.

"Hotshot, you guys got a private joke going on?" asked Booby. Because he remembered the original focus for this conversation was girl's breasts, he wasn't sure of the direction it had now taken. His tone was challenging, as it usually was when he thought anyone was poking fun at his expense. This new direction aroused his suspicions as to the meaning of their humor. Whether it was born of his Irish roots, or defensiveness about his pudgy size and shape, Booby was always primed for a fight, regardless of his opponent's size or number.

"No, Booby, there's nothing private. I wasn't talking about tit's now," Hotshot said, purposely avoiding his friend's well-known ire.

Dink's naiveté reached the irrepressible point as he waited for an explanation. The long pause was finally too much for him. "Well, what are you guys talking about?"

"Dink, think about it, what do girls have that boys don't?" Beaner made no effort to mask his sarcastic tone.

After contorting his face in confusion for a moment, Dink brightened. "Purses. They all carry purses," he said confidently. Hotshot, Suck, Jumbo, and Beaner broke into immediate laughter. The rest joined in, though uneasily, for they too were confused as to what it was all about.

"Dink," began Suck, while he was still laughing. "Sometimes you're so dumb I think you'd order cow pie for dessert."

Anyone on the entire lake who heard this resulting torrent of laughter would have believed it must have been the funniest wisecrack the entire group had ever had. However, Dink created so many mistakes and confusion, this bunch realized that funny things were so easy for them the next day may even be funnier.

As the roaring subdued, Jumbo cleared his throat, and started to speak. "You guys know that boys and girls are growing up to be men and women, and three of us have older brothers in high school who are already that age. I hide behind a small door into a closet that goes along the wall where my brother lives. Every now and then, he and two other guys who are seniors talk kind of quiet so our mom can't hear it, but they say that two other senior girls in their class will ring their bells any time they want." He did what he always does, and spat right into a can of night crawlers sitting between several of them.

Several of the boys snickered, but the rest were quiet. Dink decided to try it again. "I bet this isn't the only bell thing I know, 'cause it's probably a lot more involved in what I did. You all know I got spanked by Mr. Huey for turning the fire-alarm bells on just for the heck of it."

"Well, at least your about half right," Suck said. "When you did that stupid idea with Barnie Barnes you both got in trouble with the principal. The entire building had to clear out everybody down the emergency steps on both levels, even us. Shoot, if anybody ever does that again they'll be thrown right out of school."

Dink now had a very embarrassed look, and started hanging his head. Hotshot shook his head, "Forget it, Dink, what we are talking about now is a lot more interesting than just one more goofy thing you do. The bells Jumbo said is about messing around with one of the older boys and one of the girls in high school."

"Yeah," Beaner said, "My brother is laughing about some of the girls, too. He said most are just as good as they could be, but a couple of them are flirty, and he says that they wear sweaters one size smaller than what they should be wearing. I swear, some guys like my older brother are about as hot as some of the dogs in heat we have."

"Wow, that's wild. I never thought grown-up boys would act like they were just as wild as hot dogs," Dink said.

Several of them snickered, and even laughed, but Dink didn't see why they were cackling. "Dink, you said a silly joke, and you didn't even realize you did. We're laughing because are you talking about eating one at a baseball game or what happens to our pet dogs a couple of times a year?"

Somehow, Dink saved himself, and surprised the others by saying, "You guys, I'm talking about sex dog stuff when Jumbo and I did a marriage ceremony for Brownie and Queenie.' But the funny bit is my dad had Queenie operated on, and he said we'd never have another one in our family. Somehow Queenie doesn't ever act like she's wild anymore. I'm trying to understand why some of your brothers are acting like real wild dogs."

"Okay, you're right, Dink. Three of us have older brothers and they won't tell us one damn thing. In fact they tell me more lies than anybody else in town," Beaner said.

"Have any of you guys figured out what goes into this thing between a woman and a man?" Booby asked. "It's kind of a wild, but hidden mess. I don't have any sisters, at least not real girl, family sisters. I have to learn stuff from Sister's in St. Johns, but that isn't even close to being about what I'm talking about now."

"Yeah, I don't have a sister, either," Catfish said. "Heck, I remember when I was about seven or eight, and I had a cousin from Walnut who was two years younger than me. We were playing in the sandbox together, and somehow she said she didn't have a brother, but if I would show her mine, she would show me hers."

"Wow, that's pretty neat," Dink said, and smiled as the others also wanted to hear the rest of the story.

"Sad it ain't much to tell you. I pulled down my shorts, and she stared at my donger, and then I pulled mine back up and said pull down yours. She did, and then she covered her face with both of her hands and giggled. I looked at it for about two seconds and said what happened to you? You must have broken something off, because all you have is just a crack. She pulled her pants back up, and I said well, thanks, but I guess I'd rather play with my trucks than starin' at what you've got."

The seven boys frowned. Several were sucking weeds, and Jumbo offered a bite from a large Tootsie Role bar. A couple did, and nodded, but no one spoke.

Finally Suck said, "Based on some of these wild 8-page bibles we've seen there has to be a heck of a lot more going on with one of these days than just talking about a crack. I bet the whole deal is figuring out what that crack is all about."

"Yep, we know our peckers are probably half of the bargain, because things for us get hard pretty fast, but the worst of it is we don't know how the two sides get together," Hotshot almost softly mumbled.

"I don't know how we will get any honest news about this thing with girls," Catfish wistfully said. "Where in the world will we ever learn it?"

"In the back seat of '39 Chevy like my brother says he did," Beaner smirked.

"Yeah, but I'd like to know something serious 'fore I crawl into the back seat with some big boobed babe," Jumbo said, and laughed with several of the others.

"What is really crazy for me is that when my big sister got married last year, I heard my mom tell her in the next room that men are dirty, and they will make her life a 'deep agony.' And she will have to have sex with her husband, and then she will have about ten kids with one more baby after another. Believe it or not, I heard my mom say it just like that," Booby uttered quickly.

"I heard almost the same thing at my house," Hotshot said. "My mom was talking about one of the mothers a few doors away. She said that when she got married about 1932, she had a lot of pain, and finally had to go to the hospital. The doctor said she was going to have a baby in about ten minutes. She said she thought the baby was coming to their home because a stork was flying in to bring it to her. She cried and told my mom this stork lie was the most terrible thing she had ever heard."

"You think the stork flew to the hospital and left it there for her," Dink said, blown over in his own words.

"No, you ding dong, no, she realized that the stork was a big, phony lie," Hotshot almost yelled.

"Have any of you other moms or dads told you anything about this thing called sex? It's so damn mysterious I guess we will probably do something really wrong." Suck said. "We've just heard two sad shocks from you guys, but my folks have never told anything like that. The only thing they told me to not mess around with any girls and to behave. And then my mom told me I would never get to heaven if I ever do any bad thing with any pretty girls. The problem for me is, when I snap the back of a girls bra or get a feel with her boobs in the cloakroom, something wild happens to my pecker, and I don't give a hoot about ever worrying again over going to heaven. Boy's, I'll worry about goin' to heaven when I'm a whole lot older."

They smiled and nodded, but did not laugh. In fact, it was deadly quiet. A few birds and a distant train engine were the only thing going on right now. Fishing was even totally out of their minds. In fact several had pulled in their lines, and were just sitting, staring or talking, because this was the first time any of them had ever gotten this deep before.

"So this thing about a baby is carried over from a stork from somewhere else is just a big lie," Beaner commented. "Think about this. We all know about the terrible problems of pigeons and starlings at the park or St. John's tower. Well, if storks were delivering babies in hospitals from Timbuktu to Peoria, they would all be covered with bird shit. You know there were a lot more crazy lies that everyone of us has had to learn when we were kids, only to find out that it was bullshit,"

"Our family and friends have been pulling too many jokes. This stork thing is just as phony as when we had to understand about who Santa Claus really is," Catfish frowned again. "Can you believe that they convinced us that one fat old man in a red union suit delivered toys to every kid in the whole world?"

"Yeah, in a little sled with flying reindeer no less," Beaner added, with an incredulous smirk.

"If somebody had a whole squadron of B-29's, they couldn't deliver toys to the whole world," Booby said.

"Well, what about the Easter Bunny? I can't believe I ever thought a white rabbit could hop all over creation laying chocolate eggs in baskets filled with fake green grass," Hotshot retorted indignantly.

"Or the tooth fairy when our first teeth fell out? That sure turned out to be just another fake. Wow, we were suckers!" Jumbo exclaimed, and then spat again.

"I've got another one that is just as worse," Catfish blurted. "Now we don't buy the crap about a stork, how about the story that some of these babies come from watermelons seeds that our mom's swallowed?"

"Yeah, I mean how ridiculous can moms and dads get?" Suck said, and shook his head.

"You are right," Hotshot agreed. "When I found out that it takes nine months to have a baby everybody here would have to be born in April or May because watermelon season in Illinois lasts only to late in August. I don't think women save watermelon seeds like it was some kind of pill to raise kids."

All but five of them quickly nodded. "You sure are smart, Hotshot. I'd never have figured out that," Dink said, with undisguised admiration. Then he added, "It sounds like everything our parents have told us is just bullshit."

Jumbo had been unusually quiet with the conversation, but hearing Dink's compliment to Hotshot caused an immediate reaction. "You're right, it all gets back to the problem of what you can believe or not, whether it's really true or just one more lie. My mom and dad don't go to church at all. How about what my dad said when he told me that a lot of this stuff some of your folks believe, is even more foolish. If the Easter Bunny, and Santa Claus, and the Tooth Fairy are fake, my dad says God and Jesus and Noah are just as silly and untrue."

With that the two Catholic boys instantly crossed themselves, and Booby blurted, "Holy Mother of God, I didn't say that, he did."

"I didn't even think about it. Stop that kind of talk," Beaner commanded. "Just hearing it will get me an additional zillion 'Hail Mary' and 'Our Father' next time. I have to go to confession next Saturday afternoon."

"Wow. Me, too," Booby replied. "You better shut up like that, Jumbo, or you'll go to hell for sure. Protestants like you kind of screw up the country."

"I'm not even a member of a church, let alone something called a Protestant," Jumbo rushed. "My dad went into the Navy for three years in the big war. He said he only joined one thing, not two. He doesn't even like to go to church no matter which church we're talking about. And I damn sure don't want to go no matter what matters, either."

"Wait a minute," Hotshot urged. "We are not going to have some darn argument every time we talk about Jesus. I don't know what to say or believe about some of the church's stuff either, but if your folk's make you go, go, and if they don't care, don't go. It's that simple, right?"

All of the guys nodded, and then grabbed their brown bag with sandwiches and canteens. Hungry boys could quickly forget about sex and religion as fast as anyone else. At least almost everyone else, regardless of their age, sex or nationality. This strange conversation was just a lot more complicated than they expected, but thankfully food certainly rang a hypothetical dinner bell for these seven boys.

CHAPTER 19

▼

THE QUEST

August and Jane Peterson could easily be America's first couple who ever ran a grade school from top to bottom. August was simply called "Gus" by adults and "Mr. Gus" by the students. He was Bradford Grade School's only janitor. His wife was Aunt Jane to her friends, and Mrs. Peterson to the same students, because she was the schools principal.

After many years, both of them decided to retire, and that is when the principal took a volunteer job just for her own enjoyment. Aunt Jane was now called "The Story Lady" at the town's library. Mr. Gus was thrilled that he would never have to load the coal furnace again to heat the school all winter. He and everyone else thought that the smoke and coal smells down in the basement were as close to Hades as anyone ever dreamed.

In addition, for the past few years, eight special kids still came back to the library week after week no matter what they heard from Aunt Jane's storybooks because she also taught Bradford's piano students. Since 1946, Philip Carlton had been learning to play here because his older sister had done this plan for a number of years, and his parents pressured him into the program. Amazingly, he surprised everyone because he was getting better and better almost every month. He never told his pals much more than it was a 'pain in the butt,' however, he knew he not only liked playing the piano, he sometimes surprised even himself.

Parents interested in the library's story telling day all over town, and dozens of others who lived in farms within 15 miles or so were thrilled to bring their kids whenever this dear lady gave her weekly story telling experiences. As many kids who wanted to come could sit down, behave, and cross their legs because The Story Lady was now going to fill their minds with joy and wonder.

The seven guys who were now going to be in 8th grade in nearly three months no longer wanted to attend Mrs. Peterson's special story programs, because they felt they were too old to be sitting on the floor with a bunch of much younger children. If they were honest, however, a few of them would still have loved to hear her amazing stories. The big problem was they were embarrassed to sit beside a second grader.

One interesting occurrence last year was so vivid to them it still stuck in their minds. They heard about one of the most engaging tales she told the older kids that day. It was a child's version of Don Quixote when the challenges he and his friendly companion encountered. When the story ended Aunt Jane led them to discuss why something like a mission or pursuit in their own lives would bring them into a much higher level of their more important aspect of life. But most of these boys let this slip away in their minds because playing basketball or hockey, hunting turtle doves with their B B Guns, or just plain fishing seemed to be a lot more important for them. Except one. That young man was going to play his very first musical composition.

Not only had he been intrigued about some idea that he or even some of the others might actually plan a new mission that would make them better, stronger, or more important. It was because of the great Cervantes story, Philip convinced Jumbo that he would be leading the first serious exploration these boys would attempt to do. However, he would not be riding bikes with the other six, because this coming Saturday he was going to play something remarkable that he created himself at this year's piano recital. The name that he chose was 'The Quest.'

Occasional incidents like this from Suck might become more and more numerous as he got older and smarter. Unfortunately, his ego almost always created internal issues with the other six. To solve some of the doubts, he just dropped a word or thought into their minds. He didn't care if they began acting like they had dreamed up the new idea themselves. Even now he realized that his father was a very important businessman in this part of Illinois, and someday he wanted to be or do the exact same thing.

It's why the second Saturday of June was now going to be D-Day 2 for six tough commandos from Bradford. For one new pianist, however, he was on his own.

The day before all this was going to begin, all seven of them were sitting up in The Laughin' Tree, though no one was laughing now. "The reason why we are here is I've been thinking about an idea for our Joe Bonomo Strong Men's Club. What we need is a mission. Some new challenge that we can accomplish." Jumbo's seriousness captivated the others immediately. Even Suck was acting like he was hearing this plan for the first time.

"You mean like what we talked about a few months ago from Mrs. Peterson in that story about those two guys who tried to find their search," Dink asked intently. "It was really neat. Remember when Mrs. Peterson told us that story at Suck's birthday a year and a half ago?"

"Yeah, Dink, that's exactly what I'm talking about. "Maybe we ought to call it 'The Quest' because yesterday Suck told me that he wrote a new piano song, and he liked our idea so much he named his tune from it. I think it sounds pretty good," said Jumbo.

"Oh, come on Suck, as much as you like to brown-nose teachers I can't believe you have now even named a damn song. I'm glad I've been in St Johns for the past seven years and haven't had to watch you spend the whole year sucking ass instead of studying," Beaner sneered.

"Yeah, but we're all going to put up with this crap from him for the next four years in high school," Catfish chortled. "Besides, what was the name of that guy who got into a sword fight with a windmill? I think his name was Dan Coyote."

Hotshot smiled. "That's close, but the man wasn't named for a wild dog. Besides, who cares? If Suck is playing his piano tomorrow, we'll be running around in the woods with a ton of fun. He'll probably have Mrs. Peterson so proud she'll pat everyone's back."

Suck looked at each of them and laughed. He was so contented with himself right now he could have blown them over with what was really happening in the next twenty-four hours. But he just smiled good-naturedly at the rest of the guys. "Well, if a smart-ass guy like me can try to bump a B into an A, what's wrong with that?"

So few of the others were accustomed to even get an occasional A, they begrudgingly soon backed off with smatterings of uneasy grunts and false chuckles.

"An A," Booby muttered. "Who the heck gets an A besides you and Hotshot?"

"Okay, let's call it The Quest," Jumbo said rapidly. "When we get there to the south side of the bridge we'll go into two groups. Three will go on one side of the Mighty Spoon, and the others will do the other. We can try to find a better place to go swimming when the water gets higher."

"But what is the point of calling this thing a quest. Finding a deeper swimming hole shouldn't be that hard, either," Booby frowned.

"Yeah, I love to go back to the river once or twice a week together there, but why don't we just go fishing?" Dink said, and Catfish agreed.

"Besides, the main thing we ought to do is hunting for the closed down coal mine," Hotshot said evenly. "That's where we might find the counterfeiting gang's printing plates. Remember?"

"Wow, I thought we had forgotten about that thing," Catfish said.

"How about if any of you ever heard whether Sheck ever has found anything about the gang or those metal plates that we talked about back in the fall? He lives so close to where I bet we will find the coal mine." Hotshot raised his eyebrow, and reinforced his same questions.

"Not that I know of," Jumbo replied. "Back then we thought we were going to do a super job of spying about Sheck. But now nobody ever wonders about what else he does except growing vegetables. 'Course, if he's gone to being a crook and is printing his own money, or when my dad said he heard about a guy running a whiskey still fifteen years ago back in the same woods. Maybe we ought to check it out." He realized that his so-called idea about the Quest plan had really been dreamed up by Suck a few days ago. He was now almost over his head since several of the 'regulars' were also not too high about his first priority. It was a good time to create a shaky Plan B. "Guys, there are several good places, and other ideas that we ought to check-out, but I'm goin' tomorrow. Are you?" Jumbo said defiantly.

All but two quickly concurred. Suck knew he wasn't going anyway, but Hotshot hesitated. "How can we climb down to the mine if we can't find where it is? All of us think Sheck Dye knows where it is 'cause he digs for coal there somewhere near Harper's Woods. This place is in several hundred acres of thick trees and jungle pits. All I want to say is if we can't ever find it, let's just go up to Sheck's trolley, and ask him."

"Okay," Jumbo said, "Let's hunt for the mine, *and* we can look for a better, deeper swimming hole."

"One that has some vines or we just have to hang some rope up there. Swinging and dropping into the river is as neat as anything except when Tarzan goes in to stab a crocodile. That movie last winter so good," said Catfish, and shook his head.

"Guess good old Sheck is not doing any crazy things like this, but I still bet he might know the best place to find the mine," Beaner added.

"Well, that's what we'll be doing tomorrow. Let's ride our bikes at 9:00 a.m. At lease Suck will be doing something else while we're doing a serious job. He'll just be playing the 'peeanner' at Aunt Jane's house." This was Jumbo's silly way pronouncing it disrespectfully.

"You guys go to the river. Some of the teachers might be coming to the recital. Maybe I'll get some tips on how to get a few more A's in school this year, if Miss Fate comes." Suck started laughing as he finished his words, and the others smiled, but were secretly jealous as they all climbed down from the huge elm tree.

Without saying anything, each boy walked up to each other and quietly offered the Joe Bonamo secret strong-arm salute that Jumbo created last year as part of the club's ritual. A feeling of euphoric relief now replaced the tense confrontation of only seconds before. Though one of them would not be riding over the 'hard road' tomorrow. Philip Carlton was planning on a much more impressive achievement that any of them had ever done. These six boys were simply going on a quest, but Philip was going to perform the very one he had created.

Next morning, six of the gang had already arrived at the river's bridge and wandered across the northern section of Harper's Woods along the Mighty Spoon. They did not know it, but this is the day Hotshot would realize that finding the long lost coal mine might be sooner than even they had hoped.

One hour later, a little before ten o'clock, Aunt Jane welcomed eight Bradford girls and boys to show their families just how much they had accomplished. Miss Fate, the lady who would be teaching at their last year of grade school studies was not there, but Miss Edna Wallace walked in as the first participant, an nine year old girl, walked up to the piano and began to play. Miss Wallace looked right in the eyes of Philip, and winked. Her job for him was over, but he was now very involved in every aspect of his own life's future. The pressure began to rise.

As the next to the last piano pupil finished her piece, Suck looked over to his mother and father, and gave them a thin smile. Two weeks earlier Suck stood up as that session was over, and looked at Aunt Jane. "I have written my very first piano musical composition, Miss Jane. I made this up after a bunch of months while I was practicing so many hours. I won't tell you what the name of it is yet, and I won't play it until next week's session recital because you are such a special person to me."

"Someday, Philip, you may wear a gleaming tuxedo, and be the only piano soloist playing your own concerto that you yourself created. Eighty excellent musicians in a major symphony are now in your beck and call. I hope I live so long to stand and applaud at such a magnificent experience. However, I hope you don't feel like you have really created a true concerto. I'll be thrilled if it actually isn't quite *that* big," and Aunt Jane smiled. However, her unplanned statement wasn't to be any extra pressure for him, but it certainly was now. Both realized that no one had ever heard anything like this in Bradford.

Aunt Jane was as solid as a woman could be, considering her age and height. So what, some folks said, she was probably fifty pounds heavier than she probably should be. Her hair was now filled with silver. But her eyes were filled with both joy and satisfaction, because four decades of hundreds of young students in Bradford were now productive and successful adults all over the United States. Thanks to her and Sister Regina, Miss Vanzant, Miss Wallace, and dozens of other conscientious teachers in this great town, a new America was growing and thriving because the terrible war that ended four years ago was over.

Now, the big moment she spoke about was about to begin. As he stepped up to the bench, he looked back over at her and nodded. She was a very special lady to everyone there, but at this moment Philip Carlton realized that God almighty and Jane Peterson could be one in the same.

One, two, three. After he mentally counted those magical numbers, he inhaled through his nostrils, and instantly caressed the ivory keys as if they were eighty-eight silent children who were in his total control. It began so gentle and soft that nineteen people did not even breathe. But within ten to fifteen seconds the sounds not only went higher, the music filled the living room, as it grew stronger and louder. His eyes were now closed, but his face was glowing, and tilted his head as he moved his neck and shoulders with the movements. Several surging thrusts rose slowly and methodically to a thrilling crescendo. Though his eyes were still closed, he smiled and reached his plan to bring a discerning, triple repeating conclusion. He ended it with a final key as soft as it began with his opening touch. In just one minute and forty seconds, Philip stunned everyone in the room, including himself.

For two or three seconds nothing happened. It was because each was so caught up in their own musical experience. However, appreciation instantly now filled the entire room, not with music. This was a genuine ovation.

As the electrifying remarks and applause subsided, Aunt Jane stood up, clasped her hands, and spoke. "Oh, my goodness, Philip, you have thrilled us in a enchanting achievement. Ladies and gentlemen, and girls and boys, I told you that Philip might give us this great surprise today. You can all go back home, and remember this day. And I hope that all of the younger students will also realize that you can also start creating a new challenge for yourselves. I know Mr. and Mrs. Carlton are ecstatic right now, and we are sure of that, but all of you have heard some wonderful piano music from the other students. Next season will even be better and better. Thank you for such a wonderful morning. God bless us all."

One by one the kids and their parents departed, after enjoying peanut butter cookies and chilled Kool-Aid. As the Carlton's and their son shook hands with several of the remaining people, Miss Wallace walked over and said, "Thank you, Philip. You have given me such a joy today, I am renewed and refreshed about being a teacher…at least for one more year." At that everyone laughed, but she also added, "You have touched us deep into our minds and our hearts, young man. You told me you want to be Chief Illiwek in Champaign when you go to college in five or six years. Now you may be playing on a Steinway piano in a huge auditorium, instead of Memorial stadium. Or both."

Everyone still there laughed and nodded, and the boy called 'Suck' suddenly was abashed. Mr. Carlton solved the minor moment. "Thank you all so very much. Philip's mother and I are very happy about what he did, but the main thing we want him to do for sure is graduate from the University of Illinois with a degree in engineering. I would be very proud of that, because his grandfather told me the exact, same words about thirty years ago."

"So true, so true. Philip, I'll tell Sallie Vanzant that one year from September she is going to get you for algebra, geometry, and all the rest of what she teaches for the next four years," Miss Wallace said, and she would have quickly made her adieu, but she paused and asked one more question. "Philip, I didn't see you read one note on any sheet of music paper. Did you memorize your entire composition?"

"Uh, yes," Philip hesitated. "Ma'am, I don't know how to write music on paper. I guess, all I seem to do is create it, and remember those melodies down deep in my mind."

Everyone was now suddenly dazed. Aunt Jane was so shocked she lifted her right hand and stroked her chin. "Philip, I knew you played this entire piece with no music on paper, but you created this by yourself, and didn't write it anywhere?"

"That's the blessed truth, Aunt Jane. I play it from the memory in my mind. Quite honestly, I know all I can do is play notes that are already written in the book you teach. I don't know how to write notes I dream," he said softly.

Things were as quiet right now as when he was previously about to start playing. This remarkable news churned over in their thoughts so thoroughly, and several folks simply said one or two simultaneous words, "Astonishing," or "Remarkable." The few remaining folks seemed that the best idea was to say goodbye, and leave.

As it ended, Philip and his parents were the last to go. When they were waving as they walked over to their car, he climbed into the back seat. Surprisingly, his mother said, "Son, I want you to move up to the right front seat. You have earned a new, wonderful promotion."

When he stepped out, and moved around it, she gave him a quick, but sincere hug. He held her back just as strong. They switched their seats, and stared at each other for a couple of seconds. Mr. Carlton observed the entire brief experience, and simply smiled as he looked over at both of them.

It was so poignant for all no more words were spoken. Suck looked over through the window, but he was not really seeing anything. His mind was now back in the Spoon River basin and six pals who maybe were doing ten thousand different things that he wished he were doing right now. Then he glanced over to both of his parents, and said, "The Spoon River is a special place for us. When I dreamed up the song called 'The Quest' what I was really thinking whenever I started playing it, that river is a wonderful place. Like my song, the river begins kind of slow and quiet with small streams and brooks, and then some bubbling springs roll in with little waterfalls, and then it grows up a lot more into a big, beautiful river we call it the Mighty Spoon."

"That's incredible, son," his father almost whispered. His mother also agreed softly. He quickly glanced back at his wife, but their thoughts were equally subdued.

How a 13-year-old boy challenged their entire minds as deep as he had, caused both of them to suddenly recall several verses in St. Luke, Chapter 2. Driving home only took five or six minutes for the Carlton's, but this day's experience would be permanently stored in their personal chronicles the same way those two other parents named Mary and Joseph did a long time ago.

CHAPTER 20

▼

WHISTLING RINGS

"We've run about a quarter mile from the bridge. I see them on the west side of the river. Believe it or not, some weeds are already six feet high over there. The only way I can even know it is watching the tops of the fuzzy stuff. It moves when they walk." Whenever Booby gave them some news, he was so short, he always stood up on anything, from a stump to a fence.

Jumbo nodded, and then slid his Lone Ranger Whistling Ring off of his finger. The original, movable back fragment had now fused, and it was almost too small to even fit his left pinky. The color on both the ring and his finger were a new color version they all called crud green. Actually, they were part soap, part mustard, part colored mud, and all gross. A tiny piece of the gunk fell onto the ground when he pulled it off. A little more of it got stuck in his mouth, so he had to spit it out.

When something as serious as a real ring that makes a neat noise when you blow over it, things like this are a minor blip to a thirteen year old boy.

Unfortunately, girls and mothers are stunned that something this nasty could wind up in a boys mouth. Probably the worst realization for them is things like this can be also ignored by virtually any age in a grown man.

On the third try a loud whistle zinged across the entire river. Jumbo had hit the jackpot.

Hotshot, Catfish, and Beaner tried to see through the moving weeds, but it was much taller than they. "You blow yours, Beaner, I can't remember where I put mine," Hotshot whispered.

Beaner immediately slid his off, and blew four straight times, but no sound came out. "Darn it," he said as he shook his head. "Mine is full of too much soap. My Mom makes me wash my hands even before eating. I bet I've got enough wash bar stuff jammed in this I could probably just wear this thing, and use it to clean myself in the bathtub tonight."

"Well, this is a pickle," Hotshot muttered. "Jumbo and the other two are over on the west side, and two of us can't find ours, and your ring's wheel is jammed. We better work this out a lot better next time. We all worked out a pretty elaborate series of messages two or three weeks ago, and, stop," he suddenly interrupted himself.

Across the river a piercing, two-time, whistling sound could be heard for about four or five seconds, and then it was silent. "Guys, that's Jumbo's emergency number," Catfish urged, "We've got to either imitate some animal sound or just yell. But we can't be ignoring them."

"You're right," Hotshot expressed. He quickly started to howl as if he was a wolf.

The three boys on the West Bank looked at each other and then paused. All started giggling and then were relieved. Dink and Booby then started laughing so hard and loud, Jumbo had to yell at them. "I know it's funny, but we've got to not make a lot noise here. This is serious, Dink! I am going to howl back to them." His third long wailing cry rolled over the river.

With in a couple of seconds, one more wolf sound bounced back from Hotshot.

"That means we are supposed to ford the river and meet with the other three on the East Side, right, Jumbo?" Booby asked.

"Yep, let's sashay right over there, pilgrim," Jumbo said as close as he could imitate John Wayne. They each laughed, and with that they stood up, and began to walk closer to the edge of the river.

Dink started giggling again. "I know I shouldn't be laughing at crazy things like this, but we've already made enough noise here from six boys that we better say, thank you Lord that no wild Cherokees or Apaches still live around places like this.

"Hail Mary and saints preserve us, Dink," Booby said. "The six of us would already be scalped by now."

"That's for sure. We might as well throw those stupid rings away," Jumbo agreed.

"I don't like that blasted cereal anyway," Dink uttered. "When we each wanted a ring like this it took two box tops, and twenty-five cents cash money. My mom said if I don't eat that crap she had to buy, she's going to give the breakfast crapola to *me* in an enema."

Both of the others laughed. "I had one of those blasts about two years ago, and I wouldn't want to ever have anything like that again," Booby replied.

"How about the Captain Midnight Secret Spy Decoder Set that we got from buying three bottles of Ovaltine," Jumbo said. "After doing it seven straight shows that gave us those hidden numbers on the radio I turned the decoder just like I was supposed to do, and all I got was to drink more Ovaltine. Now that's a major, big time enema."

"The white belt that all of us got from the Lone Ranger radio show glowed in the dark. It was pretty neat, though," Dink retorted. "I scared my two brothers one night when I was just wearing my underwear. They thought I was a ghost."

"I told Sister about that story with the glowing belt I got, but she told me to stay away from that kind of thing," Booby said, then continued. "She thought it might be fooling around with Satan. She said if any boys have a 7th grade body, and a 6th grade brain, you better be studying a lot more and goofing around a lot less."

"Okay, you two," Jumbo said. "Let's pull off our high tops and socks, and roll up our overalls. We're going over the Mighty Spoon." As they laughed simultaneously each started to go over to the other side, but Jumbo led the way. For a stream like this, it was more like shuffling across a rivulet than going across a serious river. Within ten or fifteen miles north of here, the tiny brooks and little creeks that slithered along there was how Spoon River began.

"Well, guys," Hotshot said sarcastically, "Good to see you again. For two hours wandering around the northern tip of the river, it's been kind of boring. If we go any farther up that way we might as well forget about going swimming again. Maybe we could just go skipping river rocks."

Jumbo glanced over at Hotshot, and looked over to the thick woods below them. They briefly stared into each other eyes. Within just a few years at Bradford High School, these two could be colliding on the football field to see who will be the next quarterback, but no one had given any thought about that yet.

"Why not have our sandwich bags, and eat right now?" Jumbo offered. "Then we can walk back under the bridge, and climb up to say hello to Sheck Dye? He might give us the secret to where the cave is."

"That's great," Hotshot said immediately. He smiled and realized that Jumbo was not running the show now, even if it sounded as if he was. As usual, these hungry boys devoured every bit of food and candy within six minutes. Then they headed south along the river's east side to see what might happen here today. One by one, each thought about Suck, and his piano program an hour earlier, but then they forgot all about it. These woods for them were just as special as a boy they read about in second grade called Christopher Robin.

Suddenly a loud, strange, ripping sound echoed through several tall trees as they walked through them.

"Beaner is back to killing mosquitoes," Catfish said as he laughed.

Fortunately, the smell was also disintegrating, and the others just shook their heads, and smiled.

"That was pretty loud," Booby said.

"And really stinks," added Jumbo.

"Bet you guys remember watching one of the town's Saturday double feature movie where 'Eyes and the Ears' showed that huge boat called Queen Mary or some other name like that," Dink said."

"Yeah, when it arrived into New York City, it let a blast so loud it shook the theatre. And people standing around in the town had to cover their ears," Catfish said. "When it happened in the movie news, some of us laughed, but Beaner cheered."

All of the guys were shaking their heads or just laughed about the continuing story of Beaner's flatulence, as they meandered through the forest. Booby looked back at Beaner, and said, "Did Suck tell you what happened a couple of weeks ago, when he rode out to Jeannie's house with his mom visiting them with him?"

"He likes Jeannie," said Hotshot.

"He likes about ten girls," Jumbo came back.

"That's for sure," Dink added.

"Shut up you, guys, what did Booby ask about Suck going there?" Beaner asked.

"I think it's pretty funny," Booby replied right back. "Suck and Jeannie were standing out in her farm yard, and ten or twenty big cows were just outside the barn. He said one of them blasted a long fart while they were leaning against the fence. Suck said boys laugh and girls either look somewhere else, or say something to change the moment. Or, they really just get mad at a boy. Well, Suck said it lasted for about thirty seconds, and then he got embarrassed because he giggled a couple of times and was kind of shuffling. He said he asked her if the cow was playing a song."

Everybody laughed, and they stopped walking.

"He said she didn't laugh for sure, and she said folks here simply get kinda used to stuff like this living on a farm. Then he said he told her that Beaner would sure be jealous if he heard it."

Beaner exploded. "You think Suck said that to her? Oh, rats. I can't believe it. She'll probably never talk to me again. Suck says some of the most worthless, rotten, stories." He looked down in the path. "I am a champion farter, but I don't think it's fair to be in any contest with a cow. Especially a big cow."

"Don't sweat it, Beaner," Dink offered. "Just a few months ago Suck heard something stupid I said, and he told me if they had a new award for the dumb shit of the decade, I'd win for sure."

"I hope he screws up his piano playing," Beaner mumbled.

"Let's go see Sheck, if he's home," Hotshot said. Each picked up their backpacks, and started along the river. The highest hill was covered with big trees and thick jagged branches with lots of foliage. Suddenly, Hotshot yelled, "Look at this part. I just saw some coal dust and tiny chunks of it. Let's cut some of the limbs and jungle stuff, and see what that hill goes up to."

Immediately, several of them followed him right into the mess. Each opened their pocketknives, and helped clear the path. Within seconds all of them were doing it because Jumbo was now not even in the plan.

"Wow, look at this. The little path is being used more than we never knew. Holy smokes, we've hit the jackpot," Hotshot exclaimed.

They all stared at the hidden section in the 'jungle' as the lower part of the hill had secretly been cleared enough to be able to dig good, black coal.

"My gosh," Catfish whispered. "This has to be where Sheck digs this stuff."

It was deadly quiet for about ten seconds, and then Jumbo decided to eat some crow. "Congratulations, Hotshot, you found the one thing we've been talking about since that football game a long time ago."

Hotshot just nodded. "But Jumbo, you dreamed up the Quest today. So we're even," and they both quickly smiled. The other four cheered, and they all started hitting high fives together.

"You know, I bet that this is just the bottom of the coal mine, where Sheck was able to dig enough just for heating his trolley and to cook his food. Somewhere up here on this hill I bet they have closed the main mine. Let's not mess with this or Sheck will be really mad if anybody screws this up."

"Bet we don't have enough time to start trying to find the top part. It's going on three o'clock now," Jumbo said. "But the next time we ride back out here, we'll just keep hanging there long enough, and boys, we'll find it!" A few seconds earlier he had passed a penny Tootsie Roll to each of the boys as a present, and each was savoring it. When Jumbo finished this sentence, he proudly spat as loud as he could.

"Yep," Hotshot said, "We're doing a neat deal here. And we've still got enough time in July and August to make the discovery."

"I hope we find some murdered crooks who killed some sad, old bodies that have been piled high in bones," Beaner gushed.

"And the counterfeiters," Booby said.

"And the fake money plates," Catfish agreed.

"Wouldn't it be great it if some cutthroat pirates had dug coins of gold around here?" Dink's statement stopped everything. All of the other five boys stared immediately at him.

"Where in the heck would we ever have heard about ancient pirates? Especially here since there's never been a pirate ship in the middle of Illinois?" Jumbo frowned, and shook his hear. "Good lord, Dink, you *are* the dumb shit of the decade."

Everyone, especially Dink, laughed at that as they started walking south to the bridge. "Okay, there probably *aren't* any pirates around here, and I guess we'll never see any real dragons either. I just like to listen to "Let's Pretend" every Saturday morning on the radio. Some of the neatest disasters happen to brave boys and beautiful girls, and we missed it today. I was thinking about something like the station would have done. Maybe we ought to plan to ride here any day except Saturday, and listen to that show so we won't miss it."

"That's a smart thing you've said, Dink," said Booby, and then he laughed. "Not *all* of your stuff is ridiculous. Besides, I love 'Let's Pretend', too."

"Me, too," said Jumbo.

"I bet we all do," said Beaner.

"Too bad they haven't figured out how to record a radio station program when we want to hear it," Hotshot nodded.

"These records that my mom and dad play are kind of scratchy when my dad records some of us," Dink said. "Ours are either 78 pounds or speed, but I don't know what it means."

"I've heard that, too," said Jumbo. "Oh, well, let's not be dreaming about new kinds of gadgets any more. Now that the war is finally over for good, the stuff we have now may be as good as we will ever get."

These six boys were excited and fulfilled. As they arrived at the bridge, their bike ride started up the long hill going east to their homes. This was the best day they had ever had together. After they pushed up to the top, several men were cooking fish in the front yard's corner shed at the American Legion building.

While heading toward Johnston's Gas Station and Café, they were now far enough out of the three volunteer's voices, Catfish shouted. "Wait when we tell Suck what we've been doing today. Bet he'll be sick, 'cause he probably didn't even play the piano music right."

CHAPTER 21

▼

THE LITTLE LEPRECHAUN, THE SKINNY BOY, AND THE FAT MAN

Wednesday, June 15 was as perfect a day anyone would hope summer could be. However, two times a day controlled chaos entered the village. A huge and ancient two or three car train arrived around eight o'clock in the morning, and almost magically reappeared in the opposite direction in the general time of five that afternoon.

Some people called it the Milk Run. Others said it was the Spur Line. All of the kids just called it the Doodle Bug. Dink's cousin Ruthe and her friend Sharon one day rode on the train from Bradford to Brimfield to visit one of her aunts. They happily sat in the caboose, except it must have taken four hours to get forty miles. Anyone who needed a ride could do it, but the challenge was enough that few others ever did it again.

No matter how slow it went, however, everyone felt that this chugging engine was filled with an astounding mass of steel and brass belching steam, smoke, and noise. It roared and growled like a great beast. When eruptions of every size, shape, and smell happened everyone shrugged, but it certainly split their quiet sounds in the prairie countryside. Whatever the weather was doing, this engine created it's own personal pandemonium. Flecks of soot from dark gray thunder caused steam and fumes spewing out of the vents on each side. Thick, ashen smoke continuously churned out as it rumbled into town. But somehow it was the shortest train in Illinois. It usually only had one or two box cars, and was followed by an antique caboose that kids thought could have been hit by Indians with bows and arrows back in the olden days.

The Rocket and The Zephyr both were from another time. Actually, they were now in a new century. All Doodle Bug did was make such a racket coming into towns like Bradford, it must have come out of Hell at the crack of dawn every morning, and disappear back there every night.

"Someday I want to travel this train and go see what the world looks like," Catfish said in combination of wonder and awe. He and his other six friends were riding their bikes that morning. They had already planned to have a great baseball game on the north side of town. The ballpark was about two hundred yards away. In a town this small, the difference between north and south on the only Main Street was seconds away for either direction.

"Huh," Jumbo grunted. "It's so slow if you ride for twenty years you might get all the way to Galesburg. But we better never try and drop empty cans that we filled up with rocks on the engine,"

"That's for sure," Beaner added. "When we tried to see if it could blow right through the bridge, that engineer slammed his train and started screaming. Gilly even said he would arrest us if we did that again."

Engineers all seemed to wear identical stripped overalls and starched white caps, and their firemen wore blue caps and red bandannas around their necks. Some people felt the reason firemen wore this was so they could pull it off for emergency flagging. No matter here, because both of them were wary. They must have sensed that bridges in towns like this were a dangerous gauntlet. Thankfully, kids who tried to dive-bomb chugging engines with cans of rocks had that now out of everyone's plans forever.

"Lot's of us walk along the rails just for the fun of it, but where do you think Doodle Bug goes now? Dink pushed up his glasses, and his usual questions were almost frowned perpetually.

"Who cares?" Booby asked. "Let's play work-up."

That's all it took to get seven boys racing down the short hill from the bridge.

Bill Dorgan watched the boys zip through the corner between Bucher and Sullivan's Hardware, and Mowbray's Clothing Store. His wife Daisy was already warming up the great frying pan where countless pounds of beef were created for Maid-Rites.

Everyone seems to know that Bill's routine was as solid and steady as a dollar bill. Actually, the value of the dollar was not as good as what Bill Dorgan wore from day to day. The fact that he often put on and wore any of his amazing collection of personal paraphernalia, Bill and the huge Grandfather Clock that stood inside his store's front door were right on time. Even if he did wear an occasional strange outfit, his aprons were still identical to what he'd wore for sixty years.

Today he decided that one of his periodically variance was wearing his famous coonskin coat. It was now hanging out on the front of the Clock to remind him that he was going to wear it at two o'clock all over Main Street. That also told anyone else who walks in before that time they should buy a double-dip Safe-T cone, chocolate soda or ice cream shake because it was *hot outside*. People knew he was as smart as a fox, and made the best ice cream and sandwiches in this part of the state, but most didn't know that he was also one of the best advertising men since Leo Burnett opened his agency in downtown Chicago.

If you walked into his soda shop and café, and, if he looked up to see you, he'd say, "Whatdaya want?" He was so incredible that even grownups put up with anything from him to just have a good meal and a lot of laughs. Some of his most hilarious wisecracks was to tie into singing one of the radio commercials.

What he sang had no aspect of what he cooked or made, but he might be able to sell some of the products he memorized. He could instantly make a fog hound sound that pushed Lifebouy Soap. Or another soap called Lava that reminded how to spell it and most important buy it with L. A. V. A, L. A.V. A. Or he would imitate the train's chugging sound that sang Broma Seltzer. Or called "Bob White, Bob White," for Rinso White soap. Or "You'll Wonder Where the Yellow Went," with Pepsodent toothpaste. Or "Halo Everybody, Halo. He could even sing the entire Pepsi jingle that started "Twelve full ounces…"

Some of his crazy things were just meant for men. One of his favorite ads was about the Lucky Strike tobacco ads that pushed L. S. M. F. T. He would wink to some of the older men, and they laughed because they knew it really meant great women had big breasts.

As he was scrubbing some of the tall glasses that had been already dirtied this morning, Clare Breen walked in. Her father was the editor of the Bradford Republican, and she was now a junior in college. But she was just working at the paper for the summer, and always loved to walk over to Dorgan's and have whatever her pocketbook could handle.

Bill looked up and immediately smiled. He knew Clare and her family were about as good as anyone in the town. For that matter, they were so loved by everyone, her dad could have been elected for any job he wanted in Stark County.

"Now, Bill, don't tell me again about that idiot thing I did five years ago," Clare said as she smiled brightly.

"Okay, I won't bring it up. But Cliff Mokler still laughs about you. Whatdaya want today?"

"Dad and I want four Maid-Rites please, and he gave me this dollar bill. If I need a couple of pennies for the tax I'll bring it back next time," she 'begged'.

"No problem. Mother will get them ready in a couple of jerks." He then flip-flopped back to the kitchen. Whatever happened back in this room was almost a mystery. Everyone knew that Daisy Dorgan had *never* washed the huge frying pan. She and her daughters who also cooked the hamburger beef felt that the reason it had such an incredible taste was because the pan had never been cleaned. Of course, if a cockroach or a hungry mouse got a bite or two of food when it was now turned off, the big pan might have bothered some of the family, but Bill and his youngest daughter Marge didn't give a hoot about any problems like that. Taste, taste, taste was the hidden secret, and they were never going to wreck a good thing.

As Clare sat in the wire-table benches and leaned against the counter top, she mused about that experience when she drove in to buy gas from the Mokler Station. She had just got in that year even before teenage kids had to take Drivers Training courses. When she pulled up to the pump, she had driven too far to reach the hose. Cliff told her to back up about five feet, but she said he would have to back it out because she didn't know how to go backwards. All she could do is go forward. Mr. Mokler kidded her every time she arrived in the station for anything.

After he handed the bag of sandwiches to Clare as she left, Bill walked around the front room counter and checked around in the side-room. This is where dancing and fun for high school kids was perfect. It also had two fascinating pinball machines that brought some kids who blew their money much, much faster than on even ice cream.

One of them was Suck. He was now the best pinballer in the entire town. Even high school kids were in awe of his ability. It was mainly that Suck had figured out how, if he slowly lifted the front legs so they could sit on his own two feet, it changed everything. This plan kept running for long minutes because the balls could avoid dropping down into the slots. The longer he held those metal balls to score more and more, he won enough free games in ten minutes that he could keep play as long as he wanted, all for just one nickel.

Bill shook his head. Deep in his devious mind he decided that this was the day he would reconnect the machinery that could even set a better tilt for either pinball machine. If it tilts and shuts itself off faster, Suck will hear one of his precious nickels has disappeared. He had been studying some brochures that came with the machines he bought several years ago. If he was right, Suck's fake game plan was going to sink just like the balls should drop. At least as fast as Bill Dorgan hoped it would happen.

"Please Lord, help me gain some weight. You know how skinny I am. Lord, I really want to be on the football team because our coach has bought enough old war tank helmets. We're going to play this fall. And Lord, I want to be on the heavyweight basketball team. I've been playing on the lightweight team for two years, and now I'm starting eighth grade. If I don't get heavier, I will be the first eighth grader who is only on the lightweight team. I bet you know all this, Lord. But you may be so busy you didn't know that today I am mailing this envelope to Mr. Charles Atlas. He is my last hope. I've been swallowing two bottles of fat juice, and it didn't add an ounce. I took a whole box of Ex-lax and all I got was diarrhea. The comic books say that Charles Atlas will turn 98-pound weaklings into to big, strong men. Jumbo has all of us called Joe Bonomo members, and I'm not one bit bigger or stronger there, either. Please, Lord! If you will help me get this Charles Atlas book I bet it will turn me into a real strong man. And, if you will do it, I will promise that I'll donate a nickel of my allowance to the Sunday School offering every week." Dink paused, and rubbed his chin. "Uh, how about every other week? Thank you dear God, amen."

With this long prayer, Dink folded his brief letter, licked both the envelope and a three-cent stamp, and then courageously walked right out of his front door. Mailing this attempt at Lee Finnegan's post office box was truly his final attempt to be a real strong man.

Later this same day on a warm afternoon, believe it or not, there was yet another new idea that someone else decided he, too, could have a dream come true.

The Fat Man was going to get a bath.

For many years Buck Ed Minister was the biggest enigma for two reasons. The first is that he weighed about 400 pounds or more, and apparently lived in his 1938 Plymouth two-door car. The second was the fact that no one seemed to know where, how or when he got here. Now everyone could realize that he was in or around Bradford a lot of the time. No one needed to actually see him that day, however, because folks could smell him as far as across the street.

Some retired men who enjoyed going into one of the town's three bars talked about him, but no one really wanted to spend much time trying to find out the history of this huge problem. Several felt that he was originally from Wyanet, another small town about twenty miles northwest from Bradford. Just last Saturday afternoon, "Dipstick" Downs, a man who had been the towns grease jockey since Henry Ford started building Model T's and then Model A's, 'Dip' was the busiest shade tree mechanic in town. Now he was just one of the good old men in the DogHouse, and broke up the group with this statement. "Buck Ed's belly button is so big and so dirty, I bet he could grow a cash crop on it."

Apparently Buck Ed was dealing all the time day or night as a 'professional' car trader, because he had a brother who also sold cars, and the family at one time owned some land in nearby Milo township. A few folks said that he also owned a set of buildings on the West Side of the Spoon River, and could drive down a lane that led to a graveled crossing. But nobody knew for sure about anything.

However, the two things Buck Ed wanted more than anything else was to actually get a good bath, and simply wash his own filthy clothes. Today magic was going to happen as he turned his car into Bill Derick and his family's farm. They lived there near the river, and for a number of years Buck Ed felt Bill was a very good friend. Even the Derick kids were always happy to see him drive in.

As Buck Ed was rolling into the farmyard, Bill smiled. A few days ago he heard that Buck Ed drove over to see Mrs. Leonard Martin, and made an offer she couldn't turn down. The big man bought enough fresh rhubarb to bake two pies, and gave her one for her family, and he would get the other. Bill heard she watched the big man eat the entire pie in less than ten minutes.

They were now visiting to just say hello, and talk about how hot the summer was going. Then Bill told him about an old hayrack and a huge, worn-out metal tub he didn't need any more. "I'll give them to you, my friend," Bill said.

Buck Ed was flabbergasted. "This is a great gift, Bill, but how can you get the tub back over where I could get beside the river for water?"

Bill simply said he had wheels on the hayrack, but not the tub. "You can sleep on the rack out here in the barn any night you want. It'll hold you, and we can put the tub over by the river."

He and his sons immediately lifted the tub behind his tractor, and voila, ten minutes later this was as close to being a bathtub the Fat Man would probably ever see anything like this again. As they finished, Bill grinned. "Buck Ed, if we're here when you drive in, my kids and I can carry enough water to give you a bath again."

Buck Ed started sniffling, and after a second or two he almost began crying.

"Now stop getting overwhelmed, Buck Ed. These are simple things that we can do," Bill said. "Shoot, you are such a big man my son Denny here thought you might be a grizzly bear."

Everyone chuckled, but Buck Ed suddenly broke out into roaring laughter. "Maybe I am a grizzly, son. When I take off my britches to go washing in the tub, I'll be bare at night. And, son, at least I'll also be a clean bear, too."

Bill then pointed at the tractor for his kids, and said, "Maybe nobody could get you into a real bathtub, but we'll help make this the best we can." They all smiled and nodded, and with this, the Derick family climbed up and pulled away.

Tonight, as he was silently disrobing there in the moonlight, it must have been certainly a sight to be seen. Though Sheck lived on his trolley less than a mile from where Buck Ed was now bathing, not even he would believe that this mammoth man was washing both his body and his clothes in the dark along the same carefree river.

To get this done, however, it might have even taken an entire box of Rinso White.

CHAPTER 22

▼

ALMOST THE CRACK OF DAWN

Sunday mornings during this special summer were a wondrous blend of the word of God and the thoughts of women and men. Young children just enjoyed sheer, simple joys with some other little friends, but older kids who attended Sunday School, regular catechisms, and even Summer School, it was a different form of pressure. This required thought, and that meant study.

The Bible instructs all mankind to honor and hallow the Sabbath. But, even in Bradford, American's Constitution gave these same citizens both freedom *of* religion and freedom *from* it. In communities of rural America, people of either way on Sunday's dawn heralded a few special hours that were serene and peaceful.

Only the most dedicated atheist could possibly doubt that God was in His heaven, and even if they still did not believe, all enjoyed total tranquility on earth whether they liked it or not. Absence of the sounds of manual labor was the most noticeable difference. No tractor could be heard chugging laboriously through a faraway field. No push mowers or hedge clippers clattered or snipped anywhere in the distance. No fresh washed laundry billowed and flapped as it dried on backyard clotheslines. No cars were serviced at the towns three gas stations. Nor was any Main Street stores open on Sunday morning, except for Tinker Scholes Drug Store, and that was mainly for health problems.

Even the three clergymen, who were the town's busiest employees on these special mornings, didn't feel they were working at all. They and other folks, however, felt Tinker and Lefty worked as a public servant more than a violation of the Good Book's admonition. Traffic on Route 88 was also so sporadically tranquil; it was almost non-existent.

Sunday was not a day bereft of many wonderful noises, however, for serenity shares many sounds can create impromptu symphonies. Mainly, a chorus of many different birds blending their different offerings from trees throughout the village. Honey bee's or butterflies flitting from flower to flower as busy as any other day were unaware and unconcerned about their creators edict. Anywhere in town just a few hundred yards, or even a mile or so, you might hear a distant cow reminding the farmer that there were no days off for dairy cattle either.

Despite dogs startled by something real or perceived, also broke the silence periodically, and they occasionally seemed as if they would never stop barking.

Man was not to be outdone by nature however, for the beautiful sounds of church bells calling three congregations to worship began one after the other, but never out of time or tune. This small town had three different denominations, Baptist, Roman Catholic, and Methodist.

First Baptist Church was organized in 1869; the same day Bradford was an incorporated village. Members were now proud that their church was built in 1871, and still worshiped in the same building. While folks remembered that there had been some difference additions, and remodeling since those early years, they were thrilled at what their pastor, Rev. Donald Wood, had been doing to make it even better for the past two years. Anyone on Main Street, or even a block or two away could hear sawing and pounding all day long. In a few more months, a lot of new construction here was going to surprise and thrill either long time believers or brand new members.

A lot of folks were concerned about the safety of the bell that hung on the corner tower. Rev. Wood joked that one special prayer he did every day was, if the bell fell, none of the folks below including him will be hit. As of this last Sunday in June 1949, no one even heard a creak above.

Catfish and Hotshot both attended Sunday School or church here fairly often, but Hotshot probably would have been a bit more regular if he could have also not fallen asleep thirty seconds later when a sermon began.

The second church organized in our town was beatified in January 8, 1876, but the first Sunday mass of the day at St. John's the Baptist Parish was at 8 a.m. for as long as people remembered. A second mass was given two hours later, for anyone who would or could attend; there was at least one mass every day of the week. This great church had so much beauty even non-Catholic members loved to enter, and walk in awe. As people stood to look from one incredible window to another at the magnificent church it could have been called a majestic cathedral.

Even taller than the towns long, strange cylinder that was a water tower, this church was built with white cut stone or pressed brick, and it's huge tower was a new architectural treasure in 1923. The steeple soared 160 feet. Instead of just one big bell at the top, this had several, and the sounds were so melodious people could see the tower or just hear it chime for miles.

Booby and Beaner were almost always here on Sunday, and several other boys also assisted as altar boys for Father Cleary.

Two months and four days later after St. John's opened, the Bradford Methodist Episcopal Church dedicated their church on March 12. Two decades later, William Leet, the first and probably the biggest banker in the village died in 1896 after he moved to Chicago. But he was rich and generous, and still loved his friends in Bradford. His daughter and other members of their family were all staunch Methodist's who now did not live in the area anymore. Amazingly, they offered to build a new church in 1899, and wanted to name it Leet Memorial M. E. Church.

Needless to say, a vast majority of members immediately approved, and that is just what happened. Now, nearly fifty years later, Austin A. Rogers was the minister at two churches, and spoke at nearby Boyd Groves Methodist Church on Sunday morning at 8:30, and at 10:30 in Bradford.

Suck and Dink's parents would have not missed this church even if blizzards or ice storms kept their cars in the garages. Actually, this was true for any parishioner or church member who might have to walk in Bradford because it was actually just about a ten-minute trip.

When it came to attending church in Bradford, or America's small towns anywhere, rain or sleet was no different as if it was a sunny, summer day if people were believers. The sounds of contentment and commitment mingled together perfectly on those Sunday mornings reaffirming the obvious, peace on earth had indeed come to Bradford.

Goodwill toward men, especially very young men, was another matter. On this particular day, Beaner and Booby were in their usual places assisting Father Cleary. However, not even the carefully pressed scarlet robes with freshly starched white collars could transfer this pair of tough, young Irishmen into the loving angels of their mother's prayers.

"You idiot," whispered Booby sharply over his shoulder. "You stepped on my heel," as both of them followed Father Cleary going up the sacristy steps.

"I tripped. Now my candle's gone out. Give me a light at the altar," Beaner replied in hushed, but equally very annoyed tones.

Booby tilted far enough to get Beaner lit again, but as he angled his candle too close to himself, and for about two or three seconds, his hair above his forehead was now on fire. "Father, look at Beaner," urged Booby, and pointed to the small flickering blaze.

Father Cleary instantly glanced at Beaner, and quickly flipped his hand to shut off the brief problem. In just a second or two the fire was out, and Father then nonchalantly stepped up, and reached the top of the steps.

It was so fast it had not burned his skin, but Beaner was stunned because he reached up and realized that there would be no point to try and comb that part of his head for several months.

Just before he turned around, Father Cleary gave each boy such a withering glance that it seemed to them excommunication could not be far behind. With his back to the congregation, and flanked by a boy on each side, it was easy for him to speak loudly of Christ's love to the worshipers while quietly instilling the fear of God in his two clumsy acolytes.

Over at the Methodist Church, two more of the Joe Bonomo Strong Men's Club were also having their misunderstanding for a totally different set of problems. For nearly 45 years, every teenage boy in the church had been named to volunteer ringing the big bell beside the opening front door. Pulling the long rope that actually moved the clapper to ring the bell was all it took to remind folks in Bradford that church was about to begin. Whoever had the responsibility to do it, however, had to open the small door in the narthex.

Today Suck and Dink were arguing as to which one was going to pull the rope, and both were creating such a furor that neither was remembering that the regular time should be happening. This solved the obvious problem quickly as stern looks from several disapproving adults who would have gone instantly for either boy's father if it had continued one more second. Rev. Rodgers happened to walk by. As he realized the confusion was getting out of hand, he nodded to Bob Dunlap. The former Naval officer who had spent three years in the Pacific Theatre stepped up beside the boys, and quietly but forcefully announced that one would ring ten times now and the other immediately should do ten more. The most serious decision was *now*, and he instantly handed Dink, the closest one the rope.

Though the still young and handsome officer was wearing a normal navy blue suit, his former military presence was still as strong and impressive just a few years ago. Hidden memories of dangerous experiences were still very real to him, but now the war was over. Today's simple resolution for these two boys was ordering a pair of typical swabs that the church bell had to start ringing again. As he smiled while they began to instantly obey, Bob silently contemplated that other men who had to also comply immediately in places like Wake Island or Midway now seemed almost like a thousand years ago.

Sunday church members, however, are never 100% in participation or attendance. Lots of reasons why folks don't attend every week happen, and this morning one family decided that fishing was just another form of religion. Belief and faith are two of the most important aspects of any church's creed, but fishermen also have to have some skill and luck. On this great dawn, if someone had been looking out in the mirror-still surface on Lake Senachwine, they would have watched three people sitting motionless on a flat-bottomed, wooden fishing boat as it chugged steadily across the shimmering lagoon.

The boat, powered by a small 7 ½ horsepower Evinrude motor, left a perfect V-shaped wake, and would have disappeared away from you into the distance. A large, thick mist still clung in patches about the lake, and it now hid them perfectly if some other fisherman suspected they had made the flawless location. Catfish was sitting alone on the narrow bow, and the main reason he was stationary is because he was dozing quietly in his own little world.

He and his older brother left around five in the morning when their father awakened them, and drove the twenty to twenty-five minutes to the area near Henry. Today they would fish for bass in the morning, blue gills and crappies during the day, and bass again as evening approached.

Hotshot had a surprising new game plan this same morning at First Baptist Church. Catfish was not there for some reason. Regardless of that, Rev. Woods was giving such a wonderful sermon, and nearly a hundred members were thoroughly absorbed in his message. As it ended, and the closing hymn was moving into the last verse Hotshot temporarily was looking like he was singing. However, he was actually only mouthing the words because he was now staring two pews away to his left. Jeannie Houghton was there, and she looked fresh and fantastic. But she was as filled with the same spirit these brethren in their house of worship were, and he was unfortunately only consumed with a few million hormones. This unique experience created a much different prospect for the young man standing beside his sister, mother and father. He suddenly remembered about those dreams when he had to attend a program with his mother more than a month ago. Today the entire church was singing and he was getting a little sleepy again.

Around 9:30, still enveloped in a sound sleep, Jumbo abruptly awakened with a twitch. When his mother called to him from the foot of the stairs, her loud yell broke his deep sleep so abruptly he jumped right out of bed. The simple confusion had already brought her upstairs and she immediately was satisfied that he was actually getting up at the right time.

"That's better," she quietly said. "Today your father is working at the drug store. He says it's time for you to go up and see if Dad needs you to uncrate anything. And keep your hands off the new comic books this week. Somebody drove there last night from Peoria, and their shipment came in. We don't want your grubby paw prints all over them. Even if you do wash your hands, which I doubt you do very often, don't spill anything on them or fold them over so they are really used. Keep them new."

"I know, mom," he yawned as he was talking. "If I look at the top one, I can get it slid under as the bottom one. Then the weight will make the bottom look like nobody has read it yet. My brother has been doing it for two or three years."

His mother smiled. She heard these strange sounds of a body as big as he was whenever he had immediately awakened. She glanced back at him because she wanted to go back downstairs, but she saw that his answer and the fact that he was even now standing up did mean anything to either of them. "Eddy Jay, are you really awake yet?"

At the same moment, he sat back down on the side of his bed, and the response to her question was totally unintelligible.

"Are you awake? I mean really awake? Otherwise, I think I may have to grab one of your ankles, and drag your butt bouncing right on to the floor. We did put a rug on your bedroom floor for a very good reason. Some floorboards in this house are freezing cold at winter. It's not that bad now because we're well into summer. However, young man, you can still get a shock when you get dropped. Get it?"

"Yes, ma'am," Jumbo offered, the better, but still almost incoherent reply.

No matter who attended or didn't, as everyone in Bradford realized, church was a different experience for a lot of different people.

CHAPTER 23

▼

THE SON OF A GEORGIA SLAVE BOY

"My goal in life is to become the world champion farter." Beaner said it with such conviction no one else even doubted or argued his statement. All seven boys of the SMCA were now wandering south along the river and two of them had some old rope that each father offered their sons. This was the third day on the last weekend in June where the temperature was so close to hitting ninety the boys said it was finally time to go swimming.

"Come on, Beaner, we know that. But we still don't know if they really have a world champion doing this," Dink shrugged because even he didn't believe this.

"Don't rightly know either, but I sure hope so 'cause I could win a trophy that would knock your eyes off," Beaner replied.

"How do you figure on winning it," Jumbo asked, and immediately tried to spit on a butterfly. But he didn't.

"I've been thinking about it. My idea of winning a trophy is to let the most horrible fart of all time. It would be loud and so stinky it would make people's eyes water." The other six boys laughed simultaneous. Then he added, "My Uncle Dick has a Ford Convertible with a rumble seat behind it. My older brother and my sister all sit in the back. Wouldn't it be incredible if I could cut an orphan in that convertible with the top down goin' 50 miles an hour, and make everybody sick including me?"

Again they laughed as they were walking closely together in the path.

"I remember you telling about orphans," Booby asked.

"Yep, my Uncle Dick says that an orphan is the most dangerous fart there is. 'Corse, if somebody lets a silent one, nobody claims that they did it."

Hotshot snickered. "You tell us that all the time. But I've met your Uncle Dick before. He is a crazy guy. Your dad and my dad just laughed and laughed at some of the crazy things he said last year. He lives in Green Valley, but he comes up to Bradford four or five times a year."

"Right, you'd have a hard time beatin' Uncle Dick's jokes. You were there when he came to town, and our dad's were drinking beer and eatin' hard-boiled eggs and mountain oysters. After about an hour my uncle said he fired one that was so nasty, he claimed he had burned his butt."

Almost all boys have a special laughter about either farts or the Three Stooges. They were now laughing so much that Jumbo stopped, and pointed at a perfect dead tree where they could just sit and hear the rest of the story without missing anything.

"What in the world is a mountain oyster?" Suck frowned when they stopped the raucous.

"I can tell you that one," Catfish jumped in. "My dad and older brother do it, too. It's a pig's nut. I wouldn't eat one if they put a 12 gauge against my head. Did you, Beaner?"

"Only once, and the taste wasn't too bad, but when I heard that somebody cut the nuts off a lot of pigs, and then cooked them is too sick for me."

"It looks like you'll never beat a fart championship if your uncle competes," Suck said.

Each sentence brought yet more and more laughter. As they began to subside, Beaner said, "Yeah, we have laughed about him so much I was almost sick in my stomach."

"One day when I was there, the best funny part is when your uncle said he had to go take a pee, but there's no bathroom there. He stood up and said, 'I'm going to step on a frog and shake the dew off my lily.' Then he started climbing up the steps, and when he hit the first step, he let a fart. Then he took the next one, and let another," and Hotshot started grinning after he spoke.

Beaner immediately interrupted. "Yeah, Hotshot, he cut one at everyone of the fourteen steps up. My dad was sure laughing, and we were about to fall over backwards. When we quit, dad said that his brother is one of a kind. He said that Uncle Dick is the only man he ever knew who could fart the first two lines of Yankee Doodle Dandy."

As they finally stopped laughing for the umpteenth time, Jumbo grabbed a small bag of Tootsie Rolls, and threw one to each of them. His dad gave him a snack bag of penny candy, once in a while, and he shared it with the others happily, but unfortunately, greedily.

"Those things you said your dad and uncle called are 'Mountain Oysters'. Is that right, or is it just another one of the grown-up jokes we said we don't like?" Catfish questioned.

"The sound of it would probably make a goat puke, but he said they all call it instead of what it really is," Beaner offered.

"My dad loves to eat oyster stew about once a month on a Sunday night," Dink said. "He buys it in one of the restaurants in Bradford when they have it. He walks home with it in this small, white cardboard bag with a skinny little wire hook that he carries. When he gets there, mom says she will heat it, but don't let anyone else even see it, including her."

"What in the world does he think it is?" Suck asked.

It was quiet with no answer for a few seconds. As usual, Dink was the bravest of them all whenever someone needed to hear a weird guess. "Well, this is what I saw. Oysters are the sickest, ugliest looking things I've ever seen. I looked over a few nights ago at supper, and I got a sneaky glance of it. I shook my head, and said to my dad that it looks like some big gray, fish eyes are floating around in curdled milk. He looked up, and said, you're right, that's just what it looks like. And then he looked down and ate all of the bowl without saying another word."

Each stared at one another. Several of them would have to admit that vomiting was certainly a good possibility if they continued the conversation. Without even saying anything again, all seven stood up, and headed back along the path.

In less than a hundred yards, they reached a large corner of the river only a half-mile south of the bridge, and they suddenly realized that heaven had just opened one of its many magnificent locations. After early rains or lots of melting snow, flooding roars down the river from countless farms upstream. Pressure hits the bank on the opposite side, and makes it deeper than anywhere else. These seven boys now recognized what an outstanding opportunity they had.

Within minutes they were throwing two nearby ropes over strong tree limbs twenty feet away. Within seconds they were almost as naked as proverbial jaybirds, and swung out splashing into the best and deepest pool they had ever found. The sheer joy these boys were now sharing would have even made them forget anything else in the world.

Actually, almost anything. One change in the old days of skinny dipping last year had made a change. Each was either wearing a real bathing suit, or just their white underwear. These thirteen-year old boys were now growing pubic hair.

They were now having so much fun in the "Round Hole', they didn't even see someone else was leaning against a tree on the top of the bank. Sheck Dye had slipped out of the woods.

"Hi, boys," he said, when their noises had quieted down after the first few swings.

"Wow! Hi, Sheck," Dink yelled. "Ya wanta go swimming?"

"Naw, boys, I just think what you are doin' reminds me having fun just like this back in Lewistown. I grew up in this same river, but it's jus' a few miles farther down from here. But keep a look out for any water moccasins or snapping turtles. I see 'em every now and then."

Immediately, each suddenly started looking for anything around them that could be biting, striking, or even nibbling. Nothing was causing much action right now. If anything bad had been there, seven boys jumping around into the river would have quickly disappeared. They were smart enough to know that, when noise and commotion would cease, Spoon River was God's property. Crazy boys were just visitors.

"Got an idea, boys. When you decide to quit swimmin' I know where you keep the bikes under the bridge. Why don't you come up and see what my house looks like. I'se bakin' some cornbread. Does hot cornbread taste good to you?"

All seven started cheering. When ideas like these hit boys in their mind, it only takes about a second later to shock their stomachs. Five seconds ago no one was even thinking about eating anything, but fresh, hot, cornbread was now out of control for them.

"You are a wonderful friend, Sheck," Dink gushed. "I bet we don't swim more than five more minutes."

Each of the others nodded, and then Sheck said, "You're probly right, but I bet none of you have ever been to my house. You ever see a trolley car before, even in Peoria?"

"Yeah, I think almost all of us have been on one there, and my family rode one in Chicago," Hotshot said. "We left downtown and went to Wrigley Field. We watched the Cubs playing the New York Giants that day."

Sheck laughed, and said, "Well, fiddle-de-de, I ain't never even gone to anything like that. No matter what your time is, boys, I will go up to the hill, and cut it so at least you will have two good pieces."

Again the cheers erupted. Without saying another word, Sheck departed.

It only took about fifteen minutes later, but now, as they walked up to the place they began to stare at the incredible scene in Sheck's half-streetcar, half-trolley. Each boy was flabbergasted that something like this was up on the bluff in a small forest as the Spoon River meandered only about a hundred feet below. However, when the seven boys shyly walked up and knocked on the unique door, Sheck was very happy. Without saying a word, he opened it, and invited them in.

"Hot diddle do," Booby exclaimed. "Hotshot just talked about something like this when he went to Chicago, but my folks and I have gone two or three times to a town called Libertyville. It's up by Chicago, too. My cousin Marsha rides on one just like this, and she says it's almost the most fun any of us can do. She took me on one and it looks just like this. Every wall is covered with glass windows, even the side door where we stepped up and sat down."

Sheck smiled when Booby spoke, but the others were gazing in awe because this unique dwelling was now a huge, eclectic mess. They could see it looked to be about seven feet wide, and twenty feet long, and more than three-fourths of the wooden seat benches had been removed. On the side of the middle section, now an antiquated cook stove with three or four iron plates, and a bottom oven where a big pan of cornbread was coming out. A bucket of coal was sitting beside the stove and a box of kindling and corncobs were hanging just above it with a pile of big matches. Some of the windows were covered up, and sadly, some had been broken. The nutcase boys who threw green walnuts a few years ago certainly were the culprits.

Smoke rolled out of the backside of the trolley because a makeshift pipe ran through the wall at the top. There were several big candles standing around the entire room, and one big kerosene lamp was on the only table in the place. The only water was found in a well outside, but it was obvious that Sheck didn't have any electricity either.

Then he brought them back to the outside section. "Boys, I think you need to wash your hands. I have a clean towel or two, but you can wipe with your T-shirts if you want. I'll pump the well, and you can grab that big bar of lye soap there." They quietly nodded, and he began pumping the handle. In a few seconds, clean, fresh, cold water came up, and several even filled their canteens.

In just a few minutes each of the boys wedged his first fistful of cornbread. Warm chocolate cake and cold milk are two of the best combinations boys ever get, but the delicious cornbread and clear chilly water from Sheck's well was almost as good. Now they were sitting on the ground or leaning against the streetcar. When he saw wet swimming suits and underwear stuck around their back-packs, Sheck carried them around and put them over his cook stove. They all knew that in less than ten minutes, their things would be dry as can be.

As he walked back out, several big oak trees were covering the sun, and there weren't even any mosquitoes or flies that seemed to be a normal summer experience. Life was good for this group of seven boys and one old man.

"A few weeks ago I heard you north of here about five hundred yards or so. You were blowing some funny whistle toy, and then I heard some of you trying to make tweet-tweet bird calls." As soon as Sheck said this, the other's looked at each other with self-conscious giggles or moans.

"Yeah, we were trying to signal three of us on one side of the river, and three on the other. Dink started trying to sound like a cow, since he can't whistle, and most of us have jammed our Lone Ranger rings with crud," Jumbo said.

"I thought one of you got hurt, and I almost walked down there since I was fishin' near there, too. If I ever sees one of you doing somethin' crazy again like that, I might just have to come over and say 'boy, you're shakin' like a Georgia hound dog tryin' to pass a peach pit.'"

They all laughed, and Sheck lit a corn-cob pipe out of his shirt pocket. Suck then asked him, "How did you know something about Georgia, Sheck?"

"My pappy was borned there as a slave back in the 1850's. He told me that growin' up in slavery was hell on earth. But the 'mancipation war dun broke out and 'fore he was much more than a little chil', Gen'ral Sherman came through Georgia with a sword in one hand and a torch in the other. Sadly, that war dun split up his momma and daddy in the plantation where they was workin', but somehow they got back together when the war was over. My daddy told me years later that my grandaddy was sold to a slaver who took him to 'Nawlins, and we never did see him again." Sheck paused in thoughtful contemplation, and a couple of tears began a slow path downward over the parched lines in his ebony face.

It was several seconds before Dink asked, "That's sure a sad story, Sheck. But I don't know where or what 'Nawlins is?"

"Why chil', I hear it's a big, big city down in Louisiana. You know, where the Big Muddy meets the ocean gulf," Sheck replied, but slowly gave a thoughtful observation, and was almost shaken into sudden melancholia. "Someday, boys, when the good Lord calls me on, I jus will ride my soul right down this here river, and keep on goin' all the way down to the gulf in the ocean. Freedom is where I is goin'. 'Course, while I stays livin' here, that's why I call my little streetcar named 'Glory'. When I'se gone to heaven I'll just sit on a big, old leaf, and slip happily down the river. Boys, that's when I'll go to real glory."

The boys were mesmerized. They thought Aunt Jane was the best story teller they'd ever heard, but Sheck was more spellbinding than her or anyone they had ever heard before.

"You are an amazing grampa man, Sheck," said Dink softly. It was once more quiet for a few seconds.

Catfish finally asked, "How did you find out to live here, Sheck?"

"My daddy told me we were goin' to move north after the war. He said things might be a lot better then 'cause now he found momma about five miles away when it was over. He was already a blacksmith man, and he decided to move to Illinois near where some other relatives told him about. Somehow we moved to Lewistown, and his horse shed was right behind the same Spoon River down there. I jus told you about that when you was swimmin'," and he pointed down the hill.

"I'd like to ask another question, Sheck, if I can," Beaner said softly.

"Why sure," Sheck relied immediately.

"Did somebody do something terrible to you in Lewistown back a lot of years ago. And I heard that somebody did something bad here, too. It sure wasn't us, though."

Sheck looked directly over to Beaner, and shook his head. "The good bit of news is that nobody ever was bad to me or my daddy. Our momma died a lot of years earlier than that and she didn't even see Lewistown, but my daddy died there in 1913. There's somethin' kind of strange that I can tell you about, though. Boys, I don't know how to read, 'cause I never went into any kind of schoolin'. I'm sure glad that you boys can and will stay in school. But when my daddy died I heard that somebody wrote a book by a man called Masters. Some folks there told me that my daddy was the only Negro mentioned in the book. I jus figured out that some white folks might not be too glad about that to me, and a good man named Mr. Gib Jones drove there and told me he would let me live right here where we are. He bought this trolley car in Peoria ten years ago, and I am as happy as fifty-six pigs in the mud."

Once again, all seven of them laughed at his big smile, and then he chuckled, too. "As far as I got to havin' problems right here in Bradford some crazy teenage boys started throwin' green walnuts that broke two of the windows over here." He glanced over at the covered boards that were nailed into the trolley. "Nobody has done it again, and I sure hope they never will again."

"I want to ask another question, Sheck," Hotshot asked. "Do you know much about the coal mine stuff in this forest?"

The other boys were now nervous. It may be a bad question, but they also wanted to get the answer.

Sheck didn't make a sound or any change of his expression. For a few seconds he now looked perplexed, and finally said, "Yes, there is a 'bandoned mine over there," and he pointed in the northern direction of the river. "But boys, they closed this thing down twenty or thirty years ago. I got all the deadwood a man could have, but if I needs a real, hot fire all I has to do is dig along the side of the hill, and I got enough coal for cookin' and heatin' when winter hits."

That brief and honest answer was all that he wanted to say, unless one of them asked a deeper question.

Hotshot couldn't stop. "Yes, I know about digging some good coal for you here, but does anyone know if somebody could figure out how to actually climb down into the real mine?"

Again it was quiet. "That's a dangerous place, boys, and I'se glad to tell you that they closed it down. What they did is to save curious boys so they don't fall down in a terrible place like that."

The boys nodded and smiled, but it's the first time today that no one laughed.

Sheck also grinned. Deep down into his mind, however, he realized that he never had told a lie on any day of his life, but this was getting very close to being the first. Nearly ten years ago he discovered how to dig down into the mine. That day he moved some fallen trees on the top of the mound. He was surprised that when he saw two huge wooden doors which covered the entrance. By pulling them over, a ladder went down into darkness.

Six boys immediately knew that was as much as they needed to know. However, Hotshot thought he saw a glimmer of suspicion in the old man's eyes, and silently promised that he would go back in that general direction all by himself.

It was obvious now was a good time for another question, and Beaner raised his right hand, just like they all did when they wanted to ask their teachers.

"Sheck, did you ever hear about any crooks that used to live around here?" Beaner asked that, and then added, "Jumbo thought you might have known who killed Al Capone." At that they all laughed except Jumbo and Sheck, who both frowned.

"Oh, rats," Jumbo mumbled, and spat loudly. "I never said anything like that."

"Oh, yeah," Booby said. "Sheck, he is so full of crap if he ever gets an enema he'll be so little he won't even need a bed. His mom will just let him sleep in a shoe box."

Even Sheck laughed with all of them, and Jumbo finally shrugged and smiled.

"Sheck, we heard that the big crook in Chicago named Capone died two years ago. We know *you* didn't do it, but my dad said what happened was that his nose fell right off of his face," Catfish said.

"What? Cat, you are as crazy as Dink," Suck replied.

"Yeah, what is this nose thing crap," Jumbo added.

"My dad told some pals one day Big Al went muff-divin', and kissed the wrong spot on the wrong woman. The only problem with this is I don't have the slightest idea what he's talkin' about," Catfish said.

Beaner frowned. "My Uncle Dick also said the same darn thing. He said Big Al had somethin' called 'sifliss.' I just figured it was more grown-up bullshit from him like it always is."

"Let's just forget it, boys. As you get older, you'll hear more and more stuff, and some of it's probly' nothin' like he said," and Sheck smiled again at Beaner. Then he added, "Like I said, I never have been anywhere like the big city called Chicago. You want to know just how close I got north of Bradford one time? Buda, boys, Buda. And that's only about ten miles from right where we are sittin'."

"Maybe my folks will take you to Wisconsin with us next time," Dink offered. "There is a great place called Minocqua, and the fishin' is good."

"Yeah, I love Minnesota. My family rents a house on Lake Hubert in the Ten Thousand Lakes area," Suck said quickly. "I'll tell my folks, too"

"Well, I love Michigan fishing, too, Sheck. You'd like to go fishing in Escanaba," Jumbo suggested.

"Boys, boys, that's really nice of you, but I won't ever see any of those places. Gettin' some catfish down in this river is just about as good as I'll ever do."

"Yeah, and that's the same for me here and Lake Senachwine," Catfish said, laughing about his nickname.

"And I think you all better ride your bikes home now. Your momma's and daddy's are going to wonder where you is," Sheck chuckled.

They were right, but they didn't really want to leave just yet. There was something special here. Actually, there were a lot of remarkable and intriguing things here in the place where they saw the fascinating streetcar, but they knew that the most important aspect here was Sheck himself. His incredible story about how he came from Georgia all the way to Central Illinois would stay in their thoughts for many, many years. As each reluctantly stood up he handed warm, dry swimming suits and underwear. But, at this moment, all they wanted to do is give him a hug. Thirteen-year-old boys loved a million hugs when they were little, but now, as they were getting bigger and more involved with aspects of growing up, handshakes were their big step up. For them, nevertheless, Sheck Dye was a very special hugger. He even started playing his old harmonica, and the boys loved it.

For centuries, old men often have interesting conversations and memories with long time friends just sipping coffee in small cafes anywhere in America. Right now, these seven boys wouldn't even realize that something like that this might not ever happen again. No matter, here on the incredible river where they dreamed and played, this experience would stay forever in their minds. When time goes by, special experiences like this are why young boys can someday turn into real men.

However, the only thing they wanted to do now was quickly tell their parents about an amazing old man who lived along the river in a magic streetcar that he called 'Glory'.

CHAPTER 24

▼

SWEET JESUS...IS IT POLIO?

July 3, was a glorious early Sunday morning that made everyone feel as if they were as close to heaven as anyone in town. For many years, the Carlton's, and their daughter and son walked to Leet Methodist Church in time for Sunday School, and then attended the normal service there.

However, someone had just made an unexpected moaning sound and both Mr. and Mrs. Carlton woke up immediately. Most parents have a sixth sense, and this one must have set off their alarm. "Helen, what was that," he asked, as he rubbed his face and eyes.

"I don't know either, Bob. It didn't sound right. I will slip into both of their bedrooms," she quickly replied, and glanced at their clock hanging on the window side of the wall.

"I will too," he said, and grabbed his bathrobe hanging on the back of their bathroom door.

They each made no more sounds, and first walked through Sally's bedroom. She had not made a noise at all, and certainly did not hear any commotion that would have woke her up, too.

Instantly, however, when they walked into Philip's room they were terrified. This was a thirteen-year boy who was again moaning, but the biggest shock of it all was that he was drenched with sweat and almost acting as if he was in a coma.

"Oh, dear God, sweet Jesus, is it polio?" Bob Carlton was speaking almost to himself, but he was also asking their creator and his wife if the worst fears had now arrived. Everyone in America realized polio could be a personal disaster from anyone like the former President of the United States to any kid in this small town. Sadly, these two parents suddenly worried their own solitary son had been struck by the same terrible tragedy that Franklin D. Roosevelt had in 1921, more than twenty-seven years earlier. And they still talked about how Francis Clark had died so quickly in Peoria from the same epidemic.

Helen Carlton began speaking instantly. "Call either Dr. Scholes or Dr. Herrman. Ask Central who's on call, and she'll call them. Then tell her to call either Art Marsh or Bob Dunlap. It maybe best to ask Bob to drive the ambulance because his father-in-law is kind of old, and I'm sure we'll be going to Peoria for one of the hospitals in a few minutes. After you do these two calls, go wake up Sally and tell her that we have to take Philip then. She is old enough to stay here, and we will call her when we get any news there. I will start covering him with hot towels. Got it?"

She knew her husband was as successful as any husband, father, or employers in this or any other town, but mothers almost always take over when catastrophes happen. She wasn't going to waste one more second with her son now.

Actually, in just about the past thirty seconds this frightening occurrence was real, and it was serious, but they were both working quickly together. Bob immediately called Central and found out Dr. Hermann was out of town this weekend, but he was soon talking to Doc Scholes. For years the older doctor had such a permanent limp he almost looked as if he had been crippled as a kid, however, it was really from smoking too much and too long. Emphysema had taken its toll. He had believed the fake advertising in Camel Cigarettes in magazines, billboards, and newspapers that doctors said they loved something called the "T-Zone" in their throats. The full-page ads had headlines like this: "More Doctors smoke Camels than any other cigarette."

This good doctor had to temporarily stop climbing halfway up the home's beautiful second floor stairway. No matter how fast he needed to examine Philip Carlton, he had to just be able to catch his own breath.

In just another ten minutes Bob Dunlap and his father carried Philip into the long black van. Today it was called an ambulance, but the next day it could be a hearse if someone in town died unexpectedly. In thirty-eight more minutes, the boy everyone except his parents called Suck was rolled into the Emergency Station at Peoria's St. Francis Hospital.

When it comes to shocking news, people said Bradford is just as fast as a Chicago second. For year's, folks really said when something was fast, it was referred to as a New York minute. But local news was even speedier in Illinois, and that's how a Chicago second was a newer version of rapid information. Suck's story sped through town like a verbal cyclone.

After Sunday lunch, all six buddies were already sitting up in the Laughing Tree. But no one was laughing about anything in this place now. Since they had no news yet, after about ten minutes, the boys seemed to decide that riding back to their homes was probably the best thing to do.

Polio was the biggest scare any of them had ever heard about. It had a difficult medical name called poliomyelitis, but doctors simply told people it was polio. They knew it as a contagious, historically devastating disease. Though something like polio plagued humans since ancient times, its most extensive outbreak occurred fairly recently. Shrouded aspects of knowledge and understanding about where it came from, and how kids got it confused the entire county. Everyone was frightened about when it might happen again.

Scientists and doctors felt polio was a viral illness that, in about 95% of cases, actually produces no symptoms at all. Any remaining feverish patients in the hospitals that had symptoms, the illness appears in three forms. Though neither Dr.'s Hermann or Scholes had any serious knowledge of this terrible kind of plague, specialists in Peoria took over as soon as one of the patients was carried in.

Most had a mild form called abortive polio. People with this form of polio might not even suspect they had it because their sickness was limited to mild flu-like symptoms. A more serious form of polio brought sick people bigger problems such as neck stiffness, and fevers. The third, and most dangerous had a severe, debilitating form called paralysis. Thankfully, paralysis only actually hit about one or two percent of cases with this, and patients were put into an iron lung just to breath.

Some people prayed for a miracle, but many others also gave as little as a dime to a dear lady named Elizabeth Kenny from Australia. When anyone talked about her she was called Sister because everybody in Bradford thought she was probably a Roman Catholic nun. What a surprise it was when a few folks found out more than thirty-five years ago she had been in the Australia Army Nursing Service as a staff nurse. In British tradition, she was named Sister when a head nurse is given a complimentary title. An even bigger surprise was that she did not have any formal education because she had lived in her country's 'outback' area.

"Sister" may have been called that by her authoritarian manner, but colleagues would have been unlikely to question the designation, whether earned, conferred, or assumed. No matter, when she arrived in Los Angeles in 1940, at the age of 59, America was the right place at the right time, even for the President of the United States. Even some doctors and thousands of patients believed in her as much as if she was God's healing touch.

That special touch was simply called The Kenny method. It took hours and hours of therapy and 'TLC' every day of the week, but so many patients were unexpectedly getting better and better, she now was almost given another self-bestowed title, America's queen of convalescence.

Tonight, virtually everyone in town was waiting for news from the Carlton's family. Helen and Bob might just make one long-distant call to Central with a hand full of dimes and quarters because she could practically cover the town a thousand percent faster that anyone else. Phones in Bradford only had addresses with three numbers to call when you were trying to reach a neighbor, but in situations like this, Central could just plug wires and start talking.

Now two physicians in Peoria were as busy as they had ever been. Virtually all doctors everywhere take care of these challenges, even late at night. Most everyone else could only go to bed with many prayers.

Tomorrow should be a very serious visit from these doctors to a special mother and father there. For countless millions of others, however, those happy, but even more healthy Americans would be celebrating the USA's 173rd Birthday.

CHAPTER 25

▼

FIREWORKS AND FEVER

There are so many incredible places that people in Central Illinois can go to celebrate the 4th of July. Wherever fireworks are shown it's equally fun for families and friends, but fortunately not all of them ever went to the same one.

Whether folks in Bradford went to watch the show in Henry beside the Illinois River, or Riverfront Park along the same river in Peoria, or Francis Park in Kewanee, it was a wonderful holiday. Getting cotton candy, ice-cold lemonade, charred hot dogs, and even more charred marshmallows, was simply good old fun in the USA. It almost seemed that the General Assembly in Springfield banned mosquitoes for at least twenty-four hours by some other new law.

Chicago seemed to create its own laws, however, and what happened on July 4 was different. They made a decision that was so brilliant, both for performing outstanding nighttime explosions, and having it a special day of celebration early in Grant Park on July 3rd. Though million's of people enjoy the big city fireworks shows all over America, people here felt Chicago did it the best. By lighting the sky from two barges anchored a few yards away in Lake Michigan, the 4th turned into a local, family experience in everyone's own local neighborhood.

But in Bradford, most people here were quietly wondering about Philip. The other six boys were sitting in the Laughing Tree, but one of the normal, occupied limbs was now empty. They were just trying to find a new reason to be talking together. If they soon couldn't figure out something soon, they would probably be riding back to their own homes.

Beaner came up with a good idea. "My favorite movie cowboy is an injun," and he proudly said it, and laughed out loud. "You betchum, Red Ryder!" They all grinned at that again, because everyone said it a lot. Beaner kept going. "Of course, I love Red Ryder a lot, but Little Beaver is the same age as all of us. You know his real name is Robert Blake, but he is really neat. What if he grows up and becomes a real grownup actor someday?"

"So what?" Jumbo said. "Things happen in Hollywood so much maybe in some new movie he might even act like he's a bad guy. Heck, what if when he does grow up, he could even shoot Red Ryder with a real fake pistol, not just a BB gun."

"You dream a lot about bull crap, Jumbo," said Hotshot.

"Okay, you're right, there have been some crazy people in the movies," Catfish offered to stop the normal arguments with these two. "All of us have never liked any cowboy who wants to sing or kiss a girl. We won't even watch a Gene Autry or Roy Rogers movie anymore. The Durango Kid, Lash Larue and his neat whip, and the Cisco Kid are the best. Pancho is a lot funnier than Smiley Burnett, too. The one thing I just don't like in cowboy movies is when we watch the wagon wheels roll backward when the horses are going forward."

"You're right, Cat, I've never understood why that happens," Booby nodded and frowned.

"Maybe they are just trying to do magic stuff," Dink said.

"Oooooh, rats," Hotshot said. "Dink, that is really stupid. My dad said it is just a strange movie visual appearance. It isn't going backwards, it just looks like that when the camera starts filming."

The others all looked at him, and paused with no words being said. Hotshot and Suck kept the others up to snuff when questions like this happened. But Jumbo was not impressed. It still looked crazy to him, but he decided to not go any further with it, and he offered a new game plan.

"Let's all go find a great broken limb or even get a good strong, stick and ride one after another beside Mr. Horrie's house over there. He'll be out yelling within ten seconds, but we will all be gone."

"Yeah, let's go," Beaner bellowed, and he started climbing down.

"Me, too," said Catfish, and also slipped down quickly.

The reason they were going to do it was funny for them, and it was very upsetting to good old Mr. George Horrie. He had the best iron fence in Bradford, and lots of boys thought the finest sound they could ever make was to hold a strong stick against the fence while riding as fast as they could. This noise could even wake up people half a block away. George Horrie almost considered hooking electricity to run throughout the fence, but he realized that the boys would not even know it since wooden sticks had no effect. Maybe he ought to lay out some metal rods that boys would immediately love to try someday.

The only reason that he didn't or couldn't was that grownup neighbors might accidentally touch the fence. If this happened, a much bigger problem could occur then, and he didn't want to make a huge mistake.

On the other hand, if he was actually hidden and could only turn it on when some boys were coming….

Today, six boys did, but he didn't. Mr. Horrie and his wife were in Pekin for the day. Sadly, these temporarily demented boys realized that noise isn't nearly as good if the home's owner isn't there and really upset.

Ginny, Jeannie, Shirley, and Betty were baking some cookies together. Three of them lived in Bradford, and Jeannie's family resided on their farm just about a mile away. Their entire families were going to Henry to the rivers fireworks tonight, and a big box of cookies and brownies were a great idea. They were also very concerned about news from Philip, but Ginny decided to get right into the middle of another big problem for them.

"Do you think we're ever going to grow any breasts?"

"Oh, my Lord, Ginny, you should be embarrassed," Jeannie whispered.

"I can't believe it either," said Shirley.

"I can," Betty emphatically said. "Boobs are a big problem right now, and you ought to realize it. Two of our friends have grown more than any of us, and I am very jealous."

"I know you're talking about Gloria and Francis," Ginny said. "These stupid boys all want to hang around them like it's the only thing they seem to think about. I think boys have cooties!"

They all nodded, and then Shirley said, "The saddest bit of this is it's all they seem to think about those two girls. Guess I shouldn't try to be ignore this concern."

Betty replied, "How did Barbara Denton do this? Did she take pills? At least she moved."

"No, my mother said this is in our genes. I didn't know if she was talking about wearing blue jeans, but it turns out it's in our blood when we're born. This is a complicated deal, I guess," Ginny said. She had clearly wanted to grasp what was happening to their bodies.

"I guess I should agree, too," Shirley almost mumbled. "The last day of school some of those boys were obviously trying to look down Gloria's blouse, and they snapped her brassiere. She acted so upset, but she almost giggled. I can tell you giggling is not something people do when they are really angry."

"Did you know that Elaine and I went to the bathroom together about a month ago when all of you were at the Rees family. They were having a party for Tommy. We did it together because.....I guess we felt we should do it together. Anyway, when we walked out Philip and Michael were almost waiting for us, and one of them asked if I had just grown a Ping-Pong. I said, how could I grow a ping-pong ball when all we do is play it in school. Philip said maybe you should just buy one and then cut it in half. Then glue a ping on this side and a pong on the other. I was so embarrassed I wanted to cry. But I just said you are terrible, and we walked away from them." Betty did get a tear or two in her eyes when she finished.

"I am sorry about that. Maybe I am now a little less concerned about his possible polio problem," Ginny said, then she changed her thought. "Jeannie, you are being very quiet. Why don't you say what you think we are doing?"

"Somehow this is all going to happen the right way. We now know what the big differences between girls and boys. By high school it really going to be different. For heaven sakes, in ten years we all may be married by then, and having real babies, not just these fun dolls that are laying around our bedrooms."

"Sure, Jeannie, but what about you right now?" Betty was getting irked because three of them were now involved and Jeannie was acting as if it hadn't happen.

The other three began staring at her. You might say she was having a very unusual 'pregnant' pause even though pregnancy was not even in their possibilities right now.

"Well, I had another problem. Have any of you started shaving under your arms?" Though she had just said it, Jeannie was once more mortified. She didn't want to, but it had caused such a problem for her that she went ahead.

All three immediately said they hadn't done it yet.

"I made a big mistake because I didn't know how to shave. I borrowed my daddy's razor and tried to do it myself. I cut myself and that was bad enough so I stopped it. But the real problem was that the cut got infected within two days. I had to show my mother, and she almost had a fit, but the main thing is that we went immediately to Dr. Herrmann. He took care of it, and my mom will show me a better way."

"I'm so glad it worked out okay for you. Girls, we know we also have heard bits and pieces about some other changes that will soon be happening to our bodies, too," Ginny said quietly. They each nodded slightly. "Maybe we should talk more plainly to our own mothers now. Remember all those fun times when we played 'May I,' or Red Rover, Red Rover' or hide and seek yelling Olly, Olly Oxen Free. And we smoked candy cigarettes. Or swallowed and chewed wax coke-shaped bottles with colored sugar water. The young women in high school are doing a lot more new things than we ever did. I can tell you this: we were little girls then, but things are now getting a whole lot different."

"Thank God, Helen. I will put the word out as far and as fast as I can for you and Bob. At least it isn't going to be polio, but I have to admit I've never even heard about something called Undulant Fever."

Everyone knows Central was really a person, not a machine. Thankfully, today it was such a special holiday, this was the only serious phone that Fern Wiggins had to handle for the Carlton's.

"I know what you mean, Fern," Helen said back to her. "At first we thought the two doctors were saying it was a version of the polio epidemic situation, but now we feel it is a lot better than getting polio. However, it is still very serious. Philip will have to stay in his bedroom for at least two weeks because he will be quarantined for at least that much."

Just then Fern had to stop and punch in another phone call. "Thanks for holding, Helen. Did the doctors say where he got the disease? Maybe it isn't even a disease. Is it something else?"

"No, you're right, it's a disease, but it's a very infectious one caused by bacteria. You're not going to believe it any more than we did, but it seems that it happened when he drank some contaminated milk. Fern, where in God's name could anyone know how to not drink milk and be worried about this. It is amazing for us. We all get the same milk when it comes from Peoria on the truck. Since no one else ever got it, somehow Philip had the only one that caused the problem here. The doctors have called the milk company to make sure they are making sure that their pasteurization program is doing a better job. But you know what, even these two doctors say it may be something else. This is very scary for us, I can honestly say."

"I am stunned, my dear. Stunned. I will call this info to as many as I can, but what the heck can we do when we don't even know about any thing that we can do differently?" Fern paused, and both women silently thought for a moment. Helen decided to close it now.

"I know. Polio and Undulant Fever neither make any sense right now. At lease we will be bringing him back to our home within a week. His flu-like fevers and sweats are still going up and down so much that is why it's call it. He is so weak right now he can't even walk. But they feel he will be much better in a few days. You'll be calling folks who are members in St. Johns, First Baptist, and Leet Methodist. Please ask them to keep him in their prayers. This is such a shock for Bob and I we don't quite know what else to do. No matter about that now, we thank you, Fern, from our deepest feelings."

It was only about 3:30 in the afternoon, and the Central lady was as busy now as the two doctors were yesterday. Within another hour almost everyone in town would hear the news. Unfortunately, there would not be much joy at all with this kind of story.

Finding that a terrible disease has not happened to your child normally makes parents extremely gladdened. But when they are told what he did get is now so totally unknown, their happiness and his health have turned into a strange enigma.

After the news people in Bradford absorbed the story as well as they could. When you can't do what you don't know eventually forces people to make a new plan. Most everyone there soon decided they should take a welcomed break for an annual and very happy Independence Holiday.

However, a very sick boy and his parents were in Room 311 at St. Francis Hospital. Somewhere else in Peoria a lot of folks were happily sitting on blankets or just plain grass. The rockets red glare tonight was incredible.

But this mother and father were simply holding hands together in the dark. Tomorrow Bob Carlton would go back home, and run his business. All Helen could do now was to continue their vigil.

CHAPTER 26

▼

SSSSSSSSSSSSMOKE!

"Sure and I'm tellin' ya boys, Father Cleary told me what happened with Widow Mulligan. Or was it Mullicuddy? Ah, no real problem. This happened back when Father Fitzgerald first came here back in 1934. That was his first year when he began being our next priest. When he was leavin' he told Father Cleary this story but told him to never tell anyone else about this. Believe it or not, Father Cleary told me, but he told me to not tell anyone else, either. At least now I can tell it, because both the widow and one of the funniest pals in Bradford's good old past days are gone to their reward."

Late that afternoon, six or seven other men were sitting together in Kelly's Bar. They were spellbound because Belzy was off and running with one of his many tales.

"I won't get into who this happened to, but the two fathers thought this was one of the very best laughs they ever had here. One working day in the middle of the week, one of the town's farmer bachelors climbed over a fence, and slipped into his new girl friend's house. There was only one problem. She was married. Somehow she must have been looking for some 'dessert' because she brought her visitor right back to their bedroom and started some wild fun in the sack. Right at the main and exciting moment for both, she hears that her husband has just walked into the front door, and he calls her name.

"She almost goes into a panic but whispers that he has to instantly grab his clothes and jump right out of the bedroom window. Fortunately, it's already opened and on the first floor or he probably is going to hell and a hand basket because he'll break his legs jumpin' out. The word is that she grabbed a robe and walked out to their living room to tell her husband that she was goin' to take a bath. The other wild bull is now runnin' buck-naked across his neighbor's fence. Nobody is lookin' at him, and he climbs over to run into an arbor full of grape trees. However, it's a little fuller than he thought because that is where Widow Mulligan is standing while she is cutting a cluster of grapes.

"Boys, she looks over and sees a naked man who is still standin' strong and tall, as you know what I mean. The poor old widow faints right over backwards in the arbor. He pulls on his britches and his shirt and runs like hell out of the place. But he does get to his own home fast and calls Central that he thinks the widow has just had a heart attack. He hung up so fast he thinks Central won't know who he is. Central does call the fire boys, and also calls Father Fitzgerald, too, if the widow needs the last rites. When the boys realize that she just passed out and is okay, they go home. But the best is that when Central got that call she knows immediately who called her because their line has to be connected."

At this the men were snickering at almost every sentence Belzy said. Nobody in Bradford enjoyed telling a good story any better than Belzy, and he was ready for the climax.

"Father Fitz is holding the flustered old lady who is still laying there in the grass at the arbor. He says what happened to you, my dear? She looks up and says Satan himself was standin' in my arbor, Father. Our priest is relieved it was not a heart attack and says, dear Mrs. Mulligan, sure and Satan is always trying to cause terrible problems and temptations for many of our flock. Well, Father, she says, all my life I've heard that Satan has two big horns on his forehead, but this devil had just one right between his legs."

The room exploded with laughter. "I bet we could find out who Central was back in 1934 if we wanted to know," Lefty said.

"No, my friends, it's all over now. That lady who knew it then died about five years ago. Any of the other names shall be not be mentioned again," Belzy said softly. "But we can laugh our arses as much as we want to now."

Suddenly, as if this had somehow been planned by Central at another time or day, the entire room was stunned because the town's famous whistle was going on right now. Everyone called it the Noon Whistle, but since it was exactly 5:15 on this Wednesday, July 13th afternoon, a frantic phone call just changed its name to a fire alarm. Everyone here except the bartender had finished their day's work to have a simple beer, but life was about to change.

Belzy was one of the volunteers, and quickly told Mike McCree, the town's best laborer, to call Central and get the directions for the two fire trucks, and he ran across Main Street to where the fire trucks would be sitting. One of at least three trained men would surely be driving the 1939 Chevrolet Fire Truck with a Howe Pump, and probably would run the other older Chevy they got in 1929. Several of the men who owned stores or worked in one of them were already grabbing their fire helmets and yellow coats. Several were already standing outside their stores to jump on the trucks. Within another minute or two both trucks would be rolling out to get the fire out.

There was only one slight problem. Why in the world did Belzy Hooligan ask Mike, the one man in the entire town who had a bigger stuttering problem than even Arnold Bundee? Within seconds Mike ran over to the fire station and jumped up to ride the bigger truck. Belzy was going to drive.

"Sssssssssssssmoke!" Mike yelled.

"Where's the fire" called Belzy.

"Gggggggggggoooo to Arrrrrrrr!" That's as close as he got to where they had to go.

But before Belzy could get the right information they rolled up to get their last volunteer. Today it was at Jimmy Hennessey's "the Auditorium." His small store was only 9' x'21', but he added a lean-to so extra hoses could be used if they needed more for one of the fire trucks.

Just before the truck arrived Jimmy had to lay down his razor and grab his equipment. "Mr. Marsh, I've got to got to a fire. Sorry, but if I'm held up we'll meet you in the morning and finish shaving then."

Mr. Marsh was lying back on the one-chair operation, and was completely covered with a steaming towel. Some days it was so busy they had to hold their 'number' and just sit in one of the bouncy chairs with metal arms. Men loved to discuss and just cuss about politics, sports, crops, weather, and prices. Today it was unusual that there was no one else waiting there.

"No problem, Jimmy. I may take a little nap and if you get back before I wake up we'll do it then. If I have to go home for supper, I'll come back tomorrow. Putting out the fire is the most important part." Mr. Marsh and everyone else in Bradford knew when men like Jimmy hear the fire whistle blow everything else is now the main event.

As the trucks arrived Jimmy nodded and ran out of the shop. He was one of the Bradford boys who had to go into military service a few years ago. He was in the Army from 1943-45, and when he went to England for the certain, major attack to finally defeat the Nazi's across the channel, Jimmy ended up staying there. Someone made a determination that Jimmy should work in a hospital out-side of London. He took care of returning wounded boys, and when they needed it he cut their hair, too.

But even before he had to serve in the war, Jimmy Hennessey had cut a lot of little boys' first haircuts in Bradford. These seven teenage boys who were born in 1936 didn't know it then, but Jimmy opened the Auditorium the same year. By the time they were around two, every one of them had first sat in the chair Mr. Marsh was sitting right now.

They always remembered that when it was all over they got a lollypop, but even today they still love to watch the ancient cash register that rang bells and flipped drawers.

"Good lord sakes, Mikie, where are we going?"

"Arrrr…," Mike tried again, and Belzy suddenly felt he had figured out the conversation.

"We're going to Artie Brazee's house boys," and started going straight east through the four-way stop sign.

"Nnnnnnooooooo," and Mike began to wave and shout.

Belzy pulled over on East Main about where LaVerne Harris lived on one side and the Owens family on the other, and slammed his two hands on the driving wheel. "Where the hell are we goin', son?"

"Mmmmmmmiss Vvvvvanzant."

For a second or two all of the firemen were bewildered. The problem about saying a word that began with arrrr wasn't even close to either Miss or Vanzant. As both trucks began spinning around and began going back to the west, Jimmy Hennessey yelled, "Belzy, he has to be taking about going to Arbor Street because that's where this teacher lives. If she's not when we get there, he just hasn't fig-ured out where we have to go. Let's go run into somebody house and call Central again."

"Lad, that is a wonderful idea," and they turned left for the one Peoria Street block to turn west again on Arbor. Fortunately, it was only about two hundred yards before both trucks stopped right beside the Foster house. Miss Vanzant had rented this upstairs apartment for so many years most people didn't recall just how long it had been.

Smoke was coming out of the side door, and several windows in the three-room place, but whatever had caused the fire seemed was almost under con-trol.

"Well, it's about time this version of the Keystone Kops or the Katzenjammer Kids has finally arrived," Miss Vanzant said, but she was obviously very perturbed "You and your sirens got lost."

"Now, now, Miss Vanzant, sure and we had a wee misunderstanding' as to exactly where the fire was, but speaking of which, where's it now?"

She waved Belzy and several of the volunteers to come into her apartment. "This couch is what happened. Something caused the fire. When I woke up, smoke was going right out the side door there, and Mrs. Barnes across the street saw it and called Central. When I realized it was on fire, I ran over and grabbed a box of baking soda and quickly got it out. It's still smoldering, though."

"Well, lads, let's haul this out and put it out on the middle part of the grassy yard. Let's make sure it's really out." Three of the others picked it up and carried it down the steps, and left Miss Vanzant and Belzy alone.

"Now, my dear, I have to be askin' how did the fire get started in the first place?"

"Belzy, I was, uh, uh, I was apparently burning a candle over by the couch here in the living room. I think I must have fallen asleep, and maybe that candlestick got turned over....or something like that. Or maybe that Fuller Brush Man who came by here earlier did it." But her comments were not doing too well.

He instantly realized that what she just said, and what he just saw are two vastly different bits of information. The candlestick did fall over there, but he could see it hadn't been lit any time recently. Suddenly Miss Vanzant also grasped that she had just gotten caught, so to speak.

Her normal strong, dictatorial manner changed abruptly. "Belzy, go take all the boys home. I will decide if I should throw that sofa out or try to redo it again. I'll bring you boys some brownies when everyone gets together for the volunteer monthly meeting."

She was kind of cajoling him to leave as he was slowly shuffling along. He now slipped out of the side door and they both shook hands. "Well, my dear, this is in good shape now. Maybe some company can redo the sofa. Again, it was nice bein' together two months ago for the annual Lincoln speech on the park. Things are also safe and sound right now." With that they nodded, and he went down the steps, while she wheeled around and disappeared into the kitchen.

Traces of smoke were still coming from one of the charred corners of the flowery covered sofa's armrest. Jimmy applied the coup 'de grace with a brief burst of his portable fire extinguisher. Satisfied the fire was now completely out, the eight men walked back to the two trucks, and began going back up to Main Street.

"I didn't even go inside and yet I bet we know what happened here today," Keith Henson said.

"You're right as rain, Mr. Keith. It only took me about one and a half seconds to realize that 'tis my belief, and make the devil take your tongue and run it through a sausage grinder,' if any of you breath even just a word of this here speculation, thank you very much." Belzy was very concerned about nasty rumors that seemed to be out of control when mistakes and accidents were involved in fire experiences.

The other three agreed, and Mike reached up and slit his right hand across his neck to give the classic example of what happens to anyone who talks when they should be listening.

"Yes, lads, 'tis my humble opinion the old girl set it afire herself when she was smokin' a cigarette or two this afternoon. School is not going to go back 'til after next Labor Day, and it's a time when teachers can take their rest."

"Smmmmoking.... I nnnever knew any tttttteacher did anything llllike that." Mike finally finished an entire sentence. Actually, earlier he had not completely said but two, one syllable words so this achievement was good for him.

Belzy nodded, and then both trucks turned into the station and stopped. Though this truck had turned its engine off he was still sitting in the cab. He glanced and looked over at the three, and several of the others walked beside him who had also turned the other engine off. "'Tis a sad but oft true tale, lads. Society expects teachers and nuns to be even purer than Caesar's wife."

"Do the Caesar's live anywhere near Bradford?" young Willard Bonston asked seriously.

Several of the men chuckled, but Belzy interrupted so no one would be making fun of the question. "I believe this is simply a figure of speech, Will. You're smart as paint, son. We are just talkin' about the sad fire we went through a few minutes ago. Miss Vanzant is as good as the town has. Why, lads, our teachers are almost as prohibited from enjoying some of the world's 'juicier fruits' as our dear catholic sisters in the convent. Teachers and nuns are wrongly criticized for havin' gone into one our fine towns bars and establishments to just enjoy a shot and a beer with you and me. Boys, when this kind of criticism is finally happening, I am afraid they'd run the ladies outta town two fast steps ahead of the tar pot and feather bag."

With this, the men reorganized their equipment, and closed the station down. Jimmy Hennessey knew that Mr. Marsh would be back for his shave in the morning. It was now 6:30, and the amazing adventure had just gotten a little too late for business tonight. Almost no folks in Bradford ever even locked their homes, and Jimmy wasn't even interested to go back and put a key in the Auditorium.

CHAPTER 27

▼

ANGELO SICILIANO DIDN'T SHOOT POOL TODAY EITHER

Six of the gang were now riding their bikes straight into the morning sun. Suck was finally home.

Actually, he was leaning on a chair in his bedroom window on the second floor. His quarantine was now in full control. No one could even get onto his first floor let alone coming up for a normal visit like they all had done probably several dozen times before. But the best arrival that all of them enjoyed for the past few years would definitely not be happening for two more weeks. For now, the famous pool table was out the question.

Almost everyone in town had some problems or another when one of their kids got mumps, chicken pox, at least two kinds of measles or the dangerous scarlet fever. That disease could put quarantine signs on their front porch that had a simple message: stay away.

Suck's home had a huge attic on the third floor that had more room and more fun than anyone else in the bunch could have. Mainly, it was the special, full sized pool table with everything a boy could hope for. Pool balls, different length cues, chalk, a rack, and some special cues for an almost out of the question shot one of them needed to hit, were all over the huge room. The second best thing here was that it was private.

As the six started leaning or laying their bikes, they were cheering when Suck's mother opened the window ever higher, and Suck waved at all of them. They began to sit down on the grass under Suck's window, and Beaner quickly asked, "You got sick on the third of July so we haven't been able to even see you until today. How long will you have to stay in your room?"

"The doctor says I can't have anyone come in for almost two more weeks, and that is a real bummer," he replied. "I also won't be going to Minnesota to camp this year. I was going to a place called Camp Lincoln near Bemidji. My folks have an old beach house at Gull Lake there. Now the doctor has stopped the whole plan."

Everyone was kind of 'out to lunch' with this plan. No one else had the slightest idea where Brainard or Bemidji was, and finding Minnesota might even be a little tough for them.

Dink decided to ignore what had happened in some camp he hadn't heard of, but asked, "Can we come in the back door and climb up to the third floor playroom to shoot pool if you are still too sick?" Even he knew it was out of the question, and all of them laughed. Except that all of them, including Suck, really hoped it might be true.

"That was a good one, Dink. My mom heard that and shook her head no as strong as if she was going to have me arrested."

"Oh, well," Hotshot shrugged, "Maybe we can do it together in two weeks. Climbing up to your playroom has more fun than the Laughin' Tree, but it's in a better located for all of us. But when we get-together then I think I will be able to tell you about something," and he tried to whisper, but it became kind of loud, "that we have been looking to find a special place beside the Mighty Spoon."

Several nodded or said affirmative comments. Suck really wanted to talk more about this, but he was afraid his mother would come back into the bedroom and hear it at the wrong time.

Suck reached over and grabbed a big calendar hanging on a nail near the window. "How about coming here on August 5 or Saturday on the sixth. I promise I will make my mom bake some really good brownies or chocolate chip cookies." Again he glanced around to see if she was listening with 'prying eyes'. His sister was downstairs, and his mother was somewhere else.

"Has your mom done any canning this summer since you were up in the hospital so long? I bet all of our mothers have been working in the canning season doing this on and off for the past few weeks. I get worn out doing preserves with strawberries first, and then plums, and it'll be concord grapes in a month from now," Booby sighed.

"Yes, she is doing some of it, though I haven't been able to be much help," Suck said.

"Mine works like a sailor," Hotshot said. "She is boiling one kind of fruit or another one day of every week. Then she has to boil her mason jars and the rubber bands that seal it."

"I spilled some of that paraffin melting wax, last week and my mom practically hit me with her wash tub. When it got solid pretty quick, I scrapped it back up from the basement floor, but she said we had to throw it away because it was too dirty. I didn't see it was too dirty, but she did," Catfish offered.

"Hah, Cat, that's a good one, too. We all know that what we think is dirty and what our moms think are two totally different ideas," Suck said and the rest laughed.

"Bet you all have to do some other chores, too," Suck said.

"You can count on that," Jumbo said and spat loudly. "I got so lazy two weeks ago my dad got so angry he yelled at me to get your butt out of your bedroom and mow the yard right now." He laughed again, and then added, "Son, you'll get out there and do it now or I am going to grab your baseball glove and take it to Peoria and have the damn thing bronzed."

Everyone laughed, and Dink fell over backwards on the fresh, green grass. "My dad then said when he gets it back from the guy who is covering my glove at the store in Peoria, it will be sort of a hood ornament on the lawnmower. My dad by then was chuckling at himself and my mom was shaking her head and laughing, too. But he got a frown and said, Laverne, this boy is so lazy sometimes I think teenage boys are about as useless as a blind dog dry-humpin' a fire plug."

Again the laughter was so infectious they almost were getting sick from hurting their ribs. Several were now lying completely down on the grass staring and now giggling as the sun slipped in and out of huge, rolling clouds. Several of them immediately remembered that some previous summer days just like, all of them would just started spinning around and getting dizzy. Then they fell down for no other reason than tittering

"At least none of us has a blind dog," Beaner said, and still kept laughing.

"Heck, all of us has a good dog even if they're just mongrels," Hotshot offered.

"Yeah," Catfish nodded. "Mr. McNulty has a neat dog that I heard was what they call purebred, but I don't have any idea what that means."

"It's pretty simple. They take a pure kind of male and a pure kind of female and breed them," Suck called down. "But I don't anyone in town except Mr. McNulty has one."

"I don't even care. All my life we've had three dogs now, and I think they all found our house and needed some food," Dink said. "Like I said, my dad told me if our dogs are mongrels, our blood relatives are, too. Then he added, most dogs and relatives are at least first cousins."

The others laughed instantly, and Dink added, "My dad said our family is so confused and different that our ancestors are from England, Scotland, Ireland, Germany, and a great-great grandmother who was a Cherokee Indian. That's how we got to be mongrels."

"That's probably true for all of us," Jumbo laughed.

Suddenly Beaner said, "I just remembered. I bet we all have to do our work chores. I have to pick cherries off two trees in our backyard. The quicker I did it the better because those blasted robins all try to eat every one of them. But my mom baked us a bodacious cherry pie. When my dad buys a fresh dug quart of Sealtest vanilla ice cream from Dorgan's, life is as good as it can be."

"Hey Suck, when you get out, we should figure out some new games in the backyards after dinner. We're too old to be playing some of the good old best games we did for years," Booby exclaimed.

"Yeah, we did do a lot of running and laughing every night," Suck agreed. "How many times did we play Red Rover or Dodge Ball, or Kick the Can?"

"And when we boys were doing something else, the girls were playing Jacks or Jump Rope. My cousin Ruthe says sometimes they could get three girls jumping while someone was swinging each end of the rope," Dink said.

"Yeah, but everyone loved 'Simon Says'," Catfish said. "Some of us called it 'Mother May I', but it was really Simon Says."

"Everyone of our decisions then were by going 'eeny-meeny-miney-moe'but we're older. Now we vote about it," Hotshot gave his patented snicker.

"That's for sure," Suck nodded.

"We'll be playing work-up in the town's baseball field while you're gone," Beaner said. "And we'll play rounders at softball, too. But we will all have to climb over the fence in right field to get some really dry cow pies. If we don't have enough of them for all three bases somebody will have to throw their glove when the last pie finally falls apart."

"That's true, but lets really make sure they are dry. The last time Dink brought three they were so oooie we almost got sick with the smell," Booby frowned.

"Okay, guys, I screwed up then, but I'd rather remember another old fun time when we were kids pretending that we were Indians at night. We always caught as many lightning bugs as we could in a glass bottle and pretended it was a flashlight."

"Yeah, that was a lot of fun," Cat said slowly.

Hotshot glanced up to Suck, and then looked around the boys. "Like I said, we are now older. It's time for a new challenge and new fun. We still love our radio shows, but there isn't anything else that anyone will ever see or play in this town so we have to be ingenious. We'll wait until Suck gets out of his quarantine, and in less than two or three weeks we will be able to do the most exciting adventure we've ever dreamed up."

"That sounds both fun and scary, but I am going to go," Jumbo said.

With that, the boys started saying goodbye, and jumped up on their bikes. Suddenly, Suck called down, "Let me throw you some gum. This is a present. I've got one package of Blackjack and one of Teaberry. I don't like Clove." With that, he threw them down.

"Wow, thanks, Suck," Dink said.

"Yeah, that's neat. But we'll give you back what you gave us 'cause we'll just get into a fight over what's left." As Booby said this he and the others laughed, but it was also true.

No matter. It was time to have lunch at home.

Dink arrived about the same time as the others, and climbed up the one step porch in the backdoor. "Hi, mom," he called.

Mrs. Patterson smiled and walked over and gave him a brief hug. "I know you have been waiting for a special letter from you know who."

"Oh, my goodness, I bet what you are saying has finally happened. Mom, I've been running to the post office every day for four weeks, and finally it arrived. I was just having fun with the guys at Suck's house."

"Here it is, son, I hope it gives you some good news."

Dink lifted it up and held it gingerly with both hands. If he had been handed one of the original United States Constitution it couldn't have been any more important to him than this letter. He slowly walked over to the big fuzzy chair on one side of the living room and just stared at it as if it was the Holy Grail.

The envelope ripped gently, and a single page with two folds slipped out. It suddenly gave him a special reason that had concerned Dink when he wrote them his own letter last month. This one solitary page was now almost giving him a heart attack, because it seemed that he was afraid it was ringing an alarm in his mind.

The top of the letter was from Charles Atlas Ltd., in New York City. Unfortunately, the name Dink received was mailed to 'Dear Sir.' There were only three brief paragraphs

"Thank you for your recent inquiry about buying the Charles Atlas 'Dynamic-Tension' course. This program will eventually build you into a better, stronger, and bigger body through Mr. Atlas' amazing techniques.

"Mr. Atlas feels you are not yet old enough to qualify for this course at the present time. However, in a few short years, he is convinced that you, too will also be called like he is, "The World's Most Perfectly Developed Man."

"We will keep your name on file, and hope…"

"Oh, no," Dink whispered. For a few seconds he was both dazed and silent. Then he began to quietly cry. These were not soft, sad, gentle tears, they were the most bitter that had ever rolled out of his eyes.

As he silently started to climb up to his bedroom, his mother realized something was wrong. No cheering or jumping was happening in this house, and she instantly decided to find out what had transpired.

He beat her about five seconds, but as he buried his face into one of the two pillows she walked in and quickly sat beside him, caressing her hands and kissing the back of his head.

No one was speaking right now, but his sobs were so strong he was shaking the entire bed. After a few moments, she asked, "Jonathan, were they unable to let you take a course? Your father and I were very worried about how much you really hoped it would happen right for you." Like almost every mother in the world, she always called him by his full name when she was either angry or compassionate.

He lifted his head, and sobbed. "Mom, they said I couldn't take the course. They didn't even send me how much I would have to pay for it," and he stuck his head back into the pillow. More squeaks were caused when he again began sobbing, and shaking on the bed. "Mom, I weigh 82 pounds now but I am so skinny I'm even smaller than a 97 pound weakling."

"My son, you are just a young boy. You are probably not big or old enough that a coach or athlete would want you to start doing big exercises too soon. You need to know something I don't think I have ever told you. Think about this. How big do you feel your dad looks now?"

This question was a surprise. Dink paused for a second or two and answered, "Mom, he is the biggest, strongest man I have ever seen. It's why I want to make him happy and proud that he would feel that I can look like him." Dink stopped crying, and blinked his tears. She offered him a tissue.

"You father and I got married on Sunday, May 12, 1929. It was Mother's Day that year. Jonathan, the man I married that day weighed 135 pounds. He was 6' 2", the same height then as he is today. The only difference is that he now weighs 205 pounds. I don't think he ever heard about Charles Atlas or Mr. Bonomo, the man Eddy Jay thinks is a hero."

"Wow, how in the world did he get to be so strong and so heavy if he was as skinny as me?"

"It is as simple as this, son, your body will grow when it feels its ready. When you are older, I predict you will also be bigger and stronger than you will ever dream. What do you think about that, my son?"

Dink looked into his mother's eyes and smiled. Then he gave her one of the deepest, strongest hugs he had ever given her.

Somewhere in New York, Charles Atlas would have also agreed with everything Mrs. Patterson just said. He did change the bodybuilding world for a better and stronger time. But every now and then he occasionally remembered how skinny he was after moving to Brooklyn, New York in 1900 when his family migrated from Arci, Italy.

At that time, his name was Angelo Siciliano. However, 6 million other skinny boys and men bought his mail order course beginning around 1928, and the fictitious name of Charles Atlas was a lot more important than the mythical titan who held up the heavens. Interestingly, in those same years, Angelo's other big strongman buddy had a real name that he kept all his life.

This man was another magnificent Italian who was called that year, The Modern Apollo. His name was Joe Bonomo. If his physical growth finally did happen the same thing to his father, Dink would always remember those two amazing Italians for the rest of his life.

CHAPTER 28

▼

THE COAL MINE DISASTER

"Jack Armstrong, the All American Boy,,,,have you tried Wheaties, the best breakfast food in the land?"

Hotshot was listening to one of his most favorite radio shows that afternoon, but it was Thursday, August 4, and for once he was much more interested with his own program that he would be telling all six buddies tomorrow. Suck was about to be finally through his quarantine quagmire.

For several months Hotshot had been studying about what and how a coal mine works. He had gone to the library and high school to 'bone up' his enlightenment by reading their two best set of books, the Encyclopedia Britannica and the World Book. Page after page of detailed knowledge seemed to get deeper and deeper, but he kept doing it all by himself. When he finally studied enough about the inner sanctum mystery deep into coal pits in the past week, Hotshot finally figured out how to find and open the hidden cover.

When a small local company twenty or thirty years ago who had been digging all around and through what was called the Illinois Basin, large quantities of coal were found. Though it was in Indiana and Kentucky, too, this little firm found out that Bradford was just too diminutive to make any profit. A little here and a little there was way too little anywhere.

Now Sheck was the only man in this part of Stark County who cared a hoot for coal. Except this very smart young man, and he finally had put the things together that he wanted to bring tomorrow. Hotshot was going to tell them how they could go down into the mine.

All six of the others were unusually quiet, and were sitting on the floor around the pool table in Suck's third floor playroom. They knew something big was about to happen, because Hotshot called each of them for a brief phone call after supper. Now he held up a bag he that he carried this morning. "Boys, I now know how to safely go down and look around in the mine."

Surprise or shock did not register on any of their faces. In fact, none even said anything, because they had known for several months that it was not going to be *if*, but *when*.

Hotshot quickly decided to go right into his plan. "This is something I have at our home. It is a safe rope ladder that my dad put into my bedroom. If we ever get into a fire, this will be the safe way to get out through the window upstairs. We've never had a fire so this still looks as new as when he bought it five years or so ago.

"We will tie this to a tree when we go down in the mine. If the wooden ladder is too weak we will be able to go down or back up." The other six nodded and smiled. They thought it sounded like a very solid plan. "Each of us will have a flashlight. I hope your home each has one. If you need to get one I hope you can go to Mr. Sullivan or Mr. Bucher at Bradford Community Hardware. Flashlights cost about a dollar. Look at this. Bring a pair of gloves. Everyone has some at home. Here are some candles and matches to make sure we have them if we really need them." He paused for a second, and then said, "I am also bringing this."

He stared around to each face, and then held up a firecracker. It wasn't just a normal firecracker, it was a Silver Bomber TNT. When someone lit one of these it sounded like a small canon.

"Wow," Dink exclaimed. "I lit one of these a year ago on the Fourth of July and it blew up so much a small rock hit me right on my forehead fifty-feet away. It was bleeding and I didn't even know it. That's how my folks said I was never doing anything that stupid…..."

Dink suddenly stopped because he was talking to Hotshot who just said he was going to bring it this afternoon.

"No, we won't be playing with this. I am going to drop this down in the coal mine, and we'll all be hiding behind big trees as far as we can run after dropping it. We'll be able to hear it. If it has a lot of something bad or dangerous around just sitting there it may be blown up and that will be the end of the whole plan. On the other hand, if all we hear is the TNT and the area there doesn't collapse we will just find out that there is no worry about going down."

All six stared at each other. This was the most amazing idea any of them had ever considered or conceived.

Hotshot smiled, and started to speak. Jumbo interjected, "What a minute. I am still concerned about your idea to go down into that mine. I dog dare you to not do this, Hotshot."

Several of the other boys whistled softly. This statement for one boy to another was an ultimatum that a person decided to challenge someone else's statement. One to another never said it unless something was so serious it was almost considered to be law. Now six of them were staring intensely at Hotshot. He paused, and then replied, "I double-dog-dare-ya, Jumbo."

Suddenly, Hotshot's supreme declaration was over. No one said another word, because none of them, even Jumbo, wanted to argue or doubt it. After several seconds of total quiet, Hotshot said matter-a-fact, "Any questions?"

Again it was silent. "Guys, get your stuff I just mentioned, and lets bring it with our water jugs and snacks. Lets ride there tomorrow at nine o'clock. But whatever, don't tell any of the parents. You know what they will say, right?"

Saturday morning, somehow every one of them brought the exact set of material. However, they almost rode so quietly no one else would have known they had come. This was so serious but also so silent if any parent was riding with them he or she would automatically realize they were doing something wrong. Boys this age who never make a sound are certainly getting into trouble.

The first surprise was when Hotshot led the other six into the American Legion place, and rode over to the edge of Harper's Woods. He pushed his bike through a large group of bushes, and leaned it against a huge walnut tree. It was as if they had entered a concealed or secret entrance. When the last came in Hotshot said, "Our bikes are hidden here. Not even Sheck will know about this. Look over at the path. I found this when I discovered that the coal company used to drive this road to get right over to the kind of mine they would have run maybe twenty years ago. One of the farmers north of where we are told me the mine is right on the side of his cornfield and Harper's Woods. Let's walk this way."

With that Hotshot led the way though the stand of timber. This was new territory for the remaining six boys. After about a quarter of a mile they were there. "Here's where the top of the mine is. Well, I told you about this before. Here its either called a Slope Mine or a Vertical Shaft. As soon as we climb down I can tell which one we will do. Now, take a look at this." He put his gloves on and grabbed a pile of limbs and brush. Suddenly the others could see two big double hatches. He looked up, and said, "I found that I could take a hammer and a crow bar and pull all the big bolts and nails they used to close this down. Now I need at least two or three of you to help lift this thing up and over."

They were amazed at what he was saying, but they went to work, and it only took about five seconds for all other six to get their gloves on. Several lifted it about a foot high enough to push and slide the big covering. "I dug this and re-covered the panels, but I couldn't get it far enough along to be able to see down in the mine's shaft. Now, boys, let's slowly crawl over with our flashlights and see what we see. Don't be standing up! Somebody could fall down here, even if it is on a slope."

It looked as if the shaft seemed to be going straight down, but it was deep enough they couldn't see just how many feet it went down. Actually, the sunny day was so bright the flashlights here had no impact. It would have to be several feet down to began showing better light. Hotshot realized it, and looked up. A circle of eyes looked directly into him. "I will drop the TNT. You guys run over to several of the big trees there." He pointed at the ones about sixty or seventy feet away.

As they began to rapidly move out, he reached down and found a large rock. He tossed it, and let it go down into the shaft. It bounced just once, and then made a loud cracking thud. He knew it was not too deep, and he happily didn't hear any growls or any other kind of animal sounds.

"I'm going to light the firecracker. Stay behind the trees. Some rocks might blow straight up so count to at least ten before you start looking back this way." He lit the match, ignited the firecracker's fuse, threw it down in the darkness, and ran like a 'turpentined' dog.

It seemed as if each of them felt it took about ten minutes long, but seven easy seconds rocked the pit, echoing deep inside, and belching smoke right up the shaft. But there were no sounds or actions of collapsing or caving in, and not even stones or muck fell back out of the sky.

"Let's tie the rope ladder, and I will hold it and climb down the wooden one and see what's what." For some reason none of the boys were the least bit frightened, and none wanted to even offer any different thought or idea. They were there to agree and work, but Hotshot was to plan and to do it.

At the same time, as least one other person heard a strange, muffled explosion. He was casually fishing on the river several hundred yards away, and almost snoozing on such a warm, glorious Saturday afternoon. The backfire sound or concussion brought him to stand right up. It was Sheck, and he suddenly knew something wrong had just happened.

The smoke caused by the firecracker was now settling down fairly well. Hotshot went first. The acrid smell was strong, but he could see for at least fifteen feet below with his flashlight. One by one, each of the boys crawled down the black hole using a combination of the solid rope ladder, and the other, a wooden one that was half-rotten. As they began shining their flashlights it was incredible. The bottom walkway was muddy and eerie, and it wasn't very far in either direction. The smell of coal oil and seepage water was powerful, and old timbers that were still standing to support the mine's roof now looked pretty weak.

In less than a minute, all of them realized that there was nothing down in this terrible mess that they hoped might have some aspect of value. Hotshot looked over and saw a broken, old wheelbarrow. He picked it up and the left handle broke off. "Guys, this is an incredible experience, but I think we ought to start climbing back up. I guess we won't be finding any neat things today."

"Yep," Jumbo said, with a loud bit of spit, "We'll laugh about this crazy idea for a lot of years. Has anyone seen any snakes?"

"Nope," Beaner said. "And good riddance."

"There's not even anything here that the gang of counterfeiters would have hidden their stuff,…" Dink suddenly stopped. Somebody was calling down into the mine.

"Who is down thar? Is that you boys?"

"I think that's Sheck," Booby said, as he flashed his light from one boy to another.

"Sheck, is that you?" Hotshot yelled.

"Oh dear lordy," Sheck called back. "Yas'm, that is me. Come on boys. Get back up here this minute. Why, dis is the scariest idea I done have ever heard about. Come up right now, you hear!"

In the combination of flashlights all turned on in the mine, most of the boys were actually laughing. Nothing seemed too bad right now, and thought they were ready to climb back up, they thought it might be a good long last look at the place.

"Boys, I heard that 'plosion that you dropped down in here. You could be makin' the mine weaker and weaker. Why, it could fall right in there. Get's up here right now, I said, you hear?"

"Get going, he'll keep yelling at us, and it is time to get back up on the top," Hotshot said softly.

Catfish was the closest, and started going up. Within a few seconds, Booby, Suck, Dink, and Beaner emerged into the bright sunshine.

"Boys, I does think I has to tell your mommas and daddies to have a serious talkin' with you all." Sheck was relieved, but he was also angry.

"Ahhhhhhhh. Help!"

Jumbo was next, and as he was pulling himself out of the entrance he heard a scream down below. "Hotshot, what is it?"

"Oh, damn," he yelled back up. "I just stepped on the third from the bottom rung and it shattered. I slipped holding the rope ladder and fell back down on the messy bottom. I think I broke my ankle or foot. I'm trying to stand up, but it really hurts."

Jumbo lifted his head and stared at Sheck, but he was completely glancing at everyone. "Hotshot fell back down, and he's broken his leg or foot or something. The bottom rungs on the old ladder broke, and he fell back down."

At once panic was in everyone's eyes, even the old man, who was now using a strong, old limb as if it was a crutch on one thing, or a fishing pole for another.

"Boys, I'se goin' down there right now." Sheck quickly grabbed Jumbo and helped him out of the top entrance of the shaft. "I gotta get this boy up and outta here. Hand me one of your flashlights. I saw some of you havin' one." Booby was the closest and immediately handed it to Sheck. He dropped his wooden limb, and started slowly going down. Then he called to Hotshot below. "Son, are you hurtin' about somethin' else, or is it jus' your foot?"

Hotshot was running his light up to see Sheck coming down. "Just my ankle. Or maybe it's my lower leg, Mr. Sheck, but it is already swelling. If you can lift me up, I know I can lift myself up on the rope ladder with my arms, and use one step at a time with my left foot."

Sheck analyzed this as he kept going down. As he heard Hotshot's last word, he hit the bottom. For a few seconds he stared at what he could see as the flashlight danced from one ghostly clutter to another, and softly said, "Good gawd, son. This is a mighty terrible place."

Hotshot didn't even want to look at it anymore. He was also so embarrassed he couldn't even stare at the good man who might be able to get him back into sunshine once more. Sheck put the flashlight bottom into his mouth for directional light, and used his hands to help the boy standup. It took about two or three helpful hops for Hotshot to reach over to the rope ladder.

"You help pull yo'self while I'se liftin'. You try to stay high enough to be able to put most of your weight on the rope, but let your foot step one at a time and keep workin' back up as you go."

Hotshot was probably almost a hundred pounds, but the big man lifted him up as if he was a baby. He thanked Sheck softly, and then, without another word, began methodically going up. Sheck kept showing the flashlight beneath him, and followed his progress. When the other six boys saw him shove up and over they all automatically cheered, but they were shocked by how dirty Hotshot was, and how big his right ankle had swollen. They laid him down a few feet away from the shaft.

"Now we've got to help get Sheck come back up, too. Boy's, he's the best man we've ever seen." Dink said. All of the boys nodded. They each enjoyed being around with him now, because he brought the same fun and laughter that their own remaining grandparents had. Dink's sincere comment was by virtue of how much they now all respected and loved the old man.

Down below, Sheck held the flashlight that was still on, and re-stuck the back part of it into his mouth. He wanted to see what he was doing, and it took two hands to just hold the ladders. The loose bottom of the rope ladder started swinging a little as he began going up. Step by step he kept getting closer to reach the opening of the mine.

Just as he rose into the top of the hole he made a terrible, irrational decision. The long swimming rope ladder was uncomfortable, and he moved over stepping onto the wooden steps. He was now smiling at the boys as he almost reached the top, but disaster struck right in the middle of his grin.

Sheck Dye fell right out of their eyes. Some kind of collapse caused him to almost disappear. The only thing they could see was one of his frantic hands, and a few inches of his forearm. His head and face was now covered by a lot of fresh earth and dirt.

There are critical moments in a human's body, but breathing air was the one main thing Sheck abruptly needed more than anything else.

Gasps and screams instantly erupted from all seven boys.

"Dear God," Dink offered something that was a mixture of prayer and panic, and dropped down on his knees at the side of the chasm. He instantly was grabbing his hands full of dirt and started throwing them in any direction. "The rest of you grab and throw this dirt. We've got to save this man."

It was such a shock, for a moment no one else moved, but they quickly reacted and all crawled along in a circle around the mine's entrance shaft. Less than five seconds they were all throwing dirt anywhere behind themselves. Even Hotshot put his own pain out of his thoughts immediately, and went to work.

"Sheck, Sheck, we're coming. Hold your breath for another second or two," Dink called.

Amazingly, Sheck's left arm was hooked onto the rope ladder so he probably wouldn't fall any further down, and let his right hand and arm to start pushing any kind of soil away from his mouth. The boys were also frantically grabbing as much dirt away as they could. Within a couple of seconds he got his first gulp of air, and held his hands to cup away any more debris and loose dirt from falling into his throat. The seven kept going until it was obvious that he could breath normally.

"Praise the Lord, boys, I thought I was shore was goin' down," Sheck said.

"But what happened? Did one of the ladders fall?" Dink asked, but they were still getting rapid breaths.

"Guess I moved over too far. The old wooden ladder broke down jus' below where I got. It c'lapsed for me up here in the top. Now my own body is jammed by dirt into the shaft. I'se holding the rope, but I'se so jammed I might could go down farther again, but I sure can't go no where up any higher now."

They all heard this, but Dink began leaning up into the faces around the circle. They were all on their knees, and, as they stared at him he said, "I've got an idea that will get two things going to get Sheck out of here." He reached into the back seat left pocket in his overalls. "This is my ace in the hole, so to speak. This came from Junior Tracy."

Dink opened his 'toy' handcuffs and closed one part of it onto his narrow left wrist. He reached down and quickly snapped the other onto Sheck's right wrist before Sheck even realized it.

"Oh, no son, no," the old man pleaded. "You gotta take that off. If I fall down, Gawd in heaven, you is going down with me."

"Mr. Sheck, if that happens," and he paused, "Then we are both going down together."

A strange, extraordinary reaction now covered Dink's face, and he looked back up at the other six boys. "If you guys have the guts to make sure this good man doesn't go down to his tragedy, and me too, I want all of us to each grab both of my legs. I am holding his hands, and I'm already locked with him by the clicking metal cuff. But if half of you will each lay down and hold both of my legs, two will be holding one, and three will take the other. We can turn this into a human chain. Either it's just he and me or it's all of us together."

The others looked around, and silently stood up and quickly began laying down where each grabbed one of the other's legs from Dink on back. But as they were taking their places, Dink said, "No, that's not for you, Jumbo. You're the fastest we've got. You know where the McKeever's house is."

"Sure," Jumbo said.

"It's the closest farm where we are. Run like a wild man, Jumbo. I pray Mr. McKeever *is* there. If he is, tell him to get his tractor running, and he can bring it with you back here. It would be better if his son Paul is there, too. Tell them they need to bring some shovels and more ropes. Before you leave, tell Mrs. McKeever to call Central. The Volunteers can come here, too, and then say that either Mr. Marsh or Mr. Dunlap is coming with the ambulance."

Dink stopped and glanced over at him. Then he said, "But you're going to have to get a to a doctor with a broken bone. I can't think of anything else, unless the McKeever's are gone. Just run to the next farm. Can you do it, Jumbo?"

"I'm running right now," and he started away in a flash. They silently leaned up and watched him disappear into the forest.

"Thank you, Dink. You juss did a powerful lot of good thinking there. But I sure wish would take this handcuff thing away and make sure you…"

Dink interrupted Sheck's offer, and smiled. "Forget it. That keeps all of us together."

"That's for sure," Suck said.

"Yep, we're not going to let you sink, Mr. Sheck," Beaner added.

"I'll squeeze your leg so much you'll think you're leg is turning blue," Booby threatened.

"I will too," Cat agreed

"I would do it for the rest of my life if it takes that much," Hotshot said gently. "I'm the crazy clown who did all this mess."

"Like I said, forget it," Dink shrugged defiantly. "We'll either die together just like our heroes did in 1776. Or boys, we'll all just be happy together when everyone of us is safe."

"Like Mr. Sheck said, this is a good thing you've done, Dink. I haven't ever seen you do anything quite like this before," Suck said, and smiled at his friend.

Dink gulped, and pushed his glasses back up on his nose with his left hand.

Sheck smiled and slightly nodded even though his head was sure blocked into a whole lot of Illinois' black, rich, loam. All of the boys realized that they didn't want to say a simple term called 'dead-end.'

Dink paused, and then said, "I just thought of one more idea here. Why don't we make a prayer right now for each of us?"

"I shore do think that is another mighty good plan," Sheck agreed.

The others above nodded. Dink then said, "How about me saying one that we memorized at Leet Methodist church with Suck. I bet this is done by folks at St. Johns and the Baptist Church, too."

A soft breeze slipped through the many nearby trees, and a spectacular view down to the Spoon River could also be seen through the forest. Dink cleared his voice, and then began to speak. "This is called Psalm 23. The Lord is my shepherd; I shall not want. He maketh me to go down in green pasture: he leadeth me beside the still waters.

He restoreth my soul: he leadeth me in the paths of righteousness for his name's sake.

Yea, though I walk through the valley of the shadow of death, I will fear no evil: for thou art with me...."

CHAPTER 29

▼

GREATER LOVE HATH NO MAN...OR WOMAN AND TEENAGERS, TOO!

"....thy rod and thy staff they comfort me.

Thou preparest a table before me in the presence of mine enemies: thou anointest my head with oil; my cup runneth over.

Surely goodness and mercy shall follow me all the days of my life: and I will dwell in the house of the Lord forever."

Father Cleary finished reading this passage, and looked out over the large number of people who were sitting in countless folding chairs. They were carried from all three churches, and even other folks brought more from the high school.

Even before Father Cleary had first began to speak, so many of these wonderful people from Bradford were already sitting there. Belzy Hooligan dreamed this program up, and especially wanted each of the three church clergy to say a collective bit of grace for the entire village. Now several hundred folks from rural America were sitting here as if this was just an ordinary summer day.

All of them had played or laughed or taught or labored or worshipped in this town, except there was nothing similar about this clear, pleasant Saturday morning. It looked like a very sad funeral in an unexpected place.

For fifty weeks ago in a long ago football game, these seven boys first talked together about trying to find a coal mine in a beautiful forest.

Now they were sitting in the very front row with three clerics conducting a serious program just 150 feet away from disaster.

However, as usual, the good Father probably should have planned on saying a little less right now, but he almost always wound up saying too much. A number of his parish members were still smiling when a very elderly widow in Bradford finally passes away several years ago. Father Cleary announced he would give a Mass for her, and speak in Latin, of course. Unfortunately, he somehow gave the main funeral in French.

Within five minutes everyone was shaking their heads or even tickling with each other at St. John's. Naturally, no one understood a word of French except the brilliant father, but then virtually no one else understood Latin either. No matter, it's just that they recognized one and ignored the other. Father Cleary was so involved in countless other situations like this, one could say anything was the principle of the thing. That even got complicated in English, because he was also the school's principal.

"This has been decided as a serious and singular day when we all honor and remember things and people that have happened here. Seven brave, but mistaken young boys when they walked out into the edge of this beautiful forest, are now young men. And the fact that one incredible patriarchal man fell down into disaster when the old coal mine collapsed is why we are giving a brief memorial program about what happened in this spot. Today we are just about a hundred feet or so from where the terrible coal mine has been finally detonated.

"When a man sacrifices his own body to give someone else the great gift of life, it is the greatest message that every church understands and proudly proclaims. That message will now be given to you seven sitting in the front row. Believe it or no, Father Cleary paused, and then signaled Rev. Donald Woods to walk up to the make-seated little stage. .

"Thanks you, Father Cleary. Boys, I will read The Gospel of John, Chapter 15, verse 13, and I would like that each of you briefly, but symbolically hold hands together. This is the word of God. Greater love hath no man than this, that a man lay down his life for his friends."

As he began to read this message, each of the boys did hold their hands together. To the right of everyone behind them, and to the left from each of the ministers and 'Mayor' Hooligan, Michael "Hotshot" Randall was on the outside for one simple reason. His cast was sticking clear out into the side, and let his crutch lean against the chair. He had already had received a second nickname, "Crutchy."

In other towns, crazy nicknames were a dime a dozen in most places. In Bradford it was a penny a thousand. The other five, Patrick "Booby" O'Riley, Philip "Suck" Carlton, Richard "Beaner" Hurst, William "Catfish" Curtis, and Edward "Jumbo" Roberts were aiming their eyes directly into Pastor Woods.

Jonathan "Dink" Patterson was looking up into another pair of eyes, right beside him. They belonged to Sheck Dye. Both were holding hands just like the others, but they had tears streaming down their cheeks, and were staring and smiling together.

"Boys, the fact that Mr. Dye made sure that you seven were going to get out okay if he had to make the ultimate sacrifice for all of you is thankfully not what had to happen over in those lovely trees two weeks ago. Thank God, you *all* are here with us again.

"In the men sitting in the second row here are the Fire Volunteers who arrived in just fifteen minutes from Central's phone call from the McKeever's farm. Their tractor and these men were able to dig Sheck Dye out of the mire he almost had disappeared in. Marsh and Dunlap got Michael right to the hospital in Kewanee for a broken ankle. One and another, we are relieved. Now Reverend Austin Rodgers will offer these thoughts."

Rev. Rodgers stepped up to the small rostrum. "Boys, as Rev. Woods and Father Cleary have mentioned, it is about the touching power that one person can do to help save an another. However, it's also a time for each of you to consider how much that man did for you, but also what you could soon do for someone else. You will all grow up in a few more years. It is possible that one of you someday could discover a cure for polio. Or design a magnificent building. Or grow more corn than anyone else in Stark County. Or score a touchdown or paint a landscape or portrait or write a book. I understand one of you has already created a wonderful musical composition. This is what we are talking about. Your great opportunity to make something good out of your life is the gift that God has given each of you now.

"Actually, all that you need to do someday is simply be the best that you can be. That's what your mother and father would want, or Mr. Dye, too. Being the best is all anybody can ask." Rev. Rodgers then paused and looked at each of the boys. He turned around and nodded over to Belzy.

"Thank you to everyone here today, especially the fine words that the clergy have give us," Belzy began. "We are here this mornin' out on one of Bradford's beautfiful hill. Part of the words that Miss Eliza Jane Shallenberger wrote about our town in 1876 are just as true today as they were way back when." He paused, and held up this slip of paper. "The traveler sees crowning the high hill before him a busy village," and he folded it, and stuck into his front pocket. "Ladies and gentlemen, girls and boys, how true it is. This is one of our town's grand, high hills. But the great poet named Edgar Lee Masters, wrote about Lewistown near the same Spoon River where our own woods are yonder here. He was buried in Oakland Cemetery in Petersburg, but he wrote about the Hill, the Hill, all are sleepin' on the hill in Lewistown.

"Folks, today we aren't sleepin' on our hill now. I just want to say two things that we will be doing to not only be happy that these seven boys are fine, but that our Bradford Labor Day weekend a week away will have this special time together. Our leaders have voted to put Sheck Dye, the King of Labor Day a week from Monday on September 5 at the annual parade."

People cheered and clapped. Every year someone local who had done something distinguished was chosen as the titular king for a day. "Sure and our village board was so touched by what Mr. Dye did for these boys, that folks now don't have any more coal next winter, or for that matter, not even cookin' any there to have hot food later today." Suddenly a number of people were now staring at each other and hoped that he would comprehend his thoughts a little better. Everyone knew he was wandering around in his brain on one hand, and his mouth on the other.

They often did not seem to work together very well.

"Folks, I am babblin' like a little fool. What I am trying to say is that folks in town have agreed that Mr. Sheck," and he stared directly into Sheck, "You are not goin' to ever have to try and dig any more coal around this part of Illinois again."

Everyone again immediately started clapping and laughing.

"Therefore, by the powers invested to me, these here board members have agreed that once a week, Bradgas, the town's LP gas company, will make sure that you now have a new stove, and a real heating furnace. Mr. Dye, you've got enough to heat and cook for the rest of your days, my man...and for free." As Belzy finished, the entire congregation stood up and erupted.

The only thing that Sheck could do right now was shake his head slowly, and again started letting tears slip down his cheeks. Lots of folks quickly rushed all around him, and started hugging and laughing with him and everyone else in the place. If Belzy had any more words to say, it was certainly now over, pure and simple.

Back up on the top of the road behind everyone else Buck Ed was close enough to hear and see everything that had happened, but was far enough so no one else could get any strong whiffs or flies. He was so touched by the message, he reached down somewhere in the huge pile of things on the right seat floor and held up a red bandana.

For someone reason, the fat man needed to blow into his handkerchief, and dab his eyes. Bill Dorgan, who was sitting with his entire family on the fourth row, heard the incredible blast. He jumped right out of his chair, and turned his head. A big, fat man makes a lot of big, strong noises.

"Folks, either Buck Ed just blew his nose or said adios to his entire set of brains today." A number of the neighbors around them laughed and chuckled.

As many, many people started to leave the field, they were touched beyond their beliefs. Joy was almost out of control today. Teachers and Nuns were laughing and sharing together with some of their memories about these seven comrades. Most of the folks, who worked on one side of Main Street to the other, came to this great event, and many hugged and laughed. One couple was quietly walking together as they held hands, and kept staring into their eyes. It was Lynn and Dusty, and they certainly looked like the next Bradford marriage at one of the churches.

Francis Webber, the local American Legion Commander that ran the wonderful Memorial Day program three months ago, walked over to the seven boys. He announced that he was also going to be the town's first Boys Scout Leader, and he wanted all seven to be new Tenderfoot members.

The boys were smiling and laughing. Of course, they had no idea what would be happening soon, but anyone else bet these boys were going to have some new incredible experiences right back in these special woods along the Mighty Spoon. All these years of summer fun as just little boys chasing butterflies and lightning bugs were about to change even more.

An eagle anywhere is a huge, beautiful, majestic bird that people love to see every now and then. But the name Eagle Scout someday would be a whole new and different challenge for them.

As if that wasn't enough today, this special seven realized that they heard a 'moose had just arrived in Bradford.' Occasionally, an unexpected wild animal might slip into town. A skunk did a few years ago, and it caused a temporary but smelly mess.

When Gib Hall's tractor-trailer was temporarily parked at his house, the back door was knocked down and thirty cattle ran out. It created a decision for Mr.

Huey and the teachers because no kids could come out and play that day on the grade school playground for recess until they were all corralled.

But this moose was not a huge, furry northern version, and it didn't resemble anything that Dink thought looked like the hockey pond they made last fall. It was a handsome, tall, muscular, outstanding young man who was going to be a new member in this year's future 8th grade class. His name was David Raschke, and his father and mother had just bought the Lehman's Feed Store on Main Street.

Hotshot, Jumbo, and Catfish would be some of the very best guards in the conference, but this new team member who was the tallest of the tall would be their star center. He was already being compared to any other boys in the entire area, and everyone decided that someone this big had to be a moose.

"Moose" and his parents glanced over at the original seven, and they all nodded and grinned together. If any of them started laughing and talking together they would soon agree that this plan was as good as it could ever be.

A few minutes later, Sheck and all seven boys seemed to wander a few feet away from everyone else. They were looking down at the lazy stream folks named Spoon River a lot of years ago.

"Looks like it's gettin' just a little cool this afternoon," Sheck said, and smiled while he was looking around at the nearby trees. "I was starin' at a few leaves that seem like they might be going to slip away from us again in good old Injun Summer, boys."

"Yep," Suck sighed. "Today is the last Saturday in August. School will start again two days from now."

A loud moan dispersed throughout the forlorn expressions as the rest of the boys gathered together.

"No matter what happens again this new year for us, we'll always remember what you've told us and especially what you did for us, Mr. Dye," Dink said.

"Well, thank you about that. You boys are just as 'portant to me as life itself. And there's a lot of things we can see and do again. I know all of you used to say that nothin' good happens 'til summer comes, but we got a lot more neat things to do every month of the year, right? But stop callin' me Mr. Sheck or Mr. Dye. I'se just a good old grampa. You got that, boys," and he frowned, but then instantly laughed.

They smiled together and quickly agreed with that. Just then a strong gust swirled through the top branches in the nearest oak, and a still green leaf flittered as it was spinning toward the river. Dink looked up at Sheck. They both grinned.

"Mister.........er, Sheck, I hope this leaf sure isn't the one you want to go to Glory. It's a lot good years before we ever think about this again." The others again loudly concurred, immediately.

"I hope you're right, boys, but when the right leaf does fall for anyone of us, it's the good Lord who'll take folks for a happy, lazy journey downstream across the Mighty Spoon. That's when I'll be goin' toward the gulf."

Sheck was wearing a pair of brand-new overalls that someone had given him the day before. Suddenly he reached down into one of his front pockets, and pulled out his harmonica. Within seconds a haunting melody was floating across the field, and many people walking farther up the hill to get back in their cars were startled.

No matter who else was still there, they didn't care. These seven boys, some hanging together and some just standing and staring, were Stephen Foster's beautiful dreamers.

978-0-595-36346-9
0-595-36346-6

Printed in the United States
34402LVS00004B/64-306